RAYMOND

BY THE SAME AUTHOR

ALSO

RAYMOND

OR

LIFE AND DEATH

WITH EXAMPLES OF THE EVIDENCE
FOR SURVIVAL OF MEMORY AND AFFECTION
AFTER DEATH

BY

SIR OLIVER J. LODGE

WITH EIGHTEEN ILLUSTRATIONS

THIRTEENTH EDITION

METHUEN & CO. LTD.
36 ESSEX STREET W.C.
LONDON

RAYMOND

TO

HIS MOTHER AND FAMILY

WITH GRATITUDE FOR PERMISSION

TO USE PRIVATE MATERIAL

FOR PUBLIC ENDS

"Divine must be
That triumph, when the very worst, the pain,
And even the prospect of our brethren slain,
Hath something in it which the heart enjoys."

WORDSWORTH, Sonnet xxvi.

PREFACE

THIS book is named after my son who was killed in the War.

It is divided into three parts. In the first part some idea of the kind of life lived and the spirit shown by any number of youths, fully engaged in civil occupations, who joined for service when war broke out and went to the Front, is illustrated by extracts from his letters. The object of this portion is to engender a friendly feeling towards the writer of the letters, so that whatever more has to be said in the sequel may not have the inevitable dullness of details concerning an entire stranger. This is the sole object of this portion. The letters are not supposed to be remarkable ; though as a picture of part of the life at the Front during the 1915 phase of the war they are interesting, as many other such letters must have been.

The second part gives specimens of what at present are considered by most people unusual communications ; though these again are in many respects of an ordinary type, and will be recognised as such by other bereaved persons who have had similar messages. In a few particulars, indeed, those here quoted have rather special features, by reason of the assistance given by the group of my friends " on the other side " who had closely studied the subject. It is partly owing to the urgency therein indicated that I have thought it my duty to speak out, though it may well be believed that it is not without hesitation that I have ventured thus to obtrude family affairs. I should not have done so were it not that the amount of premature and unnatural bereavement at the present time is so appalling that the pain caused by exposing one's own sorrow and its alleviation, to possible scoffers, becomes almost negligible in view of the service which it is legitimate to hope may thus be rendered to mourners, if they can derive comfort by learning that communication across the gulf is possible. Incidentally I have to thank those friends, some of them previously unknown, who have in the same spirit allowed the names of loved ones to appear in this book, and I am grateful for the help which one or two of those friends have accorded. Some few more perhaps may be thus led, to pay critical attention to any assurance of continued and happy and useful existence which may reach them from the other side.

The third part of the book is of a more expository character, and is designed to help people in general to realise that this subject is not the bugbear which ignorance and prejudice have made it, that it belongs to a coherent system of thought full of new facts of which continued study is necessary, that it is subject to a law and order of its own, and that though comparatively in its infancy it is a genuine branch of psychological science. This third part is called " Life and Death," because these are the two great undeniable facts which concern everybody, and in which it is natural for every one to feel a keen interest, if they once begin to realise that such interest is not futile, and that it is possible to learn something real about them. It may be willingly admitted that these chapters are inadequate to the magnitude of the subject, but it is hoped that they are of a usefully introductory character.

The " In Memoriam " chapter of Part I is no doubt chiefly of interest to family and friends ; but everybody is very friendly, and under the circumstances it will be excused.

EXPLANATORY ADDENDUM TO THE TENTH EDITION

I PROPOSE to take advantage of the opportunity afforded by a new edition to make a short explanation or commentary, which may incidentally meet some of the objections raised by the more reasonable type of critic—one who is willing to devote some time and attention to a book in order to arrive at the real meaning.

The main object of a book like this is to help to bring comfort to bereaved persons, especially to those who have been bereaved by war. I do not indeed recommend all sorts of people to visit mediums or try to investigate the subject for themselves. If they do, it must be on their own responsibility. When sane people desire, on sound and good motives and in a reasonable spirit, to gain first-hand experience, in the hope of thereby mitigating their sorrow, there are people who do their best to help them ; but it is unwise to take the responsibility of urging such a course upon an unknown stranger. And some should be dissuaded. Nevertheless, a considerable number of bereaved people have been helped, who knew nothing of the subject beforehand. People in genuine distress have gone with careful recommendation and instructions to a reputable medium, quite anonymously, and have got into touch unmistakably with their departed. This has happened in numerous and some noteworthy cases. The result has been a considerable addition to the bulk of cumulative evidence in favour of the genuineness of the phenomenon, and incidentally of the power of mediums who normally knew nothing whatever about their visitors, but who in trance gave many intimate family details. It is absurd to suppose that people who had never been to a medium of any kind were recognised; still more absurd to suppose that every anonymous stranger is personally known and has been looked up.

The best mediums are simple straightforward people, anxious to do the best they can with their strange gift for the help of people in sorrow. Occasionally individuals may be encountered who pretend to powers which they do not possess, or who eke out their waning power by fraud; but in so far as these imitators are fraudulent they are not genuine mediums. If inexperienced novices go to charlatans who advertise by sandwich-men and other devices, they deserve what they get.

On the other hand, I have not usually found bereaved people too ready to be convinced. Some are; some are foolish enough to give things away in a careless manner; but as a rule it is a mistake to suppose that people who are really seeking for evidence are ready to be misled. They are often quite critical, and reasonably cautious. Their anxiety sometimes makes them even excessively anxious not to be deceived in so vitally important a matter. And even after they have had quite good evidence, they sometimes go back on it—very naturally—and become sceptical again. Many years of experience were needed in my own case before I was ready to admit the cumulative outcome of the whole body of evidence as finally conclusive.

Concerning the particular case of my son Raymond, I have had many further talks with him since the book was published: but the stress and anxiety to communicate has subsided. The wish to give scientific evidence remains, but, now that the fact of survival and happy employment is established, the communications are placid—like an occasional letter home. He has, however, been successful in bringing to their parents a number of youths whom he knew before death, and the weight of evidence has accordingly heavily increased. A few minor supplementary notes will be found in this edition on pages 150 and 270.

I hope that in time, when the possibility is recognised and taken under the wing of religion, that people will not need individual and specific messages to assure them of the well-being of their loved ones. They will, I hope, be able to feel assured that what has been proved true of a few must be true of all, under the same general circumstances. Moreover, it is to be hoped that they will be able to receive help and comfort and a sense of communion through their own powers, in peaceful times, without strain or special effort and without vicarious mediation. .

The power, or sensitiveness, or whatever it ought to be called, seems to be a good deal commoner than people think. I anticipate that in most families there will be found one member who may be able to help others to some knowledge in this direction. Elaborate proof is necessary at first, as it has been in connexion with many now recognised and familiar things,—such as the position of the earth in the solar system,—but when once a fact or doctrine is generally accepted, people settle down in acceptance and enjoyment of the general belief, without each striving after exceptional experience for himself. The inertia of the human mind and of the body-politic is considerable : right beliefs take time to enter, and wrong beliefs take time to disappear ; but periods of anxiety and doubt and controversy do not last as a permanent condition. They represent a phase through which we have to go.

One difficulty which good people feel, about allowing themselves to take comfort from the evidence, is the attitude of the Church to it, and the fear that we are encroaching on dangerous and forbidden ground. I have no wish to shirk the ecclesiastical point of view : it is indeed important, for the Church has great influence. But I must claim that Science can pay no attention to ecclesiastical notice-boards ; we must examine wherever we can, and I do not agree that any region of inquiry can legitimately be barred out by authority.

Occasionally the accusation is made that the phenomena we encounter are the work of devils ; and we are challenged to say how we know that they are not of evil character. To that the only answer is the ancient one—" by their fruits." I will not elaborate it. St. Paul gave a long list of the fruits of the Spirit. Yet I do not mean to say that

no precautions need be taken, and that everything connected
with the subject is wholly good : I do not regard as wholly
good any activity of man. Even the pursuit of Science can
be prostituted to evil ; as we see now only too clearly in
the war. Everything human can be used and can be abused
I have to speak in platitudes to answer these objections
they are often quite unworthy of the sacred name of religion
they savour of professionalism. Chief Priests were always
ready to attribute anything done without their sanction to
the power of Beelzebub. The Bishop of Beauvais denounced
Joan of Arc's voices as diabolic. It is a very ancient accusation. In the light of historical instances, it is an over-
flattering one : I wish to give no other answer.

Concerning the substance of the communications received
from the other side, perhaps the most difficult portion is
the account given of the similarity of the conditions as
described ' over there ' to the conditions existing on the
earth ; and it is asked, how can that be possible ? I reply
in all probability because of the identity of the observer
I do not dogmatise on the point, but I conceive that in so
far as people remain themselves, their power of interpretation will be similar to what it used to be here. Hence in
whatever way we interpret a material world here and now
so, in like manner, are we likely to interpret an etherial world
—through senses not altogether dissimilar in effect, however
they differ in detail.

Surely the external world, as we perceive it, is largely
dependent on our powers of perception and interpretation
So is a picture, or any work of art. The thing in itself—
whatever that means—can hardly be known to us. I admit
it is a difficult proposition,—but the evidence is fairly consistent on this point ever since Swedenborg,—the next world
is always represented as surprisingly like this ; and though
that obviously lends itself to scepticism, I expect it corresponds to some sort of reality. It looks almost as if that
world were an etherial counterpart of this : or else as if we
were all really in one world all the time, only they see the
etherial aspect of it and we see the material. The clue to
all this seems to depend on the similarity or rather the

identity of the observer. A nerve centre interprets or presents to the mind each stimulus in the specific way to which it has become accustomed, whatever the real nature of the stimulus ; a blow on the eye, or a pressure on the retina, is interpreted as light.

To come to smaller details. If the accusation has been brought that such things as smoking and drinking are represented as in vogue on the other side, it is unjustified and untrue. A statement detached from its context is often misleading. What is revealed in my book, if it has any trustworthy significance, implies clearly and decisively that they do *not* thus occupy their time ; nor are any such things natural to their surroundings. Nothing but common sense is needed to understand the position. If there is a community over there, it cannot be a fixed and stationary one, new-comers must be continually arriving. My son is represented as stating that when people first come over, and are in a puzzled state of mind, hardly knowing where they are, they ask for all sorts of unreasonable things ; and that the lower kind are still afflicted with the desires of earth. After all, this is really orthodox moral teaching, or I am much mistaken ; it is one of the warnings held out to sensual persons that their desires may persist and become part of their punishment.

Imagine an assembly of clergymen in some Retreat, where they give themselves to meditation and good works, and then imagine a traveller mistaking their hostel for an hotel and asking for a whisky and soda. Would that mean that alcoholic drinks were natural to the surroundings and part of the atmosphere of the place ? Would not the feeling aroused by the request mean just the contrary ? The book says that in order to wean these new-comers from sordid and unsuitable though comparatively innocuous tastes, the policy adopted is not to forbid and withhold—a policy which might over-inflame and prolong the desire—but to take steps to satisfy it in moderation until the new-comers of their own free will and sense perceive the unsuitability, and overcome the relics of earthly craving ; which they do very soon.

Whether the statement be accepted as true or not, or as containing some parabolic element of truth, I see nothing derogatory in it ; and the process of weaning may be wise.

It must be admitted, however, that games and songs are spoken of, and I have heard it claimed that " spirits of just men made perfect " ought not to be occupied in any such commonplace ways, even during their times of relaxation. To this I reply that when perfection or saintliness is attained that may be true : it is not a subject on which I am a judge. Games and exercises are harmless and beneficial here, even for good people ; and surely if young fellows remain themselves, games and exercise and songs will not seem alien to them—at any rate not for some time. People seem hardly to realise all that survival with persistent character and personal identity must really involve. It is surely clear that the majority of people, whether in this or in another life, are just average men and women, and neither saints nor devils ; and ecclesiastical teaching has surely erred in leading people to suppose that the act of death converts them into one or the other. Progress and development are conspicuously the law of the Universe. Evolution is always gradual. Youths shot out of the trenches—fine fellows as they are— are not likely to become saints all at once. They cannot be reasonably spoken of as " just men made perfect." Let a little common sense into the subject, and remember the continuity of existence and of personal identity. Do not suppose that death converts a person into something quite different. Happier and holier, pleasanter and better, the surroundings may be, than on earth ; there is admittedly room for improvement ; but sudden perfection is not for the likes of us.

It is, after all, highly unlikely that the experience of everybody on that side is the same : the few saints of the race may have quite a different experience : the few diabolical ruffians must have a different one again. I have not been in touch with either of these classes. There are many grades, many states of being ; and each goes to his own place.

If it is urged by orthodox critics that the penitent thief went to heaven, I reply, Not at all. According to the record he went to Paradise, which is different. A sort of Garden of Eden, apparently, is meant by the word, something not too far removed from earth. As far as I can make out, the ancient writers thought of it as a place or state not very different from what in the book is called " Summerland."

Against this it may be urged that Christ himself could not have stayed, even for a time, at an intermediate or comparatively low stage. But I see no reason to suppose that he exempted himself from any condition appropriate to a full-bodied humanity. Surely he would carry it through completely. Judging from the Creed, which I suppose clerical critics accept, they appear to hold that Christ even descended at first—descended into hades or the underworld, doubtless on some high missionary effort. Anyhow and quite clearly the record says that for forty days he remained in touch with earth, presumably in the state called Paradise, occasionally appearing or communicating with survivors— again after the manner of transitional humanity. And only after that sojourn, for our benefit, did he ascend to some lofty state, far above anything attainable by thieves however penitent, or by our young soldiers however magnificent and self-sacrificing. After æons of progress have elapsed, they may gradually progress thither.

Meanwhile they are happier and more at home in Paradise. There they find themselves still in touch with earth, not really separated from those left behind, still able actively to help and serve. There is nothing supine about the rest and joy into which they have entered. Under their young energy, strengthened by the love which rises towards them like a blessing, the traditional barrier between the two states is suffering violence, is being taken by force. A band of eager workers is constructing a bridge, is opening a way for us across the chasm ; communication is already easier and more frequent than ever before ; and in the long run we may feel assured that all this present suffering and bereavement will have a beneficent outcome for humanity.

TABLE OF CONTENTS

PART III

LIFE AND DEATH

LIST OF ILLUSTRATIONS

PART I
NORMAL PORTION

"And this to fill us with regard for man,
With apprehension of his passing worth."

BROWNING, *Paracelsus*

CHAPTER I

IN MEMORIAM

THE bare facts are much as reported in *The Times* :—

SECOND LIEUTENANT RAYMOND LODGE was the youngest son of Sir Oliver and Lady Lodge, and was by taste and training an engineer. He volunteered for service in September 1914 and was at once given a commission in the 3rd South Lancashires. After training near Liverpool and Edinburgh, he went to the Front in the early spring of 1915, attached to the 2nd South Lancashire Regiment of the Regular Army, and was soon in the trenches near Ypres or Hooge. His engineering skill was of service in details of trench construction, and he later was attached to a Machine-Gun Section for a time, and had various escapes from shell fire and shrapnel. His Captain having sprained an ankle, he was called back to Company work, and at the time of his death was in command of a Company engaged in some early episode of an attack or attempted advance which was then beginning. He was struck by a fragment of shell in the attack on Hooge Hill on the 14th September 1915, and died in a few hours.

Raymond Lodge had been educated at Bedales School and Birmingham University. He had a great aptitude and love for mechanical engineering, and was soon to have become a partner with his elder brothers, who highly valued his services, and desired his return to assist in the Government work which now occupies their firm.

In amplification of this bare record a few members of the family wrote reminiscences of him, and the following memoir is by his eldest brother :—

RAYMOND LODGE

(1889–1915)

By O. W. F. L.

MOST lives have marriages, births of children, productive years ; but the lives of the defenders of their Country are short and of majestic simplicity. The obscure records of childhood, the few years of school and university and constructive and inventive work, and then the sudden sacrifice of all the promise of the future, of work, of home, of love ; the months of hard living and hard work well carried through, the cheerful humorous letters home making it out all very good fun ; and in front, in a strange ruined and desolate land, certain mutilation or death.   And now that death has come.

> Unto each man his handiwork, to each his crown,
> > The just Fate gives;
> Whoso takes the world's life on him and his own lays down,
> > He, dying so, lives.[1]

My brother was born at Liverpool on January 25th, 1889, and was at Bedales School for five or six years, and afterwards at Birmingham University, where he studied engineering and was exceptionally competent in the workshop.   He went through the usual two years' practical training at the Wolseley Motor Works, and then entered his brothers' works, where he remained until he obtained a commission at the outbreak of war.

His was a mind of rare stamp.   It had unusual power, unusual quickness, and patience and understanding of difficulties in my experience unparalleled, so that he was

---

[1] Swinburne; *Super Flumina Babylonis*; *Songs before Sunrise.*

4

able to make anyone understand really difficult things. I think we were most of us proudest and most hopeful of him. Some of us, I did myself, sometimes took problems technical or intellectual to him, sure of a wise and sound solution.

Though his chief strength lay on the side of mechanical and electrical engineering it was not confined to that. He read widely, and liked good literature of an intellectual and witty but not highly imaginative type, at least I do not know that he read Shelley or much of William Morris, but he was fond of Fielding, Pope, and Jane Austen. Naturally he read Shakespeare, and I particularly associate him with *Twelfth Night, Love's Labour's Lost,* and *Henry the Fourth.* Among novelists, his favourites, after Fielding and Miss Austen, were I believe Dickens and Reade ; and he frequently quoted from the essays and letters of Charles Lamb.[1]

Of the stories of his early childhood, and his overflowing vitality made many, I was too often from home to be able to speak at large. But one I may tell. Once when a small boy at Grove Park, Liverpool, he jumped out of the bath and ran down the stairs with the nurse after him, out of the front door, down one drive along the road and up the other, and was safely back in the bath again before the horrified nursemaid could catch up with him. [*body of Memoir incomplete, and omitted here.*]

---

[1] *Note by O. J. L.*—A volume of poems by O. W. F. L. had been sent to Raymond by the author; and this came back with his kit, inscribed on the title page in a way which showed that it had been appreciated :—

" Received at Wisques (Machine-Gun School), near St. Omer, France—12*th July* 1915.
Taken to camp near Poperinghe—13*th July.*
To huts near Dickebusch—21*st July.*
To first-line trenches near St. Eloi, in front of ' The Mound of Death '—24*th July.*"

[Close of Memoir]

That death is the end has never been a Christian doctrine, and evidence collected by careful men in our own day has, perhaps needlessly, upheld with weak props of experiment the mighty arch of Faith. Death is real and grievous, and is not to be tempered by the glossing timidities of those who would substitute journalese like " passing-on," " passing-over," etc., for that awful word : but it is the end of a stage, not the end of the journey. The road stretches on beyond that inn, and beyond our imagination, " the moonlit endless way."

Let us think of him then, not as lying near Ypres with all his work ended, but rather, after due rest and refreshment, continuing his noble and useful career in more peaceful surroundings, and quietly calling us his family from intemperate grief to resolute and high endeavour.

Indeed, it is not right that we should weep for a death like his. Rather let us pay him our homage in praise and imitation, by growing like him and by holding our lives lightly in our Country's service, so that if need be we may die like him. This is true honour and his best memorial.

Not that I would undervalue those of brass or stone, for if vigorous they are good and worthy things. But fame illuminates memorials, and fame has but a narrow opening in a life of twenty-six years.

Who shall remember him, who climb
His all-unripened fame to wake,
Who dies an age before his time ?
But nobly, but for England's sake.

Who will believe us when we cry
He was as great as he was brave ?
His name that years had lifted high
Lies buried in that Belgian grave.

O strong and patient, kind and true,
Valiant of heart, and clear of brain—
They cannot know the man we knew,
Our words go down the wind like rain.

O. W. F. L.

Tintern

EPITAPH
ON THE MEMORIAL TABLET
IN ST. GEORGE'S CHURCH, EDGBASTON

REMEMBER

RAYMOND LODGE

SECOND LIEUTENANT SECOND SOUTH LANCASHIRE REGIMENT
BELOVED SON OF SIR OLIVER AND LADY LODGE OF THIS PARISH
WHO GAVE HIS LIFE FOR HIS COUNTRY.
HE WAS BORN JANUARY 25TH 1889
AND WAS KILLED IN ACTION IN FLANDERS
ABOUT NOON SEPTEMBER 14TH
IN THE YEAR OF OUR LORD 1915
AGED 26 YEARS.

Whoso bears the whole heaviness of the wronged world's weight
    And puts it by,
It is well with him suffering, though he face man's fate;
    How should he die?

Songs before Sunrise

REMINISCENCES BY O. J. L.

OF all my sons, the youngest, when he was small, was most like myself at the same age. In bodily appearance I could recognise the likeness to my early self, as preserved in old photographs; an old schoolfellow, of mine who knew me between the ages of eight and eleven, visiting Mariemont in April 1904, remarked on it forcibly and at once, directly he saw Raymond—then a schoolboy; and innumerable small mental traits in the boy recalled to me my childhood's feelings. Even an absurd difficulty he had as a child in saying the hard letters— the hard G and K—was markedly reminiscent of my own similar difficulty.

Another peculiarity which we shared in childhood was dislike of children's parties—indeed, in my own case, a party of any kind. I remember being truly miserable at a Christmas party at The Mount, Penkhull, where I have no doubt that every one was more than friendly,—though probably over - patronising, as people often are with children,—but where I determinedly abstained from supper, and went home hungry. Raymond's prominent instance was at the hospitable Liverpool house, "Greenbank," which the Rathbones annually delivered up to family festivities each Christmas afternoon and evening, being good enough to include us in their family group. On one such occasion Raymond, a very small boy, was found in the hall making a bee-line for the front door and home. I remember sympathising with him, from ancient memories, and taking him home, subsequently returning myself.

At a later stage of boyhood I perceived that his ability and tastes were akin to mine, for we had the same passionate love of engineering and machinery; though in my case, having no opportunity of exercising it to any useful extent, it gradually turned into special aptitude for physical science. Raymond was never anything like as good at physics, nor had he the same enthusiasm for

RAYMOND WHEN TWO YEARS OLD.

mathematics that I had, but he was better at engineering, was in many ways I consider stronger in character, and would have made, I expect, a first-rate engineer. His pertinacious ability in the mechanical and workshop direction was very marked. Nothing could have been further from his natural tastes and proclivities than to enter upon a military career; nothing but a sense of duty impelled him in that direction, which was quite foreign to family tradition, at least on my side.

He also excelled me in a keen sense of humour—not only appreciation, but achievement. The whole family could not but admire and enjoy the readiness with which he perceived at once the humorous side of everything; and he usually kept lively any gathering of which he was a unit. At school, indeed, his active wit rather interfered with the studies of himself and others, and in the supposed interests of his classmates it had to be more or less suppressed, but to the end he continued to be rather one of the wags of the school.

Being so desperately busy all my life I failed to see as much as I should like either of him or of the other boys, but there was always an instinctive sympathy between us; and it is a relief to me to be unable to remember any, even a single, occasion on which I have been vexed with him. In all serious matters he was, as far as I could judge, one of the best youths I have ever known; and we all looked forward to a happy life for him and a brilliant career.

His elder brothers highly valued his services in their Works. He got on admirably with the men; his mode of dealing with overbearing foremen at the Works, where he was for some years an apprentice, was testified to as masterly, and was much appreciated by his "mates"; and honestly I cannot bethink myself of any trait in his character which I would have had different—unless it be that he might have had a more thorough liking and aptitude for, and greater industry in, my own subject of physics.

When the war broke out his mother and I were in Australia, and it was some time before we heard that he had considered it his duty to volunteer. He did so in September 1914, getting a commission in the Regular

Army which was ante-dated to August ; and he threw himself into military duties with the same ability and thoroughness as he had applied to more naturally congenial occupations.   He went through a course of training at Great Crosby, near Liverpool, with the Regiment in which he was a Second Lieutenant, namely the 3rd South Lancashires, being attached to the 2nd when he went to the Front ; his Company spent the winter in more active service on the south coast of the Firth of Forth and Edinburgh ; and he gained his desired opportunity to go out to Flanders on 15 March 1915.   Here he applied his engineering faculty to trench and shelter construction, in addition to ordinary military duties ; and presently he became a machine-gun officer.   How desperately welcome to the family his safe return would have been, at the end of the war, I need not say.   He had a hard and strenuous time at the Front, and we all keenly desired to make it up to him by a course of home " spoiling."   But it was too much to hope for—though I confess I did hope for it.

He has entered another region of service now ; and this we realise.   For though in the first shock of bereavement the outlook of life felt irretrievably darkened, a perception of his continued usefulness has mercifully dawned upon us, and we know that his activity is not over.   His bright ingenuity will lead to developments beyond what we could have anticipated ; and we have clear hopes for the future.

O. J. L.

Mariemont, *September* 30, 1915

A MOTHER'S LAMENT

Written on a scrap of paper, September 26, 1915,

" To ease the pain and to try to get in touch "

"RAYMOND, darling, you have gone from our world, and *oh*, to ease the pain.   I want to know if you are happy, and that you *yourself* are really talking to me and no sham.

" No more letters from you, my own dear son, and

I have loved them so. They are all there ; · we shall have them typed together into a sort of book. " Now we shall be parted until I join you there. I have not seen as much of you as I wanted on this earth, but I do love to think of the bits I have had of you, specially our journeys to and from Italy. I had you to myself then, and you were so dear.

" I want to say, dear, how we recognise the glorious way in which you have done your duty, with a certain straight pressing on, never letting anyone see the effort, and with your fun and laughter playing round all the time, cheering and helping others. You know how your brothers and sisters feel your loss, and your poor father ! "

THE religious side of Raymond was hardly known to the family ; but among his possessions at the Front was found a small pocket Bible called " The Palestine Pictorial Bible " (Pearl 24mo), Oxford University Press, in which a number of passages are marked ; and on the fly-leaf, pencilled in his writing, is an index to these passages, which page I copy here :—

				PAGE
Ex. xxxiii. 14 .	.	.	.	63
St. John xiv. .	.	.	.	689
Eph. ii. .	.	.	.	749
Neh. i. 6, 11 .	.	.	.	337
St. John xvi. 33	.	.	.	689
Rom. viii. 35 .	.	.	.	723
St. Matt. xi. 28 .	.	.	.	616
Ps. cxxiv. 8 .	.	.	.	415
Ps. xliii. 2 .	.	.	.	468
Deut. xxxiii. 27	.	.	.	151
Deut. xxxii. 43 .	.	.	.	150
Isa. li. 12	.	.	.	473
Isa. lii. 12	.	.	.	474
Jude 24 .	.	.	.	784
Ezra ix. 9	.	.	.	335
Isa. xii. 2	.	.	.	451
Isa. i. 18 .	.	.	.	445
Isa. xl. 31	.	.	.	467
Rev. vii. 14	.	.	.	788
Rev. xxi. 4	.	.	.	795

MIZPAH. Gen. xxxi. 49.

R. L.

14/8/15

THE following poem was kindly sent me by Canon Rawnsley, in acknowledgement of a Memorial Card :—

OUR ANGEL-HOST OF HELP

IN MEMORY OF RAYMOND LODGE,
WHO FELL IN FLANDERS, 14 SEPT. 1915

"His strong young body is laid under some trees on the road from Ypres to Menin." [From the Memorial Card sent to friends.]

'Twixt Ypres and Menin night and day
  The poplar trees in leaf of gold
Were whispering either side the way
  Of sorrow manifold,

—Of war that never should have been,
  Of war that still perforce must be,
Till in what brotherhood can mean
  The nations all agree.

But where they laid your gallant lad
  I heard no sorrow in the air,
The boy who gave the best he had
  That others good might share.

For golden leaf and gentle grass
  They too had offered of their best
To banish grief from all who pass
  His hero's place of rest.

There as I gazed, the guests of God,
  An angel host before mine eyes,
Silent as if on air they trod
  Marched straight from Paradise.

And one sprang forth to join the throng
  From where the grass was gold and green,
His body seemed more lithe and strong
  Than it had ever been.

I cried, " But why in bright array
  Of crowns and palms toward the north
And those white trenches far away,
  Doth this great host go forth ? "

He answered, " Forth we go to fight
  To help all need where need there be,
Sworn in for right against brute might
  Till Europe shall be free."

H. D. RAWNSLEY

EXTRACTS FROM PLATO'S DIALOGUE
"MENEXENUS"

BEING PART OF A SPEECH IN HONOUR OF THOSE WHO
HAD DIED IN BATTLE FOR THEIR COUNTRY

" AND I think that I ought now to repeat the
message which your fathers, when they went
out to battle, urged us to deliver to you who are
their survivors, in case anything happened to them.
I will tell you what I heard them say, and what, if they
could, they would fain be saying now, judging from what
they then said ; but you must imagine that you hear it
all from their lips. Thus they spoke :—
" Sons, the event proves that your fathers were brave
men. For we, who might have continued to live, though
without glory, choose a glorious death rather than bring
reproach on you and your children, and rather than disgrace our fathers and all of our race who have gone before
us, believing that for the man who brings shame on his
own people life is not worth living, and that such an one
is loved neither by men nor gods, either on earth or in
the underworld when he is dead.
" Some of us have fathers and mothers still living, and
you must encourage them to bear their trouble, should it
come, as lightly as may be ; and do not join them in
lamentations, for they will have no need of aught that
would give their grief a keener edge. They will have
pain enough from what has befallen them. Endeavour
rather to soothe and heal their wound, reminding them
that of all the boons they ever prayed for the greatest
have been granted to them. For they did not pray that
their sons should live for ever, but that they should be
brave and of fair fame. Courage and honour are the best
of all blessings, and while for a mortal man it can hardly
be that everything in his own life will turn out as he
would have it, their prayer for those two things has
been heard. Moreover, if they bear their troubles bravely,
it will be perceived that they are indeed fathers of brave
sons, and that they themselves are like them. . . . So

minded, *we*, at any rate, bid those dear to us to be; such we would have them be; and such we say we are now showing that we ourselves are, neither grieving overmuch nor fearing overmuch if we are to die in this battle. And we entreat our fathers and mothers to continue to be thus minded for the rest of their days, for we would have them know that it is not by bewailing and lamentation that they will please us best. If the dead have any knowledge of the living, they will give us no pleasure by breaking down under their trouble, or by bearing it with impatience. . . . For our lives will have had an end the most glorious of all that fall to the lot of man; it is therefore more fitting to do us honour than to lament us."

Stat sua cuique dies; breve et irreparabile tempus
Omnibus est vitae: sed famam extendere factis,
Hoc virtutis opus.

Æn. x. 467

CHAPTER II

LETTERS FROM THE FRONT

I SHALL now, for reasons explained in the Preface, quote extracts from letters which Raymond wrote to members of his family during the time he was serving in Flanders.

A short note made by me the day after he first started for the Front may serve as a preliminary statement of fact :—

Mariemont, Edgbaston,
16 March 1915

Raymond was recently transferred back from Edinburgh to Great Crosby near Liverpool ; and once more began life in tents or temporary sheds.

Yesterday morning, Monday the 15th March, one of the subalterns was ordered to the Front ; he went to a doctor, who refused to pass him, owing to some temporary indisposition. Raymond was then asked if he was fit : he replied, Perfectly. So at 10 a.m. he was told to start for France that night. Accordingly he packed up ; and at 3.0 we at Mariemont received a telegram from him asking to be met at 5 p.m., and saying he could spend six hours at home.

His mother unfortunately was in London, and for many hours was inaccessible. At last some of the telegrams reached her, at 7 p.m., and she came by the first available (slow) train from Paddington, getting here at 11.

Raymond took the midnight train to Euston ; Alec, Lionel, and Noël accompanying him. They would reach Euston at 3.50 a.m. and have two hours to wait, when he was to meet a Captain [Capt. Taylor], and start from Waterloo for Southampton. The boys intended to see him off at Waterloo, and then return home to their war-business as quickly as they could.

He seems quite well ; but naturally it has been rather a strain for the family : as the same sort of thing has been for so many other families.   O. J. L.

First comes a letter written on his way to the Front after leaving Southampton.

"Hotel Dervaux, 75 Grande Rue,
Boulogne-s/Mer,
Wednesday, 24 March 1915, 11.30 *a.m.*
" Following on my recent despatch, I have the honour
to report that we have got stuck here on our way to the
Front. Not stuck exactly, but they have shunted us
into a siding which we reached about 8 a.m., and we are
free until 2.30 p.m. when we have to telephone for further
orders to find out where we are to join our train. I
don't know whether this is the regular way to the Front
from Rouen. I don't think it is, I fancy the more direct
way must be reserved for urgent supplies and wounded.

" My servant has been invaluable *en route* and he
has caused us a great deal of amusement. He hunted
round at the goods station at Rouen (whence we started)
and found a large circular tin. He pierced this all over
to form a brazier and attached a wire handle. As soon
as we got going he lit this, having filled it with coal
purloined from somewhere, and when we stopped by
the wayside about 10 or 11 p.m. he supplied my com-
partment (four officers) with fine hot tea. He had previously purchased some condensed milk. He also saw to
it that a large share of the rations, provided by the
authorities before we left, fell to our share, and looked
after us and our baggage in the most splendid way.

" He insists on treating the train as a tram. As soon
as it slows down to four miles an hour, he is down on the
permanent way gathering firewood or visiting some railway hut in search of plunder. He rides with a number of
other servants in the baggage waggon, and as they had no
light he nipped out at a small station and stole one of the
railway men's lamps. However, there was a good deal of
fuss, and the owner came and indignantly recovered it.

" As soon as we stop anywhere, he lowers out of his
van the glowing brazier. He keeps it burning in the van !
I wonder the railway authorities don't object. If they do,
of course he pretends not to understand any French.

" He often gets left behind on the line, and has to
scramble into our carriage, where he regales us with his
life history until the next stop, when he returns to his own
van.

" Altogether he is a very rough customer and wants a lot of watching—all the same he makes an excellent servant."

LETTERS FROM THE FRONT IN FLANDERS

" *Friday, 26 March* 1915
" I arrived here yesterday about 5 p.m., and found the Battalion resting from the trenches. We all return there on Sunday evening.

" I got a splendid reception from my friends here, and they have managed to get me into an excellent Company, all the officers of which are my friends. This place is very muddy, but better than it was, I understand. We are in tents."

" *Saturday, 27 March* 1915, 4.30 *p.m.*
" We moved from our camp into billets last night and are now in a farmhouse. The natives still live here, and we (five officers) have a room to ourselves, and our five servants and our cook live and cook for us in the kitchen. The men of our Company are quartered in neighbouring farm buildings, and other Companies farther down the road. We are within a mile of a village and about three or four miles to the southward of a fair-sized and well-known town. The weather is steadily improving and the mud is drying up—though I haven't seen what the trenches are like yet. . . .

" I am now permanently attached to C Company and am devoutly thankful. Captain T. is in command and the subalterns are Laws, Fletcher, and Thomas, all old friends of mine. F. was the man whose room I shared at Edinburgh and over whose bed I fixed the picture. . . .

" We went on a ' fatigue ' job to-day—just our Company—and were wrongly directed and so went too far and got right in view of the enemy's big guns. However, we cleared out very quickly when we discovered our error, and had got back on to the main road again when a couple of shells burst apparently fairly near where we had been. There were a couple of hostile aeroplanes about too. . . . Thank you very much for your letter wondering where I am. ' Very pressing are the Germans,' a buried city."

2

[This of course privately signified to the family that he was at Ypres.]

"1 *April* 1915, 1.15. *p.m.*

"We dug trenches by night on Monday and Wednesday, and although we were only about 300 to 500 yards from the enemy we had a most peaceful time, only a very few stray bullets whistling over from time to time."

"*Saturday*, 3 *April* 1915, 7 *p.m.*

"I am having quite a nice time in the trenches. I am writing this in my dug-out by candle-light ; this afternoon I had a welcome shave. Shaving and washing is usually dispensed with during our spell of duty (even by the Colonel), but if I left it six days I should burst my razor I think. I have got my little ' Primus ' with me and it is very useful indeed as a standby, although we do all our main cooking on a charcoal brazier. . . .

"I will look out for the great sunrise to-morrow morning and am wishing you all a jolly good Easter : I shan't have at all a bad one. It is very like Robinson Crusoe— we treasure up our water supply most carefully (it is brought up in stone jars), and we have excellent meals off limited and simple rations, by the exercise of a little native cunning on the part of our servants, especially mine."

"*Bank Holiday*, 5 *April* 1915, 4.30 *p.m.*

"The trenches are only approached and relieved at night-time, and even here we are not allowed to stir from the house by day on any pretext whatever, and no fires are allowed on account of the smoke. (Fires are started within doors when darkness falls and we have a hot meal then and again in the early morning—that is the rule— however, we do get a fire in the day by using charcoal only and lighting up from a candle to one piece and from that one piece to the rest, by blowing ; also I have my Primus stove.) . . . We are still within rifle-fire range here, but of course it is all unaimed fire from the intermittent conflict going on at the firing line. . . .

"I have a straw bed covered with my tarpaulin sheet —(it is useful although I have also the regular military rubber ground sheet as well)—and my invaluable air-pillow. I am of course travelling light and have to carry everything in my ' pack ' until I get back to my valise and ' rest billets,' so I sleep in my clothes. Simply take off my boots and puttees, put my feet in a nice clean sack, take off my coat and cover myself up with my British Warm coat (put on sideways so as to use its great width to the full). Like this I sleep like a top and am absolutely comfortable."

" I have been making up an Acrostic for you all to guess—here it is :

LIGHTS. My first is speechless, and a bell
Has often the complaint as well.
Three letters promising to pay,
Each letter for a word does stay.
There's nothing gross about this act ;—
A gentle kiss involving tact.
A General less his final ' k,'
A hen would have no more to say.
Our Neenie who is going west
Her proper name will serve you best.

WHOLE. My whole, though in a foreign tongue,
Is Richard's name when he is young.
The rest is just a shrub or tree
With spelling ' Made in Germany.'

" That's the lot. The word has ten letters and is divided into two halves for the purpose of the Acrostic.

. . . .

" My room-mate has changed for to-night, and I have got Wyatt, who has just come in covered in mud, after four days in the trenches. He is machine-gun officer, and works very hard. I am so glad to have him.

" By the way the support-trenches aren't half bad. I didn't want to leave them, but it's all right here too."

" *Thursday*, 8 *April* 1915
" Here I am back again in ' Rest Billets,' for six days' rest. When I set off for the six days' duty I was ardently looking forward to this moment, but there is not much difference ; here we ' pig ' it pretty comfortably in a house, and there we 'pig ' it almost as comfortably in a ' dug-out.' There we are exposed to rifle fire, nearly all un-aimed, and here we are exposed to shell fire—aimed, but from about five miles away.

" On the whole this is the better, because there is more room to move about, more freedom for exercise, and there is less mud. But you will understand how much conditions in the trenches have improved if comparison is possible at all.

" My platoon (No. 11) has been very fortunate ; we have had no casualties at all in the last six days. The nearest thing to one was yesterday when we were in the firing trench, and a man got a bullet through his cap quite close to his head. He was peeping over the top, a thing they are all told not to do in the daytime. The trenches at our point are about a hundred yards apart, and it is really safe to look over if you don't do it too often, but it is unnecessary, as we had a periscope and a few loopholes. . . .

" I am awfully grateful for all the things that have been sent, and are being sent. . . . I will attach a list of wants at the end of this letter. I am very insatiable (that's not quite the word I wanted), but I am going on the principle that you and the rest of the family are only waiting to gratify my every whim ! So, if I think of a thing I ask for it. . . .

" By the way we have changed our billets here. Our last ones have been shelled while we were away—a prodigious hole through the roof wrecking the kitchen, but not touching our little room at the back. However, it is not safe enough for habitation and the natives even have left !

" Things are awfully quiet here. We thought at first that it was ' fishy ' and something was preparing, but I don't think so now. It is possibly the principle of ' live and let live.' In the trenches if we don't stir them up with shots they leave us pretty well alone. Of course we are ready for anything all the same.

" Yes, we see the daily papers here as often as we want to (the day's before). Personally, and I think my view is shared by all the other officers, I would rather read a romance, or anything not connected with this war, than a daily paper. . . .

" Was the Easter sunrise a success ? It wasn't here. Cloudy and dull was how I should describe it. Fair to fine generally, some rain (the latter not to be taken in the American sense).

" I wonder if you got my Acrostic [see previous letter] and whether anybody guessed it ; it was meant to be very easy, but perhaps acrostics are no longer the fashion and are somewhat boring. I always think they are more fun to make than to undo. The solution is a household word here, because it is only a half-mile or so away, and provides most things."

[The family had soon guessed the Acrostic, giving the place as Dickebusch. The " lights " are—

D um B
I o U
Cares S
K lu Ck
E dit H.]

[*To a Brother*]

"*Billets, Tuesday*, 13 *April* 1915
" We are all right here except for the shells. When I arrived I found every one suffering from nerves and unwilling to talk about shells at all. And now I understand why. The other day a shrapnel burst near our billet and a piece of the case caught one of our servants (Mr. Laws's) on the leg and hand. He lost the fingers of his right hand, and I have been trying to forget the mess it made of his right leg—ever since. He will have had it amputated by now.

" They make you feel awfully shaky, and when one comes over it is surprising the pace at which every one gets down into any ditch or hole near.

" One large shell landed right on the field where the men were playing football on Sunday evening. They all fell flat, and all, I am thankful to say, escaped injury, though a few were within a yard or so of the hole. The other subalterns of the Company and I were (*mirabile dictu*) in church at the time.

" I wonder if you can get hold of some morphia tablets [for wounded men]. I think injection is too complicated, but I understand there are tablets that can merely be placed in the mouth to relieve pain. They might prove very useful in the trenches, because if a man is hit in the morning he will usually have to wait till dark to be removed.

" My revolver has arrived this morning."

" *Sunday*, 18 *April* 1915

" I came out of the trenches on Friday night. It was raining, so the surface of the ground was very slippery ; and it was the darkest night I can remember. There was a good deal of ' liveliness ' too, shots were flying around more than usual. There were about a hundred of us in our party, two platoons (Fletcher's and mine) which had been in the fire trenches, though I was only with them for one day, Thursday night till Friday night. Captain Taylor was in front, then Fletcher's platoon, then Fletcher, then my platoon, then me bringing up the rear. We always travel in single file, because there are so many obstacles to negotiate—plank bridges and ' Johnson ' holes being the chief.

" Picture us then shuffling our way across the fields behind the trenches at about one mile an hour—with frequent stops while those in front negotiate some obstacle (during these stops we crouch down to try and miss most of the bullets !). Every few minutes a ' Very ' light will go up and then the whole line ' freezes ' and remains absolutely stationary in its tracks till the light is over. A ' Very ' light is an ' asteroid.' (Noël will explain that.) It is fired either by means of a rocket (in the German case) or of a special pistol called a ' Very ' pistol after the inventor (in our case). The light is not of magnesium brightness, but is just a bright star light with a little parachute attached, so that it falls slowly through the air. The light lasts about five seconds. These things are being shot up at short intervals all night long. Sometimes dozens are in the air together, especially if an attack is on.

" Well, to go back to Friday night :—it took us a very long time to get back, and at one point it was hard to believe that they hadn't seen us. Lights went up and almost a volley whistled over us. We all got right down and waited for a bit. Really we were much too far off for them to see us, but we were on rather an exposed bit of ground, and they very likely fix a few rifles on to that part in the daytime and ' poop ' them off at night. That is a favourite plan of theirs, and works very well.

" We did get here in the end, and had no casualties, though we had had one just before leaving the trench. A man called Raymond (in my platoon) got shot through the left forearm. He was firing over the parapet and had been sniping snipers (firing at their flashes). Rather a nasty wound through an artery. They applied a tourniquet and managed to stop the bleeding, but he was so weak from loss of blood he had to be carried back on a stretcher.

" I had noticed this man before, partly on account of his name. Last time I was in the fire trenches (about ten days ago) I was dozing in my dug-out one evening and the Sergeant-Major was in his, next door. Suddenly he calls out ' Raymond ! ' I started. Then he calls again ' Raymond ! Come here ! ' I shouted out ' Hallo ! What's the matter ? ' But then I heard the other Raymond answering, so I guessed how it was. . . .

" While at tea in the next room the post came and brought me your letter and one from Alec. Isn't it perfectly marvellous ? You were surprised at the speed of my last letter. But how about yours ? The postmark is 2.30 p.m. on the 16th at Birmingham, and here it is in my hands at 4 p.m. on the 18th !

" I was telling you about the difficulties of going to and fro between here and the trenches, but you will understand it is not always like that. If there is a moon, or even if there is a clear sky so that we can get the benefit of the starlight (which is considerable and much more than I thought), matters are much improved, because if you can still see the man in front, when he is, say, 5 yards in front of you, and can also see the holes instead of finding them with your person, all that ' waiting for the " tail " to close up ' is done away with. . . .

" Last night Laws, Thomas, and myself each took a party of about forty-five down separately, leaving the remainder guarding the various billets. Then when we returned Fletcher took the rest down.

" It was a glorious night, starry, with a very young and inexperienced moon, and quite dry and warm. I would not have minded going down again except that I would rather go to bed, which I did.

" Do you know that joke in *Punch* where the Aunt says : ' Send me a postcard when you are safely in the trenches ! ' ? Well, there is a great deal of truth in that —one feels quite safe when one reaches the friendly shelter of the trench, though of course the approaches aren't really very dangerous. One is ' thrilled ' by the whistle of the bullets near you. That describes the feeling best, I think—it is a kind of excitement."

" *Thursday, 22 April* 1915, 6.50 *p.m.*

" I have received a most grand periscope packed, with spare mirrors, in a canvas haversack. It is a glorious one and I am quite keen to use it, thank you very much indeed for it. Thank you also for two sets of ear defenders which I am going to test when firing off a ' Very ' light. A ' parachuted ' star is fired from a brass pistol with a bore of about 1 inch and a barrel of about 6 inches. The report is very deafening, I believe—though I haven't fired one yet.

" The star, by the way, though it lights up the country for some distance, is not too bright to look at.

" I have just remembered something I wanted to tell you, so I will put it in here.

" When walking to and from the trenches in the darkness, I find it is a great help to study the stars (not for purposes of direction). I know very little about them, and I saw a very useful plan in, I think, the *Daily News* of 3 April, called ' The Night Sky in April.' It was just a circle with the chief planets and stars shown and labelled. The periphery of the circle represented the horizon.

" If you know of such a plan that is quite easily obtainable I should be glad to have one. The simpler the thing the better.

" The books you had sent me, which were passed on to me by Professor Leith, are much appreciated. They circulate among officers of this Company like a library. At the time they arrived we were running short of reading-matter, but since then our Regimental Headquarters have come to the rescue and supplied each Company with half a dozen books, to be passed on to other Companies afterwards.

" I enclose an acrostic that I made up while in the trenches during our last spell. It seems to be a prolific place for this sort of thing."

ACROSTIC

(One word of five letters)

LIGHTS. The lowest rank with lowest pay,
Don't make this public though, I pray!
Inoculation's victim, though
Defeated still a powerful foe.
When Government ' full-stop ' would say
It does so in this novel way.
The verb's success, the noun's disgrace
And lands you in a foreign place.
A king of kings without a roar,
His kingdom that no anger bore.

The final goal—the end of all—
What all desire, both great and small.
R. L., 19 *April* 1915

[The solution of this is the word *Peace* given twice—once inverted. The first ' light,' which is not ' public ' is ' Private '; the second is ' Enteric '; the third is a sign employed in Government telegrams to denote a full-stop, viz., ' aaa '; the fourth is ' Capture '; and the fifth (with apologies) is ' Emp,' and some occult reference to Edward VII, not remembered now; the kingdom without anger being Empire without ire.—O. J. L.]

" *Friday*, 30 *April* 1915, 4.10 *p.m.*
" I wish you could see me now. I am having a little holiday in Belgium. At the moment I am sitting in the shade of a large tree, leaning against its trunk, writing to you. The sun is pouring down and I have been sitting in it lying on a fallen tree, but it makes me feel lazy, so I came here to write (in the shade).

" Before me, across a moat, is the château—ruined now, but not by old age. It is quite a handsome building, two storeys high. It is built of brick with a slate roof; the bricks are colour-washed yellow with a white band 18 inches deep under the roof; there are two towers with pointed roofs that stand to the front of the house, projecting slightly from it, forming bay windows. These towers, from the roof down to the ground, are red brick, as are the fronts of the dormer windows in the main building.

" The larger and taller tower is octagonal and stands in the middle of the front, the smaller one is square and stands on the right corner. On each side of the main building are flanking buildings consisting on this (left) side of a brick-built palm-house and beyond that again a glass-covered conservatory. The other flank has a conservatory also, but I have not explored as far as that. The front of the building is about 70 to 80 yards long.

" The main entrance is on the other or northern side. It is reached by a drawbridge over the moat. The house on that (north) side is not so much damaged. It has long windows with shutters that give it a continental air.

I can't sketch it, so I have given you a rough elevation from the south. I am sitting to the south-west, just across the moat.

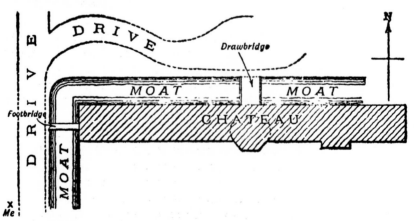

" The place is in an awful mess. In some parts it is difficult to tell how the original building went. One can see into several of the rooms ; the outer wall has fallen away, exposing about three rooms and an attic. In one room the floor has dropped at one corner to some 8 feet below its proper level, and a bed is just above poised on the edge of the room, almost falling out where the room is sectioned.

" There is no glass in any of the green-houses—it is all on the floor. The palm-house is full of green tubs with plants in them, mostly overturned.

" In the garden the trees are blossoming, some of the fruit trees are covered with white blossom ; but many, even of these, are lying flat and blossoming in the moat. The drive runs down to the road on the south side in an absolutely straight line, flanked by tall trees. But many of these are down too. I was lying on one just now. The garden is in good order, though getting a little out of hand. There is a small plantation of gooseberry bushes that looks very healthy. Shell holes are all about, however.

" The house, although it is not on an eminence, commands a good view to the southward and has a fine view of the German lines, which are slightly raised just here. The enemy evidently suspected this château was used as an observation post, as indeed it may have been.

" We came out of the trenches on Wednesday night into Reserve Billets, and I was placed with No. 9 platoon (instead of my own) in a little house not far from this château. We are not allowed to leave it by day, or rather we are not allowed to show ourselves on the south side of it, as it might draw shell-fire on to it. But I managed to sneak away to the north under cover of a hedge without any risk of being seen.

" After being relieved in the trenches on Wednesday, and marching back and having a meal with the other officers of C Company in the Reserve Billets (a brewery), it was one o'clock before I got to bed in our little house. And we had to ' stand to arms ' in the morning for an hour while dawn was breaking (we always do, and at dusk too). So after this I went to sleep till 2 p.m. I sleep in an out-house with no door, on straw laid on a brick floor. My ground-sheet on the straw, my coat over me, my feet in a sack and an air-cushion under my head, and I can sleep as peacefully as at home. The place is swarming with rats and mice, you can hear them directly you lie still. They go ' plop, plop, plop,' on the straw overhead, as if they were obliged to take long strides owing to their feet sinking into the straw. Immediately over my head, I should judge, there is a family of young rats by the noise. Occasionally they have a stampede and a lot of dust comes down on my face.

" But one gets used to this, and muttering ' Nom d'un chien ! ' one turns the other cheek. By the way, they say these rats ' stand to ' at dawn, just as we do.

" I am terrified of a rat running over my face, but my servant sleeps with me, so I console myself that the chances are just even that they won't choose me. I wish he wouldn't snore though—he's lowering the odds.

" Last night we had to turn out for fatigue parties. I took a party down to one of the fire trenches with ' knife rests.' These are sections of barbed wire entanglement. They are made by fixing cross-pieces on the ends of a long pole. The tips of these cross-pieces are joined together with barbed wire laid parallel to the centre pole. Then the whole is wound with more barbed wire laid on spirally, thus : [a sketch]
These are slung out in front of the trenches and fixed together. They are now fixed also to the trench, because the Germans used to harpoon them and draw them over to their own side !

" Well, we set off about 11 p.m. and took twenty-two of these down. We didn't exactly bless the full moon—although it showed us the holes and obstructions in the way. Still, we had no casualties and made good time. We got back about midnight. So I only slept till 12.30 this morning ! Of course I had to get up for an hour at dawn. I used the time to brew myself some cocoa. I am getting an expert cook, and can make that ' Bivouac ' cocoa taste like the very finest chocolate. . . .

" Just before going into the trenches I received another of those splendid parcels of cabbage and apples. The apples are simply splendid. The cabbage is good, but I never cared very much for it—it is medicinal in this case. However, it is great to have such a fine supply of green stuff instead of none at all. The Mess does appreciate it.

" I have been supplying our Mess (C Company) with

butter. And the supply sent up to now has just effected this with none to spare. But I don't know whether you want to do this, and that is why I suggested cutting down the supply. I don't want you to think any of it has been wasted though—it hasn't, and is splendid stuff. . . .

" In the trenches one is not always doing nothing. These last three days in I have been up all night. I had a working party in two shifts working all night and all three nights, digging communication trenches. I used to go to bed about 4.30 a.m. and sleep till lunch-time, and perhaps lie down again for a bit in the afternoon. That is why my letters have not been so frequent.

" It is extraordinary that what is wanted at the moment is not so much a soldier as a civil engineer. There are trenches to be laid out and dug, and the drainage of them to be thought out and carried through. Often the sides have to be ' riveted ' or staked, and a flooring of boards put in, supported on small piles.

" Then there is the water-supply, where one exists. I have had great fun arranging a ' source ' in my trench (the support trench that I have been in these last three days and that I have been in often before). A little stream, quite clear and drinkable after boiling, runs out at one place (at about 1 pint a minute !) and makes a muddy mess of the trenches near. By damming it up and putting a water-bottle with the bottom knocked in on top of the dam, the water runs in a little stream from the mouth of the bottle. It falls into a hole large enough to receive a stone water-jar, and then runs away down a deep trough cut beside the trench. Farther down it is again dammed up to form a small basin which the men use for washing ; and it finally escapes into a kind of marshy pond in rear of the trenches.

" I quite enjoyed this job, and there are many like it ; plank bridges to be put up, seats and steps to be cut, etc. One officer put half a dozen of his men on to making a folding bed ! But it was not for himself, but for his Captain, who has meningitis and can't sleep. The men enjoy these jobs too ; it is much better than doing nothing.

" I will creep back to my quarters now and make myself some tea on my ' Primus ' (no fires are allowed).

" A cuckoo has been singing on a tree near me—in full

view. (It left hurriedly when one of our guns went off close behind the château.) The first time I have ever seen one, I think. It is amazing how tame the animals get. They have so much ground to themselves in the daytime —the rats especially ; they flourish freely in the space between the trenches.

" Things are fairly quiet and easy here just now."

[In one of his letters to me (22 April 1915), he said he had plenty of time now to watch the stars, and would like a set of star maps or something in order to increase his knowledge of them. Accordingly, I sent him a planisphere which I happened to have—an ingenious cardboard arrangement which can be turned so as to show, in a rough way, the stars visible in these latitudes at any time of day and any period of the year.— O. J. L.]

" *May Day* 1915, 3.20 *p.m.*

" Thank you very much for the planisphere and for your letter. I have often seen the planisphere before, but never appreciated it until now.

" As to the ' Very ' pistol, I quite agree that the ' barrel ' is too short. If it were longer the light would be thrown farther, which would be much better. As it is, it falls between us and the Germans.

" The German lights, which I now learn are fired from a kind of mortar and not by a rocket as I thought, are much better than ours ; they give a better and steadier, fatter light, and they are thrown well behind our trenches. However, ours are much better, and theirs are worse than they used to be. . . .

" They have not turned the gas on to us here, though on some days I have smelled distinct traces coming down wind from the north. I should say it was chlorine rather than SO_2 that I smelled. I don't know whether the ammonia preventive would be better than the soda one. In any case, the great thing is that one is provided. The soda method is the one in use, I believe, in the chlorine works at Widnes and elsewhere."

" *Tuesday*, 3 *May* 1915, 12.40 *p.m.*
",For the first three days we are out here in new billets—officers in a comfortable little house. Last three days of our ' rest ' (!) we are going into a wood quite close

to our ' Reserve Billets.' We are in ' support ' in case of
a sudden attack. Roads are so much knocked about by
shells that traffic is limited and restricted. So we might
not be able to support quick enough unless we were
close.

" Everything is still very much upset, due to the pene-
tration of our (French) line. They have been shelling our
village from the rear (!) and most of the companies have
had to quit. *We* (C Company) are well back now. . . .

" Two of our platoons went digging last night. Mine
was one. We left here about eight o'clock, and I got
back at 1 a.m., and then I sat up with another subaltern
(Fletcher) after I had had some supper until the other
man (Thomas) had come in and eaten. We went to bed
at 3 a.m. Breakfast at nine this morning, and we are
resting. However, I am going to have an absolutely
slack day to-day. A bath too, if I can manage it. . . .

" Last night the moon got up very late and was quite
useless. They fire more when there is no light, they get
scared—at least uneasy ; they fire off ' Very ' lights constantly, and let off volleys. We lie absolutely flat while
this goes on. It is a funny sight ; the men look like a
row of starfish ! "

" *Tuesday,* 11 *May* 1915, 9.15 *a.m.*
(*really Wednesday the* 12*th. I had got wrong*)
" We are within view of a well-known place [no doubt
Ypres.—O. J. L.], and the place has been on fire in three
or four places for about two days, and is still going strong.
A magnificent spectacle at night. The place is, I believe,
a city of ruins and dead, and there is probably no one to
put a fire out. Probably, too, a fire is rather a good
thing than otherwise ; the place must be terribly in need
of purifying.

" I was awfully interested in father's dream.[1] Your
letter is dated the 8th, and you say that the other night
he dreamt that I was in the thick of the fighting, but that
they were taking care of me from the other side.

" Well, I don't know about ' the thick of the fighting,'
but I have been through what I can only describe as a
hell of a shelling with shrapnel. My diary tells me it

[1] See Note by O. J. L. at the end of this letter.

was on the 7th, at about 10.15 a.m. Our Company were ordered forward from one set of dug-outs to others nearer the firing line, and the formation adopted was platoons in single file, with intervals between. That is, four columns of about fifty men each, in single file, with about 20 to 50 yards between each column. I was the third platoon, though I was not with my own but with No. 9. Fletcher brought up the last one, thus :—

No. 10 x	No. 9 x	No. 12 x	No. 11 x
Fr.	Me	Ths.	Capt.

Direction of march ⟶

(My platoon is No. 11.—No. 9's platoon commander, Laws, is in England on sick leave, as his nerves are all wrong.)

"Well, anyhow, we had not gone far before the gunners saw us, and an aeroplane was flying along above and with us. They sent over some ' Johnsons,' but these all went too far; we were screened by a reservoir embankment. However, we had to pass through a ruined village and they knew it, so they put shrapnel over it. Still we were unaffected. But when we came out into the open on the far side, we caught it properly. Shell after shell came over and burst above us, and when I and about three men behind me had just turned a corner one burst above, in exactly the spot I should have wished it to if I had been the enemy. I looked up and saw the air full of flying pieces, some large and some small. These spattered down all round us. I was untouched, but my servant, who was immediately behind me, was hit on the knee, but only wounded slightly. He was rather scared. I led him back round the corner again and put him in a ditch. The rest of the platoon got in too, while I was doing this. I thought that was the best thing they could do until the shelling ceased, but Fletcher shouted that we must get on, whatever happened.

"So I called the men out again, and, leaving a man with the wounded, we set off. I don't believe it was right, but we just walked along. It felt rather awful. (When one is *retiring* it is important not to let the men ' double,' as they get out of hand ; but in this case we were advancing, so I think we might have done so.) I felt very much protected. It was really a miracle that we weren't nearly all ' wiped out.' The shrapnel seemed very poor stuff. As it was, we had one man killed and about five or six injured, all more or less slightly.

" We moved up into a support trench that same evening, and after a couple of days we moved a few yards farther to these trenches, which are also support trenches. Things are very quiet, and I am enjoying myself very much. If it wasn't for the unpleasant sights one is liable to see, war would be a most interesting and pleasant affair.

" My friends the other officers of C Company have given me the honorary position of ' O.C. Works.' One is always ' O.C. something or other ' out here—all but the Colonel, he is ' C.O.' Orders for the day read : ' O.C. Companies will do so-and-so.' Then there are O.C. Details, O.C. Reinforcements, etc. ' O.C.' of course stands for ' officer commanding.' Well, I am ' O.C. Works,' and have a fine time. I just do any job I fancy, giving preference to trench improvement. It is fine to have at one's disposal a large squad of men with shovels (or without). They fill sandbags and carry them, they carry timber and saw it, and in short do anything that is required. One can accomplish something under these conditions."

" 6 p.m.

" We have been told that we are being relieved to-night, and that we are going back to our old place (No. 2). So everything should be as before, once we are back. We may not manage to get *all* the way back to-night, as we cannot travel by daylight as most of the road is under direct observation. If daylight catches us we shall encamp in dug-outs *en route*.

" I am rather disappointed that we are going to-night, as Fletcher and I were going to rebuild our dug-out here. We both got very keen indeed and had laid out the plan carefully. (He has been an architect.)

" I had another disappointment when I was back in the wood (as supports). It reminds me of one of our Quartermaster-Sergeants in Edinburgh. He is an Irishman, O'Brien. I found him on the platform while we were waiting to see a draft off ; he looked very despondent

3

I asked him how he was, and was surprised when he replied, ' I've had a reverse, sorr ! ' It turned out that he had applied to headquarters for an improvement in his position, and was told he *didn't deserve any.* It had almost broken his heart !

" Well, *I* had a reverse. I was given the job of building a hut and was nearly through with it when we were ordered away. If we get back to the old wood again I shall go on with it, in spite of whatever the present tenants may have done in the way of completing it (our guns are now ' going at it ' hammer and tongs).

" I did enjoy laying the sandbags and building a proper wall with ' headers ' and ' stretchers.' I got a very good testimonial too, for the Sergeant asked me in all seriousness whether I was a brick-setter in civil life. I was awfully proud.

" *Later*

" (I had to leave off here because we were ordered to ' fire-rapid ' in between periods of our artillery fire, and I had to turn out to watch.) "

NOTE BY O. J. L.

The dream referred to, near the beginning of this long letter to his mother, Mr. J. Arthur Hill remembers that I told him of, in a letter dated 7 May 1915, which he has now returned ; and I reproduce it here :—

" To J. A. H.

" *7 May 1915*

" I do not reckon that I often have conscious intuitions ; and when I have had vivid dreams they have not meant anything, though once or twice I have recorded them because I have them seldom. I happen, however, to have had an intuition this morning, before I was more than half awake, which, though not specially vivid, perhaps I had better record, namely, that an attack was going on at the present moment, that my son was in it, but that ' they ' were taking care of him. I had this clearly in mind before seeing the morning papers ; and indeed I do not know that there is anything in the morning papers suggesting it, since of course their news is comparatively old. One might have surmised, however, that there would be a struggle for Hill 60, and I know that my son is not far off Ypres. (By the way, I have been told that the Flemish Belgians really do call it ' Wipers ' ; it does not sound likely, and it needs confirmation. I know of course that our troops are said to call it so, which is natural enough.) O. J. L."

I now (August 1916) notice for the first time that the coincidence in time between dream and fact is rather good, especially as it was the only dream or ' impression ' that I remember having during the war. Practically I do not dream.

But as this incident raises the question of possible presentiment I must deny that we had any serious presentiment about Raymond. My wife tells me that her anxiety about Raymond, though always present, was hardly keen, as she had an idea that he would be protected. She wrote to a friend on 22 March 1915 :—

" . . . I ought to get him back safe. I have a hole in my heart and shall have till he comes back. I only saw him for the inside of an hour before he left, as I was away when he came home for six hours. . . ."

At the same time I must admit that on the morning of 15 September 1915 (the day after Raymond's death, which we did not know of till the 17th) I was in an exceptional state of depression ; and though a special game, to which I had been looking forward, on the No. 1 Course at Gullane had been arranged with Rowland Waterhouse, I could not play a bit. Not ordinary bad play, but total incompetence ; so much so that after seven holes we gave up the game, and returned to the hotel. To make sure of the date, I wrote to Rowland Waterhouse, asking him when that abortive match occurred, since I knew that it was his last day at Gullane. He replies :—

" Violet and I left Gullane for Musselburgh on Wednesday, 15 September. Our final match ended that morning on the eighth tee " [which that year was on the reservoir hill].

One more dream I may as well now mention :—

After the family had returned home from Scotland and elsewhere, near the end of September 1915, and begun to settle down, Alec, who had felt Raymond's death exceedingly, told me that the night before he heard the news—or rather the early morning of the same day, 17 September—he had had an extraordinarily painful and vivid dream, quite an exceptional occurrence for him, and one of which he had spoken to a manageress in the hotel near Swansea where he was staying, describing it as the worst he had ever had in his life. He did not know that it had any significance, and neither do I, as the dream, though rather ghastly, was not about Raymond or anyone in particular ; but it seemed an odd coincidence that the ill news should be, so to speak, on the way, at the time of a quite exceptional and painful impression. The person to whom he told the dream handed him the telegram a few hours later. He has written the dream down, but it need not be reproduced.

No real prevision is involved in any of this, unless it be that of an hour or two in my own impression, in May ; but for general remarks on the question of the possibility of prevision Chapter V in Part III may be referred to

" Friday, 14 May 1915
" I had a glorious hot bath yesterday ; Fletcher and
I went up to the brewery here. The bath is zinc, and
full length, and we have as much water, and as hot, as
we like. . . .

" I spent some time too stemming the leaks in the roof
of our shed. With my *two* waterproof sheets I have rigged
up a kind of chute above my bed, so that any water that
comes through the roof is led down behind my head. I
don't know what happens to it there. I thought of leading it across on to the man next me, as the Germans used
to do in the winter campaign. They fitted a pump in
their trenches and led the delivery pipe forward, so that
the water used to run into ours—only the plan was
discovered. . . .

" I wonder if you saw the appreciation of the soda cake
on the back of my letter from the woods. M.P. stands for
Mess President. Fletcher was M.P. and was a very good
one. I am now, as he has done it for a long time and is
tired. . . .

" As cheerful and well and happy as ever. Don't
think I am having a rotten time—I am not."

" Sunday, 5.40 p.m., 16 May 1915
" We had a very fine piece of news yesterday. Over
three weeks ago we were called out one night and were
urgently required to dig a certain new trench behind our
lines. The men worked splendidly and got the job done
in a very short time (working of course in complete darkness). The next day the Brigadier-General inspected the
trench and sent in a complimentary message about it to
our Colonel. The day after he complimented us again—for
the same piece of work ! Well, we have had several such
jobs to do, and just recently we have been to Hill 60, where
the bulk of our work was deepening the trenches and improving the parapets. We were lent for this purpose to
another Division (the Division that is at the moment
occuping that area), and were away from here exactly a
week. We got a splendid testimonial from the General of
this other Division, who told our Colonel he had got 'a
top-hole battalion.' Arising out of all this, we have now

been selected as a ' Pioneer Battalion.' We are relieved from all ordinary trench work for some time to come. We simply go out at night and dig trenches or build parapets and so forth, and have the day to ourselves. This was arranged yesterday, and last night we went out and returned here at 1.30 a.m. The work is more or less under fire, but only from stray shots and nothing very serious. Our Colonel is awfully pleased that we have done so well ; and we are all pleased with the new arrangement. One great advantage is that we can settle down in our billets and are not continually having to pack up everything and move off. We can now start and make tables, chairs, beds, a proper door for the hut, a glass window, and so on. . . .

" As to aeroplanes, when one passes overhead a whistle is blown and every one either takes cover or stands perfectly still. The men are forbidden to look up. Then the whistle is blown several times when the danger is past. I am afraid, though, these regulations are more honoured in the breach than the observance.

" We had quite a nice informal service here this afternoon sitting in a field. The chaplain has the rank of Major and has been out here seven months.

" Yesterday the Captain, Fletcher, and myself went for a ride on horses. We went about five miles out, stopped for about twenty minutes at a little inn (the last in Belgium on that particular road), and then came back again. The country was perfectly lovely, though I did not appreciate it as much as I otherwise would have done, as I had a trooper's saddle and the Cap ain would trot. I got most awfully sore going out, and thought I should never be able to get back. However, I discovered a method at last, and that was to go at a full gallop. So I alternately went at a walk and ' hell for leather,' and got back in comparative comfort. I thoroughly enjoyed it ; it was very bad for the horse, I am afraid, on the stone setts (*pavé*), but sometimes I could get him on to the softer bits at the side. I was terribly afraid some one would think the horse was running away with me and ' block ' him, so I had to look as pleased as possible. And really I *was* pleased, it was such a blessed relief after that awful trotting. I trotted along in rear of the other two until I could stand it no longer, and then I encouraged my nag and hit him until he broke into a canter, and then I roared past the others, who cursed like anything because theirs wanted to gallop too. My horse's canter changed imperceptibly into a full gallop, and I ' got down to it ' and felt like a jockey. After about half a mile I would walk until the others came up and passed me, and then I would go off again. All the same, I am very sore.

" Good-bye for the present; it is lovely hot weather and we are all well—fit—and happy."

" *Tuesday*, 18 *May* 1915, 5.15 *p.m.*
" MY DEAR NORAH AND BARBARA,—I don't expect I am far wrong in attributing my ripping present of dates and figs to you two. I did enjoy them, and they are not finished yet.

" They arrived by the first post after we had returned from our little trip. We were at Hill 60; it was so interesting and rather exciting, although we were there chiefly, I think, to improve the trenches, which were very shallow and dangerous when we arrived.

" The men worked splendidly—all night and most of the day, and, when we left, the trenches were vastly improved and quite habitable. We also made some entirely new ones. We are now kept for this sort of job only, and we go out working at nights and sleep by day.

" I must explain to you about ' standing to.' A proportion of the men are always awake in the trenches to guard against surprises, for as the most likely times for an attack are at dawn and at dusk, everybody has to be awake and ready then. Of course it does interfere with your sleep, and you do not get very much as a rule in the trenches, but that is why you are not there for more than about three days at a time. In the ' supports ' you ' stand to ' so as to be ready to reinforce the front line quickly in case of an attack. Out in ' Rest Billets,' I am glad to say, it is no longer necessary.

" I am so sorry, my friend Fletcher has just gone off this morning for a rest cure. I shall miss him awfully. He is about five miles away and I am going to ride over to-morrow to see him. But later on he will probably go back to England. His nerves are all wrong and he needs a rest.

" Good-bye for now, and very best wishes to you both.
—Your very loving brother, RAYMOND "

" I hope you get my *communiqués* regularly from home
(swank). Some one must have the time of their lives
copying out all the stuff I write. I hope, however, there
are a few grains in the bundle of chaff (I'm fishing again) !
" You say, Norah, that you don't think the château
was as quiet as I described. Well, provided I mentioned
our gun, that went off at occasional intervals close behind
it with a terrific report, it was just as I described—a
peaceful summer afternoon. I know that people think
that everything in Belgium is chaos and slaughter, but it
isn't so. For instance, where Fletcher is, is a charming
country place with trees and fields and everything in full
green. Simply ripping. If I had only had a motor-cycle
to see it from instead of a trotting horse I should have
enjoyed it even more ! R."

" *Wednesday*, 19 *May* 1915, 12.50 *p.m.*
" You must know that we have now only three officers
in our Company I am very sorry indeed to lose Fletcher.
He went off for a rest cure yesterday morning to a place
about five miles from here. He is my greatest friend in
the Battalion, so I miss him very much and hope he won't
be long away. He will probably go back to England,
however, as his nerves are all wrong. He is going the
same way as Laws did and needs a complete rest. I am
going to ride over to see him this afternoon with the
Captain. I am afraid it won't be ' good going ' as the
roads are thick with mud. The slightest rain, and they
are as bad as ever.
" I told you that I was Mess President (M.P.). I am
sure you would smile to see me ordering the meals, and
inspecting the joints. I don't know anything about
them, and when the cook calls me up specially to view a
joint I have hastily to decide whether he means me to dis-
parage it—or the reverse. However, I am usually safe in
running it down."

" *Thursday*, 20 *May* 1915, 9.10 *a.m.*
" We rode over and saw Fletcher yesterday and had
tea with him. He is with about twenty other similar

cases in a splendid château (this one is not ruined and has magnificent grounds). Unfortunately this is probably the very worst possible treatment he could have. He has nothing to do, no interest in anything, and no society except people who, like himself, want cheering. He does not read, he does not even walk about the grounds. He cannot sleep much, and he said he did not know exactly *what* he did. Under these conditions I know it will not be long before he is sent home. Brooding is just the very worst thing for him. He sees all the past horrors all over again ; things which, at the time, he shut his mind to. The best treatment (even better than home, *I* think) would be to send him back for a month or so to Crosby. He would then have plenty to occupy his mind and would have cheerful companions. . . ."

" 6.20 *p.m.*

" I have attached a list of a few slang terms and curious expressions in use in this Regiment and I believe universal at the moment. Some of these are amazing, and it is difficult to trace the origin. ' Drumming up ' is one, and ' wind up ' another. I saw an old Belgian cart yesterday, a three-wheeled affair. It had been overturned on its side and the spokes of the lowest wheel had been broken. Well, some one had ' drummed up ' on them—every one had disappeared. These men here will ' drum up ' on anything. ' Drumming up ' on a thing does not mean lighting a fire *on* it but *with* it.

" When we were at that place where we were for a week, there was a most peculiar state of affairs. The Germans were holding a small piece of trench joining, and in line with, ours. They were only separated from us by double barricades—theirs and ours. They corresponded to the meat in a sandwich. [A sketch is omitted.] When I say ' ours ' I mean the English. I was not actually in this trench, but in the one just behind. The trench on one side of the ' meat ' was held by one of our Companies, and the other by another Regiment. . . ."

" *Friday*, 10.20 *a.m.*

" My nickname in the Mess is ' Maurice ' (with a French pronunciation) ; I am called after the small boy in the grocery shop here. The good dame always says

' Oui, monsieur le lieutenant ! ' ' Non, monsieur le lieutenant ! ' to everything one says ; she gets in about six to the minute. Well, we used to imitate her after our visits to the shop, and one day she called out ' Maurice ' ; so Fletcher calls me ' Maurice,' and I reply, ' Oui, monsieur le lieutenant.' "

SOME MILITARY TERMS

WATER-PARTY	A fatigue party carrying water.
TO HAVE WIND UP	(to rhyme with ' pinned up ')—To be uneasy, ' on edge.'
DRUMMING UP	Making a fire for the purpose of warming food.
BLIGHTY	England
A BLIGHTY WOUND	A wound that necessitates invaliding home.
PUCCA	Real, genuine.
RALLY UP	A short period of considerable firing in the trenches.
DUG-OUT	A cramped dwelling-place, usually above ground.
STAND-TO	An hour of preparedness at dawn and at dusk when every one is awake and wears his equipment (in trenches and supports only).
STAND-DOWN	The finish of ' stand-to.'
KNIFE-RESTS	Barbed wire in sections.
CUSHY	A ' soft ' thing.
TO GO SICK	To report oneself ill to the doctor.
TO GET DOWN TO IT	To lie down, go to bed.
CRIBBING OR GROUSING	Complaining.

R. L.

20.5.15

[*To a Brother*]

" 26 *May* 1915

" I expect you have read it, but I want to recommend to you *Simon Dale*, by Anthony Hope.

" We had the gas over here on Monday morning about 3 or 4 a.m. Although it was coming from a point about four miles away, as we learnt afterwards, it was very strong and made our eyes smart very much.

" We have got hold of some liqueurs from Railhead, a large bottle of Chartreuse and one of Curaçao.

" Good-bye and good luck."

" *Saturday,* 29 *May* 1915, 8.30 *p.m.*
" We have again done a little move, this time with

bag and baggage. We are now on the outskirts of
'No. 1,' and due west of it. The men have built themselves dug-outs along a hedge and we (C Coy. officers)
are installed in an untouched château. Quite comfortable. Fine lofty rooms. We only use part of the
house. We have the kitchen, and a large dining-room
on the ground floor. We sleep upstairs on the first floor
(our valise on hay). At least, Thomas and I do, the
Captain and Case have moved down and sleep on large
fat palliasses in the dining-room! We have the rest of
the house empty to ourselves to-night, but various head-
quarter staffs seem to come in turn and occupy two of
the other ground floor rooms occasionally.

" We have been out two nights digging on the opposite
side of the town, but we have not been ordered out
to-night, so far.

" I notice I have now been gazetted back to 15
August, the same as most of my contemporaries.

" There has been a suggestion made that I should
take a course of machine-gun instruction in order that I
might act as understudy to our present Machine-Gun
Officer (M.G.O.) who is Roscoe, and is the successor to
Wyatt. I agreed, but it may have ' fallen through '
owing to the move. If it comes off I shall go for a
fortnight's course to a place which I will call No. 3
[probably St. Omer].

" I got a letter from you to-day about 5 p.m. I was
so glad.

" No, I am not making things out better than they
really are. I like to write mostly about the pleasant
parts, of course. We have our unpleasant moments,
shelling and so on, but no very bad times as yet. Being
on tenterhooks is quite the worst part.

" As regards Fletcher being worse than us, of course
he came out much earlier. He left Edinburgh for the
Front on 4 January, and Laws left on 31 December. He
has had some awful times and the winter campaign, and
in any case the length of time one is exposed to the
mental strain and worry makes a difference. I do my
best to keep cheerful and happy all the time—I don't
believe in meeting trouble half-way. If there was some
indication of the termination of the war it would help

matters—the unending vista is apt to be rather disheartening at times. I am very glad Italy is in—at last.

" By the way, Fletcher has not been sent to England (Blighty) after all. He is at Versailles, in the No. 4 General Hospital there, having a nice time if he can enjoy it. This hospital is the Trianon Palace. The Captain had a letter from him in which he sent his love to ' Maurice ' and ' his lordship ' (that's Thomas)."

" 2 *June* 1915, 4.45 *p.m.*

" Our interpreter is a Belgian, and is a very nice man. He does our shopping for us in the town, which is ten miles or so away, and (as now arranged) he makes the journey twice a week. It is very funny to hear him talk, he picks up the soldiers' idioms and uses them in the wrong places. One he is very fond of is the expression ' Every time ' ! He puts such a funny emphasis on it.

" The last member of our Mess is a man who has just come out and has not long had his commission. He used to be Regimental Sergeant-Major to our 1st Battalion and has had about twenty-six years' service, so he knows his job.

" Unfortunately, however, his arrival is not an unmixed blessing. The Captain is seized with enthusiasm and wants to make our Company the finest Company in the Battalion. The result is that we have now nothing but parades and much less rest than before. When we were turned into a pioneer battalion the Colonel told the men that they would go digging at night and would do nothing else except for rifle inspection. Now, however, we have in addition an hour's drill of various sorts in the morning and a lecture to N.C.O.s in the afternoon, at which all subalterns have to attend and take notes. On the day following a rest night we have to be up about seven o'clock, and be on parade while the men do half an hour's physical exercise before breakfast. Then we have an hour and a half's drill afterwards and the lecture. And these parades seem to be growing. I am afraid they will wear us all out and the men as well. Thomas feels it most and is very worried—although he is Senior Subaltern in the Company he is left right out of things. I am afraid of his going like Laws and Fletcher did.

Some 'rankers' are very good fellows. They bring tremendous experience with them, but, on the other hand, we bring something too, and when they ride the high horse they can be very unbearable. . . .

"I got a supply of paraffin to-day; D Company has bought a huge barrel of it, and I sent over a petrol tin for some. They gave me nearly two gallons and asked if I could let them have a window in exchange! I hunted round and found quite a good loose one and sent it across with my compliments. The reason they have bought up so much paraffin is because their Captain has presented pocket Primuses to his men. Each section of twelve men has one between them, with one man in charge of it. It is a killing sight to see their Company sitting in a field and drumming up!

"The Belgian cooking stove is rather a curious thing. It is of the same design in every house apparently. It consists of a metal urn to hold the fire; this has a removable lid for which you can substitute a kettle or pan which just fits the round opening. The urn stands about 3 feet from the wall and has a flat-shaped iron chimney leading into the main chimney. This iron chimney can be used for heating pots or for warming plates. The base of the urn is an ash collector. You will see that there is no oven; this is built separately and is a brick affair with a separate fire to it. [Sketch.]"

"*Thursday*, 3 *June* 1915, 1.30 *p.m.*
"I am all right again to-day; you mustn't pay any attention to my grumbles, it just depends what I feel like; and I am going to stir things up about these parades. We had a fine time last night—very exciting. We went through the heart of the city and it is still very much on fire. The enemy keeps sending an occasional shell into it to keep it going. Just on the far side is a graveyard, and this has been 'crumped' out of existence nearly! It is an unpleasant place to pass now.

"The town is almost unbelievable. I don't think anyone would credit that they could do so much damage and not leave a single house untouched, without entering the place at all. [Ypres again, probably.]

"Our digging last night was near a small road much

used by transport (which is very audible at night). As the enemy can hear the rumble of the horse-drawn carts quite plainly, they kept on sending shrapnel over, and we had quite a warm time of it. We were quite glad to get away again. (No one was hit while we were there.)

" I was very interested in father's pamphlet on ' War and Christianity,' and I have passed it on to the others. I like the way he gets right outside and looks at things from above. It is a very soothing thing to read.[1] . . .

" I had such an interesting talk with the interpreter yesterday (his rank is the equivalent of one of our Sergeant-Majors). He was a merchant in Morocco, and chucked up everything and came and joined the Belgian army as a private. He fought at Namur, Antwerp, and other places, and is most awfully keen. He was offered the job of Interpreter to the British Army, and, thinking he could help more by that means and also partly for monetary considerations, he took the job. He understood he would be fighting with us in the trenches, but they have put him on to shopping for us ! He is awfully disappointed. He rides up when he can, and when we went up to Hill 60 he went up with our transports and showed them the way and helped them a lot, although shells were falling all round. He is a most gentlemanly man ; his name is Polchet. . . .

" I had a letter from Violet and another from Margaret yesterday. I understand they have gone up to Edinburgh now ; I shall like to go up there too ' after the war.' I believe Violet is getting *my* room ready for me in their house. I like everything very plain, just a valise and a little hay, and then you see if I am hungry in the night—— . . .

" P.S.—I had a most interesting letter from Oliver. His discussion of Italy's motives is fine. I like hearing what people think of events ; we are apt to get very warped views out here unless we have the other point of view occasionally."

" *Sunday*, 6 *June* 1915, 12 *p.m.*
" The Mess was thrown into the greatest state of excitement yesterday by the arrival of kippers ! How

[1] This must have been part of my book, *The War and After.*—O. J. L.

splendid! We had a grand breakfast this morning, quite like the summer holidays again—breakfast after a bathe —with Alec of course! . . .

" By the way, I did not present the last lot of asparagus to the Mess—this was not because we didn't appreciate it, but because I felt so sorry for M. Polchet (our interpreter), and I wondered if he had any green stuff or luxuries. So I sent it over to him. And do you know what he has done ? He has just sent me a shallow wooden box with a thick cotton-wool pad in it. In the pad are six hollows, and in each hollow is a ripping nectarine. Isn't it fine of him ?

" We have roses picked every day for the Mess-room ; it does improve it. The other evening we had a specially nice meal. We sat round the polished table with candles in the centre and bowls of roses round them (as a matter of fact the bowls were old tinned-fruit tins, but what of that). The food was very special, though I can't remember what it was, but to crown all there was in the room just across the passage . . . a real fiddler with a real fiddle. I really don't know how he managed to bring a fiddle out here ; he is a private in the Royal Garrison Artillery, and plays simply beautifully. He has long hair and just a suggestion of side whiskers, and large boots, and, but that he would not be complimented, looks like a Viennese.

" He started off by playing Grand Opera—I believe— and he gave us the Intermezzo from ' Cavalleria Rusticana.' Then he gave us ' Gipsy Love ' and the ' Merry Widow,' and so on. He finished up with American ragtime. We sent him in a bottle of whisky half-way through the performance, and the music got lighter thenceforward. It was most amusing to notice the effect. When we looked in later the whisky was standing on the table, and he was walking round it with his fiddle, playing hard and apparently serenading it !

" I was inoculated again on Friday evening because it is only *really* effective for about six months, and there is going to be a lot of enteric about, I expect. This apparently is just the very place for it—flat low-lying country, poor water supply, and the soil heavily manured. So I have been feeling rather weak and feverish after it, but I am better again now. I have to have it done again ten days later—but the second time is not so bad.

" Talking about roses, Thomas picked a beauty this morning (before I got up) and brought it to me in bed. It is in front of me now, and is 5 inches across, and has a very fine smell."

" *Wednesday*, 16 *June* 1915, 1.30 *p.m.*

" We made an attack early this morning, and our Company waited here to receive the prisoners. Poor devils, I do feel so sorry for them. One officer of sixteen with six weeks' service. Old men with grey beards too, and many of the student type with spectacles—not fit to have to fight.

" You remember ' Very Pressing are the Germans '; well, that's where I am, right inside the walls. Quite shell-proof, but very dank.

" I have got the machine-gun job, and am going for a fortnight's course, starting on the 26th of June."

" *Monday*, 21 *June* 1915, 4.30 *p.m.*

" We have had an extremely trying time lately, and I am very sorry to say we have lost Thomas.

" He was hit on the head by shrapnel on the night after the attack—I expect you saw the account in the papers—and died about an hour later, having never recovered consciousness.

" It was a most fatal night—the whole battalion was ordered out digging to consolidate the captured positions. We got half-way out, and then got stuck—the road being blocked by parties of wounded. We waited on a path alongside a hedge for over an hour, and though we could not be seen we had a good deal of shrapnel sent over us. To make matters worse, they put some gas shells near, and we had to wear our helmets though the gas was not very strong. It was exceedingly unpleasant, and we could hardly see at all. It was while we were waiting like this that Thomas got knocked out.

" We are all sorry to lose him, and I miss him very much, but it is nothing to the trouble there will be at his home, for he is his mother's favourite son.

" I have written to his mother, but I have not told her

what makes us feel so mad about it—namely, that we did no digging that night at all. When we got to the position we were so late, and there was still such confusion there due to the attack, that we marched back again and just got in before daylight. We might just as well never have gone out. Isn't it fairly sickening ?

" The next night we went out again, and we had a very quiet night and no casualties. The scene of the battle was pretty bad, and I put all my spare men on to burying.

" Altogether we are very thankful to have a change from ' pioneering,' and get back to the trenches !

" Our chief trouble here is snipers. We are in a wood, and parties going for water and so on to our headquarters *will* walk outside the trench instead of in it, just because the trench goes like this. [A diagram is omitted.] They take the straight course along the side in spite of repeated warnings. There is one point that a sniper has got marked. He gets our men coming back as they get into the trench just too late. We had a man hit this morning, but not badly, and a few minutes ago I had to stop this letter and go to a man of B Company who had got hit, and rather more seriously, at the same spot. I have put up a large notice there now, and hope it will prevent any more.

" I am sorry this is not a very cheerful letter, but we have all been rather sad lately. I am getting over it now. Luckily one absorbs these things very gradually ; I could not realise it at first. It was an awful blow, because, especially since Fletcher went away (he is now at home), we had become very friendly, and one is apt to forget that there is always the chance of losing a friend suddenly. As a matter of fact, Thomas is the first officer of C Company that has been killed for seven months.

" When we were up in this wood before, digging (about a fortnight ago) B Company lost Captain Salter. I dare say you saw his name in the Roll of Honour. We were just going to collect our spades and come in, when he was shot through the head by a stray bullet.

" What a very melancholy strain I am writing in, I am so sorry. I am quite well and fit. We have mislaid our mess-box coming up here with all our specially selected foods. The result is we are on short commons—great fun. I am eating awful messes and enjoying them. Fried bacon and fried cheese together! Awful; but, by Jove, when you're hungry."

LETTER FROM RAYMOND TO THE MOTHER OF AN OFFICER FRIEND OF HIS WHO HAD BEEN KILLED

" 2nd S. Lancashire Regt., B.E.F., Front,
17 June 1915

"DEAR MRS. THOMAS,—I am very sorry to say I have to tell you the very worst of bad news. I know what Humphrey's loss must be to you, and I want to tell you how much it is to all of us too. I know I have not realised it yet myself properly. I have been in a kind of trance since last night and I dread to wake up.

" He was a very fine friend to me, especially since Fletcher went away, and I miss him frightfully. Last night (16th to 17th) the whole Battalion went out digging. There had been an attack by the English early the same morning, and the enemy's guns were still very busy even in the evening. Our road was blocked in front owing to the moving of a lot of wounded, and while we were held up on a little field path alongside a hedge we had several shrapnel shells over us. To add to the horrors of the situation they had put some gas shells over too, and we were obliged to put on our gas helmets. While Humphrey was standing with his helmet on in the rear of our Company talking to the Captain of the Company behind, a shell came over and a piece of it caught him on the head. He was rendered unconscious, and it was evident from the first he had no chance of recovery. He was immediately taken a little way back to a place where there was no gas, and here the doctor dressed his wound. He was then taken back on a stretcher to the dressing-station. He died there about an hour after he had been admitted, having never recovered consciousness.

" If he had to die, I am thankful he was spared pain beforehand. It made my heart ache this afternoon packing his valise ; I have given his chocolate, cigarettes, and tobacco to the Mess, and I have wrapped up his diary and a few loose letters and made them into a small parcel which is in the middle of his valise.

" The papers and valuables which he had on him at the

4

time will be sent back through our headquarters, the other things, such as letters, etc., in his other pockets I have left just as they were. I hope the valise will arrive safely.

" He will be buried very simply, and probably due east of Ypres about three-quarters of a mile out—near the dressing-station. I will of course see he has a proper cross.

" Humphrey was splendid always when shells were bursting near. He hated them as much as any of us, but he just made himself appear unconcerned in order to put heart into the troops. Three nights ago we were digging a trench and the Germans thought our attack was coming off that night. For nearly three-quarters of an hour they put every kind of shell over us and some came very close. We all lay down in the trench and waited. On looking up once I was amazed to see a lone figure walking calmly about as if nothing was going on at all. It may have been foolish but it was grand."

———

" *Tuesday,* 22 *June* 1915, 4.45 *p.m.*
" Well ! What a long war, isn't it ? Never mind, I believe it will finish up without much help from us, and our job is really killing time. And our time is so pleasant it doesn't need much killing out here. The days roll along—nice sunny days too—bringing us nearer I suppose to Peace. (One hardly dares even to write the word now, it has such a significance.) There have been cases where the war has driven people off their heads (this applies only, I think, to the winter campaign), but I often think if Peace comes suddenly that there will be many such cases.

" It really is rather amazing the unanimity of everybody on this subject, and it must be the same behind the German front-line trenches.

" I should think that never in this world before have there been so many men so ' fed up ' before. And then the women at home too—it is wonderful where the driving force comes from to keep things going on.

" But still—I don't want to convey a false impression. If you took my last letter by itself you might think things were very terrible out here all the time. They are not. On the whole it is not a bad time at all. The life is full of interest, and the discomforts are few and far between.

Bad times do come along occasionally, but they are by way of exceptions. It is most like a long picnic in all sorts of places with a sort of constraint and uneasiness in the air. This last is purely mental, and the less one worries about it the less it is, and so one can contrive to be light-hearted and happy through it all—unless one starts to get depressed and moody. And it is just that which has happened to Laws and Fletcher and one or two others. They had been out long and had seen unpleasant times and without an occasional rest ; none but the very thick can stand it."

"*Saturday, 26 June 1915, 6.40 p.m.*

" Here I am installed in the school [Machine Gun] which is, or was, a convent. Fine large place and grounds. Two officers per bedroom and a large Mess-room ; about twenty officers up for the course (or more) which starts to-morrow (Sunday). Your solution of the Thompson acrostic [St. Omer] was perfectly right, we *are* far back. This convent is about two miles from that town.

" I am so pleased to be in the ' pleasant, sunny land of France,' amid absolute peacefulness. We had a curious journey. Last night I slept at our transport (and had a bath !). I got up soon after six, mounted a horse just before eight (after breakfast). My servant and my valise, also a groom to bring my horse back, came in a limber. And that excellent man Polchet rode all the way to *Divisional* Headquarters with me, although it was about six miles out of his way. We got to Headquarters at a quarter to ten—a motor-bus was to start at ten for here. It started at 10.30 with me, my luggage, and my servant (I don't know why he comes last) in it. The Harborne motor-buses in the Harborne High Street weren't in it. We got shaken to a jelly—we were on top. We went back about two miles to pick up some of our Division, and having done so, we set off to pick up some of the 14th Division, at a point carefully specified in our driver's instructions. This was about five miles away, in our proper direction. But when we got to the spot we discovered they (the Division) had left it a week ago and gone to a point quite close to where we had just picked up the 3rd Division men. I telephoned in vain ; we had to go all the way back. We found the place with difficulty (we found all our places with difficulty as we had no maps), collected the men, and came all the way out *again*. Then we came straight here, which was about fifteen miles at least. We got here at 4.30 p.m. ! Six hours' motor-bussing ! and the bus's maximum was 25 m.p.h. at least, I should judge. Luckily it was a glorious day, and I sat in front with the driver and enjoyed it all. . . . .

" I told you leave was starting—well, it has now started. Three of our officers have gone—and all together ! They are only getting three clear days in England—but still !

" I am going to find out when this course finishes—I think it lasts for sixteen days—and then I am going to apply for my leave to follow on. I wish—oh, how I wish—I may get it ; but of course many things may intervene.

" If it does come off I hope there will be a representative gathering to meet me at dinner. That is, I hope Violet will be back from Edinburgh, Lorna and Norah from Coniston, and perhaps Oliver and his Winifred will pay a flying visit from Cardiff. Haven't I got an enlarged opinion of my own importance ? I suppose it is too much to expect the offices to have a whole holiday ! "

" *Monday,* 28 *June* 1915, 6.15 *p.m.*
" The enemy's lines round here do not appear to be strongly held, in fact quite the reverse—that is, the front lines. But attacks on our part don't always pay—even so. Their method, as I understand it, is simply to lose less men than we do. Accordingly, they leave very few men in their front trench, but what there are have a good supply of machine guns and are well supported by artillery. We precede our attacks by heavy shelling, and the few men get into well-built dug-outs until it is over, then they come out and get to work with their machine guns on the attacking infantry. The trench ultimately falls after rather heavy loss on our side (especially if the wire isn't properly cut) and the few defenders hold up their hands. Some are made prisoners—some are not. If the enemy want the trench very badly they try and retake it by means of a strong counter-attack, trusting that our men and arrangements are in sufficient confusion to pre-

vent adequate support. That is why our attacks are sc expensive and why we aren't constantly attacking. The alternative plan is, I think, simply to shell them heavily —in all their lines—and leave out the actual attack in most cases. . . .

" I was so interested to hear that Alec had applied for me to come back. It is not at all impossible, because I have known two or three cases where officers have been recalled—one was chief chemist (or so he said) at Brunner Mond's. He was returning as I came out, and tried to make one's flesh creep by his tales of war. But I don't think it is likely to happen in my case. I only wish it would. I should love to come home again, although I don't feel as if I had done my bit yet—really. I haven't been in any big scrap, and I haven't killed my man even. . . .

" I had a ripping time at the transport ; I hope they enjoyed the peas—they deserved to. They were hospitality itself. They welcomed me, gave me three meals, lent me anything I wanted, made room for me to sleep in their large room (this necessitated the Quartermaster-Sergeant moving his bed into another room), gave me a warm bath, and generally made me feel quite at home. They have a ripping dug-out. Rooms half underground, 7 feet high, plenty of ventilation, boarded floor and walls, and a wooden roof supported on square wooden pillars and covered in earth well sodded on top. . . .

" Talking about the Major (Major Cotton), he used to be our Adjutant at Crosby—he was Captain then. He came out as second in command and has now got the Battalion while our Colonel (Colonel Dudgeon) is away sick. The latter got his C.B. in the last honours list. He is an excellent man. Lieut. Burlton, too, got a Military Cross. He has now been wounded twice ; he was the moving spirit of the hockey matches at Crosby in the old days, and, when he was recalled to the Front, his mantle fell upon me. . . .

" All the officers here are from different regiments with a very few exceptions. It is most interesting. At meals, Way and I sit among the Cavalry, Dragoons and Lancers, etc. They are fine chaps—the real Army officers of which there are now all too few."

" Machine-Gun School, G.H.Q.,
Wednesday, 7 July 1915, 5 *p.m.*
" Here I am getting towards the end of my little
holiday, only five more days to go. No word has reached
me from my Battalion on the subject of leave, or of anything else for that matter. . . .

" If this threatened push on Calais is real, or if the
higher commands have got ' wind up ' about it, they will
very likely stop all leave, and then I shall just have to
wait until it starts again. . . .

" I am sure that the fact of our nation being ' down '
and preparing for a winter campaign will materially assist
in shortening the war and rendering that preparation
unnecessary.

" We have an awfully amusing chap here who is in
the Grenadier Guards. He is always imitating Harry
Tate. A great big hefty chap, in great big sloppy clothes
(including what are known as ' Prince of Wales ' breeches).
He gets his mouth right over to the side of his face and
says ' You stupid boy ! ' in Harry Tate's voice. He does
this in the middle of our instructional squads when some
wretched person does something wrong with the gun, and
sends every one into fits of laughter. . . . [A lot more
about a motor that wouldn't go.]

" My M.G. course is going on very nicely. I have
learnt a very great deal, have been intensely interested,
and am very keen on the work. My function as a reserve
machine-gunner should really be to train the reserve team
and such parts of the main team as are not actually required in the trenches, in a safe spot behind the lines !
It sounds ' cushy,' but those in authority over us are not
sufficiently enlightened, I am afraid, to adopt such a plan.
The object of course is to prevent your reserve men from
being ' used up ' as riflemen, as otherwise when you want
them to take the place of the others they are casualties
and all their training goes for nothing.

The Cavalry officers here are a great joke. They find
this life very tiring. They are quite keen to get back
again and have been from the beginning. We, on the
other hand, fairly enjoy it and are not at all anxious to
go back to our regiments. That shows the difference

between the lives we lead. Of course they *have* been in the trenches and have had some very bad times there, but they only go in in emergencies and at long intervals. . . .

" Another difference between us is that they keep their buttons as bright as possible and themselves as spick and span as can be. The infantry officer gets his buttons as dull as possible, and if they are green so much the better, as it shows he has been through gas. He likes his clothes and especially his puttees to be rather torn, and his hat to be any old sloppy shape. If he gets a new hat he is almost ashamed to wear it—he is terrified of being mistaken for ' Kitcheners ' !

" Lord Kitchener and Mr. Asquith came here last evening. Here, to this convent. I don't know what for ; but there was of course a good deal of stir here.

" Way and I went into the town last night. We hired a *fiacre* for the return journey. It came on to rain, so it was just as well we had a hood. We both thoroughly enjoyed the journey. The *fiacre* was what would be dignified by the name of ' Victoria ' in England. But in France, where it seems to be etiquette not to take any trouble over carriage-work, *fiacre* is the only word you could apply, and it just fits it. It expresses not only its shabbiness but also hints at its broken-backed appearance.

" We went into some stables and inquired about a *fiacre*, and a fat boy in a blue apron with a white handkerchief tied over one eye said we could have one. So I said, ' Où est le cocher ? ' and he pointed to his breast and said, " C'est moi ! '

" The fare, he said, would be six francs and the *pourboire*. Thoughtful of him not to forget that. We agreed, and he eventually produced the usual French horse.

" The *fiacre* was very comfortable and we were awfully tickled with the idea of us two in that absurd conveyance, especially when we passed staff officers, which was frequently. Altogether we were quite sorry when our drive was over."

NOTE BY O. J. L.

On 16 July 1915, Raymond came home on leave, and he had a great reception. On 20 July he went back.

" Sunday, 25 July 1915, 7.30 p.m.

" I have got quite a nice dug-out, with a chair and table in it. The table was away from the door and got no light, so I have spent about two hours to-day turning things round. I went to bed about three this morning (just after 'stand-to ') and slept till nearly twelve. Then I had breakfast (bacon and eggs). As my former platoon Sergeant remarked : ' It is a great thing to have a few comforts, it makes you forget there is a war.'

" So it does until a whizz-bang comes over.

" I have just seen an aeroplane brought down (German luckily). I missed the first part, where one of ours went up to it and a flame shot across between them (machine gun, I expect). I ran out just in time to see the machine descending on fire. It came down quite steadily inside our lines (about a mile or more away), but the flames were quite clearly visible."

" Thursday, 29 July 1915, 7.35 p.m.

" Here I am in the trenches again, quite like old times, and quite in the swing again after the unsettling effect of coming home ! You know I can't help laughing at things out here. The curious aspect of things sometimes comes and hits me, and I sit down and laugh (not insanely or hysterically, *bien entendu* ; but I just can't help chuckling). It is so absurd, the reasons and causes that have drawn me to this particular and unlikely field in Belgium, and, having arrived here, that make me set about at once house-hunting—for all the world as if it was the most natural thing in life. And having selected my little house and arranged all my belongings in it, I regard it as home and spend a few days there. And then one morning my servant and I, we pack up everything once more and hoist them on to our backs and set off, staff in hand, like a pair of gipsies to another field a mile or so distant, and there make a new home. . . .

" I was very loth to leave my front line dug-out, because I had arranged things to my liking—had moved the table so that it caught the light, and so on. It had a built-in table (which took a lot of moving), a chair and a sandbag bed. Quite small and snug.

" But still—this new dug-out back here is quite nice. Large and roomy, with windows with bars in them (but no glass)—a proper square table on four legs—three chairs and a sandbag bed. So I am quite happy. The sandbag bed is apparently made as follows : Cover a portion of the floor, 6 feet 6 inches by 3 feet 6 inches, with a single layer of sandbags filled with earth. Over these place several layers of empty sandbags, and the bed is finished. If the hollows and lumps are carefully placed, the former in the middle and the latter at the head, the result is quite a success. Of course one sleeps in one's clothes covered by a coat and with an air pillow under one's head.

" We have had a very gay time in the trenches. I think I told you how I saw a hostile aeroplane brought down on fire in our lines. That was on Sunday, and the official report says both pilots killed. On Monday I went down to a support trench to have meat tea and a chat with Holden and Ventris (two of C Company officers). At a quarter to ten there was a loud rumbling explosion and the dug-out we were in rocked for several seconds. The Germans had fired a mine about 60 feet in front of our trench to try to blow in some of our workings.

" I rushed to my guns—both were quite safe. You should have heard the noise. Every man in the place got up to the parapet and blazed away for all he was worth. It was exciting ! One machine gun fired two belts (500 rounds), and the other fifty rounds. I heard afterwards that several of the enemy were seen to leap their parapets, but turned back when they heard the machine guns open fire. It took a good while for things to quieten down. Some of our miners were at work when it went off, but their gallery was some way off and they were quite all right.

" Last night they actually exploded another one ! Aren't they keen ? This was a much smaller affair, but closer to our trench. It shook down a portion of our parapet, which was easily rebuilt, and entombed temporarily two of our miners. In neither case were there any casualties. . . .

" I am so sorry the date of the wedding had to be altered, but I agree it was for the best. I only hope you remembered to inform the bridegroom—he is often forgotten on these occasions, and I have known a lot of trouble caused by just this omission."

LETTER FROM RAYMOND TO MRS. FRED STRATTON, FORMERLY MISS MARJORIE GUNN

" 1 *August* 1915, *Sunday*, 11.20 *p.m.*

" I am not actually in the trenches at the moment, though most of the Battalion is. I was in for five days, and then I was relieved about four days ago by another officer (Roscoe), who shares with me the duties of machine-gun officer. So I am in a dug-out about three-quarters of a mile behind the firing line while he is taking his turn in that line. (A mine has just gone off and shaken the ground, followed by a burst of heavy rifle firing. This makes the fourth mine this week ! Two went off while I was up there, and the whole earth rocked for several seconds. The first three mines were theirs, this last may be ours, I don't know ; we had one ready !)

" We have been at Hill 60 and also up at Ypres. At present we are south of that appalling place, but I learn with regret that to-morrow we are moving again and are going up north of Ypres. We are all depressed in consequence.

" What an awfully good letter you have written me ; but, do you know, it makes me ache all over when you write like that about the car. You have only to mention you have got a Rover, and I am as keen as mustard to come and tinker with it ! Aren't I young ?

" But you must know I want to come to New Park in any case. I am awfully keen to stay there and see it from inside, and see its inmates again after many years (it feels like). So after the war (may it be soon !) I am just going to arrive. I may let you know !

" Your remarks on weddings in general depress me very much ! I hope the bridegroom's lot is better than the poor bride's. Because my turn is bound to come !

" I am so glad Hester gave a good account of my

appearance. I *am* very fit, it is the only way to exist here. Once you begin to get ' down ' and to worry, it is all up with you. You go into a rapid decline, and eventually arrive home a wreck ! But as long as you smile and don't care a hang about anything, well the war seems to go on quite all right !

" I enjoyed my few days' leave very much indeed. I had five days in England and three full days and four nights at home. I dropped into my old life just as if no change had occurred. And the time was not long enough to make the getting back difficult.

" This life is a change for me, as you say. I haven't done laughing at its humorous side yet. In some ways we get treated like schoolboys. More so at Crosby than here, however."

_____

" *Saturday, 7 August* 1915, 7.30 *p.m.*

" I have been having rather a bad time lately,— one of those times that reminds one that it is war and not a picnic,—but, thank goodness, it is all over now.

" I think I told you that we were about to move up north of Ypres, to St. Julien or thereabouts. Well, just before we handed over these trenches to one of Kitchener's Battalions, the Germans went and knocked down a lot of our parapet, and also sent over some appalling things that we call ' sausages,' or ' aerial torpedoes,' though they are not the latter. They are great shell-shaped affairs, about 3 feet along and 9 inches in diameter, I should think. They are visible during the whole of their flight. They are thrown up about 100 yards into the air and fall down as they go up, broadside on—not point first. A few seconds after they fall there is the most appalling explosion I have ever heard. From a distance of 100 yards the rush of air is so strong that it feels as if the thing had gone off close at hand. Luckily there is a slight explosion when they are sent up, and, as I said, they are visible all the time in the air. The result is our men have time to dodge them, provided they are not mesmerised as one man was. He got stuck with his mouth open, pointing at one ! A Corporal gave him a push which sent him 10 yards, and the ' sausage ' landed not far from where he had been. Although they have sent more than twenty of these things over altogether, we have only had one casualty, and that a scratch. Their effect is to terrify every one and keep them on tenterhooks watching for them. Their purpose is to destroy mine galleries, I believe. . . .

"Monday, August the 2nd, was the day we should have been relieved, and that night I went up from headquarters and relieved Roscoe, who had had a bad time in the fire trenches. . . .

"They were firing armour-piercing shells that go right in and blow the parapet to blazes; dug-outs too, of course, if they happen to be near. After punishing the right end of the left-hand bit of trench, they traversed along, laying waste the whole of our bit.

"I was in my dug-out with Hogg, another officer. I was trying to make tea, but every shell blew out the Primus, and covered us in dust. I made it, however, eventually, and we had just drunk it when a shell blew the parados of the trench down, not far from our door, and the next wrecked the dug-out next door to mine (a man who happened to be inside having a miraculous escape). We judged it was time to clear (the machine guns had already been withdrawn to safety), and got away as best we could through and over the débris that had been a trench.

"Later in the day I made my way back, and recovered my pack and most of my belongings. It was exciting work getting back, because they were sending whizz-bangs through the gaps in the parapet, and the communication trenches in the rear were blocked in places, so that you had to get up on top and 'scoot' across and drop in the trench again.

"That evening they gave us a second shelling, and one hit my dug-out fair and square (I had quarters in a support trench). When I returned next day for the rest of my things—my equipment and some provisions—I had to put two men on to dig them out. It took three-quarters of an hour to get at them, through the wreckage of timber, corrugated iron, and earth. . . .

"On Tuesday afternoon they sent off another mine,— about the seventh since we have been in,—but they are all well in front of our parapet. And on Wednesday they gave us twelve sausages—the first I had seen.

" The trouble is, we have a number of mine shafts under the ground between our trenches and theirs, and they are fearfully ' windy ' about them. They keep trying to stop us mining them, and their shelling is with the object of blowing down our sap-heads. Their mines, too, go up short, because they are trying to blow in our galleries; or else they are so scared they send them off before they are ready. I think the last explanation is probably more near the truth, because when one of their mines went up recently a lot of Germans went up with it ! . . .

" We have been in here a fortnight to-night. You can imagine how we long for clean clothes. Most of the officers have not been out of their clothes all that time, but I have been very lucky. I had two good cold baths when I was down here before, and to-day I had a lovely hot one in a full-length wooden bath. A tremendous luxury ! Also I had some clean socks to put on. . . .

" On the day I was shelled out of my dug-out my servant, Bailey, was hit on the leg by a piece of shell and has gone down the line wounded, not very seriously, I think. He is a great loss to me, but I have got another one now, Gray, who shapes very well. He is young and willing, and quite intelligent.

" You ask whether that time when the mine went off was the first time I had used these guns. Yes, absolutely. The plan adopted in trench warfare is to place your guns in position with a good wide loophole in front of them, then block this up and keep a sharp look-out. When the enemy attacks, you blaze away at them, and then shift hurriedly to another gun-position and watch the old one being shelled to blazes.

" If you fire on other occasions you are rather apt to have your guns knocked out, and we can't afford to lose *any*. That is why I was rather horrified to find one gun had fired 500 rounds the other night. However, it was not discovered. I think the long grass in front hid the flashes. . . .

" Yes, the sandbags might be damp when used for a bed, and I always lay my waterproof ground-sheet on top of them. I either sleep on that or on some new clean bags laid above that again.   It is not only dampness, though, that one fears !

" As a matter of fact, one is not very sensitive to damp when living so much out of doors.   It is common to get one's feet slightly wet and go for about four days without removing one's boots—most unpleasant, but not in the least damaging to health."

" Monday, 16 *August* 1915, *Noon*
" We are now out and resting after doing a long spell. I did nineteen days, and some did a few more days than that.   Three weeks is a long time to live continuously in clothes, boots, and puttees. . . .

" I came out of the trenches on Thursday night, and was really a day too soon, because on Friday we were having Orderly-Room right in the country, in front of the C.O.'s tent ; the Colonel was there surrounded by most of the officers, when we heard a shell.   Well, that's nothing unusual, but this one got crescendo, and we all looked up in alarm.   Then it got very crescendo, and finally cleared us and landed with a loud explosion about 50 yards beyond us, and not far from several groups of men.   It was an 8-inch ' crump.'   One man only was killed, but we knew that more were likely to come over, and so we gradually spread out to the sides.   Four came altogether at two-minute intervals, but we only had two casualties. Rather upsetting when we were supposed to be resting. I don't know whether they could see our (officers') white tents, or whether they saw the cricket match that took place on the day before.

" Anyway we moved our tents slightly—every one put their tents where they pleased, and then the Pioneer Sergeant came and amused himself daubing green paint on them in patches.   Ours (three of C Coy.) was the best ;   the splodges looked just like hazel nuts (?) when there are three together in their little green cases, and they were interspersed with a kind of pansy-shaped flower. Altogether a very tasteful and pleasing effect. . . .

" A couple of gun stocks have come.   They arrived from Walker's, the makers, and I should very much like to know who had them sent.   They are ripping, sniping attachments with periscopes for use with the ordinary rifle. I shall stick to one, and unless I hear otherwise I shall present the other one to our sniping officer (honorary rank)."[1]

"*Wednesday*, 25 *August* 1915, 3 *p.m.*
" I am in the trenches once more. We marched in (about 10 miles) last night. We had a meal at 3 p.m., and marched off soon after six. Our rations (officers') went astray, because they were on a hand-cart in charge of our servants, who missed their way, so we have had practically nothing to eat since late lunch yesterday, and are pretty hungry. I have had a piece of chocolate, and my water-bottle was nearly full of lemon squash. . . .

" We are in support trenches at Hooge, just on the left of our former position up here. Except for some shelling (chiefly ours), things are fairly quiet.

" Since we were here last the position is greatly improved; the Germans have been driven over the ridge in front (during the recapture of trenches here), and the whole place is much ' healthier ' in consequence. . . .

" I have been out here five calendar months to-day, and in the Army just over eleven months. They will be pensioning me off soon as an old soldier."

"29 *August* 1915, 11.30 *a.m.*
" I am having a very quiet and lazy time at the moment, and feel I deserve it. We went into support trenches for three days, and worked two nights from 7.30 p.m. till 3 a.m. building and improving the fire trench. Then on the third night we had a most exciting time. One company, under Captain Taylor, was sent up right in front to dig a new fire trench to connect with another on our left. We had to go up a trench which ran right out into space, and which had only just been built itself, and when there we had to get over the parapet and creep forward to the new line we were to dig. Of course we had to be dead quiet, but there was a big moon, and of course they saw us. Most of the way we were not more than 30 yards away from their front position (and they had bombing parties out in front of that). While we were

---

[1] Thos. Walker & Son, of Oxford Street, Birmingham, had kindly given me two periscope rifle-stock attachments with excellent mirrors, so as to allow accurate sighting.—O. J. L.

digging we had one platoon with bombs to cover us, and some of this party were as close as 25 yards to their front position. It was awful work, because they kept throwing bombs at us, and what was almost worse was the close-range sniping.

"'Very' lights were going up from the German lines all the time, and you could see the bullets kicking up the dust all around. When we first got out there I picked out my ground pretty carefully before lying down (because the recent scrap there was much in evidence), but when the snipers got busy I didn't worry about what I was on, I just hugged the ground as close as I could. They would put the 'Very' lights right into us, and one just missed me by a yard. If they are not spent when they come down, they blaze fiercely on the ground, and when they finish, they look like a little coke fire. They would burn you badly if they fell on you. I have seen a dead man that one had fallen on afterwards. His clothes were fearfully burned.

"The Germans were on the edge of a wood and our ground was tipped towards them, so it was extremely difficult to get cover. Shell holes were the best. Soon the men got their trenches down, and things were a little better. The men worked extremely well, and the Wilts were working on our left, and we eventually joined up with them. After about five hours' work, the trenches were fit to hold, and we filed out and the new garrison filed in. Our casualties were much lighter than I should have thought possible. The Colonel came along the new trenches just before we left, and he was most awfully pleased with C Company, and so is the General. Captain Taylor is very bucked about it.

"The scene of this affair was right against the Château of Hooge, and close to the mine crater. We found a German machine gun half buried, but in good condition, and any number of souvenirs. The Captain has got a helmet—a dirty thing; he had to have it cleaned out, because part of the owner was still inside it! It is a rummy shape, so flat-topped and square, with a brass spike and a gold band down the back. I expect it was an officer's.

"Oh! I have seen my first German (not counting

prisoners). I was standing up and a ' Very ' light went up, so I kept perfectly still. I was looking towards the wood where the Germans were (I was 40 or 50 yards away), and I saw one quite distinctly walking into the wood.

" Our men that were killed (sniped) were buried just behind, within a quarter of an hour of being hit. Rather awful.

" The actual digging was rather trying in places, and in one case they actually came on a horse !—which dates it back to November, when we were pushed back to these positions in the first battle of Ypres.

" The men in such places work with their respirators on and are often actually sick. I have had whiffs of the smell since in my food. Once smelt never forgotten. I can tell the difference between a man and a horse, but I don't know which I like least.

" Rather a morbid topic, I am afraid. Well, after leaving the scene of our labours (and glad to get out), we called for our packs and had to march about two and a half miles. We were dead beat when we arrived here (nice safe dug-outs—roomy and comfortable—with our valises ready to sleep in when we arrived), but we found a good meal awaiting us, and about half-past four we ' got down to it ' and slept till noon. Holden and I share a palatial dug-out, and we had breakfast in bed, and I did not get up till just before our evening meal at 7. I washed and dressed in slacks—had a meal, and later on went to bed again. This morning we had breakfast in bed again about 9.30, and then I got up, washed and shaved, dressed, and am now sitting on my bed, leaning against the wall writing my letters.

" The General let us off ' stand-to ' because he knew we were fagged out ; and it is a great mercy. Turning out fully dressed at about 2.30 a.m. and remaining up for an hour does not improve one's night's rest. I suppose, though, that we shall have to start it soon—perhaps to-night.

" We are here till to-morrow night, I believe, and then we go to some fairly nice trenches near the ones we were in last. We are short of subalterns—rather—and they have taken me off machine guns for the time being. I *am* sick, but I get a bit in when I can. In the last trench we

5

built (I and my platoon), not the exposed one, there was a machine-gun position, and I took great pleasure in building it a really good emplacement. . . .

"Are you doing anything about getting me back for Munitions? I don't know what you think about it, and whether you think I ought to carry on out here. I am sure that after six months I shall be just about fed-up with this business, but am not sure that after a couple of months at home I shan't be wanting to come out again."

"*Wednesday, 1 September* 1915, 4.45 *p.m.*

"I will just write you a short letter to let you know I am still well and happy, and still leading the strange life of the picnic-hermit.

"When I last wrote to you I believe I was in the very same spot as now, namely, support trenches in the neighbourhood of a now famous château. Last time we were in for three days, and on the night we left we had a very blood-curdling experience digging a trench which was to bring us closer to our friends the enemy. But they were inclined to resent our advances, and they welcomed us, not with open arms, but with lighted bombs. However, having completed our work to the great satisfaction of those in authority over us (namely, the Colonel and the General [Brigadier]), we made good our escape.

"Then for three blissful days we lived (with our valises) in some magnificent dug-outs in one of the safest spots in this accursed though much improved neighbourhood. These days we spent competing who could sleep furthest round the clock (if that is a permissible expression). I think I won, and on my record day I got up and dressed for dinner at about 7.30 p.m., made my bed afterwards, and got back into it again. This halcyon period was only interrupted once, when we all had to go out and dig a trench one night long. However, the worst feature of this expedition was the rain, which made 'going' very difficult, and things in general rather uncomfortable (especially for the men), so we hadn't much to grumble about.

"Then we came back here and the first night we slept in peace, getting up at about 3 a.m. ostensibly for the purpose of 'stand-to,' but really to brew ourselves some cocoa. Then sleep till 9, 10, or 11, I forget which. I crawl to the door of my dug-out and shout for Gray, who lives just opposite. ' Breakfast ! ' I say, and he invariably asks, ' What will you have, sir? ' just as if he could command the larders of the Carlton or the Linga.

" Knowing my rations, and that an attempt at humour would only put me off my *plat du jour* or daily round, I usually think for a few moments and then order eggs and bacon, and face the common task. The only variation I permit myself is that on one or two days in the week I funk the bacon and have boiled eggs. Where do the eggs come from ? They are purchased out of the Mess fund by our Mess cook who lives with the Transport when we are in the trenches, and brings them up personally when the rations arrive at night. Yes, he has a ' cushy ' time of it, does our Mess cook ; and how can he avoid being happy, living as he does in a perpetual transport ?

" What of the days when no eggs are available ? Why, then, *horribile dictu*, I have fried cheese and bacon !

" It occurs to me here, although all this was not written with intention, that this could be a good place to ask whether sausages are yet in season. If they are, a few cooked ones (or half cooked) sent out now and again would make a splendid variant for our menu.

" The meat season is hard to follow out here. Bully beef is such a hardy perennial. (This does not mean that we live on it—I never eat it, there is always a good supply of fresh beef.)

" Blackberries are coming on, I notice with pleasure, and I can usually tell what shells are in season (the season for sausages in this department is, let us hope, mercifully short. I believe we are now in the middle of the close-time for this sturdy little fellow, I trust he is not utilising it to increase and multiply).

" I am sorry I have had rather a sharp attack of parentheses lately, the touch of winter in the air cramps my style. And I really did think this was going to be quite a short letter. I cannot divine my moods, I find, I did not feel like writing until I got going.

" Please thank father very much indeed for the

sniperscopes. I have given one to the Captain of D Company, who is keen on everything. He is an engineer (civil), and is a most useful man out here. I have not tried mine yet, as I haven't been in a fire trench, and it would hardly be fair to use it in a support trench, the backs of our infantry in the trench in front being too easy a target to give the thing a fair trial.

" Oh ! I was telling you about my work in this trench but got switched off on to food. Last time I was here I (and my platoon) worked for two nights from 7.30 till 3 improving the parapets. Well, the second night of *this* period (last night) I had got all sorts of plans ready and was going to have a thoroughly good night building dug-outs, draining the trench, and building a second machine-gun emplacement (not my job really at the moment). However, word came along that the platoon was wanted to dig another trench right in front again and near the other one. They said, ' A covering party with bombs will be provided, and send in your casualty report in the morning ! ' So I asked if they were supplying stretchers and all complete ! But they were not. It is a most cheering way of sending you off, is it not ? It is a wonder they did not make us take up our own grave crosses, just in case.

" (By the way, it is most impressive to meet two men walking along at night and one carrying a large white cross. The burying and decking of the graves is done very well here, and conscientiously. There is a special organisation for making the crosses, lettering them and putting them up. The position of the grave is reported to them, with the particulars, and they do the rest.)

" The great difference in last night's job was that I only had a platoon to deal with, while before the Captain had a whole company. Also I was not quite so close to the enemy (we were 30 yards off, and less, before), and the moon was mostly obscured. I determined not to let them know we were working, so I crept out and explored the ground with the Corporal of the covering party (this was the worst part of the job, because you did not know when you might not come across a party of the enemy in the many shell holes and old trenches with which the ground was covered). I had my large revolver in my pocket, but I did not want to use it, as it would have given our game away.

" All went well, and I got the men placed out in absolute silence, with the covering party pushed out in front to listen and watch. The men worked very quietly, and when a light went up they got down and kept still. Lights were very few, because the enemy had got a working party out too—at one side, and we could occasionally hear them driving in stakes for wire.

" We had to use picks in some places where the ground was stony, and these are the hardest to keep quiet. We got through it all right, and only one shot, I think, was fired all the time. It came fairly close too. I am sure they guessed we were out, because when one light went up I hadn't time to get down, so I kept still and I plainly saw a Hun standing upright on his own parapet. He straightened up as the light grew bright, and I just caught sight of the movement and saw him then distinctly.

" The ground out there has been fought over a good deal, and there are plenty of souvenirs about. I have got one myself—a Hun rifle. The original owner, who was buried with it—probably by a shell—happened to lie exactly where we dug our trench, and we were obliged to move him elsewhere. I brought his rifle home and put it over the door of my dug-out. That was early this morning. But the enemy have been putting shrapnel over us (in reply to a good 'strafing' by our guns), and one piece has gone clean through the stock.

" Our artillery are going great guns nowadays. It certainly feels as if the shell supply was all right—or nearly so.

" I don't know whether we shall be wanted for any job to-night, or whether we shall rest, or whether I can get on with my projects. I must go round and see Captain T. in the other trench. By the way, he came to see how I was getting on last night about midnight, and was very pleased with the work and with the fact that we were having no casualties.

" That cake was fine, and much appreciated in the Mess. The little knife you gave me when home on leave is proving most useful.

" Please thank Lionel for chocolate received and Alec for gourdoulis.

" I have sent another box of Surplus Kit home addressed to Noël. Rather late to do it, I know, and I shall want one or two of the things sent back later, but not for a long time, and it is a relief to get rid of some of my impedimenta. The socks returned want mending. That reminds me, thank you and please thank Miss Leith very much for the socks. They are quite all right for size. Perhaps not so long and narrow in the foot might be better, but it doesn't seem to affect the wear; they are most comfortable.

" I am still attached to the Company and not to the machine guns—much to my annoyance."

" *Monday, 6 September* 1915, 9.30 *p.m.*

" Thank you so much for your inspiring and encouraging letter. I hope I am being useful out here. I sometimes doubt if I am very much use—not as much as I should like to be. Possibly I help to keep C Company officers more cheerful ! I am very sorry they have taken me off machine guns for the present, I hope it may not be long.

" Great happenings are expected here shortly and we are going to have a share. We are resting at present and have been out a few days now. We had only two periods of three days each in the trenches last time in. . . .

" Our last two days in the trenches were appallingly wet. My conduct would have given me double pneumonia at home. My rain-coat was soaked, so I had to sleep in shirt sleeves under my tunic, and the knees of my breeches were wet.

" The next day the rain was incessant, and presently I found the floor of my dug-out was swimming—the water having welled up through the ground below and the sandbags.

" I didn't have to sleep on it luckily, because we were relieved that night. But before we went I had to turn out with fifty men and work till midnight in water up to one foot deep. So at 8.30 p.m. I got my boots full of cold water and sat out in them till 12, then marched some eight miles. After nine hours' rest and some breakfast we came here, another three or four. It was nice to get a dry pair of boots and our valises and a tent.

" That night I rode into Poperinghe with Captain Taylor, and we had a really good dinner there—great fun.

" We have a full set of parades here unfortunately, otherwise things are all right. . . .

" Alec has very kindly had a ' Molesworth ' sent me. Most useful.

" I would like a motor paper now and then, I think! *The Motor* for preference—or *The Autocar.* Aren't I young ?

" Captain Taylor has sprained his ankle by falling from his horse one night, and has gone to a rest home near. So I am commanding C Company at the moment. Hope not for long. Too responsible at the present time of crisis.

" 9 *September*, 3.30 *p.m.*

" Must just finish this off for post.

" We have just had an inspection by the Army Corps Commander, Lieut.-General Plumer [Sir Herbert].

" I am still in command of C Company, and had to call them to attention and go round with the General, followed by a whole string of minor generals, colonels, etc. He asked me a good many questions :—

" First.—How long had I had the Company ? Then, how long had I been out ? I said since March. He then asked if I had been sick or wounded even, and I said no !

" Then he said, ' Good lad for sticking it ! ' at least I thought he was going to.

" We are kept very busy nowadays. I must try and write a proper letter soon. I do apologise.

" A box of cigarettes has arrived from, I suppose, Alec. Virginias, I mean, and heaps of them.

" We have just got another tent—we have been so short and have been sleeping five in. Now we shall be two in each. The new one is a lovely dove-grey—like a thundercloud. After the war I shall buy one.

" I shall be quite insufferable, I know ; I shall want everything done for me on the word of command. Never mind—roll on the end of the war !

" Cheer-ho, lovely weather, great spirits ! Aeroplane [English] came down in our field yesterday slightly on fire. All right though.—Good-bye, much love,

"RAYMOND [MAURICE]."

"*Sunday,* 12 *September* 1915, 2 *p.m.*
"You will understand that I still have the Company to look after, and we are going into the front-line trenches this evening at 5 p.m. for an ordinary tour of duty. We are going up in motor buses ! . . .
"Capt. T. thinks he will be away a month ! "

TELEGRAM FROM THE WAR OFFICE

"17 *September* 1915
"Deeply regret to inform you that Second Lieut. R. Lodge, Second South Lancs, was wounded 14th Sept. and has since died. Lord Kitchener expresses his sympathy."

TELEGRAM FROM THE KING AND QUEEN

21 *September* 1915
"The King and Queen deeply regret the loss you and the army have sustained by the death of your son in the service of his country. Their Majesties truly sympathise with you in your sorrow."

CHAPTER III

LETTERS FROM OFFICERS

SOME letters from other officers gradually arrived, giving a few particulars. But it was an exceptionally strenuous period at the Ypres salient, and there was little time for writing. Moreover, some of his friends were killed either at the same time or soon afterwards.

The fullest account that has reached us is in the following letter, which arrived eight months later :—

LETTER FROM LIEUTENANT WILLIAM ROSCOE
TO SIR OLIVER LODGE

"*7th Brigade Machine-Gun Company,*
B.E.F., 16 *May* 1916

" DEAR SIR OLIVER LODGE,—When I was lately on leave, a brother of mine, who had met one of your relatives, encouraged me to write and tell you what I knew of your son Raymond. I was in the South Lancashire Regiment when he joined the Battalion out here last spring, and I think spent the first spell he had in the trenches in his company.

" Afterwards I became Machine Gunner, and in the summer he became my assistant, and working in shifts we tided over some very trying times indeed. In particular during August at St. Eloi. To me at any rate it was most pleasant being associated together, and I think he very much preferred work with the gunners to Company work. Being of a mechanical turn of mind, he was always devising some new ' gadget ' for use with the gun —for instance, a mounting for firing at aeroplanes, and a device for automatic traversing; and those of my men who knew him still quote him as their authority when laying down the law and arguing about machine gunning.

"I wish we had more like him, and the endless possibilities of the Maxim would be more quickly brought to light.

"I am always glad to think that it was not in any way under my responsibility that he was killed.

"During September times grew worse and worse up in the Ypres salient, culminating in the attack we made on the 25th, auxiliary to the Loos battle. The trenches were ruins, there was endless work building them up at night, generally to be wrecked again the next day. The place was the target for every gun for miles on either side of the salient.

"Every day our guns gave the enemy a severe bombardment, in preparation for the attack, and every third or fourth day we took it back from them with interest : the place was at all times a shell trap.

"It was during this time that your son was killed. He was doing duty again with the Company, which was shorthanded, and I remember one night in particular being struck with his cheerfulness on turning out to a particularly unpleasant bit of trench digging in front of our lines near the Stables at Hooge, a mass of ruins and broken trenches where no one could tell you where you might run across the enemy ; but the men had to dig for hours on end, with only a small covering party looking out a few yards in front of them.

"The morning your son was killed they were bombarding our trenches on the top of the hill, and some of the men were being withdrawn from a bad piece. He and Ventris were moving down the trench in rear of the party —which I think must have been seen—for a shell came and hit them both, but I think none of the men in front.

"Some time later, I don't know how long, I was going up to the line to visit the guns, when I saw Ventris, who was killed, laid out ready to be carried down, and presently I saw your son in a dug-out, with a man watching him. He was then quite unconscious though still breathing with difficulty. I could see it was all over with him. He was still just alive when I went away.

"Our regiment was to lose many more on that same

hill before the month was over, and those of us that remain are glad to be far away from it now ; but I always feel that anyone who has died on Hooge Hill has at all events died in very fine company.—Yours sincerely,
" (Signed) WILLIAM ROSCOE,
Lieut. 2nd S. Lancs. Regt., attached
7th Brigade, M.G. Company "

LETTER FROM LIEUTENANT FLETCHER, GREAT CROSBY, LIVERPOOL

" *21 September* 1915
" Raymond was the best pal I've ever had, and we've always been together ; in the old days at Brook Road, then in Edinburgh, and lastly in France, and nobody could ever have a better friend than he was to me.

" I'll never forget the first day he came to us at Dickebusch, and how pleased we all were to see him again ; and through it all he was always the same, ever ready to help anyone in any way he could, whilst his men were awfully fond of him and would have done anything for him."

" *24 September* 1915
" I hear that we were digging trenches in advance of our present ones at St. Eloi last week, so it must have been then that he was hit, as he was awfully keen on digging new trenches, and heaps of times I've had to tell him to keep down when he was watching the men working. . . .

" I always thought he would come through all right, and I know he thought so himself, as, the last time I saw him, we made great plans for spending some time together when we got back, and it seems so difficult to realise that he has gone.   (Signed)   ERIC S. FLETCHER "

LETTER FROM LIEUTENANT CASE TO BRODIE

" *Thursday, 23 September* 1915
" Yes, I knew Raymond Lodge very well, and he was indeed a friend of mine, being one of the nicest fellows it has ever been my privilege to meet. I was with him when he died. This was how it happened to the best of my knowledge.

" ' A ' Company (the one I am in) and ' C ' Company were in the trenches at the time.   The gunners had sent up word that there was going to be a bombardment, and so they recommended us to evacuate the front-line trenches, in case the Hun retaliated, and it was whilst C Company were proceeding down the communication trench, till the bombardment was over, that the shell came which killed your brother.   He was in command of C Company at the time, and was going down at the rear of his men, having seen them all safely out of the trenches.   His servant, Gray, was hit first, in the head (from which he afterwards died).   Then Lodge went along to tell the Sergeant-Major, and to see about assistance, farther down the trench.   Whilst talking to the Company Sergeant-Major he was hit in the left side of the back, by a piece of shell, I think.   Lower down the trench poor Ventris was hit and killed.   As soon as I heard about it I went along to see if I could be of any use.   I saw Lodge lying in a dug-out, with a servant looking after him.   I saw he was badly hit, and tried to cheer him up.   He recognised me and was just able to ask a few questions.   That must have been about twenty minutes or so after he was hit. I think he lived about half an hour, and I don't think he suffered much pain, thank God.

" I was very, very grieved at his death, for he was one of the very nicest fellows I have met.   That he was universally liked, both by officers and men, it is needless to say. . . .

" I was for nearly three months in C Company with your brother, and was thus able to see his extreme coolness and ability in military matters.

" (Signed)   G. R. A. CASE "

LETTER FROM LIEUTENANT CASE TO LADY LODGE

" *Friday*, 24 *September* 1915
" Need I say how grieved we all were at his loss ?   He was hit about midday, and died about half an hour or so afterwards.   I forget the date, but I have written more fully to his brother.   I don't think he suffered much pain. He was conscious when I arrived, and recognised me, I

think, and I remained with him for some time. I then went off to see if there was any possibility of finding the doctor, but all the telephone wires were cut, and even if we had been able to get the doctor up, it would have been of no avail. The stretcher-bearers did all that was possible. . . . Another subaltern, Mr. Ventris, was killed at the same time, as was his servant Gray as well.

"(Signed)   G. R. A. CASE"[1]

LETTER FROM CAPTAIN S. T. BOAST

"*27 September* 1915

"First of all I beg to offer you and your family my sincere sympathies in the loss of your son, 2nd Lieut. Lodge. His loss to us is very great : he was a charming young fellow—always so very cheerful and willing, hard working, and a bright example of what a good soldier ought to be. He was a most efficient officer, and only recently qualified in the handling and command of Maxim guns—a most useful accomplishment in the present war. Briefly, the circumstances which led to his death were as follows :—

"On 14 September, C Company to which 2nd Lieut. Lodge belonged, was in position in a forward fire trench. During the morning the commander of the artillery covering the position informed 2nd Lieut. Lodge, who at the time was in command of C Company, that it was intended to shell the enemy's positions, and as his trenches were only a short distance from ours, it was considered advisable to withdraw from our trench during the shelling. 2nd Lieut. Lodge gave orders for his Company to withdraw into a communication trench in the rear. He and 2nd Lieut. Ventris were the last to leave the forward trench, and in entering the communication trench both these officers were caught by enemy's shrapnel. Ventris was killed—Lodge mortally wounded and died of his wounds shortly afterwards. These are the circumstances of his death."

---

[1] Lieutenant Case himself, alas! was killed on the 25th of September 1915. It was a fatal time. Lieutenant Fletcher also has been killed now, on 3rd July 1916.

FROM CAPTAIN A. B. CHEVES, R.A.M.C.

"22 *September* 1915

" The Colonel has asked me to write you, giving some idea of the burial-ground in which your son's grave is.   I understand that he was leading his Company back from one of the communication trenches when the Germans shelled the front and rear of the column, killing your son and the officer who was at the rear.   At the same time one man was killed and two wounded.   I knew nothing about this until later in the day, as communication with my aid post was very difficult, and he was reported to me as having been killed.   I understand that he lived for about three hours after being wounded, and all the officers and men who were present speak very highly of his conduct during this time.   His wound was unfortunately in such a position that there was no chance of saving his life, and this was recognised by all, including your son himself.   When his body was brought down in the evening the expression on his face was absolutely peaceful, and I should think that he probably did not suffer a great deal of pain.   He was buried on the same evening in our cemetery just outside the aid post, side by side with Lieut. Ventris, who was unfortunately killed on the same day.   The cemetery is in the garden adjoining a ruined farm-house.   It is well enclosed by hedges, and your son's grave is under some tall trees that stand in the garden.   There are graves there of men of many regiments who have fallen, and our graves are enclosed by a wire fence, so keeping them quite distinct from the others.   There is a wooden cross marking the head of the grave, and a small one at the foot.   I am afraid that our condolences will be small consolation to you, but I can assure you that he was one of the most popular officers with the Battalion, both amongst the officers and men, and all feel his loss very greatly."

Information sent by Captain Cheves to Mrs. Ventris, mother of the Second Lieutenant who was killed at the same time as Raymond and buried with him :—

" He was buried on the right of the Menin Road, just

past where the Zonebeke Rail cuts.   If you can get hold
of Sheet 28, Belgium 1/40,000, the reference is I. 16. b 2.
Any soldier will show you how to read the map."

Letter from a Foreman Workman

[I also append a letter received from a workman who
used to be at the same bench with Raymond when he was
going through his workshop course at Wolseley Motor
Works.   Stallard is a man he thought highly of, and be-
friended.   He is now foreman in the Lodge Fume Deposit
Company, after making an effort to get a berth in Lodge
Brothers' for Raymond's sake.   He is now, and has been
since the war began, the owner of Raymond's dog Larry,
about whom some local people remember that there was
an amusing County Court case.]

" 98 *Mansel Road, Small Heath, Birmingham,*
17 *September* 1915
" DEAR MR. LIONEL,—The shock was too great for me
to speak to you this afternoon.   I should like to express
to you, and all the family, my deepest and most heartfelt
sympathy in your terrible loss.   Mr. Raymond was the
best friend I ever had.

" Truly, I thought more of him than any other man
living, not only for his kind thoughts towards me, but for
his most admirable qualities, which I knew he possessed.

" The memory of him will remain with me as long as I
live.—Believe me to be, yours faithfully,
" (Signed)   NORMAN STALLARD "

RAYMOND, 1915

PART II
SUPERNORMAL PORTION

"Peace, peace! he is not dead, he doth not sleep—
He hath awakened from the dream of life."

SHELLEY, *Adonais*

INTRODUCTION

I HAVE made no secret of my conviction, not merely that personality persists, but that its continued existence is more entwined with the life of every day than has been generally imagined ; that there is no real breach of continuity between the dead and the living ; and that methods of intercommunion across what has seemed to be a gulf can be set going in response to the urgent demand of affection,—that in fact, as Diotima told Socrates (*Symposium*, 202 and 203), LOVE BRIDGES THE CHASM.

Nor is it affection only that controls and empowers supernormal intercourse : scientific interest and missionary zeal constitute supplementary motives which are found efficacious ; and it has been mainly through efforts so actuated that I and some others have been gradually convinced, by direct experience, of a fact which before long must become patent to mankind.

Hitherto I have testified to occurrences and messages of which the motive is intellectual rather than emotional : and though much, very much, even of this evidence remains inaccessible to the public, yet a good deal has appeared from time to time by many writers in the *Proceedings* of the Society for Psychical Research, and in my personal collection called *The Survival of Man*. No one therefore will be surprised if I now further testify concerning communications which come home to me in a peculiar sense ; communications from which sentiment is not excluded, though still they appear to be guided and managed with intelligent and on the whole evidential purpose. These are what I now decide to publish ; and I shall cite them as among those evidences for survival for the publication of which some legitimate demand has of late been made, owing to my having declared my belief in continued existence without being able to give the full grounds of that belief, because much of it concerned other people. The portion of evidence I shall now cite concerns only myself and family.

I must make selection, it is true, for the bulk has become great ; but I shall try to select fairly, and especially shall give in fair fullness those early communications which, though not so free and easy as they became with more experience, have yet an interest of their own, since they represent nascent powers and were being received through members of the family to whom the medium was a complete stranger and who gave no clue to identity.

Messages of an intelligible though rather recondite character from " Myers " began to reach me indeed a week or two before the death of my son ; and nearly all the messages received since his death differ greatly in character from those which in the old days were received through any medium with whom I sat. No youth was then represented as eager to communicate ; and though friends were described as sending messages, the messages were represented as coming from appropriate people— members of an elder generation, leaders of the Society for Psychical Research, and personal acquaintances. Whereas now, whenever any member of the family visits anonymously a competent medium, the same youth soon comes to the fore and is represented as eager to prove his personal survival and identity.

I consider that he has done so. And the family scepticism, which up to this time has been sufficiently strong, is now, I may fairly say, overborne by the facts. How far these facts can be conveyed to the sympathetic understanding of strangers, I am doubtful. But I must plead for a patient hearing ; and if I make mistakes, either in what I include, or in what for brevity I omit, or if my notes and comments fail in clearness, I bespeak a friendly interpretation : for it is truly from a sense of duty that in so personal a matter I lay myself open to harsh and perhaps cynical criticism.

It may be said—Why attach so much importance to one individual case ? I do not attach especial importance to it, but every individual case is of moment, because in such a matter the aphorism *Ex uno disce omnes* is strictly applicable. If we can establish the survival of any single ordinary individual we have established it for all.

Christians may say that the case for one Individual was established nearly 1900 years ago ; but they have most of them confused the issue by excessive though perhaps legitimate and necessary emphasis on the exceptional and unique character of that Personality. And a school of thought has arisen which teaches that ordinary men can only attain immortality vicariously—that is, conditionally on acceptance of a certain view concerning the benefits of that Sacrificial Act, and active assimilation of them.

So without arguing on any such subject, and without entering in the slightest degree on any theological question, I have endeavoured to state the evidence fully and frankly for the persistent existence of one of the multitude of youths who have sacrificed their lives at the cal of their Country when endangered by an aggressor of calculated ruthlessness.

Some critics may claim that there are many stronger cases of established survival. That may be, but this is a case which touches me closely and has necessarily received my careful attention. In so far as there are other strong cases—and I know of several—so much the better. I myself considered the case of survival practically proven before, and clinched by the efforts of Myers and others of the S.P.R. group on the other side ; but evidence is cumulative, and the discussion of a fresh case in no way weakens those that have gone before. Each stick of the faggot must be tested, and, unless absolutely broken, it adds to the strength of the bundle.

To base so momentous a conclusion as a scientific demonstration of human survival on any single instance, if it were not sustained on all sides by a great consensus of similar evidence, would doubtless be unwise ; for some other explanation of a merely isolated case would have to be sought. But we are justified in examining the evidence for any case of which all the details are known, and in trying to set forth the truth of it as completely and fairly as we may.

CHAPTER I

ELEMENTARY EXPLANATION

FOR people who have studied psychical matters, or who have read any books on the subject, it is unnecessary to explain what a 'sitting' is. Novices must be asked to refer to other writings—to small books, for instance, by Sir W. F. Barrett or Mr. J. Arthur Hill or Miss H. A. Dallas, which are easily accessible, or to my own previous book on this subject called *The Survival of Man*, which begins more at the beginning so far as my own experience is concerned.

Of mediumship there are many grades, one of the simplest forms being the capacity to receive an impression or automatic writing, under peaceful conditions, in an ordinary state; but the whole subject is too large to be treated here. Suffice it to say that the kind of medium chiefly dealt with in this book is one who, by waiting quietly, goes more or less into a trance, and is then subject to what is called 'control'—speaking or writing in a manner quite different from the medium's own normal or customary manner, under the guidance of a separate intelligence technically known as 'a control,' which some think must be a secondary personality—which indeed certainly *is* a secondary personality of the medium, whatever that phrase may really signify—the transition being effected in most cases quite easily and naturally. In this secondary state, a degree of clairvoyance or lucidity is attained quite beyond the medium's normal consciousness, and facts are referred to which must be outside his or her normal knowledge. The control, or second personality which speaks during the trance, appears to be more closely in touch with what is popularly spoken of as 'the next world' than with customary human existence, and accordingly is able to get messages through from people deceased; transmitting them through the speech or writing of the medium, usually with some obscurity and misunderstanding, and with mannerisms belonging either to the medium or to the control. The amount of sophistication varies according to the quality of the medium, and to the state of the same medium at different times ; it must be attributed in the best cases physiologically to the medium, intellectually to the control. The confusion is no greater than might be expected from a pair of operators, connected by a telephone of rather delicate and uncertain quality, who were engaged in transmitting messages between two stranger communicators, one of whom was anxious to get messages transmitted, though perhaps not very skilled in wording them, while the other was nearly silent and anxious not to give any information or assistance at all ; being, indeed, more or less suspicious that the whole appearance of things was deceptive, and that his friend, the ostensible communicator, was not really there. Under such circumstances the effort of the distant communicator would be chiefly directed to sending such natural and appropriate messages as should gradually break down the inevitable scepticism of his friend.

FURTHER PRELIMINARY EXPLANATION

I must assume it known that messages purporting to come from various deceased people have been received through various mediums, and that the Society for Psychical Research has especially studied those coming through Mrs. Piper—a resident in the neighbourhood of Boston, U.S.A.—during the past thirty years. We were introduced to her by Professor William James. My own experience with this lady began during her visit to this country in 1889, and was renewed in 1906. The account has been fully published in the *Proceedings* of the Society for Psychical Research, vols. vi. and xxiii., and an abbreviated version of some of the incidents there recorded can be referred to in my book *The Survival of Man*.

It will be convenient, however, to explain here that some of the communicators on the other side, like Mr.

Myers and Dr. Richard Hodgson, both now deceased, have appeared to utilise many mediums; and that to allow for possible sophistication by normal mental idiosyncrasies, and for any natural warping due to the physiological mechanism employed, or to the brain-deposit from which selection has to be made, we write the name of the ostensible communicator in each case with a suffix—like $Myers_P$. $Myers_V$, etc. ; meaning by this kind of designation to signify that part of the Myers-like intelligence which operates through Mrs. Piper or through Mrs. Verrall, etc., respectively.

We know that communication must be hampered, and its form largely determined, by the unconscious but inevitable influence of a transmitting mechanism, whether that be of a merely mechanical or of a physiological character. Every artist knows that he must adapt the expression of his thought to his material, and that what is possible with one ' medium,' even in the artist's sense of the word, is not possible with another.

And when the method of communication is purely mental or telepathic, we are assured that the communicator ' on the other side ' has to select from and utilise those ideas and channels which represent the customary mental scope of the medium ; though by practised skill and ingenuity they can be woven into fresh patterns and be made to convey to a patient and discriminating interpreter the real intention of the communicator's thought. In many such telepathic communications the physical form which the emergent message takes is that of automatic or semiconscious writing or speech ; the manner of the utterance being fairly normal, but the substance of it appearing not to emanate from the writer's or speaker's own mind : though but very seldom is either the subject-matter or the language of a kind quite beyond the writer's or speaker's normal capabilities.

In other cases, when the medium becomes entranced, the demonstration of a communicator's separate intelligence may become stronger and the sophistication less. A still further stage is reached when by special effort what is called *telergy* is employed, *i.e.* when physiological mechanism is more directly utilised without telepathic operation on the mind. And a still further step away from personal sophistication, though under extra mechanical difficulties, is attainable in *telekinesis* or what appears to be the direct movement of inorganic matter. To this last category—though in its very simplest form—must belong, I suppose, the percussive sounds known as raps.

To understand the intelligent tiltings of a table in contact with human muscles is a much simpler matter. It is crude and elementary, but in principle it does not appear to differ from automatic writing; though inasmuch as the code and the movements are so simple, it appears to be the easiest of all to beginners. It is so simple that it has been often employed as a sort of game, and so has fallen into disrepute. But its possibilities are not to be ignored for all that ; and in so far as it enables a feeling of more direct influence—in so far as the communicator feels able himself to control the energy necessary, instead of having to entrust his message to a third person—it is by many communicators preferred. More on this subject will be found in Chapters VIII of Part II and XIV of Part III.

Before beginning an historical record of the communications and messages received from or about my son since his death, I think it will be well to prelude it by—

(i) A message which arrived before the event ;
(ii) A selection of subsequent communications bearon and supplementing this message ;
(iii) One of the evidential episodes, selected from subsequent communications, which turned out to be exactly verifiable.

A few further details about these things, and another series of messages of evidential importance, will be found in that Part of the *Proceedings* of the S.P.R. which is to be published about October 1916.

If the full discussion allowed to these selected portions appears rather complicated, an unstudious reader may skip the next three chapters, on a first reading, and may learn about the simpler facts in their evolutionary or historical order.

CHAPTER II

THE 'FAUNUS' MESSAGE

Preliminary Facts

R AYMOND joined the Army in September 1914; trained near Liverpool and Edinburgh with the South Lancashires, and in March 1915 was sent to the trenches in Flanders. In the middle of July 1915 he had a few days' leave at home, and on the 20th returned to the Front.

INITIAL 'PIPER' MESSAGE

The first intimation that I had that anything might be going wrong, was a message from Myers through Mrs. Piper in America; communicated apparently by " Richard Hodgson " at a time when a Miss Robbins was having a sitting at Mrs. Piper's house, Greenfield, New Hampshire, on 8 August 1915, and sent me by Miss Alta Piper (A. L. P.) together with the original script. Here follows the extract, which at a certain stage in Miss Robbins's sitting, after having dealt with matters of personal significance to her, none of which had anything whatever to do with me, began abruptly thus :—

R. H.—Now Lodge, while we are not here as of old, *i.e.* not quite, we are here enough to take and give messages.
      Myers says you take the part of the poet, and he will act as Faunus. FAUNUS.
MISS R.—Faunus?
R. H.—Yes. Myers. *Protect.* He will understand.
      (Evidently referring to Lodge.—A. L. P.)
      What have you to say, Lodge? Good work. Ask Verrall, she will also understand. Arthur says so. [This means Dr. Arthur W. Verrall (deceased).—O. J. L.]

MISS R.—Do you mean Arthur Tennyson ?
This absurd confusion, stimulated by the word
' poet,' was evidently the result of a long strain at
reading barely legible trance-writing for more than
an hour, and was recognised immediately afterwards with dismayed amusement by the sitter.   It
is only of interest as showing how completely
unknown to anyone present was the reference
intended by the communicator.—O. J. L.]
R. H.—*No. Myers* knows. So does   You
got mixed (to Miss R.), but Myers is straight about
Poet and Faunus.

I venture to say that to non-classical people the
above message conveys nothing.   It did not convey
anything to me, beyond the assurance, based on past
experience, that it certainly meant something definite,
that its meaning was probably embedded in a classical
quotation, and that a scholar like Mrs. Verrall would be
able to interpret it, even if only the bare skeleton of the
message were given without any details as to source.

LETTER FROM MRS. VERRALL

In order to interpret this message, therefore, I wrote
to Mrs. Verrall as instructed, asking her : " Does *The Poet
and Faunus* mean anything to you ?   Did one ' protect '
the other ? "   She replied at once (8 September 1915)
referring me to Horace, *Carm.* II. xvii. 27–30, and
saying :—

" The reference is to Horace's account of his narrow
escape from death, from a falling tree, which he ascribes
to the intervention of Faunus.   Cf. Hor. *Odes*, II. xiii. ;
II. xvii. 27 ; III. iv. 27 ; III. viii. 8, for references to
the subject.   The allusion to Faunus is in Ode II. xvii.
27–30 :—

' Me truncus illapsus cerebro
Sustulerat, nisi *Faunus* ictum
Dextra levasset, Mercurialium
Custos virorum.'

" ' Faunus, the guardian of poets ' (' poets ' being the
usual interpretation of ' Mercury's men ').

" The passage is a very well-known one to all readers of Horace, and is perhaps specially familiar from its containing, in the sentence quoted, an unusual grammatical construction. It is likely to occur in a detailed work on Latin Grammar.

" The passage has no special associations for me other than as I have described, though it has some interest as forming part of a chronological sequence among the *Odes*, not generally admitted by commentators, but accepted by me.

" The words quoted are, of course, strictly applicable to the Horatian passage, which they instantly recalled to me. (Signed) M. DE G. VERRALL "

I perceived therefore, from this manifestly correct interpretation of the ' Myers ' message to me, that the meaning was that some blow was going to fall, or was likely to fall, though I didn't know of what kind, and that Myers would intervene, apparently to protect me from it. So far as I can recollect my comparatively trivial thoughts on the subject, I believe that I had some vague idea that the catastrophe intended was perhaps of a financial rather than of a personal kind.

The above message reached me near the beginning of September in Scotland. Raymond was killed near Ypres on 14 September 1915, and we got the news by telegram from the War Office on 17 September. A fallen or falling tree is a frequently used symbol for death; perhaps through misinterpretation of *Eccl.* xi. 3. To several other classical scholars I have since put the question I addressed to Mrs. Verrall, and they all referred me to Horace, *Carm.* II. xvii. as the unmistakable reference.

Mr. Bayfield's Criticism

Soon after the event, I informed the Rev. M. A. Bayfield, ex-headmaster of Eastbourne College, fully of the facts, as an interesting S.P.R. incident (saying at the same time that Myers had not been able to ' ward off ' the blow); and he was good enough to send me a careful note in reply :—

" Horace does not, in any reference to his escape, say

clearly whether the tree struck him, but I have always thought it did. He says Faunus lightened the blow ; he does not say 'turned it aside.' As bearing on your terrible loss, the meaning seems to be that the blow would fall but would not crush ; it would be 'lightened' by the assurance, conveyed afresh to you by a special message from the still living Myers, that your boy still lives.

" I shall be interested to know what you think of this interpretation. The 'protect' I take to mean protect from being overwhelmed by the blow, from losing faith and hope, as we are all in danger of doing when smitten by some crushing personal calamity. Many a man when so smitten has, like Merlin, lain

'as dead,
And lost to life and use and name and fame.'

That seems to me to give a sufficiently precise application to the word (on which Myers apparently insists) and to the whole reference to Horace.",

In a postscript he adds the following :—

" In *Carm.* iii. 8, Horace describes himself as *prope funeratus / arboris ictu*, ' wellnigh killed by a blow from a tree.' An artist in expression, such as he was, would not have mentioned any ' blow ' if there had been none ; he would have said ' well nigh killed by a falling tree '— or the like. It is to be noted that in both passages he uses the word *ictus*. And in ii. 13. 11 (the whole ode is addressed to the tree) he says the man must have been a fellow steeped in every wickedness ' who planted thee an accursed lump of wood, a thing meant to fall (this is the delicate meaning of *caducum*—not merely "falling") on thine undeserving master's head.' Here again the language implies that he was struck, and struck on the head.

" Indeed, the escape must have been a narrow one, and it is to me impossible to believe that Horace would have been so deeply impressed by the accident if he had not actually been struck. He refers to it four times :—

Carm. ii. 13.—(Ode addressed to the tree—forty lines long.)

ii. 17. 27.

iii. 4. 27.—(Here he puts the risk he ran on a
parallel with that of the rout at
Philippi, from which he escaped.)

iii. 8. 8.

" I insist on all this as strengthening my interpretation, and also as strengthening the assignment of the
script to Myers, who would of course be fully alive to all
the points to be found in his reference to Faunus and
Horace—and, as I have no doubt, believed that Horace
did not escape the actual blow, and that it was a severe
one."

NOTE BY O. J. L.

Since some of the translators, especially verse translators, of
Horace convey the idea of turning aside or warding off the blow,
it may be well to emphasise the fact that most of the scholars
consulted gave " lightened " or " weakened " as the translation.
And Professor Strong says—" no doubt at all that ' levasset '
means ' weakened ' the blow ; the bough fell and struck the
Poet, but lightly, through the action of Faunus. ' Levo ' in this
sense is quite common and classical."

Bryce's prose translation (Bohn) is quite clear—" a tree-stem
falling on my head had surely been my death, had not good
Faunus eased the blow . . ." And although Conington's translation has " check'd the blow in mid descent," he really means the
same thing, because it is the slaying, not the wounding or striking
of the Poet that is prevented :—

" Me the curst trunk, that smote my skull,
Had slain ; but Faunus, strong to shield
The friends of Mercury, check'd the blow
In mid descent."

ADDITIONAL PIPER SCRIPT

Mr. Bayfield also calls my attention to another portion
of Piper Script—in this case not a trance or semi-trance
sitting, but ordinary automatic writing—dated 5 August,
which reached me simultaneously with the one already
quoted from, at the beginning of September, and which
he says seems intended to prepare me for some personal
trouble :—

" Yes. For the moment, Lodge, have faith and
wisdom [? confidence] in all that is highest and best.
Have you all not been profoundly guided and
cared for ? Can you answer, ' No ' ? It is by your
faith that all is well and has been."

I remember being a little struck by the wording in the above script, urging me to admit that we—presumably the family—had " been profoundly guided and cared for," and " that all is well and has been " ; because it seemed to indicate that something was not going to be quite so well. But it was too indefinite to lead me to make any careful record of it, or to send it as a prediction to anybody for filing ; and it would no doubt have evaporated from my mind except for the ' Faunus ' warning, given three days later, though received at the same time, which seemed to me clearly intended as a prediction, whether it happened to come off or not.

The two Piper communications, of which parts have now been quoted, reached me at Gullane, East Lothian. where my wife (M. F. A. L.) and I were staying for a few weeks. They arrived early in September 1915, and as soon as I had heard from Mrs. Verrall I wrote to Miss Piper to acknowledge them, as follows :—

" *The Linga Private Hotel,*
Gullane, East Lothian,
12 *September* 1915
" MY DEAR ALTA,—The reference to the Poet and Faunus in your mother's last script is quite intelligible, and a good classical allusion. You might tell the ' communicator ' some time if there is opportunity.
" I feel sure that it must convey nothing to you and yours. That is quite as it should be, as you know, for evidential reasons."

This was written two days before Raymond's death, and five days before we heard of it. The Pipers' ignorance of any meaning in the Poet and Faunus allusion was subsequently confirmed.

It so happens that this letter was returned to me, for some unknown reason, through the Dead Letter Office, reaching me on 14 November 1915, and being then sent forward by me again.[1]

[1] Further Piper and other communications, obscurely relevant to this subject, will be found in a Paper which will appear in the S.P.R. *Proceedings* for the autumn of 1916.

CHAPTER III

SEQUEL TO THE 'FAUNUS' MESSAGE

IT now remains to indicate how far Myers carried out his implied promise, and what steps he took, or has been represented as having taken, to lighten the blow—which it is permissible to say was a terribly severe one.

For such evidence I must quote from the record of sittings held here in England with mediums previously unknown, and by sitters who gave no sort of clue as to identity. (See the historical record, beginning at Chapter V.)

It may be objected that my own general appearance is known or might be guessed. But that does not apply to members of my family, who went quite anonymously to private sittings kindly arranged for by a friend in London (Mrs. Kennedy, wife of Dr. Kennedy), who was no relation whatever, but whose own personal experience caused her to be sympathetic and helpful, and who is both keen and critical about evidential considerations.

I may state, for what it is worth, that as a matter of fact normal clues to identity are disliked, and, in so far as they are gratuitous, are even resented, by a good medium ; for they are no manner of use, and yet subsequently they appear to spoil evidence. It is practically impossible for mediums to hunt up and become normally acquainted with the family history of their numerous sitters, and those who know them are well aware that they do nothing of the sort, but in making arrangements for a sitting it is not easy, unless special precautions are taken, to avoid giving a name and an address, and thereby appearing to give facilities for fraud.

In our case, and in that of our immediate friends, these

precautions have been taken—sometimes in a rather elaborate manner↙

The first sitting that was held after Raymond's death by any member of the family was held not explicitly for the purpose of getting into communication with him— still less with any remotest notion of entering into communication with Mr. Myers—but mainly because a French widow lady, who had been kind to our daughters during winters in Paris, was staying with my wife at Edgbaston —her first real visit to England—and was in great distress at the loss of both her beloved sons in the war, within a week of each other, so that she was left desolate. To comfort her my wife took her up to London to call on Mrs. Kennedy, and to get a sitting arranged for with a medium whom that lady knew and recommended. Two anonymous interviews were duly held, and incidentally I may say that the two sons of Madame communicated, on both occasions, though with difficulty ; that one of them gave his name completely, the other approximately ; and that the mother, who was new to the whole subject, was partially consoled.[1] Raymond, however, was represented as coming with them and helping them, and as sending some messages on his own account. I shall here only quote those messages which bear upon the subject of *Myers* and have any possible connexion with the 'Faunus' message.

(For an elementary explanation about 'sittings' in general, see Chapter I.)

EXTRACTS RELATING TO 'MYERS' FROM EARLY ANONYMOUS SITTINGS

We heard first of Raymond's death on 17 September 1915, and on 25 September his mother (M. F. A. L.), who was having an anonymous sitting for a friend with Mrs. Leonard, then a complete stranger, had the following spelt out by tilts of a table, as purporting to come from Raymond :—

TELL FATHER I HAVE MET SOME FRIENDS OF HIS.

[1] I realise now, though the relevance has only just struck me, that from the point of view of an outside critic, pardonably suspicious of bad faith, this episode of the bereaved French lady—an obviously complete stranger to Mrs. Kennedy as well as to the medium—has an evidential and therefore helpful side.

7

M. F. A. L.—Can you give any name ?

YES. MYERS.

(That was all on that subject on that occasion.)

On the 27th of September 1915, I myself went to London and had my first sitting, between noon and one o'clock, with Mrs. Leonard. I went to her house or flat alone, as a complete stranger, for whom an appointment had been made through Mrs. Kennedy. Before we began, Mrs. Leonard informed me that her ' guide ' or ' control ' was a young girl named " Feda."

In a short time after the medium had gone into trance, a youth was described in terms which distinctly suggested Raymond, and " Feda " brought messages. I extract the following :—

From First Anonymous Sitting of O. J. L. with Mrs. Leonard, 27 September 1915

(Mrs. Leonard's control, Feda, supposed to be speaking throughout.)

He finds it difficult, he says, but he has got so many kind friends helping him. He didn't think when he waked up first that he was going to be happy, but now he is, and he says he is going to be happier. He knows that as soon as he is a little more ready he has got a great deal of work to do. " I almost wonder," he says, " shall I be fit and able to do it. They tell me I shall."

" I have instructors and teachers with me." Now he is trying to build up a letter of some one ; M. he shows me.

(A short time later, he said :—)

" People think I say I am happy in order to make them happier, but I don't.[1] I have met hundreds of friends. I don't know them all. I have met many who tell me that, a little later, they will explain why they are helping me. I feel I have got two fathers now. I don't feel I have lost one and got another ; I have got both.

---

[1] This is reminiscent of a sentence in one of his letters from the Front: "As cheerful and well and happy as ever. Don't think I am having a rotten time—I am not." Dated 11 May 1915 (really 12).

I have got my old one, and another too—a *pro tem.*
father."
       (Here Feda ejaculated " What's that ?   Is that
right ? "   O. J. L. replied ' Yes.')
    There is a weight gone off his mind the last day or two ;
he feels brighter and lighter and happier altogether, the
last few days.   There was confusion at first.   He could
not get his bearings, didn't seem to know where he was.
" But I was not very long," he says, " and I think I was
very fortunate ; it was not very long before it was explained to me where I was."

    But the most remarkable indirect allusion, or apparent
allusion, to something like the ' Faunus ' message, came
at the end of the sitting, after " Raymond " had gone, and
just before Mrs. Leonard came out of trance :—

    " He is gone, but Feda sees something which is only
symbolic ; she sees a cross falling back on to you ; very
dark, falling on to you ; dark and heavy looking ; and as
it falls it gets twisted round and the other side seems all
light, and the light is shining all over you.   It is a sort of
pale blue, but it is white and quite light when it touches
you.   Yes, that is what Feda sees.   The cross looked
dark, and then it suddenly twisted round and became a
beautiful light.   The cross is a means of shedding **real**
light.   It is going to help a great deal.
    " Did you know you had a coloured Guide ? . . . He
says your son is the cross of light ; he is the cross of light,
and he is going to be a light that will help you ; he is
going to help too to prove to the world the Truth.   That
is why they built up the dark cross that turned to bright.
You know ; but others, they do so want to know.   Feda
is loosing hold ; good-bye."
       [This ends the O. J. L. first Leonard sitting of
              27 September 1915.]

    On the afternoon of the same day, 27 September 1915,
that I had this first sitting with Mrs. Leonard, Lady Lodge
had her first sitting, as a complete stranger, with Mr. A.
Vout Peters, who had been invited for the purpose—without any name being given—to Mrs. Kennedy's house at
3.30 p.m.

Here again, Raymond was described well enough, fairly early in the sitting, and several identifying messages were given. Presently ' Moonstone ' (Peters's chief control) asked, " Was he not associated with Chemistry ? " As a matter of fact, my laboratory has been rather specially chemical of late ; and the record continues, copied with subsequent annotations in square brackets as it stands :—

From First Anonymous Sitting of M. F. A. L. with Peters,
27 September 1915

Was he not associated with chemistry ? If not, some one associated with him was, because I see all the things in a chemical laboratory.

That chemistry thing takes me away from him to a man in the flesh [O. J. L. presumably] ; and, connected with him, a man, a writer of poetry, on our side, closely connected with spiritualism. He was very clever—he too passed away out of England.

[This is clearly meant for Myers, who died in Rome.]

He has communicated several times. This gentleman who wrote poetry—I see the letter M—he is helping your son to communicate.

[His presence and help were also independently mentioned by Mrs. Leonard.]

He is built up in the chemical conditions.

If your son didn't know this man, he knew of him.

[Yes, he could hardly have known him, as he was only about twelve at the time of Myers's death.]

At the back of the gentleman beginning with M, and who wrote poetry, is a whole group of people. [The S.P.R. group, doubtless.] They are very interested. And don't be surprised if you get messages from them, even if you don't know them.

(Then ' Moonstone ' stopped, and said :—)

This is so important that is going to be said now, that I want to go slowly, for you to write clearly every word (dictating carefully) :—

" NOT ONLY IS THE PARTITION SO THIN THAT YOU CAN HEAR THE OPERATORS ON THE OTHER SIDE, BUT A BIG HOLE HAS BEEN MADE."

This message is for the gentleman associated with the chemical laboratory.

[Considering that my wife was quite unknown to the medium, this is a remarkably evidential and identifying message. Cf. passage in my book, *Survival of Man*, containing this tunnel-boring simile; p. 337 of large edition, p. 234 of shilling edition.—O. J. L.]

' Moonstone ' continued :—

The boy—I call them all boys because I was over a hundred when I lived here and they are all boys to me—he says, he is here, but he says :—

" Hitherto it has been a thing of the head, now I am come over it is a thing of the heart."

What is more (here Peters jumped up in his chair, vigorously, snapped his fingers excitedly, and spoke loudly)—

" Good God ! how father will be able to speak out ! much firmer than he has ever done, because it will touch our hearts."

(Here ends extract from Peters sitting of 27 September 1915. A completer record will be found in Chapter VII.)

At a Leonard Table Sitting on 12 October 1915—by which time our identity was known to Mrs. Leonard—I told ' Myers ' that I understood his Piper message about Faunus and the Poet ; and the only point of interest about the reply or comment is that the two following sentences were spelt out, purporting to come either indirectly or directly from ' Myers ' :—

1. He says it meant your son's tr[ansition].
2. Your son shall be mine.

The next ' Myers ' reference came on 29 October, when I had a sitting with Peters, unexpectedly and unknown to my family, at his London room (15 Devereux Court, Fleet Street)—a sitting arranged for by Mr. J. A. Hill for an anonymous friend :—

Peters went into trance, and after some other communications, gave messages from a youth who was recognised by the control and identified as my son ; and later on

Peters's ' control,' whom it is customary to call ' Moonstone,' spoke thus :—

From Sitting of O. J. L. with Peters on 29 *October* 1915

Your common-sense method of approaching the subject in the family has been the means of helping him to come back as he has been able to do ; and had he not known what you had told him, then it would have been far more difficult for him to come back. He is very deliberate in what he says. He is a young man that knows what he is saying. Do you know F W M ?

o. j. l.—Yes, I do.

Because I see those three letters. Now, after them, do you know S T ; yes, I get S T, then a dot, and then P ? These are shown me ; I see them in light ; your boy shows these things to me.

o. j. l.—Yes, I understand. [Meaning that I recognised the allusion to F. W. H. Myers's poem *St. Paul.*

Well, he says to me : " He has helped me so much, more than you think. That is F W M."

o. j. l.—Bless him !

No, your boy laughs, he has got an ulterior motive for it ; don't think it was only for charity's sake, he has got an ulterior motive, and thinks that you will be able by the strength of your personality to do what you want to do now, to ride over the quibbles of the fools, and to make the Society, *the* Society, he says, of some use to the world. . . . Can you understand ?

o. j. l.—Yes.

Now he says, " He helped me because, with me through you, he can break away the dam that people have set up. Later on, you are going to speak to them. It is already on the programme, and you will break down the opposition because of me." Then he says, " For God's sake, father, do it. Because if you only knew, and could only see what I see : hundreds of men and women heart-broken. And if you could only see the boys on our side shut out, you would throw the whole strength of yourself into this work. But you can do it." He is very earnest. Oh, and he wants—No, I must stop him, I must prevent him, I don't want him to control the medium.—Don't think me unkind, but I must protect my medium; he would not be able to do the work he has to do; the medium would be ill from it, I must protect him, the emotion would be too great, too great for both of you, so I must prevent him from controlling.

He understands, but he wants me to tell you this :—

The feeling on going over was one of intense disappointment, he had no idea of death. The second too was grief. (Pause.)

.   .   .   .

This is a time when men and women have had the crust broken off them—a crust of convention, of . . . of indifference, has been smashed, and everybody thinks, though some selfishly.

Now, returning to him, how patient he is ! He was not always so patient. After the grief there was a glimmering of hope, because he realised that he could get back to you ; and because his grandmother came to him. Then his brother was introduced to him. Then, he says, other people. Myerse—" Myerse," it sounds like—do you know what he means ?—came to him, and then he knew he could get back. He knew.

Now he wants me to tell you this : That from his death, which is only one of thousands, that the work which he (I have to translate his ideas into words, I don't get them verbatum [sic])—the work which he volunteered to be able to succeed in,—no, that's not it. The work which he enlisted for, that is what he says, only he was only a unit and seemingly lost—yet the very fact of his death will be the means of pushing it on. Now I have got it. By his passing away, many hundreds will be benefited.

(End of extract from Peters sitting of 29 October 1915.)

(A still fuller account of the whole ' Faunus ' episode, and a further sequel to it of a classical kind, called the " Horace O. L." message, will be found in the S.P.R. *Proceedings* for the autumn of 1916.)

It will be understood, I hope, that the above extracts from sittings have been reproduced here in order to show that, if we take the incidents on their face value, Myers had redeemed his ' Faunus ' promise, and had lightened the blow by looking after and helping my son ' on the other side.' I now propose to make some further extracts—of a more evidential character—tending to establish the survival of my son's own personality and memory. There have been several of these evidential episodes, making strongly in this direction ; but I select, for description here, one relating to a certain group photograph, of which we were told through two mediums, but of which we normally knew nothing till afterwards.

CHAPTER IV

THE GROUP PHOTOGRAPH

I NOW come to a peculiarly good piece of evidence arising out of the sittings which from time to time we held in the autumn of 1915, namely, the mention and description of a group photograph taken near the Front, of the existence of which we were in complete ignorance, but which was afterwards verified in a satisfactory and complete manner. It is necessary to report the circumstances rather fully :—

Raymond was killed on 14 September 1915.

The first reference to a photograph taken of him with other men was made by Peters at M. F. A. L.'s first sitting with Peters, in Mrs. Kennedy's house, on 27 September 1915, thus :—

Extract from M. F. A. L.'s anonymous Sitting with Peters on 27 September 1915

"You have several portraits of this boy. Before he went away you had got a good portrait of him— two—no, three. Two where he is alone and one where he is in a group of other men. He is particular that I should tell you of this. In one you see his walking-stick "—('Moonstone' here put an imaginary stick under his arm).

We had single photographs of him of course, and in uniform, but we did not know of the existence of a photograph in which he was one of a group; and M. F. A. L. was sceptical about it, thinking that it might well be only a shot or guess on the part of Peters·at something probable. But Mrs. Kennedy (as Note-taker) had written down most of what was said, and this record was kept, copied, and sent to Mr. Hill in the ordinary course at the time.

I was myself, moreover, rather impressed with the emphasis laid on it—" he is particular that I should tell you of this "—and accordingly made a half-hearted inquiry or two ; but nothing more was heard on the subject for two months. On Monday, 29 November, however, a letter came from Mrs. Cheves, a stranger to us, mother of Captain Cheves of the R.A.M.C., who had known Raymond and had reported to us concerning the nature of his wound, and who is still doing good work at the Front.

Mrs. Cheves' welcome letter ran as follows :—

" 28 November 1915

" DEAR LADY LODGE,—My son, who is M.O. to the 2nd South Lancs, has sent us a group of officers taken in August, and I wondered whether you knew of this photo and had had a copy. If not may I send you one, as we have half a dozen and also a key ? I hope you will forgive my writing to ask this, but I have often thought of you and felt so much for you in yr. great sorrow. —Sincerely yours,   B. P. CHEVES"

M. F. A. L. promptly wrote, thanking her, and asking for it ; but fortunately it did not come at once.

Before it came, I (O. J. L.) was having a sitting with Mrs. Leonard alone at her house on 3 December ; and on this occasion, among other questions, I asked carefully concerning the photograph, wishing to get more detailed information about it, before it was seen. It should be understood that the subject was not introduced by Mrs. Leonard or her control. The previous mention of a photograph had been through Peters. It was I that introduced the subject through Mrs. Leonard, and asked a question ; and the answers were thus reported and recorded at the time—the typing out of the sitting being all done before the photograph arrived :—

Extract from the Record of O. J. L.'s Sitting with Mrs. Leonard, 3 December 1915

(Mrs. Leonard's child-control, Feda, supposed to be speaking, and often speaking of herself in the third person.)

FEDA.—Now ask him some more.

O. J. L.—Well, he said something about having a photograph taken with some other men. We haven't

seen that photograph yet. Does he want to say
anything more about it ? He spoke about a
photograph.

Yes, but he thinks it wasn't here. He looks at
Feda, and he says, it wasn't to you, Feda.

o. j. l.—No, he's quite right. It wasn't. Can he say
where he spoke of it ?

He says it wasn't through the table.

o. j. l.—No, it wasn't.

It wasn't here at all. He didn't know the
person that he said it through. The conditions
were strange there—a strange house. [Quite true,
it was said through Peters in Mrs. Kennedy's house
during an anonymous sitting on 27 September.]

o. j. l.—Do you recollect the photograph at all ?

He thinks there were several others taken with
him, not one or two, but several.

o. j. l.—Were they friends of yours ?

Some of them, he says. He didn't know them
all, not very well. But he knew some ; he heard
of some ; they were not all friends.

o. j. l.—Does he remember how he looked in the photograph ?

No, he doesn't remember how he looked.

o. j. l.—No, no, I mean was he standing up ?

No, he doesn't seem to think so. Some were
raised up round ; he was sitting down, and some
were raised up at the back of him. Some were
standing, and some were sitting, he thinks.

o. j. l.—Were they soldiers ?

He says yes—a mixed lot. Somebody called C
was on it with him ; and somebody called R—not
his own name, but another R. K, K, K—he says
something about K.

He also mentions a man beginning with B—
(indistinct muttering something like Berry, Burney
—then clearly) but put down B.

o. j. l.—I am asking about the photograph because we
haven't seen it yet. Somebody is going to send it
to us. We have heard that it exists, and that's all.

[While this is being written out, the above
remains true. The photograph has not yet come.]

He has the impression of about a dozen on it. A dozen, he says, if not more. Feda thinks it must be a big photograph.

No, he doesn't think so, he says they were grouped close together.

O. J. L.—Did he have a stick ?

He doesn't remember that. He remembers that somebody wanted to lean on him, but he is not sure if he was taken with some one leaning on him. But somebody wanted to lean on him he remembers. The last what he gave you, what were a B, will be rather prominent in that photograph. It wasn't taken in a photographer's place.

O. J. L.—Was it out of doors ?

Yes, practically.

FEDA (*sotto voce*).—What you mean, ' yes practically ' ; must have been out of doors or not out of doors. You mean ' yes,' don't you ?

Feda thinks he means ' yes,' because he says ' practically.'

O. J. L.—It may have been a shelter.

It might have been. Try to show Feda.

At the back he shows me lines going down. It looks like a black background, with lines at the back of them. (Feda here kept drawing vertical lines in the air.)

There was, for some reason, considerable delay in the arrival of the photograph ; it did not arrive till the afternoon of December 7. Meanwhile, on December 6, Lady Lodge had been looking up Raymond's Diary, which had been returned from the Front with his kit, and found an entry :—

" 24 *August.*—Photo taken."

(A statement will follow to this effect.)

Now Raymond had only had one " leave " home since going to the Front, and this leave was from 16 July to 20 July. The photograph had not been taken then, and so he could not have told us anything about it. The exposure was only made twenty-one days before his death, and some days may have elapsed before he saw a print, if he ever saw one. He certainly never mentioned it in his letters. We were therefore in complete ignorance concerning it ; and only recently had we normally become aware of its existence.

On the morning of 7 December another note came from Mrs. Cheves, in answer to a question about the delay ; and this letter said that the photograph was being sent off. Accordingly I (O. J. L.), thinking that the photograph might be coming at once, dictated a letter to go to Mr. Hill, recording roughly my impression of what the photograph would be like, on the strength of the communication received by me from ' Raymond ' through Mrs. Leonard ; and this was posted by A. E. Briscoe about lunch-time on the same day.   (See statement by Mr. Briscoe at the end.) My statement to Mr. Hill ran thus :—

Copy of what was written by O. J. L. to Mr. Hill about the Photograph on the morning of Tuesday, 7 December 1915

" Concerning that photograph which Raymond mentioned through Peters [saying this : ' One where he is in a group of other men. He is particular that I should tell you of this. In one you see his walking-stick.'],[1] he has said some more about it through Mrs. Leonard. But he is doubtful about the stick. What he says is that there is a considerable number of men in the photograph ; that the front row is sitting, and that there is a back row, or some of the people grouped and set up at the back ; also that there are a dozen or more people in the photograph, and that som. of them he hardly knew ; that a B is prominent in the photograph, and that there is also a C ; that he himself is sitting down, and that there are people behind him, one of whom either leant on his shoulder, or tried to.

" The photograph has not come yet, but it may come any day now ; so I send this off before I get it.

" The actual record of what was said in the sitting is being typed, but the above represents my impression of it."

The photograph was delivered at Mariemont between 3 and 4 p.m. on the afternoon of 7 December. It was a wet afternoon, and the package was received by Rosalynde, who took the wet wrapper off it. Its size was 12 by 9 inches, and was an enlargement from a 5 by 7

[1] This bit not written to J. A. H., but is copied from Peters's sitting, of which Mr. Hill had seen the record.

inch original. The number of people in the photograph
is twenty-one, made up as follows :—

> Five in the front row squatting on the grass, Raymond
> being one of these ; the second from the right.
> Seven in the second row seated upon chairs.
> Nine in the back row standing up against the outside
> of a temporary wooden structure such as might
> be a hospital shed or something of that kind.

On examining the photograph, we found that every
peculiarity mentioned by Raymond, unaided by the
medium, was strikingly correct. The walking-stick is
there (but Peters had put a stick under his arm, which is
not correct), and in connexion with the background Feda
had indicated vertical lines, not only by gesture but
by saying " lines going down," as well as " a black
background with lines at the back of them." There are
six conspicuous nearly vertical lines on the roof of the
shed, but the horizontal lines in the background generally
are equally conspicuous.

By " a mixed lot," we understood members of different
Companies—not all belonging to Raymond's Company, but
a collection from several. This must be correct, as they
are too numerous for one Company. It is probable that
they all belong to one Regiment, except perhaps one whose
cap seems to have a thistle badge instead of three feathers.

As to " prominence," I have asked several people
which member of the group seemed to them the most
prominent ; and except as regards central position, a well-
lighted standing figure on the right has usually been
pointed to as most prominent. This one is " B," as
stated, namely, Captain S. T. Boast.

Some of the officers must have been barely known to
Raymond, while some were his friends. Officers whose
names begin with B, with C, and with R were among
them; though not any name beginning with K. The
nearest approach to a K-sound in the group is one
beginning with a hard C.

Some of the group are sitting, while others are standing
behind. Raymond is one of those sitting on the ground
in front, and his walking-stick or regulation cane is lying
across his feet.

The background is dark, and is conspicuously lined. It is out of doors, close in front of a shed or military hut, pretty 'much as suggested to me by the statements made in the 'Leonard' sitting — what I called a " shelter."

But by far the most striking piece of evidence is the fact that some one sitting behind Raymond is leaning or resting a hand on his shoulder. The photograph fortunately shows the actual occurrence, and almost indicates that Raymond was rather annoyed with it ; for his face is a little screwed up, and his head has been slightly bent to one side out of the way of the man's arm. It is the only case in the photograph where one man is leaning or resting his hand on the shoulder of another, and I judge that it is a thing not unlikely to be remembered by the one to whom it occurred.

CONFIRMATORY STATEMENTS

STATEMENT BY RAYMOND'S MOTHER

Four days ago (6 December), I was looking through my son Raymond's Diary which had been returned with his kit from the Front. (The edges are soaked, and some of the leaves stuck together, with his blood.) I was struck by finding an entry " Photo taken " under the date 24 August, and I entered the fact in my own Diary at once, thus :—

" 6 December.—Read Raymond's Diary for first time, saw record of ' photo taken ' 24 August."

(Signed)   MARY F. A. LODGE

10 December 1915

STATEMENT BY A. E. BRISCOE

The dictated letter to Mr. Hill, recording roughly Sir Oliver's impression of what the photograph would be like, was written out by me on the morning of Tuesday, 7 December, at Mariemont; it was signed by Sir Oliver at about noon, and shortly afterwards I started for the University, taking that and other letters with me for posting in town. I went straight to the University, and at lunch-time (about 1.30) posted the packet to Mr. Hill at the General Post Office.

(In the packet, I remember, there was also a letter on another subject, and a printed document from Mr. Gow, the Editor of *Light.*)   (Signed)   A. E. BRISCOE,

Secretary to Sir Oliver Lodge

8 December 1915

STATEMENT BY ROSALYNDE

I was sitting in the library at Mariemont about 3.45 on Tuesday afternoon, 7 December 1915, when Harrison came in with a flat cardboard parcel addressed to Mother. Mother was resting ; and as the paper, wrapping up what I took to be the photograph, was wet from the rain, I undid it and left the photograph in tissue paper on a table, having just glanced at it to see if it was the one we'd been waiting for.

No one saw it or was shown it till after tea, when I showed it to Mother. That would be about 6. Mrs. Thompson, Lorna, and Barbara now also saw it. Honor was not at home and did not see it till later.   (Signed)   R. V. LODGE

8 *December* 1915

NOTE BY O. J. L.

In answer to an inquiry, Messrs. Gale & Polden, of Aldershot and London, the firm whose name was printed at the foot of the photograph, informed me that it was " from a negative of a group of Officers sent to us by Captain Boast of the 2nd South Lancashire Regiment " ; and having kindly looked up the date, they further tell me that they received the negative from Captain Boast on 15 October 1915.

It will be remembered that information about the existence of the photograph came through Peters on 27 September—more than a fortnight, therefore, before the negative reached England.

The photograph is only shown here because of its evidential interest. Considered as a likeness of Raymond, it is an exceptionally bad one ; he appears shrunk into an uncomfortable position.

FURTHER INFORMATION ABOUT THE PHOTOGRAPH :

Extract from a letter by Captain Boast from the Trenches, dated 7 May 1916, to Mrs. Case, and lent me to see

" Some months ago (last summer) the Officers of our Battalion had their photo taken. . . . . You see, the photographer who took us was a man who had been shelled out of house and home, and as he had no means of doing the photos for us, we bought the negatives, and sent them along to be finished in England."

GROUP OF OFFICERS, AS SENT US BY MRS. CILVES ON 7 DECEMBER, 1915, SHOWING AN ARM RESTING ON RAYMOND'S SHOULDER

A later Letter from Captain Boast

In answer to a special inquiry addressed to Captain Boast at the Front, he has been good enough to favour me with the following letter :—

" 10 *July* 1916

" DEAR SIR,—Your letter of 4 July has just reached me. The proofs of the photographs referred to were received by me from the photographer at Reninghelst two or three days after being taken. To the best of my belief, your son saw the proofs, but I cannot now say positively. I obtained particulars of requirements from the officers forming the group, but the photographer then found he was unable to obtain paper for printing. I therefore bought the negatives and sent them home to Gale & Polden. In view of the fact that your son did not go back to the trenches till 12 September 1915, it is highly probable that he saw the proofs, but he certainly did not see the negatives.—Yours faithfully,

" (Signed) SYDNEY T. BOAST "

It thus appears that Raymond had probably seen a proof of the photograph, but that there were no copies or prints available. Consequently neither we, nor any other people at home, could have received them; and the negatives were only received in England by Gale & Polden on 15 October 1915. after Peters had mentioned the existence of the photograph, which he did on 27 September 1915.

I obtained from Messrs. Gale & Polden prints of all the accessible photographs which had been taken at the same time. The size of these prints was 5 by 7 inches.

I found that the group had been repeated, with slight variations, three times—the Officers all in the same relative positions, but not in identically the same attitudes. One of the three prints is the same as the one we had seen, with some one's hand resting on Raymond's shoulder, and Raymond's head leaning a little on one side, as if rather annoyed. In another the hand had been removed, being supported by the owner's stick ; and in that one Raymond's head is upright. This corresponds

8

to his uncertainty as to whether he was actually taken with the man leaning on him or not. In the third, however, the sitting officer's leg rests against Raymond's shoulder as he squats in front, and the slant of the head and slight look of annoyance have returned.

These two additional photographs are here reproduced. Their merit is in showing that the leaning on him, mentioned by ' Raymond ' through Feda, was well marked, and yet that he was quite right in being uncertain whether he was actually being leant on while the photograph was being taken. The fact turns out to be that during two exposures he was being leaned on, and during one exposure he was not. It was, so to speak, lucky that the edition sent us happened to show in one form the actual leaning.

I have since discovered what is apparently the only other photograph of Officers in which Raymond occurs, but it is quite a different one, and none of the description applies to it. For it is completely in the open air, and Raymond is standing up in the hinder of two rows. He is second from the left, the tall one in the middle is his friend Lieutenant Case, and standing next him is Mr. Ventris (see p. 279). It is fortunate again that this photograph did not happen to be the one sent us; for we should have considered the description hopelessly wrong.

SUMMARY

CONCLUDING NOTE BY O. J. L.

As to the evidential value of the whole communication, it will be observed that there is something of the nature of cross-correspondence, of a simple kind, in the fact that a reference to the photograph was made through one medium, and a description given, in answer to a question, through another independent one.

The episode is to be published in the *Proceedings* of the S.P.R. for 1916, and a few further facts or comments are there added.

The elimination of ordinary telepathy from the living, except under the far-fetched hypothesis of the unconscious influence of complete strangers, was exceptionally comto his uncertainty as to whether he was actually taken with the man leaning on him or not. In the third, however, the sitting officer's leg rests against Raymond's shoulder as he squats in front, and the slant of the head and slight look of annoyance have returned.

These two additional photographs are here reproduced. Their merit is in showing that the leaning on him, mentioned by ' Raymond ' through Feda, was well marked, and yet that he was quite right in being uncertain whether he was actually being leant on while the photograph was being taken. The fact turns out to be that during two exposures he was being leaned on, and during one exposure he was not. It was, so to speak, lucky that the edition sent us happened to show in one form the actual leaning.

I have since discovered what is apparently the only other photograph of Officers in which Raymond occurs, but it is quite a different one, and none of the description applies to it. For it is completely in the open air, and Raymond is standing up in the hinder of two rows. He is second from the left, the tall one in the middle is his friend Lieutenant Case, and standing next him is Mr. Ventris (see p. 279). It is fortunate again that this photograph did not happen to be the one sent us ; for we should have considered the description hopelessly wrong.

SUMMARY

Concluding Note by O. J. L.

As to the evidential value of the whole communication, it will be observed that there is something of the nature of cross-correspondence, of a simple kind, in the fact that a reference to the photograph was made through one medium, and a description given, in answer to a question, through another independent one.

The episode is to be published in the *Proceedings* of the S.P.R. for 1916, and a few further facts or comments are there added.

The elimination of ordinary telepathy from the living, except under the far-fetched hypothesis of the unconscious influence of complete strangers, was exceptionally com-

ANOTHER EDITION OF THE **GROUP-PHOTOGRAPH,** WITH LEG TOUCHING SHOULDER
INSTEAD OF **HAND**

plete; inasmuch as the whole of the information was recorded before any of us had seen the photograph.

Even the establishment of a date in August for the taking of the photograph, as mentioned first in Mrs. Cheves' letter and confirmed by finding an entry in Raymond's Diary, is important, because the last time we ever saw Raymond was in July.

To my mind the whole incident is rather exceptionally good as a piece of evidence; and that ' Raymond ' expected it to be good evidence is plain from Peters's (' Moonstone's ') statement, at that first reference to a photograph on 27 September, namely, " He is particular that I should tell you of this." (This sentence it probably was which made me look out for such a photograph, and take pains to get records soundly made beforehand.) Our complete ignorance, even of the existence of the photograph, in the first place, and secondly the delayed manner in which knowledge of it normally came to us, so that we were able to make provision for getting the supernormally acquired details definitely noted beforehand, seem to me to make it a first-class case. While, as to the amount of coincidence between the description and the actual photograph, that surely is quite beyond chance or guesswork. For not only are many things right, but practically nothing is wrong.

CALENDAR

20 *July* 1915 . . .	Raymond's last visit home.
24 *August* 1915 . .	Photograph taken at the Front, as shown by entry in Raymond's private Diary, but not mentioned by him.
14 *September* 1915 . .	Raymond's death.
27 *September* 1915 . .	Peters' (' Moonstone's ') mention of the photograph as a message from ' Raymond.'
15 *October* 1915 . .	Negative sent with other negatives by Capt. Sydney T. Boast, from the Front in Flanders, to Messrs. Gale & Polden, Aldershot, for printing.
29 *November* 1915 . .	Mrs. Cheves wrote spontaueously, saying that she had a group-photograph of some 2nd South Lancashire Officers, which she could send if desired.

CHAPTER V

BEGINNING OF HISTORICAL RECORD OF SITTINGS

ALTHOUGH this episode of the photograph is a good and evidential one, I should be sorry to base an important conclusion on any one piece of evidence, however cogent. All proofs are really cumulative ; and though it is legitimate to emphasise anything like a crucial instance, it always needs supplementing by many others, lest there may have been some oversight. Accordingly, I now proceed to quote from sittings held by members of the family after Raymond's death—laying stress upon those which were arranged for, and held throughout, in an anonymous manner, so that there was not the slightest normal clue to identity.

The first message came to us through a recent friend of ours in London, Mrs. Kennedy, who herself has the power of automatic writing, and who, having lost her specially beloved son Paul, has had her hand frequently controlled by him—usually only so as to give affectionate messages, but sometimes in a moderately evidential way. She had been sceptical about the genuineness of this power apparently possessed by herself ; and it was her painful uncertainty on this point that had brought her into correspondence with me, for she was trying to test her own writing in various ways, as she was so anxious not to be deceived. The first I ever heard of her was the following letter which came while I was in Australia, and was dealt with by Mr. Hill :—

FIRST LETTER FROM MRS. KENNEDY TO O. J. L.

" 16 *August* 1914

" SIR OLIVER LODGE.

" DEAR SIR,—Because of your investigations into spirit life, I venture to ask your help.

" My only son died 23 June, eight weeks after a terrible accident. On 25 June (without my asking for it or having thought of it) I felt obliged to hold a pencil, and I received in automatic writing his name and ' yes ' and ' no ' in answer to questions.

" Since then I have had several pages of writing from him every day and sometimes twice daily. I say ' from him '; the whole torturing question is—is it from him or am I self-deceived ?

" My knowledge is infinitesimal.   Nineteen years ago a sister who had died the year before suddenly used my hand, and after that wrote short messages at intervals ; another sister a year later, and my father one message sixteen years ago ; but I felt so self-deceived that I always pushed it aside, until it came back to me, unasked, after my son's passing over.

" Your knowledge is what I appeal to, and the deep, personal respect one has for you and your investigations.   It is for my son's sake—he is only seventeen—and he writes with such intense sadness of my lack of decided belief that I venture to beg help of a stranger in a matter so sacred to me.

" Do you ever come to London, and, if so, could you possibly allow me to see you for even half an hour ? and you might judge from the strange and holy revelations (I know no other way to express many of the messages that are sent) whether they can possibly be only from my own subconscious mind. . . . Pardon this length of letter.—Yours faithfully,

" (Signed)   KATHERINE KENNEDY "

Ultimately I was able to take her anonymously and unexpectedly to an American medium, Mrs. Wriedt, and there she received strong and unmistakable proofs.[1]   She also received excellent confirmation through several other mediums whom she had discovered for herself— notably Mr. Vout Peters and Mrs. Osborne Leonard. Of Mrs. Leonard I had not previously heard ; I had heard of a Madame St. Leonard, or some name like that, but this is somebody else.   Mrs. Kennedy tells me that she herself had not known Mrs. Leonard long, her own first sitting with that lady having been on 14 September 1915.   I must emphasise the fact that Mrs. Kennedy is keen and careful about evidential considerations.

As Mrs. Kennedy's son Paul plays a part in what

---

[1] I think it only fair to mention the names of professional mediums, if I find them at all genuine.   I do not guarantee their efficiency, for mediumship is not a power that can always be depended on,—it is liable to vary; sitters also may be incompetent, and conditions may be bad. The circumstances under which sensitives work are difficult at the present time and ought to be improved.

follows, perhaps it is permissible to quote here a description of him which she gave to Mr. Hill in October 1914, accompanying an expression of surprise at the serious messages which she sometimes received from him—interspersed with his fun and his affection :—

K. K.'s DESCRIPTION OF PAUL

" Picture to yourself this boy : not quite eighteen but always taken for twenty or twenty-two ; an almost divine character underneath, but exteriorly a typical 'motor knut,' driving racing-cars at Brooklands, riding for the Jarrott Cup on a motor cycle, and flying at Hendon as an Air Mechanic ; dining out perpetually, because of his charm which made him almost besieged by friends ; and apparently without any creed except honour, generosity, love of children, the bringing home of every stray cat to be fed here and comforted, a total disregard of social distinctions when choosing his friends, and a hatred of hurting anyone's feelings."

On seeing the announcement of Mr. R. Lodge's death in a newspaper, Mrs. Kennedy ' spoke ' to Paul about it, and asked him to help ; she also asked for a special sitting with Mrs. Leonard for the same purpose, though without saying why. The name Raymond was on that occasion spelt out through the medium, and he was said to be sleeping. This was on 18 September. On the 21st, while Mrs. Kennedy was writing in her garden on ordinary affairs, her own hand suddenly wrote, as from her son Paul :—

> " I am here. . . . I have seen that boy Sir Oliver's son ; he's better, and has had a splendid rest, tell his people."

Lady Lodge having been told about Mrs. Leonard, and wanting to help a widowed French lady, Madame Le Breton, who had lost both her sons, and was on a visit to England, asked Mrs. Kennedy to arrange a sitting, so as to avoid giving any name. A sitting was accordingly arranged with Mrs. Leonard for 24 September 1915.

On 22 September, Mrs. Kennedy, while having what she called a ' talk ' with Paul, suddenly wrote automatically :—

> " I shall bring Raymond to his father when he comes to see you. . . . He is so jolly, every one loves him ;

he has found heaps of his own folks here, and he is settling down wonderfully. DO TELL HIS FATHER AND MOTHER. . . . He spoke clearly to-day. . . . He doesn't fight like the others, he seems so settled already. It is a ripping thing to see one boy like this. He has been sleeping a long time, but he has spoken to-day. . . .

" If you people only knew how we long to come, they would all call us."

[Capitals indicate large and emphatic writing.]

On the 23rd, during Lady Lodge's call, Mrs. Kennedy's hand wrote what purported to be a brief message from Raymond, thus :—

" I am here, mother. . . . I have been to Alec already, but he can't hear me. I do wish he would believe that we are here safe; it isn't a dismal hole like people think, it is a place where there is life."

And again :

" Wait till I have learned better how to speak like this. . . . We can express all we want later; give me time."

I need hardly say that there is nothing in the least evidential in all this. I quote it only for the sake of reasonable completeness, so as to give the history from the beginning. Evidence comes later.

Next day, 24 September 1915, the ladies went for an interview with Mrs. Leonard, who knew no more than that friends of Mrs. Kennedy would accompany her. The following is Lady Lodge's account of the sitting :—

First Sitting of any Member of the Family (Anonymous)
with Mrs. Leonard

GENERAL ACCOUNT BY M. F. A. L.
24 SEPTEMBER 1915

Mrs. Leonard went into a sort of trance, I suppose, and came back as a little Indian girl called ' Freda,' or ' Feda,' rubbing her hands, and talking in the silly way they do.

However, she soon said there was an old gentleman and a young one present, whom she described ; and Mrs. Kennedy told me afterwards that they were her father and her son Paul. There seemed to be many others standing beside us, so ' Feda ' said.

Then Feda described some one brought in lying down—about twenty-four or twenty-five, not yet able to sit up; the features she described might quite well have belonged to Raymond. (I forgot to say Mrs. Leonard did not know me or my name, or Madame Le Breton's.) Feda soon said she saw a large R beside this young man, then an A, then she got a long letter with a tail, which she could not make out, then she drew an M in the air, but forgot to mention it, and she said an O came next, and she said there was another O with a long stroke to it, and finally, she said she heard ' Yaymond ' (which is only her way of pronouncing it). [The name was presumably got from ' Paul.'—O. J. L.] Then she said that he just seemed to open his eyes and smile; and then he had a choking feeling, which distressed me very much; but he said he hadn't suffered much—not nearly as much as I should think; whether he said this, or Paul, I forget; but Paul asked me not to tell him to-morrow night that I was not with him, as he had so much the feeling that I was with him when he died, that he (Paul) wouldn't like to undeceive him.

I then asked that some one in that other world might kiss him for me, and a lady, whom they described in a way which was just like my mother, came and kissed him, and said she was taking care of him. And there was also an old gentleman, full white beard, etc. (evidently my stepfather, but Feda said with a moustache, which was a mistake), with W. up beside him, also taking care; said he had met Raymond, and he was looking after him, and lots of others too; but said he [W.] belonged to me and to ' O.' [Correct.] I asked how and what it was he had done for me, and Feda made a movement with her fingers, as though disentangling something, and then putting it into straight lines. He then said he had made things easier for me. So I said that was right, and thanked him gratefully. I said also that if Raymond was in his and Mama's hands, I was satisfied.

[I do not append the notes of this sitting, since it was held mainly for Madame and her two sons, both of whom were described, and from whom some messages appeared to come.]

Table Sitting at Mrs. Leonard's

Next day (Saturday, 25 September 1915), as arranged partly by Paul, the three ladies went to Mrs. Leonard's house again for a sitting with a table, and Dr. Kennedy kindly accompanied them to take notes.

The three ladies and the medium sat round a small table, with their hands lightly on it, and it tilted in the usual way. The plan adopted here is for the table to tilt as each letter of the alphabet is spoken by the medium, and to stop, or 'hold,' when a right letter is reached. For general remarks on the rationale, or what most people will naturally consider the absurdity, of intelligent movements of this kind, see Chapter XIV, Part III.

It was a rather complicated sitting, as it was mainly for Madame who was a novice in the subject. Towards the end unfortunately, though momentarily and not at all pronouncedly, she spoke to Lady Lodge by name. At these table sittings the medium, Mrs. Leonard, is not unconscious; accordingly she heard it in her normal self, and afterwards said that she had heard it. The following extracts from the early part of the sitting may be quoted here, as answers purporting to be spelt out by Raymond :—

QUESTIONS	ANSWERS
Are you lonely ?	No.
Who is with you ?	Grandfather W.
Have you anything to say to me ?	You know I can't help missing you, but I am learning to be happy.
Have you any message for any of them ?	Tell them I have many good friends.
Can you tell me the name of anyone at home ?	Honor. [One of his sisters.]

(Other messages of affection and naturalness.)

Have I enough to satisfy them at home ?	No.
Is there anything you want to send ?	Tell father I have met some friends of his.
Any name ?	Yes ; Myers.
Have you anything else to say?	(No answer.)
Is some one else there ?	Yes ; Guy. (This was a son of Madame, and the sitting became French.)

Reasonable and natural messages were spelt out in French. The other son of Madame was named Didier, and an unsuccessful attempt to spell this name was made, but the only result was Dodi.

Automatic Writing by Mrs. Kennedy, 26 September

On 26 September Mrs. Kennedy (alone) had a lot of automatic writing, with her own hand, mainly from Paul, who presently wrote, " Mother, I have been let to bring Raymond."

(After a welcome, Raymond was represented as sending this message :—)

" I can speak easier than I could at the table, because you are helping all the time. It is easy when we are alone with you, but if I go there it confuses me a little. . . . I long to comfort them. Will you tell them that Raymond had been to you, and that Paul tells me I can come to you whenever I like ? It is so good of you to let the boys all come. . . ."

" Paul tells me he has been here since he was seventeen ; he is a jolly chap ; every one seems fond of him. I don't wonder, for he helps every one. It seems a rule to call Paul if you get in a fix."

(Then Paul said he was back, and wrote :—)

" He is quite happy really since he finds he can get to his people. He has slept ever since last night, till I was told to fetch him to-night."

(Asked about the French boys, Paul said :—)

" I saw them when I brought them, but I don't see them otherwise ; they are older than I am . . . they hardly believe it yet that they have spoken. All the time they felt it was impossible, and they nearly gave it up, but I kept on begging them to tell their mother they lived."

" I do hope she felt it true, mother. . . ."

" It is hard to think your sons are dead ; but such a lot of people do think it. It is revolting to hear the boys tell you how no one speaks to'them ever ; it hurts me through and through."

(Interval. Paul fetched Guy [one of Madame Le Breton's sons], saying :—)

" I can't stand it when they call out for help. Speak to him please, mother."

(Mrs. Kennedy spoke to Guy, saying that she felt he could not believe any of it, but would he give time and trouble to studying the subject as she was doing ? The following writing came :—)

GUY.--I think you hear me because it is just as I am feeling ; how CAN I believe we can speak to you who live where we once lived ? It was not possible then for us to speak to dead people ; and why should it be possible for us to speak. Will you keep on helping me, please, for I can't follow it, and I long to ?

(Mrs. Kennedy asked him to ask Paul, that being an easier method, probably, than getting information through her. She asked him to ' excuse ' Paul's youth.)

GUY.—I like Paul ; he is good to us. I shall be glad to talk to him constantly if he has time for all of us ; he seems a sort of messenger between us and you, isn't he ?

[Guy had been to school in England, his brother had not.]

CHAPTER VI

FIRST SITTING OF O. J. L. WITH MRS. LEONARD

ON 27 September, as already stated in Chapter III, I myself visited Mrs. Leonard, going anonymously and alone, and giving no information beyond the fact that I was a friend of Mrs. Kennedy. I lay no stress on my anonymity, however.

In a short time Feda controlled, and at first described an elderly gentleman as present. Then she said he brought some one with the letter R ; and as I took verbatim notes I propose to reproduce this portion in full, so as to give the general flavour of a 'Feda' sitting; only omitting what has already been extracted and quoted in Chapter III.

O. J. L. at Mrs. Leonard's, Monday, 27 September 1915,
12 noon to 1 o'clock

(Mrs. Leonard's control 'Feda' speaking all the time.)

There is some one here with a little difficulty; not fully built up ; youngish looking ; form more like an outline ; he has not completely learnt how to build up as yet. Is a young man, rather above the medium height ; rather well-built, not thick-set or heavy, but well-built. He holds himself up well. He has not been over long. His hair is between colours. He is not easy to describe, because he is not building himself up so solid as some do. He has greyish eyes ; hair brown, short at the sides ; a fine-shaped head ; eyebrows also brown, not much arched ; nice-shaped nose, fairly straight, broader at the nostrils a little ; a nice-shaped mouth, a good-sized mouth it is, but it does not look large because he holds the lips nicely together ; chin not heavy ; face oval. He is not built up quite clearly, but it feels as if Feda knew him. He must have been here waiting for you. Now he looks at Feda and smiles ; now he laughs, he is having a joke with Feda, and Paulie laughs too. Paul says he has been here before, and that Paul brought him. But Feda sees many hundreds of people, but they tell me this one has been brought quite lately. Yes, I have seen him before. Feda remembers a letter with him too. R, that is to do with him.

(Then Feda murmured, as if to herself, " Try and give me another letter.") (Pause.)

It is a funny name, not Robert or Richard. He is not giving the rest of it, but says R again ; it is from him. He wants to know where his mother is ; he is looking for her ; he does not understand why she is not here.

o. j. l.—Tell him he will see her this afternoon, and that she is not here this morning, because she wants to meet him this afternoon at three o'clock.

[Meaning through another medium, namely Peters. But that, of course, was not said.]

He has been to see you before, and he says that once he thought you knew he was there, and that two or three times he was not quite sure. Feda gets it mostly by impression ; it is not always what he says, but what she gets ; but Feda says "he says," because she gets it from him somehow.[1] He finds it difficult, he says, but he has got so many kind friends helping him. He didn't think when he waked up first that he was going to be happy, but now he is, and he says he is going to be happier. He knows that as soon as he is a little more ready, he has got a great deal of work to do. " I almost wonder," he says, " shall I be fit and able to do it. They tell me I shall."

[And so on as reported in Chapter III.]

He seems to know what the work is. The first work he will have to do, will be helping at the Front ; not the wounded so much, but helping those who are passing over in the war. He knows that when they pass on and wake up, they still feel a certain fear—and some other word which Feda missed. Feda hears a something and

[1] Note this, as an elucidatory statement.

' fear.' Some even go on fighting ; at least they want to ; they don't believe they have passed on. So that many are wanted where he is now, to explain to them and help them, and soothe them. They do not know where they are, nor why they are there.

> [I considered that this was ordinary ' Feda talk,' such as it is probably customary to get through mediums at this time ; therefore, though the statements are likely enough, there is nothing new in them, and I thought it better to interrupt by asking a question. So I said :—]

O. J. L.—Does he want to send a message to anyone at home ? Or will he give the name of one of his instructors ?

> [I admit that it is stupid thus to ask two questions at once.]

He shows me a capital H, and says that is not an instructor, it is some one he knows on the earth side. He wants them to be sure that he is all right and happy. He says, " People think I say I am happy in order to make them happier, but I don't.

> [*And so on as already reported in Chapter III.*]

Now the first gentleman with the letter W is going over to him and putting his arm round his shoulder, and he is putting his arm round the gentleman's back. Feda feels like a string round her head ; a tight feeling in the head, and also an empty sort of feeling in the chest, empty, as if sort of something gone. A feeling like a sort of vacant feeling there ; also a bursting sensation in the head. But he does not know he is giving this. He has not done it on purpose, they have tried to make him forget all that, but Feda gets it from him. There is a noise with it too, an awful noise and a rushing noise.

He has lost all that now, but he does not seem to know why Feda feels it now. " I feel splendid," he says, " I feel splendid ! But I was worried at first. I was worried, for I was wanting to make it clear to those left behind that I was all right, and that they were not to worry about me."

You may think it strange, but he felt that you would not worry so much as some one else ; two others, two ladies, Feda thinks. You would know, he says, but two ladies would worry and be uncertain ; but now he believes they know more.

Then, before Mrs. Leonard came out of trance, came the description of a falling dark cross which twisted round and became bright, as reported in Chapter III.

After the sitting, and before I went away, I asked Mrs. Leonard if she knew who I was. She replied, " Are you by chance connected with those two ladies who came on Saturday night ? " On my assenting, Mrs. Leonard added, " Oh ! then I know, because the French lady gave the name away ; she said ' Lady Lodge ' in the middle of a French sentence."

I also spoke to her about not having too many sittings and straining her power. She said she " preferred not to have more than two or three a day, though sometimes she could not avoid it ; and some days she had to take a complete rest." But she admitted that she was going to have another one that day at two o'clock. I told her that three per day was rather much. She pleaded that there are so many people who want help now, that she declined all those who came for only commercial or fortune-telling motives, but that she felt bound to help those who are distressed by the war. I report this to show that she saw many people totally disconnected with Raymond or his family : so that what she might say to a new unknown member of the family could be quite evidential.

CHAPTER VII

FIRST PETERS SITTING (ANONYMOUS)

MRS. KENNEDY desired Lady Lodge to try with a different and independent medium, and therefore kindly arranged with Mr. A. Vout Peters to come to her house on Monday afternoon and give a trance sitting to ' a friend of hers ' not specified. Accordingly, at or about 3 p.m. on Monday, 27 September 1915, Lady Lodge went by herself to Mrs. Kennedy's house, so as not to have to give any name, and awaited the arrival of Peters, who, when he came, said he would prefer to sit in Mrs. Kennedy's own room in which he had sat before, and which he associated with her son Paul. No kind of introduction was made, and Peters was a total stranger to Lady Lodge ; though to Mrs. Kennedy he was fairly well known, having several times given her first-rate evidence about her son, who had proved his identity in several striking ways.

When Peters goes into a trance his personality is supposed to change to that of another man, who, we understand, is called ' Moonstone ' ; much as Mrs. Piper was controlled by apparent personalities calling themselves ' Phinuit ' or ' Rector.' When Peters does not go into a trance he has some clairvoyant faculty of his own.

The only other person present on this occasion was Mrs. Kennedy, who kindly took notes.

This is an important sitting, as it was held for a complete stranger, so I propose to report it practically in full.

9

M. F. A. L. Sitting with A. Vout Peters, in Mrs. Kennedy's House, on 27 September 1915, at 3.30 p.m.

MEDIUM . . . . A. VOUT PETERS.
SITTER . . . . Lady LODGE (M. F. A. L.).
RECORDER . . . Mrs. KATHERINE KENNEDY (K. K.).

The record consists of Mrs. Kennedy's notes.   Annotations in square brackets have been added subsequently by O. J. L.

While only partially under control, Peters said : " I feel a lot of force here, Mrs. Kennedy."

Peters was controlled quickly by ' Moonstone,' who greeted K. K. and reminded her of a prophecy of his. (This prophecy related to the Russian place Dvinsk, and to the important actions likely to be going on there—as if the decisive battle of the war was to be fought there.) Then he turned to L. L. and said :—

What a useful life you have led, and will lead.

You have always been the prop of things.

You have always been associated with men a lot.

You are the mother and house prop.

You are not unacquainted with spiritualism.

You have been associated with it more or less for some time.

I sense you as living away from London—in the North or North-West.

You are much associated with men, and you are the house prop—the mother.   You have no word in the language that quite gives it—there are always four walls, but something more is needed—you are the house prop.

You have had a tremendous lot of sadness recently, from a death that has come suddenly.

You never thought it was to be like this.   (Peters went on talking glibly, and there was no need for the sitter to say anything.)

There is a gentleman here who is on the other side—he went very suddenly.   Fairly tall, rather broad, upright (here the medium sat up very straight and squared his shoulders)—rather long face, fairly long nose, lips full, moustache, nice teeth, quick and active, strong

sense of humour—he could always laugh, keen sense
of affection.

He went over into the spirit world very quickly.
There is no idea of death because it was so sudden,
with no illness.

Do you know anything connected with the letter L ?
(No answer was given to this.)

What I am going to say now is from Paul—he says :
"Tell mother it is not one L, it is double L." He
says : "Tell mother she always loved a riddle"—
he laughs.

(L. L. and K. K. both said they could not understand.[1]
' Moonstone ' continued :—-)

They don't want to make it too easy for you, and
funnily enough, the easier it seems to you sometimes
the more difficult it seems to them.

This man is a soldier—an officer. He went over
where it is warm.

You are his mother, aren't you—and he does not call
you ma, or mama, or mater—just mother, mother.
[True.]

He is reticent and yet he told you a tremendous lot.
You were not only his mother but his friend.

Wasn't he clever with books ? He laughs and says :
"Anyhow I ought to be, I was brought up with them."
He was not altogether a booky person.

He knew of spiritualism before he passed over, but
he was a little bit sceptical—he had an attitude of
carefulness about it. He tells me to tell you this :

The attitude of Mr. Stead and some of those people
turned him aside ; on one side there was too much
credulity—on the other side too much piffling at trifles.
[See also Appendix to this sitting.]

He holds up in his hand a little heap of olives, as a
symbol for you—then he laughs. Now he says—for a
test—Associated with the olives is the word Roland.[2]
All of this is to give you proof that he is here.

---

[1] Though K. K.'s record, being made at the time, reads L. L.
(meaning Lady Lodge) throughout. When she speaks, later on, I
change the L. L. of the record to her proper initials to avoid confusion.—O. J. L.

[2] This is clear, though apparently it was not so recognised at the
time. See later, pp. 135 and 144.

Before you came you were very down in the dumps.
Was he ill three weeks after he was hurt ? [More
like three hours, probably less.]
(Various other guesses were made for the meaning of 3.)
I see the figure 3 so plainly—can't you find a meaning
for it ?
(L. L. suggested 3rd Battalion, and ' Moonstone '
continued :—)
He says " Yes "—and wasn't he officially put down on
another one ? [Perfectly true, he was attached to
the 2nd Battalion at the Front, to the 3rd or reserve
Battalion while training.] [1]
He says : " Don't forget to tell father all this."
His home is associated with books—both reading and
writing books. Wait a minute, he wants to give me a
word, he is a little impatient with me. Manuscripts,
he says, manuscripts—that's the word.
He sends a message, and he says—this is more for
father—" It is no good his attempting to come to the
medium here, he will simply frighten the medium for
all he is worth, and he will not get anything. But he
is not afraid of you, and if there is communication
wanted with this man again, *you* must come."
You have several portraits of this boy. Before he
went away you had got a good portrait of him—2—
no, 3. [Fully as many as that.]
Two where he is alone and one where he is in a group
of other men. [This last is not yet verified.] [2]
He is particular that I should tell you of this. In one
you see his walking-stick (' Moonstone ' here put an
imaginary stick under his arm). [Not known yet.]
He had particularly strong hands.
When he was younger, he was very strongly associated
with football and outdoor sports. You have in your
house prizes that he won, I can't tell you what.
[Incorrect ; possibly some confusion in record here ; or
else wrong.]
Why should I get two words—' Small ' and ' Heath.'

---

[1] Let it be understood, once for all, that remarks in square brackets
represent nothing said at the time, but are comments afterwards by me
when I read the record.—O. J. L.

[2] The photograph episode is described above, in Chapter IV, in the
light of later information.

[Small Heath is a place near Birmingham with which he had some but not close associations.]

Also I see, but very dimly as in a mist, the letters B I R. [Probably Birmingham.]

You heard of either his death or of his being hurt by telegram.

He didn't die at once. He had three wounds.

I don't think you have got details yet. [No, not fully.]

If he had lived he would have made a name for himself in his own particular line.

Was he not associated with chemistry? If not, some one associated with him was, because I see all the things in a chemical laboratory.

[The next portion has already been reported in Chapter III, but I do not omit it from its context here.]

That chemistry thing takes me away from him to a man in the flesh.

And connected with him a man, a writer of poetry, on our side, closely connected with spiritualism.

He was very clever—he too passed away out of England.

He has communicated several times.

This gentleman who wrote poetry—I see the letter M—he is helping your son to communicate.

He is built up in the chemical conditions.

If your son didn't know this man, he knew of him.

At the back of the gentleman beginning with M and who wrote poetry is a whole group of people.

They are very interested. And don't be surprised if you get messages from them, even if you don't know them.

This is so important that is going to be said now, that I want to go slowly, for you to write clearly every word (dictates carefully).

"Not only is the partition so thin that you can hear the operators on the other side, but a big hole has been made."

This message is for the gentleman associated with the chemical laboratory.

The boy—I call them all boys, because I was over a

hundred when I lived here and they are all boys to me—he says, he is here, but he says : " Hitherto it has been a thing of the head, now I am come over it is a thing of the heart. What is more (here Peters jumped up in his chair vigorously, snapped his fingers excitedly, and spoke loudly) :

" Good God ! how father will be able to speak out ! much firmer than he has ever done, because it will touch our hearts."

M. F. A. L.—Does he want his father to speak out ?

     Yes, but not yet—wait, the evidence will be given in such a way that it cannot be contradicted, and his name is big enough to sweep all stupid opposition on one side.

     I was not conscious of much suffering, and I am glad that I settled my affairs before I went.

> [He did ; he made a will just before leaving England, and left things in good order. He also cleared up things when he joined the Army.]

     Have you a sister of his with you, and one on our side ? A little child almost, so little that you never associated her with him.

     There are two sisters, one on each side of him, one in the dark and one in the light.

> [Raymond was the only boy sandwiched in between two sisters ; Violet older than he, and still living (presumably in the dark), and Laura [1] younger than he, died a few minutes after birth (in the light). Raymond was the youngest boy, and had thus a sister on either side of him.]

     Your girl is standing on one side, Paul on the other, and your boy in the centre. (Here ' Moonstone ' put his arm round K. K.'s shoulder to show how the boy was standing.) Now he stoops over you and kisses you there (indicating the brow).

     Before he went away he came home for a little while. Didn't he come for three days ?

     (There is a little unimportant confusion in the record about ' days.')

[1] Now apparently called Lily : see later.

Then, with evident intention of trying to give a ' test,' some trivial but characteristic features were mentioned about the interior of three houses—the one we are in now, the one we had last occupied at Liverpool, and the one he called ' Mother's home.' But there is again some confusion in the record, partly because M. F. A. L. didn't understand what he was driving at, partly because the recorder found it difficult to follow ; and though the confusion was subsequently disentangled through another medium next day, 28 September, it is hardly worth while to give as much explanation as would be needed to make the points clear. So this part is omitted. (See p. 145.)

And he wanted me to tell you of a kiss on the forehead.

M. F. A. L.—He did not kiss me on the forehead when he said good-bye.

Well he is taller than you, isn't he ?

(Yes.)

Not very demonstrative before strangers. But when alone with you, like a little boy again.

M. F. A. L.—I don't think he was undemonstrative before strangers.

Oh yes, all you English are like that. You lock up your affection, and you sometimes lose the key.

He laughs. He says you didn't understand about Rowland. He can get it through now, it's a Roland for your Oliver [p. 131].

[Excellent. By recent marriages the family has gained a Rowland (son-in-law) and lost (so to speak) an Oliver (son).]

He is going. He gives his love to all.

It has been easy for him to come for two reasons : First, because you came to get help for Madame.[1] Secondly, because he had the knowledge in this life.

M. F. A. L.—I hope it has been a pleasure to him to come ?

Not a pleasure, a joy.

M. F. A. L.—I hope he will come to me again.

As much as he can.

Paul now wants to speak to his mother.

---

[1] This is curious, because it was with Mrs. Leonard that Madam had sat, not with Peters at all. It is a simple cross-correspondence.

Appendix to First Peters Sitting

NOTE ON RAYMOND'S OLD ATTITUDE TO PSYCHO-PHYSICAL PHENOMENA

Mrs. Rowland Waterhouse has recently found among her papers an old letter from Bedales School which she received from her brother Raymond when she was in Paris during the winter 1905–1906. The concluding part of it is of some small interest in the light of later developments :—

" I should like to hear more about table turning. I don't believe in it. The girls here say they have done it at Steephurst, and they attribute it to some sense of which we know nothing, and which I want to turn to some account, driving a dynamo or something, if it is possible, as they make out, to cause a table to revolve without any exertion —I am your affectionate brother,

" RAYMOND "

CHAPTER VIII

A TABLE SITTING

ON 28 September my wife and I together had a table sitting with Mrs. Leonard, which may be reported nearly in full together with my preliminary note written immediately afterwards. This is done not because it is a particularly good specimen, but because these early sittings have an importance of their own, and because it may be instructive to others to see the general manner of a table sitting. It was, I think, the first joint-sitting of any kind which we had had since the old Piper days.

NOTE BY O. J. L. ON TABLE TILTINGS

A table sitting is not good for conversation, but it is useful for getting definite brief answers—such as names and incidents, since it seems to be less interfered with by the mental activity of an intervening medium, and to be rather more direct. But it has difficulties of its own. The tilting of the table need not be regarded as a 'physical phenomenon' in the technical or supernormal sense, yet it does not *appear* to be done by the muscles of those present. The effort required to tilt the table is slight, and evidentially it must, no doubt, be assumed that so far as mechanical force is concerned, it is exerted by muscular action. But my impression is that the tilting is an incipient physical phenomenon, and that though the energy, of course, comes from the people present, it does not appear to be applied in quite a normal way (XIV, Pt. III).

As regards evidence, however, the issue must be limited to intelligent direction of the energy. All that can safely be claimed is that the energy is intelligently directed, and the self-stoppage of the table at the right letter conveys by touch a sort of withholding feeling—a kind of sensation as of inhibition—to those whose hands lie flat on the top of the table. The light was always quite sufficient to see all the hands, and it works quite well in full daylight. The usual method is for the alphabet to be called over, and for the table to tilt or thump at each letter, till it stops at the right one. The table tilts three times to indicate " yes," and once to indicate " no " ; but as one tilt also represents the letter A of the alphabet, an error of interpretation is occasionally made by the sitters. So also C might perhaps be mistaken for " yes," or *vice versa* ; but that mistake is not so likely.

Unconscious guidance can hardly be excluded, *i.e.* cannot be excluded with any certainty when the answer is of a kind expected. But first, our desire was rather in the direction of avoiding such control ; and second, the stoppages were sometimes at unexpected places ; and third, a long succession of letters soon becomes meaningless, except to the recorder who is writing them down silently, as they are called out to him *seriatim*, in another part of the room.

It will also be observed that at a table sitting it is natural for the sitters to do most of the talking, and that their object is to get definite and not verbose replies.

On this occasion the control of the table seemed to improve as the sitting went on, owing presumably to increased practice on the part of the communicator, until towards the end, when there seemed to be some signs of weariness or incipient exhaustion ; and, since the sitting lasted an hour and a half, tiredness is in no way surprising.

No further attempt was made to keep our identity from Mrs. Leonard : our name had been given away, as reported near the end of Chapter VI.

Table Sitting with Mrs. Leonard, Tuesday, 28 September 1915, at 5.30 p m.

Present—O. J. L., M. F. A. L., K. K., WITH DR. KENNEDY AT ANOTHER TABLE AS RECORDER

A small partly wicker table with a square top was used, about 18 inches square. O. J. L. and M. F. A. L. sat opposite to each other; **K. K.** and Mrs. Leonard occupied the other positions, Mrs. Leonard to the right of O. J. L. After four minutes' interval, the table began to tilt.

Medium.—Will you tilt three times to show you understand ?
(It did.)

Medium.—Will you like to give your name ?
(It gave three tilts indicating YES.)

Medium.—Very well, then, the alphabet. Spell it, please.
(Mrs. Leonard here repeated the alphabet fairly quickly, while the table tilted slightly at each letter as it was said,

stopping first at the letter	**P**
then at the letter	**A**
then	**U**
then	**L.**

O. J. L.—Yes, very well, Paul ; we know who you are, and you know who we are, and we know that you have brought Raymond, and have come to help.
YES.

O. J. L.—We that are here know about this, and you have given us evidence already, but I am here to get evidence for the family.
YES.

O. J. L.—Would you like to say something first, before I ask a question ?
(Silence.)

Then the table moved and shook a little, indicating that it wanted the alphabet ; and when the medium recited the letters, it spelt out in the same manner as before, *i.e.* by stopping at the one desired by whatever intelligence was controlling the table :—

RAYMOND WANTS TO COME HIMSELF.

Here M. L. ejaculated : " Dear Raymond," and sighed unconsciously.

The table spelt—it being understood that Raymond had now taken control :—

DO NOT SIGH.

M. F. A. L.—Was I sighing ?

O. J. L.—Yes, but you must not be so distressed ; he doesn't like it. He is there all right, and I am glad to have some one on the other side.
YES.

O. J. L.—Raymond, your mother is much happier now.
YES.

O. J. L.—Now then, shall I ask you questions ?
YES.

O. J. L.—Well now, wait a minute and take your time, and I will ask the first question :—
" What did the boys call you ? "

The medium now again repeated the alphabet, the
table tilting to each letter as before,

> first stopping at   P
> then at   A
> then at   P again ;

it then shook as if something was wrong.

O. J. L.—Very well, try again, begin once more.

Again it spelt PAP, but again indicated dissent, and
tried again : at the third trial it appeared to
spell

PAS.

M. F. A. L.—Raymond dear, you have given two letters right,
try and give the third.

It now stopped at T ; making PAT.

M. F. A. L.—Yes, that is right.

[This was, of course, well in our knowledge and therefore not strictly evidential, but it would not be in
the knowledge of the medium.]   (Cf. p. 148.)

YES.

O. J. L.—Well, now, you have done that, shall I ask another ?

YES.

O. J. L.—Will you give the name of a brother ?

The alphabet was repeated as usual by the medium,
in a monotonous manner, the table tilting as before

> and stopping first at   N
> then at   O
> then going past E, it stopped at   R
> and the next time at   M

then, by a single tilt, it indicated   A or else "No."

O. J. L., thinking that the letters R and M were wrong,
because the (to him) meaningless name NORMAN
was evidently being given, took it as " No," and
said :—

O. J. L.—You are confused now, better begin again.

The name accordingly was begun again, and this time
it spelt

NOEL

O. J. L.—That is right.   [But see Appended Note, p. 147.]

A slight pause took place here ; the table then indicated
that it wanted the alphabet again, and spelt out
an apparently single meaningless word which Dr.
Kennedy, as he wrote the letters down, perceived
to be

FIRE AWAY.

O. J. L.—Oh ! You want another question ! Would you like
to say the name of an officer ?

YES.

O. J. L.—Very well then, spell it.

Table spelt :—

MIP,

then indicated error.

O. J. L.—Not P ?

No.

O. J. L.—Well, begin again.

MITCHELL.

O. J. L.—Then the officer's name is Mitchell ?

YES.

O. J. L.—Was he a captain ?

(Silence.)

O. J. L.—Was he a lieutenant ?

(Silence.)

O. J. L.—Was he a second lieutenant perhaps ?

(Apparent assent, but nothing forcible)

O. J. L.—I am now going to give a name away on purpose : I am going to ask—Do you remember Case ?

YES.

O. J. L.—Would you like to say anything about him ?

YES.

O. J. L.—Very well then, let us have the alphabet.
Table spelt :—

HE IS A GOING A LLONG ALL RRIGHT.

[Erasures signify errors which were made either by the communicator or the interpreter, and are in accordance with the record. The method was that each letter, as understood, was called out, usually by me, to the recorder. When a wrong letter was indicated, or when there was obviously a duplication, it was scratched out as above.]

(After a short silence the spelling began again, it being easy for the table to indicate to the medium, by shaking or fidgeting, that she is wanted to repeat the alphabet.)

HE IS HERE.

O. J. L.—What, on your side ?
[Thinking it referred to Lieutenant Case.]

A loud " No."

HE IS HERE SPEAK.

K. K. (interpreting for us).—It only means Raymond is here and waiting.

O. J. L.—Under what circumstances did you see him last ?

(The answer was apparently a faint " YES.")

O. J. L.—Have you any special message, or did you give Case a special message ?

YES.

O. J. L.—What was it ?

SO IM NOT   SO IM WUO.

(Here some confusion was indicated ; and M. F. A. L. said, " Try and spell the name "—meaning for whom the message was, if it was a message that was intended, which was very doubtful.

It seemed to me that he was trying to say, or remember, what he had said to Lieutenant Case, who saw him after he had been struck ; and that what he thought he had said was " So I'm wounded " ; but I thought it unadvisable to continue on this tack, and rather regretted that I had begun it, since it was liable to put him back into a period of reminiscence which his friends would prefer that he did not dwell upon. Moreover, these last few questions did not seem particularly to interest him, and the responses were comparatively weak. Accordingly, I decided to switch him on to a topic that would be more likely to interest him.)

O. J. L.—Would you like your mother to go and see a friend of yours ?

(Some names of friends of his were now correctly given, but as we knew them I need not reproduce this part.)

O. J. L.—I say, Raymond, would you like a Ford ? [motor].
(After a moment's apparent surprise :—)
YES.

O. J. L.—Aren't you tired now ?
Loud " No."

M. F. A. L.—Raymond, I don't know Mitchell.
No.

O. J. L.—Well, that will be better evidence.
YES.

O. J. L.—Is that why you chose it ?
YES.
AER

MEDIUM (sotto voce).—No, that can't be right.
O J. L. (ditto).—I don't know , it may be. Go on.
OPLANE.

O. J. L.—You mean that Mitchell is an aeroplane officer ?
" YES " (very loud).

M. F. A. L. (misunderstanding, and thinking that he had said that he would like an aeroplane in preference to a Ford).—Still at your jokes, Raymond !
YES.

(Then again the table indicated, by slight rocking, that the alphabet was wanted ; and it spelt :—)
RAYMOND IS BEATING U.

(The sitters here made a little explanatory comment to each other on what they understood this unimportant sentence to mean ; after which O. J. L. appears to have said :—)

O. J. L.—I don't like bothering you.
Table moved, indicating that it was no trouble.

M. F. A. L.—Raymond, can you see us ?
YES.

M. F. A. L.—Can you see that I have been writing to you ? [See Part I, p. 10.]
YES.

M. F. A. L.—Can you read what I am writing ?
> YES.

M. F. A. L.—How do you read it ? By looking over my shoulder ?
Table again called for alphabet and spelt :—
> SENSE IT.

M. F. A. L.—Shall you ever be able to write through my hand
do you think ?
> (Silence.)

M. F. A. L.—Well, anyhow, you would like me to try ?
> YES.

O. J. L.—Raymond, have you plenty to do over there ?
> Loud " YES."

O. J. L.—Well, look here, I am going to give another name away.
> No.

O. J. L.—Oh ! You prefer not ! Very well, I will ask you in
this way : Have you met any particular friend of mine ?
> YES.

O. J. L.—Very well then, spell his name.
The table spelt :—
> MYERS AND GRA

Here O. J. L. thought that he had got wrong—rather
suspected that the A meant " No," and stupidly
said :—

O. J. L.—Well, it doesn't matter, it won't be evidential, so I
may as well guess what you mean · Is it Gurney ?
The table assented. But it still went on spelling. It
again spelt :—
> GRA

and then
> ND,

at which O. J. L. queried : Grand men ?
The table dissented, and went on and spelt :—
> FATHER.

O. J. L.—Oh ! You mean Grandfather !
> YES.

M. F. A. L.—Is he with Myers and Gurney ?
> Emphatic " No."

M. F. A. L.—Which grandfather is it that you mean ? Give
the first letter of his Christian name.
> W.

M. F. A. L.—Dear Grandpapa ! He would be sure to come
and help you !

O. J. L.—I say, do you like this table method better than the
' Feda ' method ?
> YES.

O. J. L.—But you remember that you can send anything you
want specially through Paul always ?
> YES.

O. J. L.—That was a grand sitting yesterday that your mother
had ! [i.e. the one with Peters.]
> YES.

M. F. A. L.—Do you remember showing olives ?
YES.

M. F. A. L.—What did you mean by them ?
OLIVER.

M. F. A. L.—Then we now understand—A Roland for an Oliver
YES.

O. J. L.—You intended no reference to Italy ?   [We had been doubtful at first of the significance of the olives ;   see p. 131.]
No.

O. J. L.—But you were interested in Italy ?
YES.

O. J. L.—Do you remember anyone special in Italy ?
YES.

O. J. L.—Well, spell the name.
(A name was spelt correctly.)

O. J. L.—You *are* clever at this !
Loud " YES."

O. J. L.—You always did like mechanical things.
YES.

O. J. L.—Can you explain how you do this ?   I mean how you work the table ?

The table then spelt with the alphabet for a long time, and as the words were not divided up, the sitters lost touch, one after the other, with what was being said. I, for instance, lost touch after the word " magnetism," and, for all I knew, it was nonsense that was being said ; but the recorder put all the letters down as they came, each letter being called out by me according to the stoppages of the table, and the record reads thus :—

YOU ALL SUPPLY MAGNETISM GATHERED IN MEDIUM, AND THAT GOES INTO TABLE ; AND WE MANIPULATE.

[The interest of this is due to the fact that the table was spelling out coherent words, although the sitters could hardly, under the circumstances, be exercising any control. Naturally, this does not prevent the medium from being supposed to be tilting out a message herself, and hence it is quite unevidential of course ; but, in innumerable other cases, the things said were quite outside the knowledge of the medium.]

O. J. L.—It is not what *I* should call " magnetism," is it ?
No.

O. J. L.—But you do not object to the term ?
No.

O. J. L.—Paul's mother offers to take messages from you, and if she gets them, she will transmit them to us.
YES.

O. J. L.—So when you want to get anything special through, just speak to Paul.
YES.

O. J. L.—And sometimes I shall be able to get a message back to you.

Loud " YES."

(In answer to a question about which of his sisters were at school with a specified person, the names of the right two sisters were now spelt out :—)

ROSALIND.

[We generally spell the name Rosalynde, but it was spelt here Rosalind as shown.]

BARBARA.

M. F. A. L.—Isn't it clever of him ?

Loud and amusing " YES."

O. J. L.—I never thought you would do it so quickly.

No.

O. J. L.—Can you still make acrostics ? [O. J. L. immediately regretted having asked this leading sort of question, but it was asked.]

YES.

K. K.—You are not going to make one now ?

No.

M. F. A. L.—Can you see me, Raymond, at other times when I am not with a medium ?

Alphabet called for, and spelt :—
SOMETIMES.

M F. A. L.—You mean when I think of you ?

YES.

O. J. L.—That must be very often.

Loud " YES."

[When a 'loud' YES or No is stated, it means that the table tilted violently, bumping on the floor and making a noise which impressed the recorder, so that the words " loud bumps " were added in the record.]

[I then asked him about the houses (of which he had specified some identifying features at a previous sitting through Peters on 27 September). He seemed to regret that there had been some confusion, and now correctly spelt out GROVEPARK as the name of one house, and NEWCASTLE as the place where 'Mother's home' was. But I omit details, as before.] (See p. 135.)

O. J. L.—Tell Mr. Myers and Mr. Gurney that I am glad to hear from them and that they are helping you.

YES.

M. F. A. L.—Give my affectionate regards to Mr. Gurney for a message which he got through for me some time ago.

YES.

O. J. L.—Now you must rest.

YES.

M. F. A. L.—One of your record sleeps.

Loud " YES."

10

O. J. L.—Good-bye, I will tell the family to-morrow.
YES.

O. J. L.—Alec especially.
YES.

M. F. A. L.—Noel will love to have his name spelt out.
YES.

O. J. L.—Well, good-bye, old man, we shall hear from you again.
M. F. A. L.—Good-bye, Raymond darling.
O. J. L.—Before we stop, does Paul want to say a word ?
> (Paul was then understood to take control, and spelt out :—)

HE IS GETTING ON WELL.

(We then thanked Paul for helping, and said good-bye.)

(End of sitting.)

To complete the record I shall append the few annotations which I made a couple of days afterwards, before I supplement them with later information.

Contemporary Annotations for Table Sitting on 28 September

Very many things were given right at the sitting above recorded, and in most cases the rightness will be clear from the comments of the sitters as recorded. But two names are given on which further annotation is necessary, because the sitters did not understand them ; in other words, they were such as, if confirmed, would furnish excellent and indeed exceptional evidence.

The first is ' Norman,' about which a very important report could be made at once ; but I think it better not to put anything in writing on that subject even now, at the present stage, since it is quite distinct, unforgettable, and of the first importance.

The other is the name ' Mitchell,' which at present we have had no opportunity for verifying ; hence annotation on that must be postponed. Suffice it to say that to-day (6 October 1915) it remains unknown. Whether an Army List has been published this year seems doubtful, and on the whole unlikely ; and no Army List later than 1909 has been so far accessible. Such few inquiries as have up to now been made have drawn blank. [See, however, three pages further on.]

Later Information

On 10 October Mrs. Kennedy, alone, had some automatic writing as follows :—

> Mother, Paul is bringing Raymond. I have him here ; he will speak to you. . . .
> " Please listen carefully now I want to speak to you about NORMAN. There is a special meaning to that because we always called my brother Alec Norman, the (muddle . . .)."

(K. K. said that she couldn't get the rest clearly.)

On 12 October we had a sitting with Mrs. Leonard, K. K. also present, and I said to ' Raymond ' :—

> Do you want to say anything more about that name ' Norman ' ? You gave a message about it to Mrs. Kennedy, but I don't know whether she got it clearly. Perhaps you want to amplify it ? If so, now is your chance. (The reply spelt out was :—)
> I TOLD HER THAT I CALLED LIONEL.

On which K. K. said : " I am afraid I often get names wrong. I suppose I got the name of the wrong brother."

NOTE BY O. J. L. ABOUT THE NAME ' NORMAN '

It appears that ' Norman ' was a kind of general nickname ; and especially that when the boys played hockey together, which they often did in the field here, by way of getting concentrated exercise, Raymond, who was specially active at this game, had a habit of shouting out, " Now then, Norman," or other words of encouragement, to any of his other brothers whom he wished to stimulate, especially apparently Lionel, though sometimes Alec and the others. That is what I am now told, and I can easily realise the manner of it. But I can testify that I was not aware that a name like this was used, nor was Lady Lodge, we two being the only members of the family present at the Leonard table sitting where the name ' Norman ' was given. (See p. 140.)

It will be remembered that at that sitting I first asked

him what name the boys had called him, and, after a few partial failures, obviously only due to mismanagement of the table, he replied, ' Pat,' which was quite right. I then asked if he would like to give the name of a brother, and he replied ' Norman,' which I thought was quite wrong. I did not even allow him to finish the last letter. I said he was confused, and had better begin again ; after which he amended it to ' Noel,' which I accepted as correct. But it will now be observed that the name ' Norman ' was the best he could possibly give, as a kind of comprehensive nickname applicable to almost any brother. And a nickname was an appropriate kind of response, because we had already had the nickname ' Pat.' Furthermore, on subsequent occasions he explained that it was the name by which he had called Lionel ; and, through Mrs. Kennedy—if she did not make a mistake—that it was a name he had called Alec by. It is quite possible, however, that he had intended to say ' Lionel ' on that occasion, and that she got it wrong. I am not sure how that may be. Again, at a later stage, in a family sitting— no medium present—one of the boys said, " Pat, do you remember ' Norman '?" at which with some excitement, the girls only touching the table, he spelt out ' HOCKEY ' ; thus completing the whole incident.

The most evidential portions, however, are those obtained when nobody present understood what was being said—namely, first, the spelling of the name ' Norman ' when those present thought that it was all a mistake after the first two letters ; and secondly, the explanation to Mrs. Kennedy that it was a name by which he had called one of his brothers, showing that it was originally given by no accident, but with intention.

As to the name ' Pat ' (p. 140), I extract the following from a diary of Noël, as evidence that it was very much Raymond's nickname ; but of course we knew it :—

1914
" Sept. 9. Pat goes to L'pool *re* Commission.
,, 10. Pat gets commission in 3rd South Lanc's.
,, 14. Pat collecting kit. We inspect revolvers.
,, 18. Pat comes up to Harborne for some rifle practice. Does not find it too easy.
,, 19. I become member of Harborne Rifle Club.
,, 20. Pat shoots again.

Sept. 23. Pat leaves for L'pool to start his training at Great Crosby.

I give up commission-idea for the present.

Oct. 17. Pat comes home to welcome Parents back from Australia.

  ,, ⌐20. Pat returns to L'pool."

Note on the name ' Mitchell ' (added later)

It can be remembered that, when asked on 28 September for the name of an officer, Raymond spelt out MITCHELL, and indicated decisively that the word AEROPLANE was connected with him ; he also assented to the idea that he was one whom the family didn't know, and that so it would be better as evidence (pp. 141, 142).

After several failures at identification I learnt, on 10 October, through the kind offices of the Librarian of the London Library, that he had ascertained from the War Office that there was a 2nd Lieut. E. H. Mitchell now attached to the Royal Flying Corps. Accordingly, I wrote to the Record Office, Farnborough ; and ultimately, on 6 November, received a post card from Captain Mitchell, to whom I must apologise for the, I hope, quite harmless use of his name :—

" Many thanks for your kind letter. I believe I have met your son, though where I forget. My wounds are quite healed, and I am posted to Home Establishment for a bit, with rank of Captain. Your letter only got here (Dover) from France this morning, so please excuse delay in answering.

                                    E. H. MITCHELL "

In concluding this chapter, I may quote a little bit of non-evidential but characteristic writing from ' Paul.' It was received on 30 September 1915 by Mrs. Kennedy, when alone, and her record runs thus :—

(After writing of other things, I *not* having asked anything about Raymond.)

  " I think it hardly possible for you to believe how quickly Raymond learns ; he seems to believe all that we have to fight to teach the others.

  " Poor chaps, you see no one has told them before they come over, and it is so hard for them when they see us and they feel alive, and their people keep on sobbing.

" The business for you and me gets harder and harder as the days go on, mother ; it needs thousands at this work, and you are so small.

" I feel that God helps us, but I want Him to find others, darling ; there is no time to waste either in your place or mine, but I know you are trying ever so hard."

NOTE IN TENTH EDITION

I have recently received a letter from Captain Mitchell's father, previously quite unknown to me, which, as it adds something evidential, I here quote extracts from :—

" 32 PEMBRIDGE SQUARE, LONDON, W. 2,
10 *March* 1918

" My reason for intruding upon you is this : Only last night I was reading in your book *Raymond*, and was first astonished and then deeply interested when I read on pages 141 to 149 of a young officer of the R.F.C., E. H. Mitchell, being mentioned by Raymond at the sitting you had on 28 September 1915. For this dear boy (Erik Harrison Mitchell)—who passed over on the last Saturday of the following April—was or rather *is* my only son.

" I think I can see why Raymond's thoughts were directed to him on that day, also why he was silent when questioned as to the boy's rank. In the first place, probably your son was engaged in tending the wounded—as I learn my boy now is ; and Erik had been wounded only two days before your sitting, viz. on Sunday, 26 September 1915 ; and may not your son have tended my boy during some part of those forty-eight hours ? And as to rank. When the war began Erik was an apprentice at Vickers' at Erith, and was a 2nd Lieut. in the 4th Home Counties Howitzer Brigade, consisting of Vickers' boys principally, if not entirely. He then became 1st Lieut. in this territorial brigade and later joined the regulars, being gazetted 2nd Lieut. in the R.F.A. When he was wounded, therefore, he was 2nd Lieut. R.F.*A.*, seconded to R.F.C. For his exploit on 26 September 1915 he was promoted to the post of Flight Commander with rank of Captain. Does not all this account for the silence and apparent doubt of Raymond when questioned as to rank ?

" If you will bear with me a little longer I should like to refer to the sitting I had a few days ago with Mrs. Brittain. It was the first such sitting I had ever had, and my dear boy was so grateful to me for taking the step, for he explained that he had been trying during all these months to communicate with his mother and me without success. And he was so glad and happy and so wonderfully affectionate. Without my mentioning even that it was he I had come to seek, Mrs. Brittain told me she saw an aeroplane with a broken propeller and a boy beside it—describing him in great detail and most faithfully. And when I said she had not given me his name she said, ' Why, there's a boy calling him now, " Erik." ' "

" (Signed)   H. BEAUFORT MITCHELL "

CHAPTER IX

ATTEMPTS AT STRICTER EVIDENCE

IN a Table Sitting it is manifest that the hypothesis of unconscious muscular guidance must be pressed to extremes, as a normal explanation, when the communications are within the knowledge of any of the people sitting at the table.

Many of the answers obtained were quite outside the knowledge of the medium or of Mrs. Kennedy, but many were inevitably known to us ; and in so far as they were within our knowledge it might be supposed, even by ourselves, that we partially controlled the tilting, though of course we were careful to try not to do so. And besides, the things that came, or the form in which they came, were often quite unexpected, and could not consciously have been controlled by us. Moreover, when the sentence spelt out was a long one, we lost our way in it and could not tell whether it was sense or nonsense ; for the words ran into each other. The note-taker, who puts each letter down as it is called out to him by the sitters at the table, has no difficulty in reading a message, although, with the words all run together, it hardly looks intelligible at first sight, even when written. For instance :—

BELESSWORRIEDALECPLEASEOLDCHAP,

which was one message, or :—

GATHEREDINMEDIUMANDTHATGOESINTOTABLEAN
DWEMANIPULATE,

which was part of another. Neither could be readily followed if called out slowly letter by letter.

Still, the family were naturally and properly sceptical about it all.

Accordingly, my sons devised certain questions in the

nature of tests, referring to trivial matters which they thought would be within Raymond's recollection, but which had happened to them alone during summer excursions or the like, and so were quite outside my knowledge. They gave me a few written questions, devised in conclave in their own room ; and on 12 October I took them to London with me in a sealed envelope, which I opened in the train when going up for a sitting ; and after the sitting had begun I took an early opportunity of putting the questions it contained. We had already had (on 28 September, reported in last chapter) one incident of a kind unknown to us, in the name ' Norman,' but they wanted more of the same or of a still more marked kind. I think it will be well to copy the actual contemporary record of this part of the sitting in full :—

Second Table Sitting of O. J. L. and M. F. A. L. with Mrs. Leonard, 12 October 1915, 5.30 p.m.

Present—O. J. L., M. F. A. L., K. K., WITH DR. KENNEDY AS RECORDER

At the beginning of the sitting O. J. L. explained that they were now engaged in trying to get distinct and crucial evidence ; that preparations had been made accordingly ; and that no doubt those on the other side approved, and would co-operate.

A pause of three and a half minutes then ensued, and the table gave a slow tilt.

O. J. L.—Is Paul there ?
            YES.
O. J. L.—Have you brought Raymond ?
            YES.
O. J. L.—Are you there, Raymond ?
            YES.
O. J. L. (after M. F. A. L. had greeted him).—Well now, look here, my boy, I have got a few questions which your brothers think you will know something about, whereas to me they are quite meaningless. Their object is to make quite sure that we don't unconsciously help in getting the answers because we know them. In this case that is impossible,

because nobody here knows the answers at all. Do you understand the object ?

YES.

O. J. L.—Very well then, shall I begin ?

NO.

O. J. L.—Oh! You want to say something yourself first ?

YES.

O. J. L.—Very well then, the alphabet.

TELLTHEMINOWTRYTOPROVEIHAVEMESSAGESTOTHEWORLD.

> [Taking these long messages down is rather tedious, and it is noteworthy that the sitters lose their way sooner or later—I had no idea what was coming or whether it was sense—but of course when it is complete the recorder can easily interpret, and does so.]

O. J. L.—Is that the end of what you want to say yourself ?

YES.

O. J. L.—Well then, now I will give you one of the boys' questions, but I had better explain that you may not in every case understand the reference yourself. We can hardly expect you to answer all of them, and if you don't do one, I will pass on to another. But don't hurry, and we will take down whatever you choose to say on each of them. The first question is :—

O. J. L.—" Do you remember anything about the Argonauts ? "

(Silence for a short time.)

O. J. L.—' Argonauts' is the word. Does it mean anything to you ? Take your time.

YES.

O. J. L.—Well, would you like to say what you remember ?

YES.

Then, by repeating the alphabet, was spelt :—

TELEGRAM.

O. J. L.—Is that the end of that answer ?

YES.

O. J. L.—Well, now I will go on to the second question then. " What do you recollect about Dartmoor ? "
The time for thought was now much briefer, and the table began to spell pretty soon :—
COMING DOWN.

O. J. L.—Is that all ?
No.

O. J. L.—Very well then, continue.
HILL FERRY.

O. J. L.—Is that the end of the answer ?
YES.

O. J. L.—Very well then, now I will go on to the third question, which appears to be a bit complicated. " What do the following suggest to you :—
Evinrude
O. B. P.
Kaiser's sister."

(No good answers were obtained to these questions : they seemed to awaken no reminiscence.
Asked the name of the man to whom Raymond had given his dog, the table spelt out STALLARD quite correctly. But this was within our knowledge.)

(*End of extract from record.*)

NOTE ON THE REMINISCENCES AWAKENED BY THE WORDS 'ARGONAUTS' AND 'DARTMOOR'

On reporting to my sons the answers given about ' Argonauts ' and ' Dartmoor ' they were not at all satisfied.

I found, however, from the rest of the family that the word TELEGRAM had a meaning in connexion with ' Argonauts '—a meaning quite unknown to me or to my wife—but it was not the meaning that his brothers had expected. It seems that in a previous year, while his mother and I were away from home, the boys travelled by motor to somewhere in Devonshire, and (as they think) at Taunton Raymond had gone into a post office, sent a telegram home to say that they were all right, and had signed it ' Argonauts.' The girls at home remembered the telegram quite well ; the other boys did not specially remember it.

The kind of reference they had wanted, Raymond gave ultimately though meagrely, but only after so much time had elapsed that the test had lost its value, and only after I had been told to switch him on to " Tent Lodge, Coniston," as a clue.

Now that I know the answer I do not think the question was a particularly good one ; and the word ' telegram,' which they had not expected and did not want, seems to me quite as good an incident as the one which, without a clue, they had expected him to recall in connexion with ' Argonauts.'   Besides, I happened myself to know about an Iceland trip in Mr. Alfred Holt's yacht ' Argo ' and its poetic description by Mr. Mitchell Banks and Dr. Caton in a book in the drawing-room at Tent Lodge, Coniston (though the boys were not aware of my knowledge), but it never struck me that this was the thing wanted ; and if it had come, the test would have been of inferior quality.

Concerning the answer to ' Dartmoor,' his brothers said that COMING DOWN HILL was correct but incomplete ; and that they didn't remember any FERRY.   I therefore on another occasion, namely, on 22 October, during a sitting with Feda (that is to say, not a table sitting, but one in which Mrs. Leonard's control Feda was speaking and reporting messages), said—still knowing nothing about the matter beyond what I had obtained in the table sitting— " Raymond, do you remember about ' Dartmoor ' and the hill ? "

The answer is recorded as follows, together with the explanatory note added soon afterwards—though the record is no doubt a little abbreviated, as there was some dramatic representation by Feda of sudden swerves and holding on :—

From Sitting of O. J. L. and M. F. A. L. on
22 October 1915.   ' *Feda* ' *speaking*

O. J. L.—Raymond, do you remember about Dartmoor and the hill ?

> Yes, he said something about that.   He says it

was exciting. What is that he says? Brake—
something about a brake—putting the brake on.
Then he says, sudden curve—a curve—he gives
Feda a jerk like going round a quick curve.

[I thought at the time that this was only
padding, but subsequently learnt from Alec
that it was right. It was on a very long
night-journey on their motor, when the
silencer had broken down by bursting, at
the bottom of an exceptionally steep hill,
and there was an unnerving noise. The
one who was driving went down other steep
hills at a great pace, with sudden applica-
tions of the brake and sudden quick curves,
so that those at the back felt it dangerous,
and ultimately had to stop him and insist on
going slower. Raymond was in front with
the one who was driving. The sensations
of those at the back of the car were strongly
connected with the brake and with curves;
but they had mainly expected a reference
from Raymond to the noise from the broken
silencer, which they ultimately repaired
during the same night with tools obtained
at the first town they stopped at.]

O. J. L.—Did he say anything about a ferry?

No, he doesn't remember that he did.

O. J. L.—Well, I got it down.

There is one : all the same there is one. But
he didn't mean to say anything about it. He says
it was a stray thought that he didn't mean to give
through the table. He has found one or two things
come in like that. It was only a stray thought.
You have got what you wanted, he says. ' Hill,'
he meant to give, but not ' ferry.' They have
nothing to do with each other.

On a later occasion I took an opportunity of cate-
chising him further about this word FERRY, since none of
the family remembered a ferry, or could attach any
significance to the word. He still insisted that his
mention of a ferry in connexion with a motor trip was not

wrong, only he admitted that "some people wouldn't call it a ferry." I waited to see if any further light would come ; and now, long afterwards, on 18 August 1916 I receive from Alec a note referring to a recent trip, this month, which says :—

> " By the way, on the run to Langland Bay (which is the motor run we all did the year before the run to Newquay) we pass through Briton Ferry ; and there is precious little ferry about it."

So even this semi-accidental reminiscence seems to be turning out not altogether unmeaning ; though probably it ought not to have come in answer to ' Dartmoor.' (See more about Dartmoor on p. 211.)

GENERAL REMARKS ON THIS TYPE OF QUESTION

It will be realised, I think, that a single word, apart from the context, thus thrown at a person who may be in a totally differen mood at the time, is exceedingly difficult ; and on the whole I think he must be credited with some success, though not with as much as had been hoped for. If his brothers had been present, or had had any interview with him in the meantime, it would have spoilt the test, considered strictly ; nevertheless, it might have made the obtaining of the answers they wanted much more feasible, inasmuch as in their presence he would have been in their atmosphere and be more likely to remember their sort of surroundings. Up to this date they had not had any sitting with a medium at all. In presence of his mother and myself, and under all the circumstances, and what he felt to be the gravity of some of his recent experiences, it is not to me surprising that the answers were only partially satisfactory ; though, indeed, to me they seem rather good. Anyhow, they had the effect of stimulating his brothers to arrange some sittings with a table at home on their own account.

CHAPTER X

RECORD CONTINUED

I MIGHT make many more extracts from this sitting of 22 October, of which a short extract has just been quoted, because, though not specially evidential, they have instructive and so to speak common-sense features, but it is impossible to include everything. I will therefore omit most of it, but quote a little, not because it is evidential, but because what is said may be instructive to inquirers.

FROM O. J. L. AND M. F. A. L. SITTING WITH MRS. LEONARD, 22 OCTOBER 1915

He wants to gather evidence and give something clearly. He seems to think that his brother had been coming here (looking about).

O. J. L.—Your brother will come to see you to-morrow. [He was not coming to Mrs. Leonard.]

Where is he ? He got the impression that he had either been here or should be here now ; he has got the thought of him. He has been trying to get into touch with him himself ; he has been trying to speak to him. Seems to have something to do with Mrs. Kathie,[1] and he has tried to write to him. The trouble is, that he can't always see distinctly. He feels in the air, but can't see always distinctly. (To M. F. A. L.) When you are sitting at the table he sees you, and can see what you have got on. When he tries to come to you, he can only sense you ; but at the table he can see you.

O. J. L.—Has he seen his brothers at a table ?

No, not at the table. He sensed them, and he thought they were trying to speak to him ; but didn't feel as if he was going to get near. It has something to do with a medium. Medium. [Meaning that they were trying to do without a medium.]

---

[1] Mrs. Kennedy's name is Katherine, and Feda usually speaks of her as Mrs. Kathie.

M. F. A. L.—When did he see me ?

When a medium is present he sees you quite distinctly. He saw you, not here, but at another place. Oh, it was in London, another place in London, some time ago. He was surprised to see you, and wondered how he could. [Presumably the occasion intended was when Mrs. Kennedy, who herself has power, was present as well as Peters.] He can only think the things he wants to say.[1] [Then reverting to his brothers' attempts at Mariemont.] " Tell them to go on. I shall never get tired. Never ! Tell them to have patience. It is more interesting to me than to them." He does not seem sure if he got anything through. It is so peculiar. Even here, he is not always quite certain that he has said what he wanted to say, except sometimes when it is clear and you jump at it. Sometimes then he feels, " I've got that home, anyway ! " He has got to feel his way. They must go easy with him— not ask too much all at once. If they have plenty of patience, in a while he will be able to come and talk as if he were there.

M. F. A. L.—Do you mean with the voice ?

No, with the table.

More important than talking is to get things through with his own people, and to give absolute evidence. He doesn't want them to bother him with test questions till he feels at home. It doesn't matter here, where there is a medium, but the conditions there are not yet good. Tell them to take for granted that it is he, and later on he will be able to talk to them and say all he wishes to say. The boys are so eager to get tests. When grandpapa comes, it is to relieve him a little, while he is not there. He doesn't himself want to speak.

Twice a week, he says.

He is bringing a girl with him now—a young girl, growing up in the spirit world. She belongs to Raymond : long golden hair, pretty tall, slight, brings a lily in her hand. There is another spirit too who passed out very young—a boy ; you wouldn't know him as he is now ; he looks about the same age as Raymond, but very spiritual in appearance ; he brings a W with him ; he doesn't know much of the earth plane, nor the lily either ; he passed over too young. They are both with Raymond now. They look spiritual and young. Spirit people look young if they passed on young. Raymond is in the middle between them. He says this is not very scientific. [All this is appropriate to a deceased brother and sister; the brother older, the sister younger.]

Raymond really is happy now. He doesn't say this to make you feel satisfied. He is really happy now. He says

---

[1] This corresponds with an early statement made by " Myers " through Mrs. Thompson. See *Proceedings*, S.P.R., vol. xxiii. p. 221.

this is most interesting, and is going to be fifty times more interesting than on the earth plane. There is such a big field to work in. Father and he are going to do such a lot together. He says, " I am going to help for all I am worth." (To M. F. A. L.) If you are happy, I will be happier too. You used to sigh ; it had an awful effect on him, but he is getting lighter with you. Father has been wonderful. He is often with Paulie, and has been to see Mrs. Kathie too.
[Meaning Mrs. Katherine Kennedy. Feda, of course, is speaking throughout.]

M. F. A. L.—Which way does he find the easiest to come ?

He is able to get to you by impression, and not only by writing. He thinks he can make you hear. He is trying to make you clair-audient. Let there be no misapprehension about that. He does it in order to help himself. He hopes to get something through.

O. J. L.—You might send the same thing through different channels.

Yes, he says. He need not say much, but is going to think it out. He can get Mrs. K. to write it out, and then get it through the table with them. He thinks he will be able to do a lot with you, Mrs. Kathie. You know that Paulie's here ?

(K. K. spoke to Paul for a short time.)

O. J. L.—Do you think it had better be tried on the same evening, or on different evenings ?

Try it on the same evening at first, and see what success is got ; if only one word came through the same, he would be very pleased. He might get one word first, then two, then two or three. Tell them to reserve a little time for just that, and give him some time specially for it, not mix it up with other things in the sittings.

K. K.—Shall I ask him to write some word ?

He will think of some word—no matter if it is meaningless. What you have to do is, not to doubt, but take it down. One word might be much more valuable than a long oration. One word would do, no matter how silly it sounded ; even if it is only a jumble, so long as it is the same jumble. He is jumping now. [Meaning, he is pleased with the idea.] He says he finds it difficult owing to the medium. He is not able to get through all he wants to say, but on the whole thinks he got it pretty straight to-night.

[The quickness with which the communicator jumped at the idea of a cross-correspondence was notable, because I do not think he had known anything about them. It sounded rather like the result of rapid Myersian instruction. I rather doubt if cross-correspondences of this kind can be got through Mrs. Kennedy, though she knows we are going to try for them. The boys are quite willing to take

down any jumble, but she herself likes to understand
what she gets, and automatically rejects gibberish.—
O. J. L.]

On 13 October, through the kind arrangement of Mrs.
Kennedy, we had an anonymous sitting with a medium
new to us, a Mrs. Brittain, of Hanley, Staffordshire, in
Mrs. Kennedy's house.

It was not very successful—the medium seemed tired
and worried—but there were a few evidential points
obtained, though little or nothing about the boy ; in the
waking stage, however, she said that some one was calling
the name ' Raymond.'

At an interview next day with Mrs. Kennedy, Mrs.
Brittain said that a boy named ' Pat ' had come with
Paul to see her on the evening after the sitting (see p. 148
for the significance of ' Pat ') ; and she described it in
writing to Mrs. Kennedy thus :—

14 October 1915

" I was just resting, thinking over the events of the day,
and worrying just a little about my ordeal of next Monday,
when I became conscious of the presence of such a dear soldier
boy. He said, ' I am Pat, and oh, I did want to speak to my mother.'
Then I saw with him your dear boy [Paul] ; he asked me to tell
you about Pat, and to give the message to his father that he would
get proof without seeking it."

CHAPTER XI

FIRST SITTING OF ALEC (A. M. L.)

Introduction by O. J. L.

A WORD may be necessary about the attitude of Raymond's family to the whole subject. It may be thought that my own known interest in the subject was naturally shared by the family, but that is not so. So far as I can judge, it had rather the opposite effect; and not until they had received unmistakable proof, devised largely by themselves, was this healthy scepticism ultimately broken down.

My wife had had experience with Mrs. Piper in 1889, though she continued very sceptical till 1906 or thereabouts, when she had some extraordinarily good evidence. But none of this experience was shared by the family, who read neither my nor anyone else's books on the subject, and had no first-hand evidence. For the most part they regarded it without interest and with practical scepticism. If in saying this I convey the impression of anything like friction or disappointment, the impression is totally false. Life was full of interest of many kinds, and, until Raymond's death, there was no need for them to think twice about survival or the possibility of communication.

The first sitting held by any of his brothers, apart from private amateur attempts at home,—the first sitting, I may say, held by any of them with any medium,—took place on 23 October, when Alec had a sitting with Peters; his mother also was present, but no names were given. Alec's record of this sitting, together with his preliminary Note, I propose to quote practically in full.

Alec and his mother went in the morning to Mrs. Kennedy's house, where the sitting was to take place. M. F. A. L. stopped on the way to buy a bunch of violets, which she put on Peters' table. When he arrived and saw them, he was very pleased; ejaculated " my flower," and said that he could not have had anything that gave him more pleasure.

I may here remark, incidentally, that Peters is a man who takes his mediumship seriously, and tries to regulate his life so as to get good conditions. Thus, he goes into the country at intervals, and stops all work for a time to recuperate. He lives, in fact, at Westgate-on-Sea, and only has a room in London. He seems to lead a simple life altogether, and his " control " spoke of his having been prepared since six o'clock that morning for this sitting

Alec went up prepared to take notes, and after the sitting wrote the following preliminary account :—

A. M. L.'s Remarks on the Sitting

Mother and I arrived at Mrs. Kennedy's house at five minutes to eleven. We saw Mrs. Kennedy, who asked us if we would like her to be present. We said yes. Then she told us that Peters had come, and that she would ask him. Peters wanted her to be present.

Mrs. Kennedy brought Peters up; he shook hands, without any introduction. We had all gone up to Mrs. Kennedy's private room, where Peters likes the sittings to take place. We four sat round a table about four feet in diameter. A. and M. with backs to one or other of the two windows, K. and P. more or less facing them. A. was opposite P.; M. was opposite K. There was plenty of light, but the room was partly shaded by pulling down blinds. They talked about street noises at first. P. held K.'s and M.'s hands for a time. K. and M. talked together a little. P. now moved about a little and rubbed his face and eyes. Suddenly he jerked himself up and began talking in broken English.

During the trance his eyes were apparently closed all the time; and when speaking to anyone he ʻlookedʼ at them with his eyelids screwed up. Sometimes a change of control occurred. While that was taking place, he sat quiet, and usually held K.'s and M.'s hands until another sudden jerk occurred, when he let go and started talking.

The sitting was rather disjointed, and most of it apparently not of much importance, but for a few minutes in the middle it was very impressive. It then felt to me exactly as if my hand was being held in both Raymond's, and as if Raymond himself was speaking in his own voice. My right hand was being held, but even if I had had it free I could not possibly have taken notes under the circumstances.

(M. F. A. L. adds that neither could she nor anyone, while that part of the sitting was going on.)

Peters spoke often very quickly, and sometimes indistinctly, so that the notes are rather incomplete.

(To this O. J. L. adds that it was Alec's first experience of a sitting, and that, even with experience, it is difficult to take anything like full notes.)

Report of Peters Sitting in Mrs. Kennedy's Room, at
11 *a.m. on Saturday,* 23 *October* 1915

(Revised by the Sitters)

Present—MRS. KENNEDY (K. K.), LADY LODGE (M. F. A. L.), ALEC M. LODGE, and the Medium—VOUT PETERS

REPORT BY A. M. L.

In a short time Peters went into trance, and ' Moonstone·' was understood to be taking control. He first made some general remarks :—

> Good morning! I generally say, " Good evening," don't I ? Don't be afraid for Medie ; he has been prepared since six o'clock this morning Magnetism has to be stored up, and therefore it is best to use the same room and the same furniture every time.

Then he spoke to K. K. :—

> Will you call on little woman close to ? It will mean salvation to two people [Abbreviated.]

(K. K. understood.)

Then the medium took M.'s hand.

> Somebody not easy to describe ; old lady ; not tall ; grey hair, parted in centre ; grey eyes ; nose thin ; mouth fairly large and full. This describes her as she was before she passed away. Had big influence on your early life. Good character ; loving, but perhaps lived in narrow outlook ; not only a mother to her own belongings, but she mothered every man, woman, or child she came into contact with. She is here this morning and has been before. Is it not your Mother ?

M. F. A. L.—If it is my Mother, it is a great pleasure to me.

She has been with you and comforted you through this trial.

She has been, and will go on, looking after the boy. You must not think she is not just as much with you because she has no body. She is just as much your mother. She *has* a body, though it is different.

(Pointing to A.) She is related to *him*. She puts her hand on his shoulder. She is very proud of what he is doing at the present time. He has been a great help to you. Since the passing away of him who is loved by you both, he has looked on spiritualism with much more respect, because previously it has not touched his heart. It is not only a thing of the head, it is now a thing of the heart.

She suffered terribly before passing away. She bore her suffering patiently.

She put her finger on her lips and says : " I am so proud of O. ! " (Medium puts one finger on middle of lips.)

It has always been what I thought : the triumph (?) has been a long time coming, but it will come greater than had been anticipated. There have been difficulties. I am glad of success. It will come greater than before. The book that is to be will be written from the heart, and not the head. But the book will not be written now. NOT NOW ! NOT NOW ! NOT NOW ! (loud). Written later on. THE BOOK which is going to help many and convert many. The work done already is big. But what is coming is bigger.

(Interval.)

(Paul, sending a message to K. K. :—)

I have been drilling her to link up. You don't know what it is. It is like teaching people to transmit messages by the telegraph. Don't let the boy come, let Granny come. (The medium here imitated Paul's manner of sitting down and pulling up the knees of his trousers.) She laughs at the idea of being drilled.

He says (Paul still communicating) : You know,

little Mother, you wonder why I was taken ; but it is a great deal better like this. Thousands of people can be helped like this. You are the link, and the means of reaching thousands of mothers.

(Then ' Moonstone ' was understood to say :—)

Returning to Madam (*i.e.* the old lady again, and medium turning to M. F. A. L.), she says " I am so glad you not only told him what you did —this is not to you but some one away (finger on lips), somebody she will not give—and reached out as you did."

This is from Madam. She is going away.

M. F. A. L.—My love to her.

No, no, no, she does not go away ; she stands back, to let some one else come forward—like actors take turns at a theatre.

> [Then an impersonation of my Uncle Jerry was represented, with the statement, "Your husband will know who he is"; but this part of the record is omitted as comparatively unimportant. It was unintelligible to the sitter.—O. J. L.]

(Then a new control came in, which was by K. K. understood to be ' Redfeather.' When he arrived, the medium smacked his hands and spoke to K. K. :—)

I come dis little minute to try experiment. If we succeed, all right ; if we don't, don't mind. There will be some difficulties.

You know me ? (To K. K.)

K. K.—Yes. It is ' Redfeather.'

Glad to see you better. You used to feel—a hand on your head. It was a little girl. It was your boy who brought her. Now I go. Just talk a little.

(K. K. then thanked the speaker for his help.)

Who could help better than me ?

. . . long ago I was killed.

Who could help better ?

> (Then there was an interval, and evident change of control. And speech very indistinct at first.)

I want to come.

Call Mother to help me.

Because you know.

You understand.

It wasn't so bad.

Not so bad.

I knew you knew the possibility of communicating, so when I went out as I did, I was in a better condition than others on the other side. We had often talked about this subject, father understanding it as he did ; and now, coming into touch with his strength, makes it easy.

(Medium here reached out across the table to A. and grasped his right hand, so that the notes were temporarily interrupted. The medium's arms were now both stretched out across the table, with his head down on them, and he held A.'s hand in both his. All this time he spoke with great emotion : the medium was shaken with sobs ; his head and neck were suffused with blood ; the whole circumstances were strained, and strongly emotional ; and the voice was extraordinarily like Raymond's. A., too, felt that his hands were being gripped in a grasp just like Raymond's. This was the central part of the sitting ; and for the time no notes could be taken, even by Mrs. Kennedy. But after a bit the hand was released, the strain rather lightened, and notes continue which run thus :—)

[A. M. L. says, " In time the interval was brief," but it was surcharged with emotion, strongly felt by all present.]

But no, wait.

Because they tell me.

I am not ashamed.

I am glad.

I tell you, I would do it again.

I realise things differently to what one saw here.

And oh, thank God, I can speak !

But . . .

The boys help me.

You don't know what he has done.

Who could help ?

But I must keep quiet, I promised them to keep calm.

The time is so short.

Tell father that I am happy.

That I am happy that he has not come.

If he had come here, I couldn't have spoken.

I find it difficult to express what I want.

Every time I come back it is easier.

The only thing that was hard was just before.

The 15th, do you understand ?

And the 12th.

[We do not clearly understand these dates.]

But every time I come it is better.

Grandmama helped or I couldn't.

Now I must go.

. . . broken . . .

But I have done it, thank God !

(Then this special control ended ; while the medium murmured, as to himself, first the word ' John,' and then the word ' God.' Then the strain was relieved by a new control, understood to be ' Biddy.')

Surely it's meself that has come to speak. Here's another mother. I am helping the boy. I said to him to come out.

(To A. M. L.) Just you go and do your work. When the boy comes as he did, it upsets the body. I come to help to soothe the nerves of the medium. It is a privilege to help. I am an old Irishwoman.

(To K. K.) You don't realise that the world is governed by chains, and that you are one of the links. I was a washerwoman and lived next a church, and they say cleanliness comes next to godliness ! One of my chains is to help mothers. Well, I am going. But for comfort, —the boy is glad he is come. (To K. K.) Your husband is a fine man. I love him. His

heart's as big as his body, and it is not only
medicine, but love that he dispenses.

(Then an interval; and another control—
probably ' Moonstone ' again, or else Peters
himself clairvoyantly :—)

We succeeded a little in our experiment.

Now the boy is with . . .

(Here the medium seized *both* Alec's hands, and
K. K. continues the notes.)

[But they may be abbreviated here, as they
represent only Peters's ordinary clairvoyance
—probably.]

You bring with you a tremendous force. You
don't always say what you think. A quick way
of making up your mind. Your intuitional force
is very strong. Your mind is very evenly balanced,
[and so on] . . . The last three months, things
have altered. It has stirred you to the depths
of your innermost being. You had no idea how
strong the bond was between you and one who has
been here to-day. Want to shield and take care of
your mother. You know her devotion to both you
and the one gone over. . . .

The one gone over is a brother. He wants to
send a message.

(Some messages omitted.)

You did not cry, but heart crying inside.

Help others. You are doing it If you ever
tried to do what he did, you would physically break
down. All this is from him.

(To Mother) So glad about the photograph.
Something you have had done that is satisfactory.

[This is good, but it only occurred to me to-day,
31 October. It evidently relates to two
photographs in a pocket case, found on his
body, which Raymond carried with him, and
which had been returned to the original by
us.—A. M. L.]

Wants to convey message to father, but it is not
about himself this time. I get the initials F W M
—not clear about all the letters — but F M
wishes to be remembered. He says : I am still

very active.   Get into touch with Crookes *re* the Wireless.

>   [O. J. L. was at Muirhead's works in Kent on this subject, at this moment.—A. M. L.]

Still active, still at work.

>   [Spoken like " I see you are still active, still at work."—A. M. L.]

Then he gives me a curious thing, and laughs. One of the things I am most proud of is " St. Paul."

>   [This puzzled K. K., the note-taker.]

(To Alec.) So glad you *came*, boy !   What a lot you think !

>   (Medium came-to, breathing and struggling. Said he had been under *very* deep — like coming-to after an anæsthetic.)

NOTE BY O. J. L.

Lady Lodge impressed me considerably with the genuine and deeply affecting character of the above episode of personal control.   It was evidently difficult to get over for the rest of the day.   I doubt if the bare record conveys much : though it may to people of like experience.

CHAPTER XII

GENERAL REMARKS ON CONVERSATIONAL REPORTS AND ON CROSS-CORRESPONDENCES

IT may be asked why I report so much of what may be called ordinary conversation, instead of abbreviating and concentrating on specific instances and definite statements of fact. I reply :—

1. That a concentrated version is hard to read, while a fuller version is really less tedious in spite of its greater length. A record is always a poor substitute for actual experience ; and too much abbreviation might destroy whatever relic of human interest the records possess.

2. That abbreviation runs the risk of garbling and amending ; it is undesirable in reports of this kind to amend style at the expense of accuracy.

3. That the mannerisms and eccentricities of a ' control ' (or secondary personality) are interesting, and may be instructive ; at any rate they exhibit to a novice the kind of thing to be expected.

4. A number of inquirers want to know—and I think properly want to know—what a sitting is like, what kind of subjects are talked about, what the ' communicators ' —*i.e.* the hypothetical personalities who send messages through the ' control '—have to say about their own feelings and interests and state of existence generally. Hence, however the record be interpreted, it seems better to quote some specimens fully.

5. I am aware that some of the records may appear absurd. Especially absurd will appear the free-and-easy statements, quoted later, about the nature of things ' on the other side,'—the kind of assertions which are not only unevidential but unverifiable, and which we usually either discourage or suppress. I have stated

elsewhere my own reasons for occasionally encouraging statements of this kind and quoting them as they stand. (See beginning of Chapter XVI.)   And though I admit that to publish them is probably indiscreet, I still think that the evidence, such as it is, ought to be presented as a whole.

6. The most evidential class of utterance, what we call cross-correspondence, is not overlooked ; and while every now and then it occurs naturally and spontaneously, sometimes an effort is made to obtain it.

Note about the Meaning of Cross-Correspondence

It will be convenient to explain that by the term " cross-correspondence " is meant the obtaining through two or more independent mediums, at about the same time, a message from a single communicator on any one definite subject.

It is usually impossible for the coincidence of time to be exact, because both mediums may not be sitting at the same time.   But in some cases, wherein coincidence of subject is well marked, coincidence in time is of little moment ; always provided that the subject is really an out-of-the-way or far-fetched one, and not one common to every English-speaking person, like Kitchener or Roberts or Jellicoe.

Cross-correspondences are of various grades.   The simplest kind is when two mediums both use the same exceptional word, or both refer to the same non-public event, without any normal reason that can be assigned.   Another variety is when, say, three mediums refer to one and the same idea in different terms,—employing, for instance, different languages, like ' mors,' ' death,' and ' thanatos.' (See *Proc.*, S.P.R., xxii. 295-304.) Another is when the idea is thoroughly masked and brought in only by some quotation—perhaps by a quotation the special significance of which is unknown to the medium who reproduces it, and is only detected and interpreted by a subsequent investigator to whom all the records are submitted.   Sometimes a quotation is maltreated, evidently with intention by the communicator ; the important word to which attention is being directed being either omitted or changed.

A large number of examples of this more complex kind of cross-correspondence are reported at length in the *Proceedings* of the Society for Psychical Research ; see especially vol. xxi. p. 369 and xxii. *passim*, or a briefer statement in *Survival of Man*, chap. xxv.

Some of these instances as expounded by Mr. Piddington may seem extraordinarily complicated and purposely concealed. That is admitted.   They are specially designed to eliminate the possibility of unintended and unconscious telepathy direct from one medium to another, and to throw the investigator back on what is asserted to be the truth, namely that the mind of one single communicator, or the combined mind of a group of communicators,— all men of letters,—is sending carefully designed messages through different channels, in order to prove primarily the reality of the operating intelligence, and incidentally the genuineness of the mediums who are capable of receiving and transmitting fragments of messages so worded as to appear to each of them separately mere meaningless jargon ; though ultimately when all the messages are put together by a skilled person the meaning is luminous enough.   Moreover, we are assured that the puzzles and hidden allusions contained in these messages are not more difficult than literary scholars are accustomed to ; that, indeed, they are precisely of similar order

This explanation is unnecessary for the simple cross-correspondences (c.c.) sometimes obtained and reported here ; but the subject itself is an important one, and is not always understood even by investigators, so I take this opportunity of referring to it in order to direct the attention of those who need stricter evidence to more profitable records.

GENERAL NOTE

Returning to the kind of family records here given, in which evidence is sporadic rather than systematic though none the less effective, one of the minor points, which yet is of interest, is the appropriate way in which different youths greet their relatives.   Thus, while Paul calls his father ' Daddy ' and his mother by pet names, as he used to ; and while Raymond calls us simply ' Father ' and ' Mother,' as he used to ; another youth named Ralph —an athlete who had fallen after splendid service in the war—greeted his father, when at length that gentleman was induced to attend a sitting, with the extraordinary salutation " Ullo 'Erb ! ", spelt out as one word through the table ; though, to the astonishment of the medium, it was admitted to be consistent and evidential.   The ease and freedom with which this Ralph managed to communicate are astonishing, and I am tempted to add as an appendix some records which his family have kindly allowed me to see, but I refrain, as they have nothing to do with Raymond.

CHAPTER XIII

AN O. J. L. SITTING WITH PETERS

ON the 29th of October I had a sitting with Peters alone, unknown to the family, who I felt sure were still sceptical concerning the whole subject. It was arranged for, as an anonymous sitting, by my friend Mr. J. Arthur Hill of Bradford. The things said were remarkable, and distinctly pointed to clairvoyance. I am doubtful about reporting more than a few lines, however. There was a great deal that might be taken as encouraging and stimulating, intermixed with the more evidential portions. A small part of this sitting is already reported in Chapter III, and might now be read by anyone interested in the historical sequence.

A few unimportant opening lines I think it necessary to report, because of their connexion with another sitting :—

Anonymous O. J. L. Sitting with A. Vout Peters at 15 *Devereux Court, Fleet Street, on Friday,* 29 *October* 1915, *from* 10.30 *to* 11.45 *a.m.*

(Sitter only spoken of as a friend of Mr. Hill) [1]

PETERS.—Before we begin, I must say something : I feel that I have a certain fear of you, I don't know what it is, but you affect me in a most curious way. I must tell you the honest truth before I am controlled. . . .

> [Whatever this may mean it corresponds with what was said at the previous M. F. A. L. Sitting, p. 132, though M. F. A. L. had sat as a friend of Mrs. Kennedy in her house,

---

[1] Whether it be assumed that I was known or not, does not much matter ; but I have no reason to suppose that I was. Rather the contrary. Peters seems barely to look at his sitters, and to be anxious to receive no normal information.

and I sat as a friend of Mr. Hill in Peters's room, and no sort of connexion was indicated between us.]

(Soon afterwards the medium twitched, snapped his fingers, and began to speak as ' Moon-stone ' :—)

" I come to speak to you, but I must get my Medie deep ; we get superficial control first, and then go deeper and deeper ; with your strong personality you frighten him a little ; I find a little fear in the medium. . . . You bring with you a tremendous amount of work and business," etc.

Now I get a new influence : an old lady, medium height, rounded face ; light eyes ; grey hair ; small nose ; lips somewhat thin, or held together as suppressed ; a lady with very strong will ; tremendously forcible she is. She passed away after leading a very active life. . . .

She's a very good woman. It is not the first time she has come back. She tells me to tell you that they are all here. ALL. Because they are trying to reach out to you their love and sympathy at the present occasion, and they are thanking you both for the opportunity of getting back to you. " We are trying all we can also to bring him back to you, to let you realise that your faith, which you have held as a theory "—it is curious, but she wants me to say her message word for word—" as a theory for years, shall be justified." Then she rejoices . . . (and refers to religious matters, etc.). [This clearly suggested the relative whose first utterance of this kind is reported so long ago as 1889 in *Proc.*, S.P.R., vi. 468 and 470.]

Now she brings up a young man from the back. I must explain what we mean by ' the back ' some time.

o. j. l.—But I understand.

He is of medium height ; somewhat light eyes ; the face browned somewhat ; fairly long nose ; the lips a little full ; nice teeth. He is standing pretty quiet.

Look here, I know this man ! And it is not

the first time he has been to us. Now he smiles,
'cos I recsonise him [so pronounced], but he comes
back very, very strongly. He tells me that he is
pushing the door open wider. Now he wants me
to give you a message. He is going to try to come
down with you ; because it looks to me as though
you are travelling to-day. " Down," he says.
" I come down with you. We will try " (he says
' we,' not ' I '), " we will try to bring our united
power to prove to you that I am here ; I and the
other young man who helped me, and who will
help me."

>[The association of Raymond with ' another
>young man,' and his intention to come ' down '
>with me when I travelled back home on the
>same day to meet Mrs. Kennedy there, are
>entirely appropriate.—O. J. L.]

Look here, it is your boy ! Because he calls
you ' Father ' ; not ' Pa,' nor anything, but
' Father.' [True.]

O. J. L.—Yes, my son.

Wait a minute ; now he wants to tell me one
thing : " I am so glad that you took such a
common-sense view of the subject, and that you
didn't force it on mother. But you spoke of it as
an actuality. She treated it like she treats all your
things that she couldn't understand ; giving you,
as she always has done, the credit of being more
clever than herself. But when I came over as I
did, and in her despair, she came to you for help ;
but she wanted to get away from anything that
you should influence."

>[Unfortunately, some one knocked at the door
>—a servant probably, wanting to come in
>and clear the room. The medium jerked
>and said, " Tell them to go away." I called
>out, " Can't come in now, private, engaged."
>Some talking continued outside for a little
>time—very likely it was some one wanting
>an interview with Peters. After a time the
>disturbance ceased. It was not very loud ;
>the medium ignored it, except for the rather

loud and strong knock, which certainly
perturbed him.]
Tell me where I was.
(I repeated : " She wanted to get away from
anything that you should influence.")
Oh yes. He wants to say that you were quite
right in staying away and letting her work altogether by herself. She was able to do better than
if you had been there. You would have spoilt it.

Your common-sense method of approaching the
subject in the family has been the means of helping him to come back as he has been able to do ;
and had he not known what you had told him,
then it would have been far more difficult for him
to come back. He is very deliberate in what he
says. He is a young man that knows what he is
saying.
Do you know F. W. M. ?
O. J. L.—Yes, I do.
[The next portion, relating to Myers, has
been already reported in Chapter III ; and
the concluding portion, which is rather
puzzling, shall be suppressed, as it relates
to other people.]

Towards the end ' Moonstone ' began talking about
himself, which he does in an interesting manner, and I
shall perhaps give him an opportunity of saying more
about the assumption of ' control ' from his point of view.
Meanwhile I quote this further extract :—

' MOONSTONE'S ' ACCOUNT OF HIMSELF

Have you been suffering inside ?
O. J. L.—No, not that I know of.
Your heart's been bleeding. You never thought you
could love so deep. There must be more or less suffering.
Even though you are crucified, you will arise the stronger,
bigger, better man. But out of this suffering and crucifixion, oh, how you are going to help humanity ! This is a
big work. It has been prophesied. It is through the
sufferings of humanity that humanity is reached. It
must be through pain. Let me tell you something about
myself. I was Yogi—do you understand ?
O. J. L.—Yes ; a kind of hermit.

12

I lived a selfish life : a good life, but a selfish one, though I didn't know it then.   I isolated myself and did not mix with people, not even with family life.   When I go over, I find it was a negative goodness, so then I wanted to help humanity, because I hadn't helped it.   I had not taken on the sufferings even of a family man.   It was useless.   And so that is why I came back to my Medie, and try to bear through him the sorrows of the world.   It is through suffering that humanity is helped.   That is one great thing in your beautiful religion ; you know what I mean—the sacrifice of Jesus.   He demonstrated eternity, but to do it He must be sacrificed and taste death.   So all who teach the high . . . must tread the same path ; there's no escaping the crucifixion, it comes in one way or another.   And you must remember, back in the past, when the good things came to you, how you began to realise (?) that there was a spirit world and a possibility of coming back.   Though you speak cautiously, yet possibly in your prayers to God you say, " Let me suffer, let me know my cross, so that I can benefit humanity " ;   and when you make a compact with the unseen world, it is kept.   You have told no one this, but it belongs to you and to your son.   Out of it will come much joy, much happiness to others.

Mr. Stead was, I understand, a friend to Peters, and how much of the above is tinged by Mr. Stead's influence, I cannot say : but immediately afterwards his name was mentioned, in the following way :—

Flashing down the line comes a message from Mr. Stead.   I can't help it, I must give it.   He says : " We did not see eye to eye ; you thought I was too impetuous and too rash, but our conclusions are about the same now. We are pretty well on a level, and I have realised, even through mistakes, that I have reached and influenced a world that is suffering and sorrowing.   But you have a world bigger and wider than mine, and your message will be bigger and will reach farther."

SUMMARY

As far as evidence is concerned, Peters has done well at each of the three sittings any member of my family has had with him since Raymond's death.   On the whole, I think he has done as well as any medium ; especially as the abstention from supplying him normally with any identifying information has been strict.

It is true that I have not, through Peters, asked test questions of which the answers were unknown to me, as I did at one sitting with Mrs. Leonard (Chapter IX). But the answers there given, though fairly good, and in my view beyond chance, were not perfect. Under the circumstances I think they could hardly have been expected to be perfect. It was little more than a month since the death, and new experiences and serious surroundings must have been crowding in upon the youth, so that old semi-frivolous reminiscences were difficult to recall. There was, however, with Peters no single incident so striking as the name ' Norman,' to me unknown and meaningless, which was given in perfectly appropriate connexion through the table at Mrs. Leonard's.

CHAPTER XIV

FIRST SITTING OF LIONEL (ANONYMOUS)

AT length, on 17 November 1915, Raymond's brother Lionel (L. L.) went to London to see if he could get an anonymous sitting with Mrs. Leonard, without the intervention of Mrs. Kennedy or anybody. He was aware that by that time the medium must have sat with dozens of strangers and people not in any way connected with our family, and fortunately he succeeded in getting admitted as a complete stranger. This therefore is worth reporting, and the contemporary record follows. A few portions are omitted, partly for brevity, partly because private, but some non-evidential and what may seem rather absurd statements are reproduced, for what they are worth. It must be understood that Feda is speaking throughout, and that she is sometimes reporting in the third person, sometimes in the first, and sometimes speaking for herself. It is unlikely that lucidity is constant all the time, and Feda may have to do some padding. She is quite good and fairly careful, but of course, like all controls, she is responsible for certain mannerisms, and in her case for childishly modified names like ' Paulie,' etc. The dramatic circumstances of a sitting will be familiar to people of experience. The record tries to reproduce them—probably with but poor success. And it is always possible that the attempt, however conscientious, may furnish opportunity for ridicule, if any hostile critic thinks ridicule appropriate.

L. L.'s Sitting with Mrs. Leonard at her house, as a stranger, no one else being present, 12 o'clock, Wednesday, 17 November 1915

INTRODUCTION BY O. J. L.

Lionel wrote to Mrs. Leonard at her old address in Warwick Avenue, for I had forgotten that she had moved, and I had not told him her new address.   He wrote on plain paper from Westminster without signing it, saying that he would be coming at a certain time.   But she did not get the letter ; so that, when he arrived about noon on Wednesday, 17 November, he arrived as a complete stranger without an appointment.   He had at first gone to the wrong house and been redirected.   Mrs. Leonard answered the door.   She took him in at once when he said he wanted a sitting.   She drew the blind down, and lit a red lamp as usual.   She told him that she was controlled by ' Feda.'   Very quickly—in about two minutes—the trance began, and Feda spoke.

Here follows his record :—

REPORT BY L. L.

Subsequent annotations, in square brackets, are by O. J. L.

Good morning !

Why, you are psychic yourself !

L. L.—I didn't know I was.

It will come out later.

There are two spirits standing by you ; the elder is fully built up, but the younger is not clear yet.

The elder is on the tall side, and well built ; he has a beard round his chin, but no moustache.

(This seemed to worry Feda, and she repeated it several times, as if trying to make it clear.)

A beard round chin, and hair at the sides, but upper lip shaved. A good forehead, eyebrows heavy and rather straight—not arched—eyes greyish ; hair thin on top, and grey at the sides and back. It looks as if it had been brown before it went grey. A fine-looking face.   He is building up something. He suffered here before he passed out (medium indicating chest or stomach). Letter W is held up. (See photograph facing p. 258.)

[This is the one that to other members of the family had been called Grandfather W., p. 143.]

There is another spirit.

Somebody is laughing.

Don't joke—it is serious.

(This was whispered, and sounded as if said to some one else, not to me.)

It's a young man, about twenty-three, or

might be twenty-five, judging only by appearance.
Tall ; well-built ; not stout, well-built ; brown hair,
short at the sides and back ; clean shaven ; face
more oval than round ; nose not quite straight,
rather rounded, and broader at the nostrils.

(*Whispering.*) Feda can't see his face.

(*Then clearly.*) He won't let Feda see his face ;
he is laughing.

(*Whispered several times.*) L, L, L.

(*Then said out loud.*) L. This is not his name ;
he puts it by you.

(*Whispering again.*) Feda knows him—Raymond.

Oh, it's Raymond !

(The medium here jumps about, and fidgets with
her hands, just as a child would when pleased.)

That is why he would not show his face,
because Feda would know him.

He is patting you on the shoulder hard. You
can't feel it, but he thinks he is hitting you hard.

[It seems to have been a trick of his to pat a
brother on the shoulder gradually harder and
harder till humorous retaliation set in.]

He is very bright.

This is the way it is given—it's an impression.

He has been trying to come to you at home, but
there has been some horrible mix-ups ; not really
horrible, but a muddle. He really got through
to you, but other conditions get through there,
and mixes him up.

[This evidently refers to some private ' Mariemont ' sittings, without a medium, with
which neither Feda nor Mrs. Leonard had
had anything to do. It therefore shows
specific knowledge and is of the nature
of a mild cross-correspondence ; cf. p. 217.]

L. L.—How can we improve it ?

He does not understand it sufficiently himself
yet. Other spirits get in, not bad spirits, but
ones that like to feel they are helping. The
peculiar manifestations are not him, and it only
confuses him terribly. Part of it was him, but

when the table was careering about, it was not him at all. He started it, but something comes along stronger than himself, and he loses the control.

(*Whispered.*) Feda, can't you suggest something ? "

[This seemed to be a reported part of conversation on the other side.]

Be very firm when it starts to move about.

Prayer helps when things are not relevant.

He is anxious about F.

L. L.—I don't know who F. is. Is it some friend ?

(Medium here fidgets.)

Letter F. all right ; it's some one he is interested in.

He says he is sorry he worried his mother about [an incident mentioned at some previous sitting].

L. L.—Was it a mistake ?

Yes, tell her, because (etc. etc.). When I thought it over I knew it was a mistake. If it had been now, and I had a little more experience in control, I should not have said so ; but it was at the beginning—everything seemed such a rush—and I was not quite sure of what I did get through. He did not look at things in the right pers—perpec——

L. L.—Perspective ?

Yes, that's what he said.

Do you follow me, old chap ?

L. L.—Perfectly.

L. L.—Do you remember a sitting at home when you told me you had a lot to tell me ?

Yes. What he principally wanted to say was about the place he is in. He could not *spell* it all out—too laborious. He felt rather upset at first. You do not feel so real as people do where he is, and walls appear transparent to him now. The great thing that made him reconciled to his new surroundings was—that things appear so solid and substantial. The first idea upon waking up was, I suppose, of what they call ' passing over.' It was only for a second or two, as you count time, [that it seemed a] shadowy vague place, everything vapoury and vague. He had that feeling about it.

The first person to meet him was Grandfather.

(This was said very carefully, as if trying to get it right with difficulty.)

And others then, some of whom he had only heard about. They all appeared to be so solid, that he could scarcely believe that he had passed over.

He lives in a house—a house built of bricks—and there are trees and flowers, and the ground is solid. And if you kneel down in the mud, apparently you get your clothes soiled. The thing I don't understand yet is that the night doesn't follow the day here, as it did on the earth plane. It seems to get dark sometimes, when he would like it to be dark, but the time in between light and dark is not always the same. I don't know if you think all this is a bore.

(I was here thinking whether my pencils would last out ; I had two, and was starting on the second one.)

What I am worrying round about is, how it's made, of what it is composed. I have not found out yet, but I've got a theory. It is not an original idea of my own ; I was helped to it by words let drop here and there.

People who think everything is created by thought are wrong. I thought that for a little time, that one's thoughts formed the buildings and the flowers and trees and solid ground ; but there is more than that.

He says something of this sort :—

[This means that Feda is going to report in the third person again, or else to speak for herself.—O. J. L.]

There is something always rising from the earth plane—something chemical in form. As it rises to ours, it goes through various changes and solidifies on our plane. Of course I am only speaking of where I am now.

He feels sure that it is something given off

from the earth, that makes the solid trees and flowers, etc.

He does not know any more. He is making a study of this, but it takes a good long time.

L. L.—I should like to know whether he can get into touch with anybody on earth ?

Not always.

Only those wishing to see him, and who it would be right for him to see. Then he sees them before he has thought.

I don't seem to wish for anything.

He does not wish to see anybody unless they are going to be brought to him.

I am told that I can meet anyone at any time that I want to ; there is no difficulty in the way of it. That is what makes it such a jolly fine place to live in.

L. L.—Can he help people here ?

That is part of his work, but there are others doing that ; the greatest amount of his work is still at the war.

I've been home—only likely I've been home— but my actual work is at the war.

He has something to do with father, though his work still lies at the war, helping on poor chaps literally shot into the spirit world.

L. L.—Can you see ahead at all ?

He thinks sometimes that he can, but it's not easy to predict.

I don't think that I really know any more than when on earth.

L. L.—Can you tell anything about how the war is going on ?

There are better prospects for the war. On all sides now more satisfactory than it has been before.

This is not apparent on the earth plane, but I feel more . . . the surface, and more satisfied than before.

I can't help feeling intensely interested. I believe we have lost Greece, and am not sure that it was not due to our own fault. We have

only done now what should have been done
months ago.

He does not agree about Serbia. Having left
them so long has had a bad effect upon Roumania.
Roumania thinks will she be in the same boat, if
she joins in.

All agree that Russia will do well right through
the winter. They are going to show what they
can do. They are used to their ground and winter
conditions, and Germany is not. There will be
steady progress right through the winter.

I think there is something looming now.

Some of the piffling things I used to be interested in, I have forgotten all about. There is such
a lot to be interested in here. I realise the
seriousness sometimes of this war. . . . It is like
watching a most interesting race or game gradually
developing before you. I am doing work in it,
which is not so interesting as watching.

L. L.—Have you any message for home ?

Of course love to his mother, and to all, specially to mother. H. is doing very well. [Meaning
his sister Honor.]

L. L.—In what way ?

H. is helping him in a psychic way ; she makes it
easy for him. He doesn't think he need tell father
anything, he is so certain in himself meaning
Raymond, in spite of silly mistakes. It disappoints
him. We must separate out the good from the
bad, and not try more than one form; not the
jig—jig——

L. L.—I know ; jigger. [A kind of Ouija.]

No. He didn't like the jigger. He thinks he
can work the table. [See Chapter XIX.]

L. L.—Would you tell me how I could help in any way?

Just go very easily, only let one person speak,
as he has said before. It can be H. or L. L. Settle
on one person to put the questions, the different
sound of voices confuses him, and he mixes it up
with questions from another's thoughts. In time
he hopes it will be not so difficult. He wouldn't
give it up, he loves it. Don't try more than twice

a week, perhaps only once a week. Try to keep the same times always, and to the same day if possible.

He is going.

Give my love to them all. Tell them I am very happy. Very well, and plenty to do, and intensely interested. I did suffer from shock at first, but I'm extremely happy now.

I'm off. He won't say good-bye.

A lady comes too : A girl, about medium height ; on the slender side, not thin, but slender ; face, oval shape ; blue eyes ; lightish brown hair, not golden.

L. L.—Can she give a name—I cannot guess who she is from the description ?

She builds up an L.

Not like the description when she was on earth. Very little earth life. She is related to you. She has grown up in the spirit life.

Oh, she is your sister !

She is fair ; not so tall as you ; a nice face ; blue eyes.

L. L.—I know her name now. [See at a previous sitting where this deceased sister is described, p. 159.]

Give her love to them at home, but also principally to mother. And say that she and her brother, not Raymond, have been also to the sittings at home.

She is giving his name. She gives it in such a funny way, as if she was writing, so—— She wrote an N, then quickly changed it into a W. [See also pp. 134, 159, and 190.]

She brings lilies with her ; she is singing—it's like humming ; Feda can't hear the words.

She is going too—power is going.

L. L.—Give my love to her.

Feda sends her love also.

Raymond was having a joke by not showing his face to Feda.

Good-bye.

(*Sitting ended at* 1.30 *p.m.*)

CHAPTER XV

SITTING OF M. F. A. L. WITH MRS. LEONARD

Friday, November 26, 1915

A FEW things may be reported from a sitting which Lady Lodge had with Mrs. Leonard on 26 November, however absurd they may seem. They are of course repeated by the childish control Feda, but I do not by that statement of bare fact intend to stigmatise them in any way. Criticism of unverifiable utterances seems to me premature.

The sitting began without preliminaries as usual. It is not a particularly good one, and the notes are rather incomplete, especially near the end of the time, when Feda seemed to wander from the point, and when rather tedious descriptions of people began. These are omitted.

Sitting of M. F. A. L. with Mrs. Leonard at her house on Friday, 26 November 1915, from 3 to 4.30 p.m.

(No one else present.)

(The sitting began with a statement from Feda that she liked Lionel, and that Raymond had taken her down to his home. Then she reported that Raymond said :—)

"Mother darling, I am so happy, and so much more so because you are."

M. F. A. L.—Yes, we are ; and as your father says, we can face Christmas now.

Raymond says he will be there.

M. F. A. L.—We will put a chair for him.

Yes, he will come and sit in it.

He wants to strike a bargain with you. He

says, " If I come there, there must be no sadness. I don't want to be a ghost at the feast. There mustn't be one sigh. Please, darling, keep them in order, rally them up. Don't let them. If they do, I shall have the hump." (Feda, *sotto voce.*— ' hump,' what he say.)

M. F. A. L.—We will all drink his health and happiness.

Yes, you can think I am wishing you health too.

M. F. A. L.—We were interested in hearing about his clothes and things ; we can't think how he gets them ! [The reference is to a second sitting of Lionel, not available for publication.]

They are all man-u-fac-tured. [Feda stumbling over long words.]

Can you fancy you see me in white robes ? Mind, I didn't care for them at first, and I wouldn't wear them. Just like a fellow gone to a country where there is a hot climate—an ignorant fellow, not knowing what he is going to ; it's just like that. He may make up his mind to wear his own clothes a little while, but he will soon be dressing like the natives. He was allowed to have earth clothes here until he got acclimatised ; they let him ; they didn't force him. I don't think I will ever be able to make the boys see me in white robes.

Mother, don't go doing too much.

M. F. A. L.—I am very strong.

You think you are, but you tire yourself out too much. It troubles me.

M. F. A. L.—Yes, but I should be quite glad to come over there, if I could come quickly, even though I am so happy here, and I don't want to leave people.

Don't you think I would be glad to have you here ! If you do what he says, you will come over when the time comes—quick, sharp.

He says he comes and sees you in bed. The reason for that is the air is so quiet then. You often go up there in the spirit-land while your body is asleep.

M. F. A. L.—Would you like us to sit on the same night as Mrs. Kennedy sits, or on different nights ? [Meaning in trials for cross-correspondences.]

On the same night, as it wastes less time. Besides, he forgets, if there is too long an interval. He wants to get something of the same sort to each place.

William and Lily come to play with Raymond. Lily had gone on, but came back to be with Raymond. [These mean his long-deceased infant brother and sister.]

(More family talk omitted.)

Get some sittings soon, so as to get into full swing by Christmas. Tell them when they get him through, and he says, " Raymond," tell them to go very easily, and not to ask too many questions. Questions want thinking out beforehand. They are not to talk among themselves, because then they get part of one thing and part of another. And not to say, " No, don't ask him that," or he gets mixed.

Do you know we sometimes have to prepare answers a little before we transmit them ; it is a sort of mental effort to give answers through the table. When they say, do you ask, we begin to get ready to speak through the table. Write down a few questions and keep to them.

CHAPTER XVI

O. J. L. SITTING OF DECEMBER 3

WITH SOME UNVERIFIABLE MATTER

AT a sitting which I had with Mrs. Leonard on 3 December 1915, information was given about the photograph—as already reported, Chapter IV. In all these ' Feda ' sittings, the remarks styled *sotto voce* represent conversation between Feda and the communicator, not addressed to the sitter at all. I always try to record these scraps when I can overhear them ; for they are often interesting, and sometimes better than what is subsequently reported as the result of the brief conversation. For she appears to be uttering under her breath not only her own question or comment, but also what she is being told ; and sometimes names are in that way mentioned correctly, when afterwards she muddles them. For instance, on one occasion she said *sotto voce,* " What you say ? Rowland ? " (in a clear whisper) ; and then, aloud, " He says something like Ronald." Whereas in this case ' Rowland ' proved to be correct. The dramatically childlike character of Feda seems to carry with it a certain amount of childish irresponsibility. Raymond says that he " has to talk to her seriously about it sometimes."

A few other portions, not about the photograph, are included in the record of this sitting, some of a very non-evidential and perhaps ridiculous kind, but I do not feel inclined to suppress them. (For reasons, see Chapter XII.) Some of them are rather amusing. Unverifiable statements have hitherto been generally suppressed, in reporting Piper and other sittings ; but here, in deference partly to the opinion of Professor Bergson—

who when he was in England urged that statements about life on the other side, properly studied, like travellers' tales, might ultimately furnish proof more logically cogent than was possible from mere access to earth memories—they are for the most part reproduced. I should think, myself, that they are of very varying degrees of value, and peculiarly liable to unintentional sophistication by the medium. They cannot be really satisfactory, as we have no means of bringing them to book. The difficulty is that Feda encounters many sitters, and though the majority are just inquirers, taking what comes and saying very little, one or two may be themselves full of theories, and may either intentionally or unconsciously convey them to the ' control ' ; who may thereafter retail them as actual information, without perhaps being sure whence they were derived. Some books, moreover, have been published of late, purporting to give information about ill-understood things in a positive and assured manner, and it is possible that the medium has read these and may be influenced by them. It will be regrettable if these books are taken as authoritative by people unable to judge of the scientific errors which are conspicuous in their more normal portions ; and the books themselves seem likely to retard the development of the subject in the minds of critical persons.

Sitting with Mrs. Leonard at her House on Friday, 3 December 1915, *from* 6.10 *p.m. to* 8.20 *p.m.*

(O. J. L. alone.)

This is a long record, because I took verbatim notes, but I propose to inflict it all upon the reader, in accordance with promise to report unverifiable and possibly absurd matter, just as it comes, and even to encourage it.

Feda soon arrived, said good evening, jerked about on the chair, and squeaked or chuckled, after her manner when indicating pleasure. Then, without preliminaries, she spoke :—

He is waiting ; he's looking very pleased. He's awful anxious to tell you about the place where he lives ; he doesn't understand *yet* how it looks so solid. (Cf. p. 184.)

(Feda, *sotto voce.*—What you say ? Yes, Feda knows.) He's been watching lately different kinds of people what come over, and the different kinds of effect it has on them.

Oh, it is interesting, he says—much more than on the old earth plane. I didn't want to leave you and mother and all of them, but it *is* interesting. I wish you could come over for one day, and be with me here. There are times you do go there, but you won't remember. They have all been over with him at night-time, and so have you, but he thought it very hard you couldn't remember. If you did, he is told (he doesn't know it himself, but he is told this), the brain would scarcely bear the burden of the double existence, and would be unfitted for its daily duties ; so the memory is shut out. That is the explanation given to him.

(Feda, *sotto voce.*—What, Raymond ? Al—lec, he says, Al—lec, Al—lec.)

He keeps on saying something about Alec. He has been trying to get to Alec, to communicate with him ; and he couldn't see if he made himself felt—whether he really got through.

> (The medium hitherto had been holding O. J. L.'s left hand ; here she let go, Feda saying : He will let you have your own hand back.)

He thought he had got into a bedroom, and that he knocked ; but there wasn't much notice taken.

O. J. L.—Alec must come here sometime.[1]

Yes, he wanted to see him.

And he also hopes to be able to talk to Lionel with the direct voice ; not here, he says, but somewhere else. He is very anxious to speak to him. Through a chap, he says, a direct voice chap.

O. J. L.—Very well, I will take the message.

[1] Alec had had a sitting with Peters, not with Mrs. Leonard.

13

Well, he says, he wants to try once or twice. He wants to be able to say what he says to Feda in another way. He thinks he could get through in his own home sometime. He would much rather have it there. And he thinks that if he got through once or twice with direct voice, he might be able to do better in his own home. H. is psychic, he says, but he is afraid of hurting her; he doesn't want to take too much from her. But he really is going to get through. He really has got through at home; but silly spirits wanted to have a game. There was a strange feeling there; he didn't seem to know how much he was doing himself, so he stood aside part of the time. [Mariemont sittings are reported later. Chapter XIX.]

Then the photograph episode came, as reported in Chapter IV.

Then it went on (Feda talking, of course, all the time) :—

He says he has been trying to go to somebody, and see somebody he used to know. He's not related to them, and the name begins with S. It's a gentleman, he says, and he can't remember, or can't tell Feda the name, but it begins with S. He was trying to get to them, but is not sure that he succeeded.

O. J. L.—Did he want to ?

He says it was only curiosity; but he likes to feel that he can look up anybody. But he says, if they take no notice, I shall give up soon, only I just like to see what it feels like to be looking at them from where I am.

O. J. L.—Does he want to say anything more about his house or his clothes or his body ?

Oh yes. He is bursting to tell you.

He says, my body's very similar to the one I had before. I pinch myself sometimes to see if it's real, and it is, but it doesn't seem to hurt as much as when I pinched the flesh body. The internal organs don't seem constituted on the same lines as before. They can't be quite the same. But to all appearances, and outwardly, they are the same as before.   I can move somewhat more freely, he says.

Oh, there's one thing, he says, I have never seen anybody bleed.

o. j. l.—Wouldn't he bleed if he pricked himself?

He never tried it.   But as yet he has seen no blood at all.

o. j. l.—Has he got ears and eyes?

Yes, yes, and eyelashes, and eyebrows, exactly the same, and a tongue and teeth.   He has got a new tooth now in place of another one he had—one that wasn't quite right then.   He has got it right, and a good tooth has come in place of the one that had gone.

He knew a man that had lost his arm, but he has got another one.   Yes, he has got two arms now.   He seemed as if without a limb when first he entered the astral, seemed incomplete, but after a while it got more and more complete, until he got a new one.   He is talking of people who have lost a limb for some years.

o. j. l.—What about a limb lost in battle?

Oh, if they have only just lost it, it makes no difference, it doesn't matter; they are quite all right when they get here.   But I am told—he doesn't know this himself, but he has been told—that when anybody's blown to pieces, it takes some time for the spirit-body to complete itself, to gather itself all in, and to be complete.   It dissipated a certain amount of substance which is undoubtedly theric, theric—etheric, and it has to be concentrated again.   The *spirit* isn't blown apart, of course,—he doesn't mean that,—but it has an effect upon it.   He hasn't seen all this, but he has been inquiring because he is interested.

o. j. l.—What about bodies that are burnt?

Oh, if they get burnt by accident, if they know about it on this side, they detach the spirit first. What we call a spirit-doctor comes round and helps. But bodies should not be burnt on purpose.   We have terrible trouble sometimes over people who are cremated too soon; they shouldn't be.   It's a terrible thing; it has worried me. People are so careless. The idea seems to be—"hurry up and get them out of the way now that they are dead." Not until seven days, he says. They shouldn't be cremated for seven days.

O. J. L.—But what if the body goes bad?

When it goes bad, the spirit is already out. If that much (indicating a trifle) of spirit is left in the body, it doesn't start mortifying. It is the action of the spirit on the body that keeps it from mortifying. When you speak about a person 'dying upwards,' it means that the spirit is getting ready and gradually getting out of the body. He saw the other day a man going to be cremated two days after the doctor said he was dead. When his relations on this side heard about it, they brought a certain doctor on our side, and when they saw that the spirit hadn't got really out of the body, they magnetised it, and helped it out. But there was still a cord, and it had to be severed rather quickly, and it gave a little shock to the spirit, like as if you had something amputated; but it had to be done. He believes it has to be done in every case. If the body is to be consumed by fire, it is helped out by spirit-doctors. He doesn't mean that a spirit-body comes out of its own body, but an essence comes out of the body—oozes out, he says, and goes into the other body which is being prepared. Oozes, he says, like in a string. String, that's what he say. Then it seems to shape itself, or something meets it and shapes round it. Like as if they met and went together, and formed a duplicate of the body left behind. It's all very interesting.[1]

He told Lionel about his wanting a suit at first [at an unreported second sitting]. He never thought that they would be able to provide him with one.

O. J. L.—Yes, I know, Lionel told us; that you wanted

---

[1] I confess that I think that Feda may have got a great deal of this, perhaps all of it, from people who have read or written some of the books referred to in my introductory remarks. But inasmuch as her other utterances are often evidential, I feel that I have no right to pick and choose; *especially as I know nothing about it, one way or the other.*

something more like your old clothes at first, and that they didn't force you into new ones, but let you begin with the old kind, until you got accustomed to the place (p. 189).

Yes, he says, they didn't force me, but most of the people here wear white robes.

O. J. L.—Then, can you tell any difference between men and women ?

There are men here, and there are women here. I don't think that they stand to each other quite the same as they did on the earth plane, but they seem to have the same feeling to each other, with a different expression of it. There don't seem to be any children born here. People are sent into the physical body to have children on the earth plane; they don't have them here. But there's a feeling of love between men and women here which is of a different quality to that between two men or two women ; and husband and wife seem to meet differently from mother and son, or father and daughter. He says he doesn't want to eat now. But he sees some who do ; he says they have to be given something which has all the appearance of an earth food. People here try to provide everything that is wanted. A chap came over the other day, who *would* have a cigar. " That's finished them," he thought. He means he thought they would never be able to provide that. But there are laboratories over here, and they manufacture all sorts of things in them. Not like you do, out of solid matter, but out of essences, and ethers, and gases. It's not the same as on the earth plane, but they were able to manufacture what looked like a cigar. He didn't try one himself, because he didn't care to ; you know he wouldn't want to. But the other chap jumped at it. But when he began to smoke it, he didn't think so much of it ; he had four altogether, and now he doesn't look at one.[1] They don't seem to get the same satisfaction out of it, so gradually it seems to drop from them. But when they first

---

[1] Some of this Feda talk is at least humorous.

come they do want things. Some want meat,
and some strong drink ; they call for whisky sodas.
Don't think I'm stretching it, when I tell you that
they can manufacture even that. But when they
have had one or two, they don't seem to want it
so much—not those that are near here. He has
heard of drunkards who want it for months and
years over here, but he hasn't seen any. Those
I have seen, he says, don't want it any more—
like himself with his suit, he could dispense with it
under the new conditions.

He wants people to realise that it's just as
natural as on the earth plane.

O. J. L.—Raymond, you said your house was made of
bricks. How can that be ? What are the bricks
made of ?

That's what he hasn't found out yet. He is
told by some, who he doesn't think would lead him
astray, that they are made from sort of emana-
tions from the earth. He says there's something
rising, like atoms rising, and consolidating after
they come ; they are not solid when they come,
but we can collect and concentrate them—I
mean those that are with me. They appear to
be bricks, and when I touch them, they feel like
bricks ; and I have seen granite too.

There's something perpetually rising from
your plane ; practically invisible—in atoms when
it leaves your plane—but when it comes to the
ether, it gains certain other qualities round each
atom, and by the time it reaches us, certain people
take it in hand, and manufacture solid things from
it. Just as you can manufacture solid things.

All the decay that goes on on the earth plane
is not lost. It doesn't just form manure or dust.
Certain vegetable and decayed tissue does form
manure for a time, but it gives off an essence or
a gas, which ascends, and which becomes what
you call a ' smell.' Everything dead has a smell,
if you notice ; and I know now that the smell is
of actual use, because it is from that smell that
we are able to produce duplicates of whatever

form it had before it became a smell. Even old
wood has a smell different from new wood; you
may have to have a keen nose to detect these
things on the earth plane.

Old rags, he says (*sotto voce.*—Yes, all right,
Feda will go back), cloth decaying and going
rotten. Different kinds of cloth give off different
smells—rotting linen smells different to rotting
wool. You can understand how all this interests
me. Apparently, as far as I can gather, the
rotting wool appears to be used for making things
like tweeds on our side. But I know I am jumping, I'm guessing at it. My suit I expect was made
from decayed worsted on your side.[1]

Some people here won't take this in even yet—
about the material cause of all these things. They
go talking about spiritual robes made of light,
built by the thoughts on the earth plane. I
don't believe it. They go about thinking that it is
a thought robe that they're wearing, resulting
from the spiritual life they led ; and when we try
to tell them that it is manufactured out of
materials, they don't believe it. They say,
" No, no, it's a robe of light and brightness which
I manufactured by thought." So we just leave it.
But I don't say that they won't get robes quicker
when they have led spiritual lives down there ;
I think they do, and that's what makes them
think that they made the robes by their lives.

You know flowers, how they decay. We have
got flowers here ; your decayed flowers flower again
with us—beautiful flowers. Lily has helped me a
lot with flowers.

O. J. L. —Do you like her ?

Yes, but he didn't expect to see her.

(Feda, *sotto voce.*—No, Raymond, you don't
mean that.)

Yes, he does. He says he's afraid he wasn't very
polite to her when he met her at first ; he didn't
expect a grown-up sister there. Am I a little
brother, he said, or is she my little sister ? She

I have not yet traced the source of all this supposed information.

calls me her little brother, but I have a decided impression that she should be my little sister.

He feels a bit of a mystery : he has got a brother there he knows, but he says *two*.

(*Sotto voce.*—No, Yaymond, you can't have two. No, Feda doesn't understand.) Is it possible, he says, that he has got another brother—one that didn't live at all ?

O. J. L.—Yes, it is possible.

But he says, no earth life at all ! That's what's strange. I've seen some one that I am told is a brother, but I can't be expected to recognise him, can I ? I feel somehow closer to Lily than I do to that one. By and by I will get to know him, I dare say.

I'm told that I am doing very well in the short time I have been here. Taking to it—what he say ?—duck to water, he say.

O. J. L.—You know the earth is rolling along through space. How do you keep up with it ?

It doesn't seem like that to him.

O. J. L.—No, I suppose not. Do you see the stars ?

Yes, he sees the stars. The stars seem like what they did, only he feels closer to them. Not really closer, but they look clearer ; not appreciably closer, he says.

O. J. L.—Are they grouped the same ? Do you see the Great Bear, for instance ?

Oh yes, he sees the Great Bear. And he sees the ch, ch, chariot, he says.

O. J. L.—Do you mean Cassiopeia ?

Yes. [But I don't suppose he did.]

There's one more mystery to him yet, it doesn't seem day and night quite by regular turns, like it did on the earth.

O. J. L.—But I suppose you see the sun ?

Yes, he sees the sun ; but it seems always about the same degree of warmth, he doesn't feel heat or cold where he is. The sun doesn't make him uncomfortably hot. That is not because the sun has lost its heat, but because he hasn't got the same body that sensed the heat. When he comes into contact with the earth plane, and is manifesting, then he feels a little cold or warm— at least he does when a medium is present— not when he comes in the ordinary way just to look round. When he sang last night, he felt cold for a minute or two.

O. J. L.—Did he sing ?

Yes, he and Paulie had a scuffle. Paulie was singing first, and Yaymond thought he would like to sing too, so he chipped in at the end. He sang about three verses. It wasn't difficult, because there was a good deal of power there. Also nobody except Mrs. Kathie knew who he was, and so all eyes were not on him, and they were not expecting it, and that made it easier for him. He says it wasn't so difficult as keeping up a conversation ; he just took the organs there, and materialised his own voice in her throat. He didn't find it very difficult, he hadn't got to think of anything, or collect his ideas ; there was an easy flow of words, and he just sang. And I *did* sing, he says ; I thought I'd nearly killed the medium. She hadn't any voice at all after. When he heard himself that he had really got it, he had to let go. Raised the roof, he says, and he *did* enjoy it !

(Here Feda gave an amused chuckle with a jump and a squeak.)

He was just practising there, Yaymond says. At first he thought it wouldn't be easy.

[This relates to what I am told was a real occurrence at a private gathering ; but it is not evidential.]

O. J. L.—Raymond, you know you want to give me some proofs. What kind of proofs do you think are best ? Have you talked it over with Mr. Myers, and have you decided on the kind of proof that will be most evidential ?

I don't know yet. I feel divided between two ways : One is to give you objective proof, such as simple materialisations and direct voice, which you can set down and have attested. Or else I should have to give you information about my different experiences here, either something like what I am doing now, or through the table, or some other way. But he doesn't know whether he will be able to do the two things together.

O. J. L.—No, not likely, not at the same time. But you can take opportunities of saying more about your life there.

Yes, that's why he has been collecting information. He does so want to encourage people to look forward to a life they will certainly have to enter upon, and realise that it is a rational life. All this that he has been giving you now, and that I gave to Lionel, you must sort out, and put in order, because I can only give it scrappily. I want to study things here a lot. Would you think it selfish if I say I wouldn't like to be back now?—I wouldn't give this up for anything. Don't think it selfish, or that I want to be away from you all. I have still got you, because I feel you so close, closer even. I wouldn't come back, I wouldn't for anything that anyone could give me.

He hardly liked to put it that way to his mother.

Is Alec here ?   (Feda looking round.)

O. J. L.—No, but I hope he will be coming.

Tell him not to say who he is.   I did enjoy myself that first time that Lionel came—I could talk for hours.

(O. J. L. had here looked at his watch quietly.)

I could talk for hours ; don't go yet.

He says he thinks he was lucky when he passed on, because he had so many to meet him. That came, he knows now, through your having been in with this thing for so long. He wants to impress this on those that you will be writing for : that it makes it so much easier for them if they and their friends know about it beforehand.   It's awful when they have passed over and won't believe it for weeks,—they just think they're dreaming. And they won't realise things at all sometimes. He

doesn't mind telling you now that, just at first,
when he woke up, he felt a little depression.   But
it didn't last long.   He cast his eyes round, and soon
he didn't mind.   But it was like finding yourself in a
strange place, like a strange city ; with people you
hadn't seen, or not seen for a long time, round you.
Grandfather was with me straight away ; and
presently Robert.   I got mixed up between two
Roberts.   And there's some one called Jane comes
to him, who calls herself an aunt, he says.   Jane.
He's uncertain about her.   Jane—Jennie.   She
calls herself an aunt ; he is told to call her ' Aunt
Jennie.'   Is she my Aunt Jennie ? he says.

O. J. L.—No, but your mother used to call her that.

[And so on, simple talk about family and friends.]

He has brought that doggie again, nice doggie.
A doggie that goes like this, and twists about
(Feda indicating a wriggle).   He has got a nice tail,
not a little stumpy tail, nice tail with nice hair on it.
He sits up like that sometimes, and comes down
again, and puts his tongue out of his mouth.   He's
got a cat too, plenty of animals, he says.   He
hasn't seen any lions and tigers, but he sees horses,
cats, dogs, and birds.   He says you know this
doggie ; he has nice hair, a little wavy, which sticks
up all over him, and has twists at the end.   Now
he's jumping round.   He hasn't got a very pointed
face, but it isn't like a little pug-dog either ; it's
rather a long shape.   And he has nice ears what
flaps, not standing up ; nice long hairs on them
too.   A darkish colour he looks, darkish, as near
as Feda can see him.   [See photograph, p. 278.]

O. J. L.—Does he call him by any name ?

He says, ' Not him.'

(Sotto voce.—What you mean ' not him ' ?   It
is a ' him ' ; you don't call him ' it.')

No, he won't explain.   No, he didn't give it a
name.   It can jump.

[All this about a she-dog called Curly, whose
death had been specially mentioned by
' Myers ' through another medium some
years ago,—an incident reported privately

to the S.P.R. at the time,—is quite good as far as it goes ?

He has met a spirit here, he says, who knows you—G. Nothing to do with the other G. Some one that's a very fine sort indeed. His name begins with G—Gal, Gals, Got, Got,—he doesn't know him very well, but it sounds like that. It isn't who you feel, though it might have been, nothing to do with that at all. Some one called Golt— he didn't know him, but he is interested in you, and had met you.

It's surprising how many people come up to me, he says, and shake me by the hand, and speak to me. I don't know them from Adam. (*Sotto voce.*—Adam, he say.) But they are doing me honour here, and some of them are such fine men. He doesn't know them, but they all seem to be interested in you, and they say, " Oh, are you his son? —how-do-you-do ? "

Feda is losing control.

O. J. L.—Well, good-bye, Raymond, then, and God bless you.

God bless *you.* I do so want you to know that I am very happy. And bless them all. My love to you. I can't tell what I feel, but you can guess. It's difficult to put into words. My love to all. God bless you and everybody. Good-bye, father.

O. J. L.—Good-bye, Raymond. Good-bye, Feda.

(Feda here gave a jerk, and a ' good-bye.')

Love to her what 'longs to you, and to Lionel Feda knows what your name is. ' Soliver,' yes. (Another squeak.)

(*Sitting ended 8.20 p.m.*)

The conclusion of sittings is seldom of an evidential character, and by most people would not be recorded ; but occasionally it may be best to quote one completely, just as a specimen of what may be called the ' manner ' of a sitting.

CHAPTER XVII

K. K. AUTOMATIC WRITING

ON 17 December 1915, I was talking to Mrs. Kennedy when her hand began to write, and I had a short conversation which may be worth reporting:—

I have been here such a long time, please tell father I am here—Raymond.

o. j. l.—My boy !

Dear father !

Father, it was difficult to say all one felt, but now I don't care. I love you. I love you intensely. Father, please speak to me.

o. j. l.—I recognise it, Raymond. Have you anything to say for the folk at home ?

I have been there to-day ; I spoke to mother. I don't know if she heard me, but I rather think so. Please tell her this, and kiss her from me.

o. j. l.—She had a rather vivid dream or vision of you one morning lately. I don't know if it was a dream.

I feel sure she will see me, but I don't know, because I am so often near her that I can't say yes or no to any particular time.

o. j. l.—Raymond, you know it is getting near Christmas now ?

I know. I shall be there ; keep jolly or it hurts me horribly. Truly, I know it is difficult, but you *must* know by now that I am so splendid. I shall never be one instant out of the house on Christmas Day. (Pause.)

He has gone to fetch some one.—Paul.

(This is the sort of interpolation which frequently happens. Paul signs his explanatory sentence)

(K. K. presently said that Raymond had returned, and expected me to be aware of it.)

I have brought Mr. Myers. He says he doesn't often come to use this means, but he wants to speak for a moment.

" Get free and go on," he says. " Don't let them trammel you. Get at it, Lodge."—Myers.

He has gone, tell my father.

(O. J. L., *sotto voce*.—What does that mean ?)

(K. K.—I haven't an idea.)

O. J. L.—Has Myers gone right away ?

" I have spoken, but I will speak again, if you keep quiet (meaning K. K.). Do cease to think, or you are useless. Tell Lodge I can't explain half his boy is to me. I feel as if I had my own dearly loved son here, yet I know he is only lent to me.

" Pardon me if I rarely use you (to K. K.) ; I can't stand the way you bother."—Myers.

K. K.—Do you mean the way I get nervous if I am taking a message from you ?

" Yes I do."

This interpolated episode was commented on by O. J. L. as very characteristic.]

O. J. L.—Is Raymond still there ?

Yes.

O. J. L.—Raymond, do you know we've got that photograph you spoke of ? Mrs. Cheves sent us it, the mother of Cheves—Captain Cheves, you remember him ?

Yes, I know you have the photograph.

O. J. L.—Yes, and your description of it was very good. And we have seen the man leaning on you. Was there another one taken of you ?

K. K.—' Four,' he says ' four.' Did you say ' four,' Raymond ?

Yes, I did.

O. J. L.—Yes, we have those taken of you by yourself, but was another taken of you with other officers ?

I hear, father ; I shall look, but I think you have had the one I want you to have ; I have seen you looking at it. I have heard all that father has said. It is ripping to come like this. Tell my father I have enjoyed it.—Raymond.

O. J. L.—Before you go, Raymond, I want to ask a serious question. Have you been let to see Christ ?

Father, I shall see him presently. It is not time yet. I am not ready. But I know he lives, and I know he comes here. All the sad ones see him if no one else can help them. Paul has seen him : you see he had such a lot of pain, poor chap. I am not expecting to see him yet, father. I shall love to when it's the time.—Raymond.

O. J. L.—Well, we shall be very happy this Christmas I think.

Father, tell mother she has her son with her all day on Christmas Day. There will be thousands and thousands of us back in the homes on that day, but the horrid part is that so many of the fellows don't get welcomed. Please keep a place for me. I must go now. Bless you again, father.—Raymond.

(Paul then wrote a few words to his mother.)

CHAPTER XVIII

FIRST SITTING OF ALEC WITH
MRS. LEONARD

ON 21 December 1915 Alec had his first sitting with Mrs. Leonard ; but he did not manage to go quite anonymously—the medium knew that he was my son. Again there is a good deal of unverifiable matter, which whether absurd or not I prefer not to suppress ; my reasons are indicated in Chapters XII and XVI, Part II, and Chapter XI, Part III.

Alec's (A. M. L.'s) Sitting with Mrs. Leonard at her House on Tuesday Afternoon, 21 *December* 1915, 3.15 *to* 4.30 *p.m.*

(Medium knows I am Sir Oliver Lodge's son.)

Front room ; curtains drawn ; dark ; small red lamp.
No one else present.
Mrs. Leonard shook hands saying, " Mr. Lodge ? "
(Medium begins by rubbing her own hands vigorously.)

Good morning ! This is Feda.
Raymond's here. He would have liked A *and* B.
(Feda, *sotto voce.*—What you mean, A and B ?)
Oh, he would have like to talk to A and B. [See Note A.] He says : " I wish you could see me, I am so pleased ; but you know I am pleased."
He has been trying hard to get to you at home. He thinks he is getting closer, and better able to understand the conditions which govern this way of communicating. He thinks that in a little while he will be able to give actual tests

at home. He knows he has got through, but not
satisfactorily. He gets so far, and then flounders.

(Feda, *sotto voce.*—That's what fishes do !)

He says he is feeling splendid. He did not
think it was possible to feel so well.

He was waiting here ; he knew you were
coming, but thought you might not be able to
come to-day. [Train half an hour late.]

Did you take notice of what he said about
the place he is in ?

A. M. L.—Yes. But I find it very difficult to understand.

He says, it is such a solid place, I have not
got over it yet. It is so wonderfully real.

He spoke about a river to his father ; he has
not seen the sea yet. He has found water, but
doesn't know whether he will find a sea. He is
making new discoveries every day. So *much*
is new, although of course not to people who
have been here some time

He went into the library with his grandfather—Grandfather William—and also somebody called Richard, and he says the books
there seem to be the same as you read.

Now this is extraordinary : There are books
there not yet published on the earth plane. He
is told—only told, he does not know if it is correct
—that those books will be produced, books like
those that are there now ; that the matter in them
will be impressed on the brain of some man, he
supposes an author.

He says that not everybody on his plane is
allowed to read those books ; they might hurt
them—that is, the books not published yet. Father
is going to write one—not the one on now, but a
fresh one.

Has his father found out who it was, beginning with G, who said he was going to help
(meaning help Raymond) for his father's sake ?
It was not the person he thought it was at the
time (p. 204).

It is very difficult to get things through. He
wants to keep saying how pleased he is to come.

There are hundreds of things he will think of after he is gone.

He has brought Lily, and William—the young one——

(Feda, *sotto voce*.—I don't know whether it is right, but he appears to have two brothers.)

> [Two brothers as well as a sister died in extreme infancy. He would hardly know that, normally.—O. J. L.]

A. M. L.—Feda, will you ask Raymond if he would like me to ask some questions ?

Yes, with pleasure, he says.

A. M. L.—A little time ago, Raymond said he was with mother. Mother would like to know if he can say what she was doing when he came ? Ask Raymond to think it over, and see if he can remember ?

Yes, yes. She'd got some wool and scissors. She had a square piece of stuff—he is showing me this—she was working on the square piece of stuff. He shows me that she was cutting the wool with the scissors.

Another time, she was in bed.

She was in a big chair—dark covered—— This refers to the time mentioned first. [Note B.]

A. M. L.—Ask Raymond if he can remember which room she was in ?

(Pause.)

He can't remember. He can't always see more than a corner of the room—it appears vapourish and shadowy.

He often comes when you're in bed.

He tried to call out loudly : he shouted, ' Alec, Alec ! ' but he didn't get any answer. That is what puzzles him. He thinks he has shouted, but apparently he has not even manufactured a whisper.

A. M. L.—Feda, will you ask Raymond if he can remember trivial things that happened, as these things often make the best tests ?

He says he can now and again.

A. M. L.—The questions that father asked about ' Evinrude,' ' Dartmoor,' and ' Argonauts,' are all trivial, but make good tests, as father knows nothing about them.

Yes, Raymond quite understands. He is just as keen as you are to give those tests.

A. M. L.—Ask Raymond if the word ' Evinrude ' in connexion with a holiday trip reminds him of anything ?

Yes. (Definitely.)

A. M. L.—And ' Argonauts ' ?

Yes. (Definitely.)

A. M. L.—And ' Dartmoor ' ?

Yes. (Definitely.)

A. M. L.—Well, don't answer the questions now, but if father asks them again, see if you can remember anything.

(While Alec was speaking, Feda was getting a message simultaneously :—)

He says something burst.

[This is excellent for Dartmoor, but I knew it.— A. M. L.]   [Note C.]

A. M. L.—Tell Raymond I am quite sure he gets things through occasionally, but that I think often the meaning comes through altered, and very often appears to be affected by the sitter. It appears to me that they usually get what they expect.

Raymond says, " I only wish they did ! " But in a way you are right. He is never able to give all he wishes. Sometimes only a word, which often must appear quite disconnected. Often the word does not come from his mind ; he has no trace of it. Raymond says, for this reason it is a good thing to try, more, to come and give something definite at home. When you sit at the table, he feels sure that what he wants to say is influenced by some one at the table. Some one is helping him, some one at the table is guessing at the words. He often starts a word, but somebody finishes it.

He asked father to let you come and not say who you were ; he says it would have been a bit of fun.

A. M. L.—Ask Raymond if he can remember any characteristic things we used to talk about among ourselves ?

Yes.   He says you used to talk about cars.

(Feda, *sotto voce*.—What you mean ?   Everybody talks about cars !)

And singing.   He used to fancy he could sing. He didn't sing hymns.   On Thursday nights he has to sing hymns, but they are not in his line.

> [On Thursday nights I am told that a circle holds sittings for developing the direct voice at Mrs. Leonard's, and that they sing hymns. Paul and Raymond have been said to join in. Cf. near end of Chapter XVI, p. 201.]

A. M. L.—What used he to sing ?

Hello—Hullalo—sounds like Hullulu—Hullulo. Something about ' Hottentot ' ; but he is going back a long way, he thinks. [See note in Appendix about this statement.]

(Feda, *sotto voce*.—An orange lady ?)

He says something about an orange lady.

(Feda, *sotto voce*.—Not what sold oranges ?)

No, of course not.   He says a song extolling the virtues and beauties of an orange lady.

> [Song : " My Orange Girl.   Excellent.   The last song he bought.—A. M. L.]

And a funny song which starts ' Ma,' but Feda can't see any more—like somebody's name.   Also something about ' Irish eyes.'   [See Note D.]

(Feda, *sotto voce*.—Are they really songs ?)

Very much so.

(A number of unimportant incidents were now mentioned.)

He says it is somebody's birthday in January.

A. M. L.—It *is*.

(Feda, *sotto voce*.—What's a beano ?   Whose birthday ?)

He won't say whose birthday.   He says, *He* knows (meaning A.).

[Raymond's own birthday, 25 Jan., was understood.]

(More family talk.)

Yes, he says he is going now.   He says the power is getting thin.

A. M. L.—Wish him good luck from me, Feda.

Love to all of them.

My love to you, old chap.

Just before I go : Don't ever any of you regret my going.   I believe I have got more to do than I could have ever done on the earth plane.   It is only a case of waiting, and just meeting every one of you as you come across to him.   He is going now.   He says Willie too—young Willie.   [His deceased brother.]

(Feda, *sotto voce*.—Yes, what ?   Proclivities ?)

Oh, he is only joking.

He says : Not Willie of the weary proplic—propensities—that's it.

He is joking.   Just as many jokes here as ever before.   Even when singing hymns.   When he and Paul are singing, they do a funny dance with their arms.   (Showing a sort of cake-walk—moving arms up and down.)

(Feda.—It's a silly dance, anyway.)

Good-bye, and good luck.

> [Characteristic ; see, for instance, a letter of his on page 41 above.   I happen to have just seen another letter, to Brodie, which concludes : "Well good-bye, Brodie, and good luck."—O. J. L.]

Yes, he is going.   Yes.   He is gone now, yes.

Do you want to say anything to Feda ?

A. M. L.—Yes, thank you very much for all your help.   The messages are sometimes difficult, but it is most important to try and give exactly what you hear, and nothing more, whether you understand it or not.

Feda understands.   She only say exactly what she hear, even though it is double-Dutch.   Don't forget to give my love to them all.

A. M. L.—Good-bye, Feda.   (Shakes hands.)

Medium comes-to in about two to three minutes.

(Signed)   A. M. L.

21 *December* 1915

> [All written out fair same evening.   Part on way home, and part after arriving, without disturbance from seeing anybody.]

Notes by O. J. L. on the A. M. L. Record

This seems to have been a good average sitting; it contains a few sufficiently characteristic remarks, but not much evidential. What is said about songs in it, however, is rather specially good. In further explanation, a few notes, embodying more particular information obtained by me from the family when reading the sitting over to them, may now be added :—

NOTE A

The ' A *and* B ' manifestly mean his brothers Alec and Brodie; and there was a natural reason for bracketing them together, inasmuch as they constitute the firm Lodge Brothers, with which Raymond was already to a large extent, and hoped to be still more closely, associated. But there may have been a minor point in it, since between Alec and Brodie long ago, at their joint preparatory school, there was a sort of joke, of which Raymond was aware, about problems given in algebra and arithmetic books : where, for instance, A buys so many dozen at some price, and B buys some at another price ; the question being to compare their profits. Or where A does a piece of work in so many days, and B does something else. It is usually not at all obvious, without working out, which gets the better of it, A or B ; and Alec seems to have recognised, in the manner of saying A and B, some reference to old family chaff on this subject.

NOTE B

The reference to a square piece of stuff, cut with scissors, suggests to his mother, not the wool-work which she is doing like everybody else for soldiers, but the cutting of a circular piece out of a Raymond blanket that came back with his kit, for the purpose of covering a round four-legged table which was subsequently used for sittings, in order to keep it clean without its having to be dusted or otherwise touched by servants. It is not distinct enough to be evidential, however.

NOTE C

About Dartmoor, "he says something burst." Incidents referred to in a previous sitting, when I was there alone, were the running downhill, clapping on brake, and swirling round corners (p. 156); but all this was associated with, and partly caused by, the bursting of the silencer in the night after the hilly country had been reached. And it was the fearful noise subsequent to the bursting of the silencer that the boys had expected him to remember.

NOTE D

The best evidential thing, however, is on p. 212—a reference to a song of his called " My Orange Girl." If the name of the song merely had been given, though good enough, it would not have been quite so good, because the name of a song is common property. But the particular mode of describing it, in such a way as to puzzle Feda, namely, " an orange lady," making her think rather of a market woman, is characteristic of Raymond—especially the sentence about " extolling her virtues and beauties," which is not at all appropriate to Feda, and is exactly like Raymond. So is " Willie of the weary proclivities."

The song " Irish Eyes " was also, I find, quite correct. It seems to have been a comparatively recent song, which he had sung several times.

Again, the song described thus by Feda :—

" A funny song which starts MA. But Feda can't see any more—like somebody's name."

I find that the letters M A were pronounced separately—not as a word. To me the MA had suggested one of those nigger songs about ' Ma Honey '—the kind of song which may have been indicated by the word ' Hottentot ' above. But, at a later table sitting at Mariemont, he was asked what song he meant by the letters M A, and then he spelt out clearly the name ' Maggie.' This song was apparently unknown to those at the table, but was recognised by Norah, who was in the room, though not at the table, as a still more recent song of Raymond's, about " Maggie Magee." (See Appendix also.)

Appendix to Sitting of 21 December 1915
(Written 3½ Months Later)

(Dictated by O. J. L., 12 April 1916.)

Last night the family were singing over some songs, and came across one which is obviously the one referred to in the above sitting of A. M. L. with Mrs. Leonard, held nearly four months ago, of which a portion ran thus (just before the reference to Orange Girl) :—

" A. M. L.—What used he to sing ?
　　　　Hello—Hullalo—sounds like Hullulu,—Hullulo.
　　　　Something about ' Hottentot '; but he is
　　　　going back a long way, he thinks."

References to other songs known to the family followed, but this reference to an unknown song was vaguely remembered by the family as a puzzle;

and it existed in A. M. L.'s mind as "a song about 'Honolulu,'"—this being apparently the residual impression produced by the 'Hullulu' in combination with 'Hottentot'; but no Honolulu song was known.

A forgotten and overlooked song has now (11 April 1916) turned up, which is marked in pencil "R. L. 3.3.4.," *i.e.* 3 March 1904, which corresponds to his "going back a long way"—to a time, in fact, when he was only fifteen. It is called, "My Southern Maid"; and although no word about 'Honolulu' occurs in the printed version, one of the verses has been altered in Raymond's writing in pencil; and that alteration is the following absurd introduction to a noisy chorus :—

> " Any little flower from a tulip to a rose,
> If you'll be Mrs. John James Brown
> Of Hon-o-lu-la-lu-la town."

Until these words were sung last night, nobody seems to have remembered the song "My Southern Maid," and there appears to be no reason for associating it with the word 'Honolulu' or any similar sound, so far as public knowledge was concerned, or apart from Raymond's alterations.

Alec calls attention to the fact that, in answer to his question about songs, no songs were mentioned which were not actually Raymond's songs; and that those which were mentioned were not those he was expecting. Furthermore, that if he had thought of these songs he would have thought of them by their ordinary titles, such as "My Orange Girl" and "My Southern Maid"; though the latter he had forgotten altogether.

(A sort of disconnected sequel to this song episode occurred some months later, as reported in Chapter XXIII.)

CHAPTER XIX

PRIVATE SITTINGS AT MARIEMONT

IT had been several times indicated that Raymond wanted to come into the family circle at home, and that Honor, whom he often refers to as H., would be able to help him. Attempted private sittings of this kind were referred to by Raymond through London mediums, and he gave instruction as to procedure, as already reported (pp. 160 and 190).

After a time some messages were received, and family communications without any outside medium have gradually become easy.

Records were at first carefully kept, but I do not report them, because clearly it is difficult to regard anything thus got as evidential. At the same time, the naturalness of the whole, and the ready way in which family jokes were entered into and each new-comer recognised and welcomed appropriately, were very striking. A few incidents, moreover, were really of an evidential character, and these must be reported in due course.

But occasionally the table got rather rampageous and had to be quieted down. Sometimes, indeed, both the table and things like flower-pots got broken. After these more violent occasions, Raymond volunteered the explanation, through mediums in London, that he couldn't always control it, and that there was a certain amount of sky-larking, not on our side, which he tried to prevent (see pp. 182, 194, and 273); though in certain of the surprising mechanical demonstrations, and, so to speak, tricks, which certainly seemed beyond the normal power of anyone touching the table, he appeared to be decidedly interested, and was represented as desirous of repeating a few of the more remarkable ones for my edification.

I do not, however, propose to report in this book concerning any purely physical phenomena. They require a more thorough treatment. Suffice it to say that the movements were not only intelligent, but were sometimes, though very seldom, such as apparently could not be accomplished by any normal application of muscular force, however unconsciously such force might be exerted by anyone—it might only be a single person—left in contact with the table.

A family sitting with no medium present is quite different from one held with a professional or indeed any outside medium. Information is freely given about the doings of the family ; and the general air is that of a family conversation ; because, of course, in fact, no one but the family is present.

At any kind of sitting the conversation is rather one-sided, but whereas with a medium the sitter is reticent, and the communicator is left to do nearly all the talking, in a family group the sitters are sometimes voluble ; while the ostensible control only occasionally takes the trouble to spell out a sentence, most of his activity consisting in affirmation and negation and rather effective dumb show.

I am reluctant to print a specimen of these domestic chats, though it seems necessary to give some account of them.

On Christmas Day, 1915, the family had a long table sitting. It was a friendly and jovial meeting, with plenty of old songs interspersed, which he seemed thoroughly to enjoy and, as it were, ' conduct ' ; but for publication I think it will be better to select something shorter, and I find a description written by one to whom such things were quite new except by report—a lady who had been governess in the family for many years, when even the elder children were small, and long before Raymond was born. This lady, Miss F. A. Wood, commonly called ' Woodie ' from old times, happened to be staying on a visit to Mariemont in March 1916, and was present at two or three of the family sittings. She was much interested in her first experience, and wrote an account immediately afterwards, which, as realistically giving the impression of a witness, I have obtained her permission to copy here.

At this date the room was usually considerably darkened for a sitting ; but even partial darkness was unnecessary, and was soon afterwards dispensed with, especially as it interfered with easy reading of music at the piano.

Table Sitting in the Drawing-room at Mariemont, Thursday, 2 March 1916, about 6 p.m.

Sitters—LADY LODGE, NORAH, and WOODIE ; later, HONOR

Report by Miss F. A. Wood

As it was the first time that I had ever been at a sitting of any kind, I shall put down the details as fully as I can remember them.

The only light in the room was from the gas-fire, a large one, so that we could see each other and things in the room fairly distinctly ; the table used at this time was a rather small octagonal one, though weighty for its size, with strong centre stem, supported on three short legs, top like a chess-board. Lady Lodge sat with her back to window looking on to drive, Norah with back to windows looking on to tennis-lawn, and I, Woodie, had my back to the sofa.

As we were about to sit down, Lady Lodge said : " We always say a little prayer first."

I had hoped that she intended to pray aloud for us all, but she did it silently, so I did the same, having been upstairs before and done this also.

For some time nothing whatever happened. I only felt that the table was keeping my hands extremely cold.

After about half an hour, Lady Lodge said : " I don't think that anyone is coming to-night ; we will wait just a little longer, and then go."

LADY LODGE.—Is anyone here to-night to speak to us ? Do come if you can, because we want to show Woodie what a sitting is like. Raymond, dear, do you think you could come to us ?

(No answer.)

During the half-hour before Lady Lodge asked any questions I had felt every now and then a curious tingling in my hands and fingers, and then a much stronger drawing sort of feeling through my hands and arms, which caused the table to have a strange intermittent trembling sort of feeling, though it was not a movement of the *whole* table. Another ' feeling ' was as if a ' bubble ' of the table came up, and tapped gently on the palm of my left hand. At first I only felt it once ; after a short interval three times ; then a little later about twelve times. And once (I shall not be able to explain this) I felt rather than heard a faint tap in the centre of the table (away from people's hands).

Nearly every time I felt these queer movements Lady Lodge asked, "Did you move, Woodie?" I had certainly not done so consciously, and said so, and while I was feeling that 'drawing' feeling through hands and arms, I said nothing myself, till Lady Lodge and Norah both said, "What *is* the table doing? It has never done like this before." Then I told of my strange feelings in hands and arms, etc. Lady Lodge said it must be due to nerves, or muscles, or something of the sort. These strange feelings did not last long at a time, and generally, but not always, they came after Lady Lodge had asked questions (to some one on the other side).

After a bit, when the 'feelings' had gone from me at least, Lady Lodge suggested Norah's going for Honor, who came, but said on first sitting down that the table felt dead, and she did not think that anyone was there.

LADY L.—Is anyone coming? We should be so pleased if any-one could; we have been sitting here some time very patiently.

Nothing happened for a bit, and Lady Lodge said, "I don't think it is any good."

But I said, "Oh, do wait a little longer, that tingling feeling is coming back again."

And Honor said, "Yes, I think there is something."

And then the table began to move, and Lady Lodge asked :—

LADY L.—Raymond, darling, is that you?

(The table rocked three times.)

LADY L.—That is good of you, because Woodie did so want you to come.

(The table rocked to and fro with a pleased motion, most difficult to express on paper.)

WOODIE.—Do you think that I have any power?

No.

[Personally, I do not feel so sure of this. After the sitting and during it, I felt there might be a possibility.—Woodie.]

LADY L.—Lorna has gone to nurse the soldiers, night duty. They are typhoid patients, and I do not like it. Do you think it will do her any harm?

No.

LADY L.—Do you like her doing this?

YES.

LADY L.—You are rocking like a rocking-horse. Do you remember the rocking-horse at Newcastle?

YES.

LADY L.—Can you give its name? (They went through the alphabet, and it spelt out :—)

PRINCE.

[It used to be called Archer Prince.]

(Soon after this the table began to show signs of restlessness, and Honor said : " I expect he wants to send a message." So Lady Lodge said :—)

LADY L.—Do you want to send a message ?

YES.

HONOR.—Well, we're all ready ; start away.

YOURLOVETOMYRTYPEKILL.

HONOR.—Raymond, that is wrong, isn't it ? Was " Your love to my " right ?

YES.

HONOR.—Very well, we will start from there.

(The message then ran :—)

YOUR LOVE TO MY LITTLE SISTER.

(Before the whole of ' sister ' was made out, he showed great delight ; and when the message was repeated to him in full to see if it was right, he was so pleased, and showed it so vigorously, that *he*, and we, all laughed together.

I could never have believed how real the feeling would be of his presence amongst us.)

LADY L.—Do you mean Lily ?

YES.

LADY L.—Is she here ?

YES.

LADY L.—Are you here in the room ?

YES.

LADY L.—Can Lily see us ?

No.

LADY L.—Lily, darling, your mother does love you so dearly. I have wanted to send you my love. I shall come to see you some time, and then we shall be so happy, my dear, dear little girl. Thank you very much for coming to help Raymond, and coming to the table sometimes, till he can come himself. My love to you, darling, and to Brother Bill too.

(Raymond seemed very pleased when Brother Bill was mentioned.)

(The table now seemed to wish to get into Lady Lodge's lap, and made most caressing movements to and fro, and seemed as if it could not get close enough to her.

Soon we realised that he was wanting to go, so we asked him if this was so, and he said :—)

YES.

(So we said ' good night ' to him, and after giving two rather slight movements, which I gather is what he generally does just as he is going, we said 'good night' once more, and came away.)

(Signed) WOODIE

One other family sitting, a still shorter one, may be quoted as a specimen also; though out of place. A question asked was suggested by something reported on page 230. It appears that Miss Wood was still here, but that on this occasion she was not one of those that touched the table.

At this date the table generally used happened to be a chess-table with centre pillar and three claw feet. After this table and another one had got broken during the more exuberant period of these domestic sittings, before the power had got under control, a stronger and heavier round table with four legs was obtained, and employed only for this purpose.

Table Sitting in the Drawing-Room at Mariemont,
9 p.m., Monday, 17 April 1916

REPORT BY M. F. A. L.

Music going on in the drawing-room at Mariemont.

The girls (four of them) and Alec singing at the piano. Woodie and Honor and I sitting at the other end of the room. Lionel in the large chair.

The Shakespeare Society was meeting in the house, and at that time having coffee in the dining-room, so O. J. L. was not with us.

Woodie thought Raymond was in the room and would like to hear the singing, but Honor thought it too late to begin with the table, as we should shortly be going into the dining-room.

However, I got the table ready near the piano, and Honor came to it, and the *instant* she placed her hands on it, it began to rock. I put my hands on too.

We asked if it was Raymond, and if he had been waiting, and he said :—

YES.

He seemed to wish to listen to the music, and kept time with it gently. And after a song was over that he liked, he very distinctly and decidedly applauded.

Lionel came (I think at Raymond's request) and sat at the table with us. It was determined to edge itself close to the piano, though we said we must pull it back, and did so. But it would go there, and thumped Barbie, who was playing the piano, in time to the music. Alec took one of the black satin cushions and held it against her as a buffer. The table continued to bang, and made a little hole in the cushion.

It then edged itself along the floor, where for a minute or two it could make a sound on the boards beyond the carpet. Then it seemed to be feeling about with one foot (it has three).

It found a corner of the skirting board, where it could lodge one foot about 6 inches from the ground. It then raised the other two level with it, in the air ; and this it did many times, seeming delighted with its new trick.

It then laid itself down on the ground, and we asked if we should help it and lift it up, but it banged a

No

on the floor, and raised itself a little several times without having the strength to get up. It lifted itself quite a foot from the ground, and was again asked if we might not lift it, but it again banged once for

No.

But Lionel then said :—

ᴸIONEL.—Well, Pat, my hand is in a most uncomfortable position ; won't you let me put the table up?

It at once banged three times for

YES.

So we raised it.

I then said :—

ᴹ. ꜰ. ᴀ. ʟ.—Raymond, I want to ask you a question as a test : What is the name of the sphere on which you are living ?

[I did this, because others beside Raymond have said, through Mrs. Leonard, that they were living on the third sphere, and that it was called ' Summerland,' so I thought it might be an idea of the medium's.[1] I don't much like these 'sphere' messages, and don't know whether they mean anything; but I assume that 'sphere' may mean condition, or state of development.]

We took the alphabet, and the answer came at once :—

SUMMERRLODGE.

We asked, after the second R, if there was not some mistake; and again when O came, instead of the A we had expected for 'Summerland.'

But he said No.

So we went on, though I thought it was hopelessly wrong, and ceased to follow. I felt sure it was mere muddle.

So my surprise was the greater when the notetaker read out, 'Summer R. Lodge,' and I found he had signed his name to it, to show, I suppose, that it was his own statement, and not Feda's.

[Lorna reports that the impression made upon them was that Raymond knew they had been expecting one ending, and that he was amused at having succeeded in giving them another. They enjoyed the joke together, and the table shook as if laughing.]

We talked to him a little after this, and Alec and Noël put their hands on the table, and we said good night.

It is only necessary to add that the mechanical movements here described are *not* among those which, on page 218, I referred to as physically unable to be done by muscular effort on the part of anyone whose hands are only on the table top. I am not in this book describing any cases of that sort. Whatever was the cause of the above mechanical trick movements, which were repeated on a subsequent occasion for my observation, the circumstances were not strictly evidential. I ought to say, however, that most certainly I am sure that no *conscious* effort was employed by anyone present.

[1] The statement will be found on page 230, in the record of a sitting preceding this in date.

MARIEMONT

RAYMOND AND BRODIE WITH THE PIGEONS AT MARIEMONT

WARNING

It may be well to give a word of warning to those who find that they possess any unusual power in the psychic direction, and to counsel regulated moderation in its use. Every power can be abused, and even the simple faculty of automatic writing can with the best intentions be misapplied. Self-control is more important than any other form of control, and whoever possesses the power of receiving communications in any form should see to it that he remains master of the situation. To give up your own judgement and depend solely on adventitious aid is a grave blunder, and may in the long run have disastrous consequences. Moderation and common sense are required in those who try to utilise powers which neither they nor any fully understand, and a dominating occupation in mundane affairs is a wholesome safeguard.

CHAPTER XX

A FEW MORE RECORDS, WITH SOME UNVERIFIABLE MATTER

AFTER Christmas I had proposed to drop the historical order and make selections as convenient, but I find that sequence must to some extent be maintained, because of the interlocking of sittings with different mediums and development generally. I shall, however, only preserve historical order so far as it turns out useful or relevant, and will content myself with reporting that on 3 January 1916 Raymond's eldest sister, Violet (the one married to the ' Rowland ' that he mentioned through Feda), had a good sitting with him, and was not only recognised easily, but knowledge was shown of much that she had been doing, and of what she was immediately planning to do. Reference was also made by Raymond to what he called his special room in her house (p. 45); and, later, he said that that room was bare of furniture, which it was.

And at some of the sittings now, deceased friends, not relatives, were brought by Raymond, and gave notable evidence both to us and to other people ; especially to parents in some cases, to widows in others ; some of which may perhaps be partially reported hereafter.

I propose now to pass on to some unverifiable matter (see Chapters XII and XVI), and especially to a strange and striking sitting which Lady Lodge had with Mrs. Leonard on 4 February 1916.

This may as well be reported almost in full, in spite of unimportant and introductory portions, since it seems fairer to give the context, especially of unverifiable matter. But I feel bound to say that there is divergence of opinion as to whether this particular record ought to be published or not. I can only say that I recognise the responsibility, and hope that I am right in partially accepting it.

Non-Evidential Sitting of M. F. A. L. with Mrs. Leonard at her House on Friday, 4 February 1916, *from* 8.30 *p.m. to* 11.10 *p.m.*

(M. F. A. L. alone.)

Feda.—Oh, its Miss Olive !

M. F. A. L.—So glad to meet you, Feda !

Feda love you and Soliver best of all. SLionel and SAlec too she love very much.

Yaymond is here. He has been all over the place with Paulie, to all sorts of places to the mediums, to try and get poor boys into touch with their mothers. Some are very jealous of those who succeed. They try to get to their mothers, and they can't—they are shut out. They make me feel as though I could cry to see them. We explain that their mothers and fathers don't know about communicating. They say, why don't they all go to mediums ?

Yaymond say, it makes me wonder too.

He say, he was telling Feda, it was awful funny the things some of them did—it has a funny side, going to see the mediums. You see, Paul and he couldn't help having a joke ; they are boys themselves, laughing over funny things.

He says he was listening to Paul, and he was describing the drawing-room at home. (A good description was now given of the drawing-room at Mariemont, which the medium had never seen.)

Feda sees flowers ; they're Feda's, not Gladys's.

[M. F. A. L. had brought flowers for Mrs. Leonard.]

M. F. A. L.—Don't you have flowers, then ?

Yes, lots of flowers. But Feda like to have them in Gladys's room. [Apparently this must be Mrs. Leonard's name.]

There's a lot in prayer. Prayer keeps out evil things, and keeps nice clean conditions. Raymond says, keeps out devils.

Mother, I don't want to talk about material

things, but to satisfy anxiety.   I was very uneasy
on Monday night.   I tried to come near, but there
was a band round me.   We were all there.

M. F. A. L.—The Zeppelins did come on Monday night,
but they did not touch us.   [We went to bed and
didn't worry about them.]

He says, they worked in a circular way, east and
south of you.   Awful !   He hoped it wouldn't upset you ; he didn't want them to come too close.   I
know you're not nervous, but I fear for you.   If
he'd been on the earth plane, he'd have been flying
home.   He says *New Street* was the mark.

Some one called 'M.' sent you a message through
Mrs. F. (?), and wanted her dearest love given.
She's had to be away rather from the earth plane
for some time, but he actually has seen M. several
times.   Conditions of war have brought her back.
She had progressed a good way.   She wondered if
you realised it was not her will to leave you so long,
but progression.   She belongs to a higher plane.

M. knew something about this before she passed
on, though perhaps it makes it easier to be always
communicating.

> [Some friends will know for whom this is in-
> tended—a great friend of our and many
> other children.   She had had one sitting with
> Mrs. Piper at Mariemont, not a good one.—
> O. J. L.]

Her life on the earth plane made it easier for
her to go on quickly after she passed out.

(Feda, *sotto voce*.—What you say ?)

M. says, it will be a test, that she was with
his father at a medium's, where she saw a control named Alice Anne, a little girl control ; she
didn't speak to Soliver, but was with him at the
medium's.   "The old Scotch lady" what Paulie
calls her.

> [This is correct about a sitting with Miss
> McCreadie, when this 'M.' had unmistak-
> ably sent messages through Miss McC.'s
> usual control.—O. J. L.]

(Added later.)

Some friends will be interested in this lady,—a really beautiful character, with initials M. N. W.,—so I record something that came through from Feda on a much later occasion—in July 1916:—

Raymond's got rather a young lady with him. Not the sister who passed away a little baby. But she's young—she looks twenty-four or twenty-five. She's rather slender, rather pretty. Brown hair, oval face. Not awful handsome, but got a nice expression. She's very nice, and comes from a high sphere. She's able to come close to-night, but can't always come. Name begins with an M. And she says, " Don't think that because she didn't come, she didn't want to come. She had to keep away for so long. It was necessary for her to stay away from the earth for a while, because she had work in high spheres for three years, and it's difficult for her to come through.

Good, good—something about the lady, lady—two people, she says. Lady and good man. Feda ought to remember it—a lady and good man.

Between them Soliver and her, Soliver and Miss Olive, and her. Lady and good man and M. She must have been very good on the earth plane, she wasn't ordinary at all. Quite unusual and very very good. You can tell that by what she looks like now.

She brings a lot of flowers—pansies, not quite pansies, flower like a pansy, and not quite a pansy. Heartsease, that's what it is. She brings lots of those to you. She brought a lot of them when Raymond wented over there. But not for very long, she didn't— they wasn't wanted very long.

M. F. A. L. *Record of February 4—continued*

He said about some one, that she'd gone right on to a very high sphere indeed, as near celestial as could possibly be. His sister, he says—can't get her name. [He means Lily, presumably.] He says William had gone on too, a good way, but not too far to come to him. [His brother.]

Those who are fond of you never go too far to come back to you—sometimes too far to communicate, never too far to meet you when you pass over.

M. F. A. L.—That's so comforting, darling. I don't want to hold you back.

You gravitate here to the ones you're fond of. Those you're not fond of, if you meet them in the street, you don't bother yourself to say ' how-do-you-do.'

M. F. A. L.—There are streets, then ?

Yes. He was pleased to see streets and houses.

At one time, I thought it might be created by one's own thoughts. You gravitate to a place you are fitted for. Mother, there's no judge and jury, you just gravitate, like to like.

I've seen some boys pass on who had nasty ideas and vices. They go to a place I'm very glad I didn't have to go to, but it's not hell exactly. More like a reformatory—it's a place where you're given a chance, and when you want to look for something better, you're given a chance to have it. They gravitate together, but get so bored. Learn to help yourself, and immediately you'll be helped. Very like your world ; only no unfairness, no injustice—a common law operating for each and every one.

M. F. A. L.—Are all of the same rank and grade ?

Rank doesn't count as a virtue. High rank comes by being virtuous. Those who have been virtuous have to pass through lower rank to understand things. All go on to the astral first, just for a little.

He doesn't remember being on the astral himself. He thinks where he is now, he's about third. Summerland—Homeland, some call it. It is a very happy medium. The very highest can come to visit you. It is just sufficiently near the earth plane to be able to get to those on earth. He thinks you have the best of it there, so far as he can see.

Mother, I went to a gorgeous place the other day.

M. F. A. L.—Where was it ?

Goodness knows !

I was permitted, so that I might see what was going on in the Highest Sphere. Generally the High Spirits come to us.

I wonder if I can tell you what it looked like !

[Until the case for survival is considered established, it is thought improper and unwise to relate an experience of a kind which may be imagined, in a book dealing for the most part with evidential matter. So I have omitted the description here, and the brief reported utterance which followed. I think it fair, however, to quote the record so far as it refers to the youth's own feelings, because otherwise the picture would be incomplete and one-sided, and he might appear occupied only with comparatively frivolous concerns.]

I felt exalted, purified, lifted up. I was kneeling. I couldn't stand up, I *wanted* to kneel.

Mother, I thrilled from head to foot. He didn't come near me, and I didn't feel I wanted to go near him. Didn't feel I ought. The Voice was like a bell. I can't tell you what he was dressed or robed in. All seemed a mixture of shining colours.

No good ; can you imagine what I felt like when he put those beautiful rays on to me ? I don't know what I've ever done that I should have been given that wonderful experience. I never thought of such a thing being possible, not at any rate for years, and years, and years. No one could tell what I felt, I can't explain it.

Will they understand it ?

I know father and you will, but I want the others to try. I can't put it into words.

I didn't walk, I had to be taken back to Summerland, I don't know what happened to me. If you could faint with delight ! Weren't those beautiful words ?

I've asked if Christ will go and be seen by everybody ; but was told, " Not quite in the same sense as you saw Him." I was told Christ was always in spirit on earth—a sort of projection, something like those rays, something of him in every one.

People think he is *a* Spirit, walking about in a particular place. Christ is everywhere, not as a personality. There *is* a Christ, and He lives on the higher plane, and that is the one I was permitted to see.

There was more given me in that beautiful message ; I can't remember it all. He said the whole of it, nearly and word for word, of what I've given you. You see from that I'm given a mission to do, helping near the earth plane. . . .

Shall I tell you why I'm so glad that is my work, given me by the Highest Authority of all !

First of all, I'm proud to do His work, no matter what it is ; but the great thing is, I can be near you and father.

M. F. A. L.—If we can only be worthy !

You are both doing it, every bit you can.

M. F. A. L.—Well, I'm getting to love people more than I used to do.

I have learnt over here, that every one is not for you. If not in affinity, let them go, and be with those you *do* like.

Mother, will they think I'm kind of puffing myself up or humbugging? It's so wonderful, will they be able to understand that it's just Raymond that's been through this? No Sunday school.

I treasured it up to give you to-night. I put it off because I didn't know if I could give it in the right words that would make them feel like I feel —or something like. Isn't it a comfort? You and father think it well over. I didn't ask for work to be near the earth plane! I thought that things would be made right. But think of it being given me, the work I should have prayed for!

M. F. A. L.—Then you're nearer?

Much nearer! I was bound to be drawn (?). So beautiful to think, now I can *honestly* stay near the earth plane. Eventually, instead of going up by degrees, I shall take, as Feda has been promised, a jump. And when you and father come, you will be on one side, and father on the other. We shall be a while in Summerland, just to get used to conditions. He says very likely we shall be wanted to keep an eye on the others. He means brothers and sisters. I can't tell you how pleased I feel— ' pleased ' is a poor word!

M. F. A. L.—About what, my dear?

About being very near the earth plane.

I've pressed on, getting used to conditions here, and yet when I went into the Presence I was over-awed.

How can people . . .

It made me wish, in the few seconds I was able to think of anything, that I had led one of the purest lives imaginable. If there's any little tiny thing I've ever done, it would stand out like a mountain. I didn't have much time to think, but I did feel in that few seconds . . .

I felt when I found myself back in Summerland that I was *charged* with something—some wonderful power. As if I could stop rivers, move mountains ; and so wonderfully glad.

He says, don't bother yourself about trying to like people you've got an antipathy for, it's waste of you. Keep love for those who want it, don't throw it away on those who don't ; it's like giving things to over-fed people when hungry chaps are standing by.

Do you know that I can feel my ideas altering, somehow.

I feel more naturally in tune with conditions very far removed from the earth plane ; yet I like to go round with Paul, and have fun, and enjoy myself.

After that wonderful experience, I asked some one if it wasn't stupid to like to have fun and go with the others. But they said that if you've got a work to do on the earth plane, you're not to have all the black side, you are allowed to have the lighter side too, sunshine and shadow. One throws the other up, and makes you better able to judge the value of each. There are places on my sphere where they can listen to beautiful music when they choose. Everybody, even here, doesn't care for music, so it's not in my sphere compulsory.

He likes music and singing, but wouldn't like to live in the middle of it always, he can go and hear it if he wants to, he is getting more fond of it than he was.

Mr. Myers was very pleased. He says, you know it isn't always the parsons, not always the parsons, that go highest first. It isn't what you professed, it's what you've done. If you have not believed definitely in life after death, but have tried to do as much as you could, and led a decent life, and have left alone things you don't understand, that's all that's required of you. Considering how simple it is, you'd think everybody would have done it, but very few do.

On our side, we expect a few years will make a great difference in the conditions of people on the earth plane.

In five years, ever so many more will be wanting to know about the life to come, and how they shall live on the earth plane so that they shall have a pretty good life when they pass on. They'll do it, if only as a wise precaution. But the more they know, the higher lines people will be going on.

M. F. A. L.—Did you see me reading the sitting to your father ?

I'm going to stop father from feeling tired. Chap with red feather helping. Isn't it wonderful that I can be near you and father ?

Some people ask me, are you pleased with where your body lies ? I tell them I don't care a bit, I've no curiosity about my body now. It's like an old coat that I've done with, and hope some one will dispose of it. I don't want flowers on my body. Flowers in house, in Raymond's home.

M. F. A. L.—Can he tell the kind of flowers I put for him on his birthday ?

(Feda, *sotto voce*.—Try and tell Feda.)
Doesn't seem able to get it.

Don't think he knew. I can't get it through. Don't think I don't appreciate them. Sees some yellow and some white.

He thinks it is some power he takes from the medium which makes for him a certain amount of physical sight. He can't see properly.

M. F. A. L.—Can he tell me where I got the flowers from for his birthday ?

(Feda, *sotto voce*.—Flowers doesn't grow now. Winter here !)

Yes, they do. Thinks they came from home.

(Feda, *sotto voce*.—Try and tell me any little thing.)

He means they came from his own garden.

[Yes, they did, It was yellow jasmine, cut
from the garden at Mariemont.—M. F. A. L.]

Paul's worried 'cos medium talk like book. Paul calls Feda ' Imp.' Raymond sometimes calls Feda ' Illustrious One.' I think Yaymond laughing ! Always pretending Feda very little, and that they've lost Feda, afraid of walking on her, but Feda pinches them sometimes, pretend they've trodden on Feda. But Feda just as tall as lots of Englishes.

M. F. A. L.—Isn't Feda tired now?

No.

M. F. A. L.—I think Raymond must be.

Well, power is going.

M. F. A. L.—Anyhow, I must go. Some one perhaps of your brothers will come soon.

I want no heralds or flourish of trumpets, let them come and see if I can get through to them.

M. F. A. L.—(I here said something about myself, I forget; I think it was about being proud.)

If I see any signs, I'll take you in hand at once; it shall be nipped in the bud!

Good night.

M. F. A. L.—Do you sleep?

Well, I doze.

M. F. A. L.—Do you have rain?

Well, you can go to a place where rain is.

M. F. A. L.—Do you know that your father is having all the sittings bound together in a book?

It will be very interesting to see how I change as I go on.

Good night.

NOTE BY O. J. L.

It must be remembered that all this, though reported in the first person, really comes through Feda; and though her style and grammar improve in the more serious portions, due allowance must be made for this fact.

CHAPTER XXI

TWO RATHER EVIDENTIAL SITTINGS BY O. J. L. ON MARCH 3, 1916

ON the morning of 3 March I had a sitting in Mrs. Kennedy's house with a Mrs. Clegg, a fairly elderly dame whose peculiarity is that she allows direct control by the communicator more readily than most mediums do.

Mrs. Kennedy has had Mrs. Clegg two or three times to her house, and Paul has learnt how to control her pretty easily, and is able to make very affectionate demonstrations and to talk through the organs of the medium, though in rather a jerky and broken way. She accordingly kindly arranged an anonymous sitting for me.

The sitting began with sudden clairvoyance, which was unexpected. It was a genuine though not a specially successful sitting, and it is worth partially reporting because of the reference to it which came afterwards through another medium, on the evening of the same day; making a simple but exceptionally clear and natural cross correspondence —

Anonymous Sitting of O. J. L. with Mrs. Clegg

At 11.15 a.m. on Friday, 3 March 1916, I arrived at Mrs. Kennedy's, went up and talked to her in the drawing-room till nearly 11.30, when Mrs. Clegg arrived.

She came into the room while I was seeing to the fire, spoke to Mrs. Kennedy, and said, " Oh, is this the gentleman that I am to sit with ? " She was then given a seat in front of the fire, being asked to get quiet after her omnibus journey. But she had hardly seated herself before she said :—

" Oh, this room is so full of people ; oh, some one so eager to come ! I hear some one say ' Sir Oliver Lodge.' Do you know anyone of that name ? "

I said, yes, I know him.

Mrs. Kennedy got up to darken the room slightly, and Mrs. Clegg ejaculated :—

" Who is Raymond, Raymond, Raymond ? He is standing close to me."

She was evidently going off into a trance, so we moved her chair back farther from the fire, and without more preparation she went off.

For some time, however, nothing further happened, except contortions, struggling to get speech, rubbings of the back as if in some pain or discomfort there, and a certain amount of gasping for breath.

Mrs. Kennedy came to try and help, and to give power. She knelt by her side and soothed her. I sat and waited.

Presently the utterance was distinguished as, " Help me, where's the doctor ? "

After a time, with K. K.'s help, the control seemed to get a little clearer, and the words, " So glad ; father ; love to mother ; so glad," frequently repeated in an indistinct and muffled tone of voice, were heard, followed by, " Love to all of them."

Nothing was put down at the time, for there seemed nothing to record—it seemed only preliminary effort ; and in so far as anything was said, it consisted merely of simple messages of affection, and indications of joy at being able to come through, and of disappointment at not being able to do better. The medium, however, went through a good deal of pantomime, embracing me, stroking my arm, patting my knees, and sometimes stroking my head, sometimes also th-owing her arms round me and giving the impression of being overjoyed, but unable to speak plainly.

Then other dumb show was begun. He seemed to be thinking of the things in his kit, or things which had been in his possession, and trying to enumerate them. He indicated that his revolver had not come back, and that in his diary the last page was not written up. I promised to complete it.

After a time, utterance being so difficult, I gave the

medium a pad and pencil, and asked for writing. The writing was large and sprawly, single words: 'Captain' among them.

While Raymond was speaking, and at intervals, the medium kept flopping over to one side or the other, hanging on the arm of her chair with head down, or else drooping forward, or with head thrown back—assuming various limp and wounded attitudes. Though every now and then she seemed to make an effort to hold herself up, and once or twice crossed knees and sat up firm, with arms more or less folded. But the greater part of the time she was flopping about.

Presently Raymond said 'Good-bye,' and a Captain was supposed to control. She now spoke in a vigorous martial voice, as if ordering things, but saying nothing of any moment.

Then he too went away, and 'Hope' appeared, who, I am told, is Mrs. Clegg's normal control. Hope was able to talk reasonably well, and what she said I recorded for what it might be worth, but I omit the record, because though it contained references to people and things outside the knowledge of the medium or Mrs. Kennedy, and was therefore evidential as regards the genuineness and honesty of the medium, it was not otherwise worth reporting, unless much else of what was said on the same subjects by other mediums were reported too.

———

On the evening of this same 3rd of March—*i.e.* later in the same day that I had sat with Mrs. Clegg—I went alone to Mrs. Leonard's house and had rather a remarkable sitting, at which full knowledge of the Clegg performance was shown. It is worthy therefore of some careful attention.

After reading this part, the above very abbreviated record of the Clegg sitting, held some hours before in another house and other conditions, should again be read. I wish to call attention to the following 3rd of March sitting as one of the best; other members of the family have probably had equally good ones, but my notes are fuller. I hope it is fully understood that the mannerisms are Feda's throughout.

Sitting of O. J. L. with Mrs. Leonard at her House on Friday,
3 *March* 1916, *from* 9.15 *p.m. to* 11.15 *p.m.*

(O. J. L. alone.)

No preliminaries to report. Feda came through quickly, jerked in the chair, and seemed very pleased to find me.

(I asked if she had seen Raymond lately.)

Oh yes, Yaymond's here.

He came to help Feda with the lady and gentleman—on Monday, Feda thinks it was. Not quite sure when. But there was a lady and gentleman, and he came to help ; and Feda said, " Go away, Yaymond ! " He said, " No, I've come to stay." He wouldn't go away, and he did help them through with their boy.

[The reference here is to a sitting which a colleague of mine, Professor and Mrs. Sonnenschein, had had, unknown to me, with Mrs. Leonard. I learnt afterwards that the arrangements had been made by them in a carefully anonymous manner, the correspondence being conducted *via* a friend in Darlington ; so that they were only known to Mrs. Leonard as " a lady and gentleman from Darlington." They had reported to me that their son Christopher had sent good and evidential messages, and that Raymond had turned up to help. It was quite appropriate for Raymond to take an interest in them and bring their son, since Christopher Sonnenschein had been an engineering fellow-student with Raymond at Birmingham. But there was no earthly reason, so far as Mrs. Leonard's knowledge was concerned, for him to put in an appearance ; and indeed Feda at first told him to ' Go away,' until he explained that he had come to help. Hence the mention of Raymond, under the circumstances, was evidential.]

He's only been once to help beside this, and then he said, Don't tell the lady he was helping. [See below.]

He's been with Paulie to-day, to Paulie's mother's. He says he's been at Paulie's house, but not with Mrs. Kathie, with another lady, a medie, Feda thinks. She was older than this one ; a new one to him.[1]   He wanted to speak through her, but he found it was difficult   Paul manages it all right, he says, but *he* finds it difficult.   He says he started to get through, and then he didn't feel like himself.   It's awful strange when one tries to control anybody.   He wanted to very bad ; he almost had them.   (*Sotto voce.*—What you mean, Yaymond ?)   He says he thought he almost had them.   He means he nearly got through.   Oh, he says, he's not given it up ; he's going to try again. What worries him is that he doesn't feel like himself.   You know, father, I might be anybody.   He says, Do you believe that in that way, practice makes perfect ?

o. j. l.—Yes, I'm sure it gets easier with practice.

Oh, then he'll practise dozens of times, if he thinks it will be any good.

o. j. l.—Did he like the old woman ?

Oh yes ; she's a very good sort.

o. j. l.—Who was there sitting ?

[This question itself indicates, what was the fact, that I had so far given no recognition to the statement that Raymond had been trying to control a medium on the morning of that same day.   I wanted to take what came through, without any assistance.]

He's not sure, because he didn't seem to get all properly into the conditions ; it was like being in a kind of mist, in a fog.   He felt he was getting hold of the lady, but he didn't quite know where he was.   He'd got something ready to say, and he

---

[1] This shows clear and independent knowledge of the sitting which I had held with Mrs. Clegg that same morning (see early parts of this chapter).

16

started to try and say it, and it seemed as if he didn't know where he was.

[Feda reports sometimes in the third person, sometimes in the first.]

What does she flop about for, father ? *I* don't want to do that ; it bothered me rather, I didn't know if I was making her ill or something. Paulie said she thought it was the correct thing to do ! But I wish she wouldn't. If she would only keep quiet, and let me come calmly, it would be much easier. Mrs. Kathie [Feda's name for Mrs. Katherine Kennedy] tries to help all she can, but it makes such a muddled condition. I might not be able to get a test through, even when I controlled better ; I should have to get quite at home there, before I could give tests through her. He and Paulie used to joke about the old lady, but they don't now. Paul manages to control ; he used to see Paulie doing it. I will try again, he says, and I will try again. It's worth trying a few times, then I can get my bearings, and I feel that what I wanted to say beforehand I will be able to get through.

Feda has an idea that what he had saved up to say was only just the usual messages. He had got them ready in his head ; he had learnt it up—just a few words. Paulie told him he had better do that, and then (oh, you had better not tell Mrs. Kathie this, for it isn't polite !)—and then Paulie told him to spit it out. And that's what he tried to do—just to say the few words that he had learnt up. He just wanted to say how pleased he was to see you. He wanted also to speak about his mother, and to bring in, if he could, about having talked to you through Feda. Just simple things like that. He had to think of simple things, because Paulie had told him that it was no good trying to think of anything in-tri-cate.

[Feda always pronounces what she no doubt considers long words in a careful and drawn-out manner.]

He didn't see clearly, but he felt. He had a

good idea that you were there, and that Mrs. Kathie was there, but he wasn't sure; he was all muddled up. Poor Mrs. Kathie was doing her best. He says, Don't change the conditions, if you try it again. He never quite knows whether he is going to have good conditions or not. He wanted to speak about all this. That's all about that.

[This is a completely accurate reference to what had happened with Mrs. Clegg in the morning of the same day. Everything is properly and accurately represented. It is the best thing about the sitting perhaps, though there are many good things in it.]

[The next incident concerns other people—and I usually omit these—but I propose to include this one.]

About the lady he tried to help—the one that he didn't want Feda to tell who he was (p. 241).

He was helping through a man who had got drownded. This lady had had no belief nor nothing in spiritual things before. The guides brought her to Feda, that she might speak with a dear friend of hers. I helped him, he says, and got both of his initials through to her—E. A.

o. j. l.—Do I know these people ?

Yes, you write a lot to the lady.

[I remembered afterwards that I had had some correspondence with a lady who was told at a sitting, apparently by Raymond, that I knew a Dr. A. She was and is a stranger, but for this curious introduction.]

o. j. l —Is A the surname ?

Yes, the spirit's, not the lady's. The lady doesn't know that he [Raymond] is telling you this. And she doesn't know that he helped her. He says, It's for your own use, father. It's given her a new outlook on life.

o. j. l.—I have no idea who she is. Can you get her name ?

Oh yes, she's a lady called Mrs. D. [Full name given easily, but no doubt got from the sitter in ordinary course.] And before, you see, she was living a worldly life. She was interested in a way, but not much. She never tried to come into it. When she came, she thought she would have her fortune told. Raymond was waiting for her to come, and brought up the right conditions at once. The man was a nice man, he liked him, and he wanted to bring her into it. The man was fond of her. Raymond has been helping him a lot. He says, I can only help in a small way, but if you could go round and see the people just on the verge of learning something ! I can't help them in a big way, but still, it's something important even what I can do. For every one I bring in like that lady, there will be a dozen coming from that.

o. j. l. (still remembering nothing about these people).— Did the man drown himself ?

Oh no, he wented down in a boat ; they nearly all wented down together.

The lady wasn't expecting him—she nearly flopped over when he came.

o. j. l.—Was he related to the lady ?

No, but he had been the biggest thing in her life. He says it seemed as though she must have felt something, to make her write to you.

o. j. l.—However did Raymond know that she had written to me ?

Feda doesn't know. (*Sotto voce.*—Tell Feda, Yaymond.)

Do you believe me, father, I really can't tell you how I know some things. It's not through inquiry, but sometimes I get it just like a Marconi apparatus receives a message from somewhere, and doesn't know where it comes from at first. Sometimes I try to find out things, and I can't.

[I perceived gradually that this episode related to some one named E. A. (unknown to me), about whom I had been told at a Feda sitting on Friday, 28 January 1916, Raymond seeming to want me to speak to E. A.'s father about him. And in a note to that sitting it is explained how I received a letter shortly afterwards from a stranger, a Mrs. D.;

who consulted me about informing Dr. A. of the appearance of his son. The whole episode is an excellent one, but it concerns other people, and if narrated at all must be narrated more fully and in another place. Suffice it to say that the son had been lost in tragic circumstances, and that the father is impressed by the singular nature of the evidence that has now been given through the lady—a special visit to Scotland having been made by her for that express purpose. She had not known the father before, but she found him and his house as described ; and he admits the details as surprisingly accurate.]

Here is the extract from my sitting of 28 January 1916 relating to this affair :—

EXTRACT FROM O. J. L.'S SITTING WITH MRS. LEONARD, FRIDAY, 28 JANUARY 1916

He has met somebody called E., Raymond has. He doesn't know who it is, but wonders if you do.

O. J. L.—Is she an old lady ?

It's a man, he says. He was drownded. I have helped him a bit, at least I tried, he says. He passed on before Raymond did.

O. J. L.—Did he drown himself ?

Raymond doesn't say that. His name was E. He was from Scotland. You will know his father.

Raymond says, I have got a motive in this, father ; I don't want to say too much, and I don't want to say too little. You have met E.'s father, and you will meet him again ; he comes from Scotland. Raymond is not quite certain, but he thinks he is in Scotland now. His father's name begins with an A, so the other man is E. A. He was fighting his ship. Raymond thinks they was all drownded. He's older than Raymond. Raymond says he's a pretty dark chap. You know his father best, I don't know whether you knew the other chap at all. You have known his father for some years, but you don't often get a chance of meeting. I have got an idea that you will be hearing from him soon. Then you will be able to unload this on to him. They are trying to bring it about, that meeting with the father of E.

O. J. L.—I could make a guess at the surname, but perhaps I had better not.

No, don't.   You know I'm not always sure of my facts. I know pretty well how things are, and I think I am pretty safe in saying that it is Scotland.   He gives D. also, That's not a person, it's a place.   Some place not far from it, called D., he says.   It's near, not the place, where he lives.   'Flanked,' he calls it, 'flanked' on the other side by L.   They never knew how E. passed on really. They know he was drowned, but not how it happened.

On receiving this message I felt that the case was a genuine one, and that I did know a Dr. A. precisely as described.   And I also gradually remembered that he had lost a son at sea, though I did not know the son.   But I felt that I must wait for further particulars before broaching what might be an unpalatable subject to Dr. A.

(*End of extract from* 28 *January* 1916.)

Ultimately I did receive further particulars as narrated above, and so a month later I did go to call on the old Doctor, after the ice had been broken by Mrs. D.,—who in some trepidation had made a special journey for the purpose, and then nearly came away without opening the subject,—and I verified the trance description of his house which Mrs. D. had received and sent me.   Indeed, all the facts stated turned out to be true.

The sitting of 3 March, now being reported, and interrupted by this quotation from a previous sitting, went on thus :—

He took his mother some red roses, and he wants you to tell her.   He took them to her from the spirit world, they won't materialise, but I gathered some and took them to her.   This isn't a test, father.

O. J. L.—No.   Very well, you just want her to know.   I will tell her.

(A little talk omitted.)

O. J. L.—Do you want to say anything about the other two people that you helped—last Monday, I think it was? [The Sonnenscheins; still only known to Mrs. Leonard as a lady and gentleman from Darlington.]

No, there's nothing much to tell you about that, or about them.   But he brought a son to them. He stood on one side so as not to take any of the power. He just came at first to show Feda it was all right, and he just came in at the end to send his love.

O. J. L.—Why did he help those particular people?

[I knew why, but I thought proper to ask, since from the medium's point of view there was no reason at all.]

He says he had to. They have been worrying about whether their son had suffered much pain before he passed on. There seems to have been some uncertainty about as to whether he had or not. His body wasn't recovered as soon as it ought to have been. But he didn't suffer much. He was numbed, and didn't as a matter of fact feel much. He throwed up his arms, and rolled down a bank place.

[Christopher Sonnenschein was killed by falling down a snow mountain, and his body was not recovered for five days.]

O. J. L.—Did you know these people before?

Yes. He says, yes. But he won't tell Feda who they is.

O. J. L.—Does he want to send them any message?

He says nothing further has come out, except that he is getting on very well, and that he was pleased. You might tell them that he is happier now. Yes, he is, since he seed them.

[The sitting referred to here, as having been held by a lady and gentleman last Monday, refers to my colleague and his wife and their deceased son Christopher. Their identity had been completely masked by the arrangements they had made, without my knowledge. The letters making arrangements were sent round by Darlington to be posted, in order to cover up tracks and remove all chance of a discoverable connexion with me. (See p. 240.) Hence it is interesting that Raymond turned up to help, for in their normal life the two youths had known each other.]

He has been trying to help you since he saw
you here last time. He thought that you knew
that he was. He did try hard. He says, I helped
you in such a funny way. I got near you and felt
such a desire to help you and prevent you from
getting tired. He was concentrating on the
back of your head, and sort of saying to himself, and impressing the thought towards you :
" It's coming easy, you shan't get tired, the brain
is going to be very receptive, everything is going
to flow through it easily in order." I feel myself
saying it all the time, and I get so close I nearly
lean on you. To my great delight, I saw you sit
up once, and you said : " Ah, that's good." It was
some little time back.

O. J. L.—I speak to your photograph sometimes.

Yes. I can speak to you without a photograph ! I am often with you, very often.

He's taking Feda into a room with a desk in it ;
too big for a desk, it must be a table. A sort of a
desk, a pretty big one. A chair is in front of it,
not a chair like that, a high up chair, more wooden,
not woolly stuff ; and the light is falling on to the
desk ; and you are sitting there with a pen or
pencil in your hand ; you aren't writing much,
but you are looking through writing, and making
bits of writing on it ; you are not doing all the
writing yourself, but only bits on it. Raymond is
standing at the back of you ; he isn't looking at
what you are doing. [The description is correct.]

He thought you were tired out last time you
came here. He knows you are sometimes. He's
been wanting to say to you, " Leave some of it."

O. J. L.—But there's so much to be done.

Yes, he knows it isn't easy to leave it. But it
would be better in the end if you can leave a bit,
father. You are doing too much.

You know that I am longing and dying for the
day when you come over to me. It will be a
splendid day for me. But I mustn't be selfish.
I have got to work to keep you away from us, and
that's not easy for me.

He says that lots over here talk, and say that you will be doing the most wonderful work of your life through the war. People are ready to. listen now. They had too many things before to let them think about them ; but now it's the great thing to think about the after-life.

I want you to know that when first I came over here, I thought it a bit unfair that such a lot of fellows were coming over in the prime of life, coming over here. But now he sees that for every one that came over, dozens of people open their eyes, and want to know where he has gone to. Directly they want to know, they begin to learn something. Some of them never stopped to think seriously before. " He must be somewhere," they say, " he was so full of life; can we find out ? " Then I see that through this, people are going to find out, and find out not only for themselves, but will pass it on to many others, and so it will grow.

He wants to tell you that Mr. Myers says that in ten years from now the world will be a different place. He says that about fifty per cent. of the civilised portion of the globe will be either spiritualists, or coming into it.

O. J. L.—Fifteen per cent. ?

Fifty, he said.

Raymond says, I am no judge of that, but he isn't the only one that thinks it. He says, I've got a kind of theory, in a crude sort of way, that man has made the earth plane into such a hotbed of materialism and selfishness, that man again has to atone by sacrifices of mankind in the prime of their physical life. So that by that prime self-effacement, they will bring more spiritual conditions on to the earth, which will crush the spirit of materialism. He says that isn't how I meant to put it, but I've forgotten how I meant to say it.

O. J. L.—Well now, Raymond, Mr. Myers sent me a message to say that you had got some tests ready to get through, and that I was to give you an opportunity of giving them.

Oh yes, he says. But I can't get anything

through about the Argonauts : that seems worst of anything.

He's showing Feda a thing that looks like a canvas house. Yes, it must be a canvas house. And it looks to Feda as though it's on a place that seems to be open—a wide place. Yes, no, there's not much green showing where Feda can see. There's a kind of a door in it, like that. (Feda made some sign I didn't catch.) The canvas is sort of grey, quite a light colour, but not quite white. Oh yes, Feda feels the sound of water not far from it—ripple, ripple. Feda sees a boy—not Raymond—half lying, half sitting at the door of the tent place, and he hasn't got a proper coat on ; he's got a shirt thing on here, and he's like spreaded out. It's a browny-coloured earth, not nice green, but sandy-coloured ground. As Feda looks at the land, the ground rises sharp at the back. Must have been made to rise, it sticks up in the air. He's showing it as though it should be in some photograph or picture. Feda got wondering about it, what it was for. It's a funny-shaped tent, not round, sort of lop-sided. The door isn't a proper door, it flops. You ought to be able to see a picture of this. [See photographs opposite.]

O. J. L.—Has it got to do with the Argonauts ?

No.

O. J. L.—Oh, it's not Coniston then ?

No.

O. J. L.—Is it by the sea ?

Near the water, he says ; he doesn't say the sea. No, he won't say that ; he says, near water. It looks hot there.

O. J. L.—Will the boys know ?

You will know soon about it, he says.

Feda gets a feeling that there are two or three moving about inside that tent.

O. J. L.—Is it all one chamber in the tent ?

He didn't say that. He was going to say, no, and then he stopped to think. No, I don't think it was, it was divided off.

LARGE DOUBLE-COMPARTMENT TENT IN ITS FIRST FORM (1905)
(BUILT AT MORIEMONT AND TAKEN TO WOOLACOMBE)

[See photographs of two forms of this tent.]

Now he is showing something right on top of that. Now he is showing Feda a yacht, a boat with white sails. Now he is going back to the tent again. The raised up land is at the back of the tent, well set back. It doesn't give an even sticking up, but it goes right along, with bits up and bits lower down.

> [The description could not be completely taken down, but it gave the impression of a raised bank of varying height, behind an open space, and a tent in front of it. It quite suggested that sort of picture.]

[See photograph facing p. 252.]

Maps, what's that? Maps, maps, he says. He's saying something about maps. This is something that the boys will know. Poring, he says. Not pouring anything out, but poring over maps. Ask the boys. [See note after further reference to maps later in the sitting.]

O. J. L.—What about that yacht with sails; did it run on the water?

> No. (Feda, *sotto voce.*—Oh, Raymond, don't be silly!) He says, no. (Feda.—It must have done!) He's showing Feda like a thing on land, yes, a land thing. It's standing up, like edgeways. A narrow thing. No, it isn't water, but it has got nice white sails.

O. J. L.—Did it go along?

> He says it DIDN'T! He's laughing! When he said ' didn't ' he shouted it. Feda should have said, ' He laid peculiar emphasis on it.' This is for the boys.

O. J. L.—Had they got to do with that thing?

> Yes, they will know, they will understand. Yes, he keeps on showing like a boat—a yacht, he calls it, a yacht.

[See note below and photographs.]

Now he is showing Feda some figures. Something flat, like a wall. Rods and things, long rods. Some have got little round things shaking on them, like that. And he's got strings, some have got strings. ' Strings ' isn't the right word, but it will do. Smooth, strong, string-like. In the corner, where it's a little bit dark, some one is standing up and leaning against something, and a piece of stuff is flapping round them.

Now he is saying again something about maps. He's going to the maps again. It isn't a little map, but it's one you can unfold and fold up small. And they used to go with their fingers along it, like that—not he only, but the boys. And it wasn't at home, but when they were going somewhere— some distance from home. And Feda gets the impression as though they must be looking at the map when it was moving. They seem to be moving smoothly along, like in one of those horrible trains. Feda has never been in a train.

> [The mention of folded-up maps cannot be considered important, but it is appropriate, because many of the boys' common reminiscences group round long motor drives in Devonshire and Cornwall, when they must frequently have been consulting the kind of map described.]

> [*Note by O. J. L. on Tent and Boat.*—All this about the tent and boat is excellent, though not outside my knowledge. The description of the scenery showed plainly that it was Woolacombe sands that was meant— whither the family had gone in the summer for several years—a wide open stretch of sand, with ground rising at the back, as described, and with tents along under the bank, one of which—a big one—had been made by the boys. It was on wheels, it had two chambers with a double door, and was used for bathing by both the boys and girls. Quite a large affair, oblong in shape, like a small cottage. One night a gale carried it up to the top of the sand-hills and wrecked it. We saw it from the windows in the morning.

FIRST EDITION OF THE SAND-BOAT (1906) AT WOOLACOMBE
WITH ALEC ON BOARD

RISING GROUND BEHIND OLDER TENTS ON WOOLACOMBE BEACH

The boys pulled it to pieces, and made a smaller tent of the remains, this time with only one chamber, and its shape was now a bit lop-sided. I felt in listening to the description that there was some hesitation in Raymond's mind as to whether he was speaking of the first or the second stage of this tent.

As for the sand-boat, it was a thing they likewise made at Mariemont, and carted down to Woolacombe. A kind of long narrow platform or plank on wheels, with a rudder and sails. At first, when it had small sails, it only went with a light passenger and a strong wind behind. But in a second season they were more ambitious, and made bigger sails to it, and that season I believe it went along the sands very fast occasionally ; but it still wouldn't sail at right angles to the wind as they wanted. They finally smashed the mast by sailing in a gale with three passengers. There had been ingenuity in making it, and Raymond had been particularly active over it, as he was over all constructions. On the whole it was regarded as a failure, the wheels were too small ; and Raymond's ' DIDN'T ' is quite accepted.

References to these things were evidently some of the tests (p. 249) which he had got together for transmission to me. [See photographs.]

The rod and rings and strings, mentioned after the ' boat,' I don't at present understand. So far as I have ascertained, the boys don't understand either, at present.]

I don't know whether I have got anything more that I can really call a test. You will have to take, he says (he's laughing now)—take the information about the old lady as a test.

o. j. l.—You mean what he began with ? [*i.e.* about Mrs. Clegg.]
                Yes.

o. j. l.—Well, it's a very good one.

He's been trying to find somebody whose name begins with K. But it isn't Mrs. Kathie, it's a gentleman. He's been trying to find him.

o. j. l.—What for ?

He thought his mother would be interested. There's something funny about this. One is in the spirit world, but one they believe is still on the earth plane. He hasn't come over yet. [One of the two referred to is certainly dead ; the other may possibly, but very improbably, be a prisoner.] There's a good deal of mystery about this, but I'm sure he isn't actually come over yet. Some people think that because we are here, we have only to go anywhere we choose, and find out anything we like. But that's Tommy-rot. They are limited, but they send messages to each other, and what he sincerely believes is, that that man has not passed on.

o. j. l.—Mother thinks he has, and so do his people.

Yes, yes. I don't know whether it would be advisable to tell them anything, but I have a feeling that he isn't here. I have been looking for him everywhere.

He keeps on building up a J. He doesn't answer when Feda asks what that is. He says there will be a few surprises for people later on.

o. j. l.—Well, I take it that he wants me to understand that J. K. is on our side ?

Yes, he keeps nodding his head. Yes, in the body. Mind, he says, I've got a feeling—I can only call it a feeling—that he has been hurt, practically unconscious. Anyway, time will prove if I am right.

o. j. l.—I hope he will continue to live, and come back.

I hope so too. Except for the possible doubt about it, I would say tell them at once. But after all they are happier in thinking that he has gone over, than that he's in some place undergoing terrible privations.

Now he's saying something carefully to Feda. He says they should not go by finding a stick. He

wants you to put that down—they ought not to
go by finding a stick.

o. j. l.—Oh, they found a stick, did they?

Yes, that's how, yes.

[I clearly understood that this statement referred to a certain Colonel, about whom
there was uncertainty for months.   But
a funeral service has now been held
—an impressive one, which M. F. A. L.
attended.   On inquiry from her, I find
(what I didn't know at the time of the
sitting) that the evidence of his death is a
riding-whip, which they found in the hands
of an unrecognisable corpse.   From some
initials on this riding-whip, they thought it
belonged to him ; and on this evidence have
concluded him dead.   So far as I know,
they entertain no doubt about it.   At any
rate, we have heard none expressed, either
publicly or privately.   Hence, the information now given may possibly turn out of
interest, though there is always the possibility that, if he is a prisoner in Germany,
he may not survive the treatment.   He was
leading an attack on the Hohenzollern Re-
doubt when he fell ; he was seen to fall,
wounded ; there was great slaughter, and
when at night his man returned to try and
find him, he could not be found.   This is
my recollection of the details, but of course
they can be more accurately given.   At
what period the whip was found, I don't
know, but can ascertain.]   (See also p. 266.)

[No further news yet—September 1916.   But
I must confess that I think the information
extremely unlikely.—O. J. L.]

o. j. l.—Does he remember William, our gardener?

Yes.

Feda doesn't know what he means, but he says
something about coming over.   (Feda, *sotto voce.*—
Tell Feda what you mean.)

He doesn't give it very clearly. Feda gets an idea that he means coming over there. Yes, he does mean into the spirit world. Feda asks him, did he mean soon ; but he shakes his head.

o. j. l.—Does he mean that he has come already ?

He doesn't get that very clearly. He keeps saying, coming over, coming over, and when Feda asked ' Soon ? ' he shook his head, as if getting cross.

o. j. l.—If he sees him, perhaps he will help him.

Of course he will. He hasn't seen him yet. No, he hasn't seen him.

[I may here record that William, the gardener, died within a week before the sitting, and that Raymond here clearly indicates a knowledge, either of his death or of its imminence.]

It's difficult when people approach you, and say they knew your father or your mother ; you don't quite know what to say to them !

o. j. l.—Yes, it must be a bother. Do you remember a bird in our garden ?

(Feda, *sotto voce.*—Yes, hopping about ?)

o. j. l.—No, Feda, a big bird.

Of course, not sparrows, he says ! Yes, he does. (Feda, *sotto voce.*—Did he hop, Yaymond ?) No, he says you couldn't call it a hop.

o. j. l.—Well, we will go on to something else now ; I don't want to bother him about birds. Ask him does he remember Mr. Jackson ?

Yes. Going away, going away, he says. He used to come to the door. (Feda, *sotto voce.*—Do you know what he means ? Anyone can come to the door !) He used to see him every day, he says, every day. (*Sotto voce.*—What did he do, Yaymond ?)

He says, nothing. (I can't make out what he says.) He's thinking. It's Feda's fault, he says.

o. j. l.—Well, never mind. Report anything he says, whether it makes sense or not.

He says he fell down. He's sure of that. He hurt himself. He builds up a letter T, and he shows a gate, a small gate—looks like a foot-path ; not one in the middle of a town. Pain in hands and arms.

O. J. L.—Was he a friend of the family ?

No. No, he says, no. He gives Feda a feeling of tumbling, again he gives a feeling as though— (Feda thinks Yaymond's joking)—he laughed. He was well known among us, he says; and yet, he says, not a friend of the family. Scarcely a day passed without his name being mentioned. He's joking, Feda feels sure. He's making fun of Feda.

O. J. L.—No, tell me all he says.

He says, put him on a pedestal. No, that they put him on a pedestal. He was considered very wonderful. And he 'specs that he wouldn't have appreciated it, if he had known; but he didn't know, he says. Not sure if he ever will, he says. It sounds nonsense, what he says. Feda has got an impression that he's mixing him up with the bird, because he said something about ' bird ' in the middle of it—just while he said something about Mr. Jackson, and then he pulled himself up, and changed it again. Just before he said ' pedestal ', he said ' fine bird,' and then he stopped. In trying to answer the one, he got both mixed up, Mr. Jackson and the bird.

O. J. L.—How absurd ! Perhaps he's getting tired.

He won't say he got this mixed up ! But he did ! Because he said ' fine bird,' and then he started off about Mr. Jackson.

O. J. L.—What about the pedestal ?

On a pedestal, he said.

O. J. L.—Would he like him put on a pedestal ?

No, he doesn't say nothing.

[*Contemporary Note by O. J. L.*—The episode of Mr. Jackson and the bird is a good one. ' Mr. Jackson ' is the comic name of our peacock. Within the last week he has died, partly, I fear, by the severe weather. But his legs have been rheumatic and troublesome for some time ; and in trying to walk he of late has tumbled down on them. He was found dead in a yard on a cold morning with his neck broken. One of the last people I saw before leaving home for this sitting was a man whom Lady Lodge had sent to take the bird's body and have it stuffed. She showed him a wooden pedestal on which she thought it might be placed, and tail feathers were being sent with it. Hence, the reference to the pedestal, if not telepathic from me, shows a curious knowledge of what was going on. And the jocular withholding from Feda of the real meaning of Mr. Jackson, and the appropriate remarks made concerning him which puzzled Feda, were quite in Raymond's vein of humour.

Perhaps it was unfortunate that I had mentioned a bird first, but I tried afterwards, by my manner and remarks, completely to dissociate the name Jackson from what I had asked before about the bird ; and Raymond played up to it.

It may be that he acquires some of these contemporary items of family information through sittings which are held in Mariemont, where of course all family gossip is told him freely, no outsider or medium being present. But the death of Mr. Jackson, and the idea of having him stuffed and put on a pedestal, were very recent, and I was surprised that he had knowledge of them. I emphasise the episode as exceptionally good.]

He's trying to show Feda the side of a house ; not a wall, it has got glass. He's taking Feda round to it ; it has got glass stuff. Yes, and when you look in, it's like flowers inside and green stuff. He used to go there a lot—be there, he says. Red-coloured pots.

O. J. L.—Is that anything to do with Mr. Jackson ?

He's shaking his head now. That's where mother got the flowers from. Tell her, she will know.

[There is more than one greenhouse that might be referred to. M. F. A. L. got the yellow jasmine, which she thinks is the flower re-

"GRANDFATHER W."

"MR. JACKSON" WITH M.F.A.L. AT MARIEMONT

ferred to, from the neighbourhood of one of them. And it is one on which the peacock used commonly to roost ; though whether the reference to it followed on, or had any connexion with, the peacock is uncertain, and seems to be denied.]

Yes, he's not so clear now, Soliver. He *has* enjoyed himself. Sometimes he enjoys himself so much, he forgets to do the good things he prepared. I could stay for hours and hours, he says. But he's just as keen as you are in getting tests through. I think I have got some. When I go away, I pat myself on the back and think, That's something for them to say, " Old Raymond does remember something." What does aggravate him sometimes is that when he can't get things through, people think it's because he has forgotten. It isn't a case of forgetting. He doesn't forget anything.

Father, do you remember what I told mother about the place I had been to, and whom I had been allowed to see ? What did they think of it ?

[See M. F. A. L. sitting with Mrs. Leonard, 4 February 1916, Chapter XX.]

O. J. L.—Well, the family thought that it wasn't like Raymond.

Ah, that's what I was afraid of. That's the awful part of it.

O. J. L.—Well, I don't suppose they knew your serious side.

Before he gave that to his mother, he hesitated, and thought he wouldn't. And then he said, Never mind what they think now, I must let mother and father know. Some day they will know, and so, what does it matter ?

He knew that they might think it was something out of a book, not me ; but perhaps they didn't know that side of me so well.

O. J. L.—No. But among the things that came back, there was a Bible with marked passages in it, and so I saw that you had thought seriously about these things. [Page 11.]

Yes, he says. Yet there's something strange

about it somehow.　We are afraid of showing that
side ; we keep it to ourselves, and even hide it.

o. j. l.—It must have been a great experience for you.

I hadn't looked for it, I hadn't hoped for it, but
it was granted.

o. j. l.—Do you think you could take some opportunity
of speaking about it through some other medium,
not Feda ?　Because at present the boys think
that Feda invented it.

Yes, that's what they do think.　He says he
will try very hard.

o. j. l.—Have you ever seen that Person otherwise than
at that time ?

No, I have not seen Him, except as I told you ;
he says, father, he doesn't come and mingle
freely, here and there and everywhere.　I mean,
not in that sense ; but we are always conscious,
and we feel him.　We are conscious of his presence.
But you know that people think that when they
go over, they will be with him hand in hand, but
of course they're wrong.

He doesn't think he will say very much more
about that now, not until he's able to say it through
some one else.　It may be that they will say it
wrong, that it won't be right ; it may get twisted.
Feda does that sometimes.　(Feda, *sotto voce.*—No,
Feda doesn't !)　Yes she does, and that's why I
say, go carefully.

o. j. l.—Has he been through another medium to a
friend of mine lately ?

[This was intended to refer to a sitting which
Mr. Hill was holding with Peters about
that date, and, as it turned out, on the same
day.]

He doesn't say much.　No, he doesn't say
nothing about it.　He hasn't got much power, and
he's afraid that he might go wrong.

Good-bye, father, now.　My love to you, my
love to mother.　I am nearer to you than ever
before, and I'm not so silly about [not] showing it.
Love to all of them.　Lionel is a dear old chap.
My love to all.

SECOND EDITION OF SAND-BOAT, AT MARIEMONT, BEFORE BEING
UNSHIPPED AND TAKEN TO WOOLACOMBE, 1907

RAYMOND WORKING AT THE SAND-BOAT IN THE BOYS
LABORATORY AT MARIEMONT

Don't forget to tell mother about the roses I brought her.   There's nothing to understand about them ; I just wanted her to know that I brought her some flowers.

Good night, father.   I am always thinking of you.   God bless you all.

Give Feda's love to SrAlec.

O. J. L.—Yes, I will, Feda.   We are all fond of you.

Yes, Feda feels it, and it lifts Feda up, and helps her.

Mrs. Leonard speedily came-to, and seemed quite easy and well, although the sitting had been a long one, and it was now nearly 11.30 p.m.

[I repeat in conclusion that this was an excellent sitting, with a good deal of evidential matter.—O. J. L.]

CHAPTER XXII

MORE UNVERIFIABLE MATTER

ON 24 March, we had some more unverifiable material through Mrs. Leonard ; it was much less striking than that given on 4 February, and I am inclined myself to attribute a good deal of it to hypothetical information received by Feda from other sitters : but it seems unfair to suppress it. In accordance with my plan I propose to reproduce it for what it is worth.

Sitting with Mrs. Leonard at our Flat, Friday, 24 March 1916, from 5.45 p.m. to 8 p.m.

*(Present—*O. J. L. AND M. F. A. L.)

REPORT BY O. J. L.

(Mrs. Leonard arrived about 5.30 to tea, for a sitting with M. F. A. L. I happened to be able to come too, in order to take notes. She had just come away from another sitting, and had had some difficulty in getting rid of her previous sitter in time, which rather bothered her. The result was not specially conducive to lucidity, and the sitting seemed only a moderately good one.

When Feda arrived she seemed pleased, and said :—)

Yes it is, yes, it's Soliver !

How are you ? Raymond's here !

M. F. A. L.—Is he here already ?

Yes, of course he is !

(Feda, *sotto voce.*—What's he say ?) He says he hasn't come to play with Feda, or make jokes ; he's come about serious things.

Do you remember, Miss Olive [Feda's name for Lady Lodge], some time ago, about that beautiful experience what he had ?   He's so glad that you and Soliver know about it, even though the others can't take it in.   Years hence he thinks they may. He says, over there, they don't mind talking about the real things, over there, 'cos they're the things that count.

He thinks the one that took it in mostly was Lionel.   Yes, it seemed to sink in mostly ; he was turning it over afterwards, though he didn't say much.   He's more ready for that than the others. He says he would never have believed it when he was here, but he is.

He hasn't been to that place again, not that same place.   But he's been to a place just below it. He's been attending lectures, at what they call, " halls of learning " : you can prepare yourself for the higher spheres while you are living in lower ones. He's on the third, but he's told that even now he could go on to the fourth if he chose ; but he says he would rather be learning the laws ap-per-taining to each sphere while he's still living on the third, be-cause it brings him closer—at least until you two have come over.   He will stay and learn, where he is. He wouldn't like to go on there and then find it to be difficult to get back.   He will wait till we can go happily and comfortably together !

Would it interest you for him to tell you about one of the places he's been to ?   It's so interesting to him, that he might seem to exaggerate ; but the experience is so wonderful, it lives with him.

He went into a place on the fifth sphere—a place he takes to be made of alabaster.   He's not sure that it really was, but it looked like that.   It looked like a kind of a temple—a large one.   There were crowds passing into this place, and they looked very happy.   And he thought, " I wonder what I'm going to see here."   When he got mixed up with the crowd going into the temple, he felt a kind of— (he's stopping to think).   It's not irreverency what he says, but he felt a kind of feeling as if he had had too much champagne—it went to his head, he felt too buoyant, as if carried a bit off the ground.

That's 'cos he isn't quite attuned to the conditions
of that sphere.   It's a most extraordinary feeling.
He went in, and he saw that though the building
was white, there were many different lights : looked
like certain places covered in red, and . . . was blue,
and the centre was orange.   These were not the
crude colours that go by those names, but a soft-
ened shade.   And he looked to see what they came
from.   Then he saw that a lot of the windows were
extremely large, and the panes in them had glass
of these colours.   And he saw that some of the
people would go and stand in the pinky coloured
light that came through the red glass, and others
would stand in the blue light, and some would
stand in the orange or yellow coloured light.   And
he thought, "What are they doing that for?"
Then some one told him that the pinky coloured
light was the light of the love-colour ; and the blue
was the light of actual spiritual healing ; and the
orange was the light of intellect.   And that, according to what people wanted, they would go and
stand under that light.   And the guide told him
that it was more important than what people on
earth knew.   And that, in years to come, there
would be made a study of the effect of different
lights.

    The pinky people looked clever and developed
in their attitude and mentality generally ; but they
hadn't been able to cultivate the love-interest much,
their other interests had overpowered that one.
And the people who went into the intellectual light
looked softer and happy, but not so clever looking.
He says he felt more drawn to the pink light himself, but some one said, "No, you have felt a good
deal of that," and he got out and went into the
other two, and he felt that he liked the blue light
best.   And he thinks that perhaps you will read
something into that.   I had the other conditions,
but I wanted the other so much.   The blue seemed
to call me more than the others.   After I had been
in it some time, I felt that nothing mattered much,
except preparing for the spiritual life.   He says

that the old Raymond seemed far away at the time, as though he was looking back on some one else's life—some one I hadn't much connexion with, and yet who was linked on to me. And he felt, "What does anything matter, if I can only attain this beautiful uplifting feeling." I can't tell you what I felt like, but reading it over afterwards, perhaps you will understand. Words feel powerless to describe it. He won't try, he will just tell you what happened after.

We sat down—the seats were arranged something like pews in a church—and as he looked towards the aisle, he saw coming up it about seven figures. And he saw, from his former experience, that they were evidently teachers come down from the seventh sphere. He says, they went up to the end part, and they stood on a little raised platform ; and then one of them came down each of the little aisles, and put out their hands on those sitting in the pews. And when one of the Guides put his hand on his head, he felt a mixture of all three lights—as if he understood everything, and as if everything that he had ever felt, of anger or worry, all seemed nothing. And he felt as if he could rise to any height, and as if he could raise everybody round him. As if he had such a power in himself. He's stopping to think over it again.

They sat and listened, and the first part of the ceremony was given in a lecture, in which one of the Guides was telling them how to teach others on the lower spheres and earth plane, to come more into the spiritual life, while still on those lower planes. I think that all that went before was to make it easy to understand. And he didn't get only the words of the speaker, words didn't seem to matter, he got the thought—whole sentences, instead of one word at a time. And lessons were given on concentration, and on the projection of uplifting and helpful thoughts to those on the earth plane. And as he sat there—he sat, they were not kneeling—he felt as if something was going from him, through the other spheres on to the earth, and was helping somebody, though he didn't know who it was. He can't tell you how wonderful it was ; not once it happened, but several times.

He's even been on to the sixth sphere too. The sixth sphere was even more beautiful than the fifth, but at present he didn't want to stay there. He would rather be helping people where he is.

O. J. L.—Does he see the troubles of people on the earth ?

Yes, he does sometimes.

I do wish that we could alter people so that they were not ashamed to talk about the things that matter. He can see people preparing for the summer holidays, and yet something may prevent them. But the journey that they have got to go some time, that they don't prepare for at all.

M. F. A. L.—How can you prepare for it ?

Yes, by speaking about it openly, and living your life so as to make it easier for yourself and others.

O. J. L.—Is Raymond still there ? Has he got any more tests to give, or anything to say, to the boys or anybody ?

Did they understand about the yacht ?

O. J. L.—Yes, they did.

And about the tent ?

O. J. L.—Yes, they did.

He's very pleased—it bucks him up when he gets things through.

O. J. L.—Have you learnt any more about [the Colonel [1]] ?

He's not on the spirit side. He feels sure he isn't. Somebody told him that there was a body found, near the place where he had been, and it was dressed in uniform like he had had. But something had happened to it here (pointing to her head).

O. J. L.—Who was it told you ?

Some one on the other side ; just a messenger, not one who knew all about it. No, the messenger didn't seem to know J. K. personally, but he had

[1] See record on p. 254.

gathered the information from the minds of people on the earth plane. And Feda isn't quite sure, but thinks that there was something missing from the body—missing from the body that they took to be him, which would have identified him.

O. J. L.—Do you mean the face ?

No, he doesn't mean the face.

(M. F. A. L., here pointing to her chest, signified to me that she knew that it was the identification disk that was missing.)

M. F. A. L.—Why was it missing ?

Because it wasn't he ! In the first place, it couldn't be, but if that had only been there, they would have known. He can't say where he is at the present moment, but he heard a few days ago that he is being kept somewhere, and as far as he can make out, in Belgium. It's as though he had been taken some distance.

Raymond's not showing this—but Feda's shown in a sort of flash a letter. First a B, and then an R. But the B doesn't mean Belgium ; it's either a B or an R, or both. It just flashed up. It may mean the place where he is. But Raymond doesn't know where he is, only he's quite sure that he isn't on the spirit side. But he's afraid he's ill.

O. J. L.—Have you anything more to say about E. A. ? [See 3 March record, p. 243.]

No, no more. Raymond came to Feda to help the lady who came. Feda started describing Raymond. And he said, no, only come to help. And then he brought the one what was drownded. He came to help also with another, but Feda didn't tell that lady, 'cos she didn't know you. He doesn't like Feda to tell. Feda couldn't understand why he wanted to help, because she didn't know he knew that gentleman. He helped E. A. to build up a picture of his home. Perhaps she thinks it was Feda being so clever !

O. J. L.—Yes, I know, she's been there to see it. [See p. 245.]

Yes, and she found it what she said. He told

her that she wouldn't be seeing his mother. She couldn't see why she shouldn't see his mother ; but she didn't. [True.]

Raymond hasn't got any good tests. He can't manufacture them, and they are so hard to remember.

o. j. l.—Is he still in his little house ?

Oh yes, he feels at home there.

o. j. l.—He said it was made of bricks—I could make nothing of that.

I knew you couldn't ! It's difficult to explain. At-om- ; he say something about at-om-ic principle. They seem to be able to draw (?) certain unstable atoms from the atmosphere and crystallise them as they draw near certain central attraction. That isn't quite what Feda thinks of it. Feda has seen like something going round—a wheel—something like electricity, some sparks dropping off the edge of the wheel, and it goes crick, crick, and becomes like hard ; and then they falls like little raindrops into the long thing under the wheel—Raymond calls it the accumulator. I can't call them anything but bricks. It's difficult to know what to call them. Wait until you come over, and I'll show you round. And you will say, " By Jove, so they are ! " Things are quite real here. Mind, I don't say things are as heavy as on the earth, because they're not. And if he hit or kicked something it wouldn't displace it so much as on the earth, because we're lighter. I can't tell you exactly what it is ; I'm not very interested in making bricks, but I can see plainly how it's apparently done.

He says it appears to him too, that the spirit spheres are built round the earth plane. and seem to revolve with it. Only, naturally, the first sphere isn't revolving at such a rate as the third, fourth, fifth, sixth, and seventh spheres. Greater circumference makes it seem to revolve more rapidly. That seems to have an actual effect on the atmospheric conditions prevailing in any one of the spheres. Do you see what he's getting at ?

o. j. l.—Yes. He only means that the peripheral

velocity is greater for the bigger spheres, though the angular velocity is the same.

Yes, that's just what he means. And it does affect the different conditions, and that's why he felt a bit careful when he was on a higher sphere, in hanging on to the ground.

[A good deal of this struck me as nonsense ; as if Feda had picked it up from some sitter. But I went on recording what was said.]

Such a lot of people think it's a kind of thought-world, where you think all sort of things—that it's all "think." But when you come over you see that there's no thinking about it ; it's *there*, and it does impress you with reality. He does wish you would come over. He will be as proud as a cat with something tails—two tails, he said. Proud as a cat with two tails showing you round the places. He says, father will have a fine time, poking into everything, and turning everything inside out.

There's plenty flowers growing here, Miss Olive, you will be glad to hear. But we don't cut them here. They doesn't die and grow again ; they seem to renew themselves. Just like people, they are there all the time renewing their spirit bodies. The higher the sphere he went to, the lighter the bodies seemed to be—he means the fairer, lighter in colour. He's got an idea that the reason why people have drawn angels with long fair hair and very fair complexion is that they have been inspired by somebody from very high spheres. Feda's not fair ; she's not brown, but olive coloured ; her hair is dark. All people that's any good has black hair.

Do you know that [a friend] won't be satisfied unless he comes and has a talk through the table. Feda doesn't mind now, 'cos she has had a talk. So she will go now and let him talk through the table all right.

Give Feda's love to all of them, specially to SLionel—Feda likes him

(Mrs. Leonard now came-to, and after about ten minutes she and M. F. A. L. sat at a small octagonal table, which, in another five minutes, began to tilt.)
[But the subject now completely changed, and, if reported at all, must be reported elsewhere.]

I may say that several times, during a Feda sitting, some special communicator has asked for a table sitting to follow, because he considers it more definite and more private. And certainly some of the evidence so got has been remarkable ; as indeed it was on this occasion. But the record concerns other people, distant friends of my wife, some of whom take no interest in the subject whatever.

NOTE IN TENTH EDITION

The episode of " E. A." has developed a good deal since the book appeared. " Dr. A." himself has died, and has proved unexpectedly competent in giving messages himself—giving them through several independent mediums, and in a very characteristic style. He has clearly shown that he remembers some of our talks on the subject, and has described the circumstances under which they occurred. Mrs. D. also has had further communications from E. A. ; and the whole episode has now grown so much that a detailed account of it must be reported either in the *Proceedings S.P.R.* or elsewhere.

CHAPTER XXIII

A FEW ISOLATED INCIDENTS

THERE are a number of incidents which might be reported, some of them of characteristic quality, and a few of them of the nature of good tests. The first of these reported here is decidedly important.

I. SIMULTANEOUS SITTINGS IN LONDON AND EDGBASTON

SPECIAL "HONOLULU" TEST EPISODE

Lionel and Norah, going through London on the way to Eastbourne, on Friday, 26 May 1916, arranged to have a sitting with Mrs. Leonard about noon. They held one from 11.55 to 1.30, and a portion of their record is transcribed below.

At noon it seems suddenly to have occurred to Alec in Birmingham to try for a correspondence test; so he motored up from his office, extracted some sisters from the Lady Mayoress's Depot, where they were making surgical bandages, and took them to Mariemont for a brief table sitting. It lasted about ten minutes, between 12.10 and 12.20 p.m. And the test which he then and there suggested was to ask Raymond to get Feda in London to say the word " Honolulu." This task, I am told, was vigorously accepted and acquiesced in.

A record of this short sitting Alec wrote on a letter-card to me, which I received at 7 p.m. the same evening at Mariemont : the first I had heard of the experiment. The postmark is " 1 p.m. 26 My 16," and the card runs thus :—

" *Mariemont, Friday,* 26 *May,* 12.29 *p.m.*

Honor, Rosalynde, and Alec sitting in drawing-room at table. Knowing Lionel and Norah having Feda sitting in London simultaneously. Asked Raymond to give our love to Norah and Lionel and to try and get Feda to say Honolulu. Norah and Lionel know nothing of this, as it was arranged by A. M.•L. after 12 o'clock to-day.

" (Signed)   ALEC M. LODGE
HONOR G. LODGE
ROSALYNDE V. LODGE "

It is endorsed on the back in pencil, " Posted at B'ham General P.O. 12.43 p.m." ; and, in ink, " Received by me 7 p.m.—O. J. L. Opened and read and filed at once."

The sitters in London knew nothing of the contemporaneous attempt ; and nothing was told them, either then or later. Noticing nothing odd in their sitting, which they had not considered a particularly good one, they made no report till after both had returned from Eastbourne a week later.

The notes by that time had been written out, and were given me to read to the family. As I read, I came on a passage near the end, and, like the few others who were in the secret, was pleased to find that the word " Honolulu " had been successfully got through. The subject of music appeared to have been rather forced in by Raymond, in order to get Feda to mention an otherwise disconnected and meaningless word ; the time when this was managed being, I *estimate,* about 1.0 or 1.15. But of course it was not noted as of any interest at the time.

Here follow the London Notes. I will quote portions of the sitting only, so as not to take up too much space :—

Sitting of Lionel and Norah with Mrs. Leonard in London, Friday, 26 *May* 1916, *beginning* 11.55 *a.m.*

EXTRACTS FROM REPORT BY L. L.

After referring to Raymond's married sister and her husband, Feda suddenly ejaculated :—
How is Alec ?

L. L.—Oh, all right.

He just wanted to know how he was, and send his love to him.   He does not always see who is at the table ; he feels some more than others.[1]

He says you (to Norah) sat at the table and Lionel.

He felt you (Norah) more than any one else at the table.

[This is unlikely.   He seems to be thinking that it is Honor.]

Feda feels that if you started off very easily, you would be able to see him.   Develop a normal . . . [clairvoyance probably].

Raymond says, go slowly, develop just with time, go slowly.   Even the table helps a little.

He can really get through now in his own words.   When he is there, he now knows what he has got through.

The Indians have got through their hanky-panky.   [We thought that this meant playing with the table in a way beyond his control.]

He says that Lily is here.   (Feda, *sotto voce.*— Where is she ?)

She looks very beautiful, and has lilies ; she will help too, and give you power.

Sit quietly once or twice a week, hold your hands, the right over the left, so, for ten minutes, then sit quiet—only patience.   He could wait till doomsday.

He says, Wait and see ; he is laughing !

He has seen Curly (p. 203).

L. L.—Is Curly there now ?

No, see her when we wants to.   That's the one that wriggles and goes . . . (here Feda made a sound like a dog panting, with her tongue out— quite a good imitation).

Raymond has met another boy like Paul, a boy called Ralph.   He likes him.   There is what you call a set.   People meet there who are interested

---

[1] It is noteworthy, in connexion with these remarks, that Honor and Alec were sitting for a short time at Mariemont just about now.— O. J. L.

18

in the same things.   Ralph is a very decent sort of chap.[1]

(To Norah).—You could play.

N. M. L.—Play what ?

Not a game, a music.

N. M. L.—I am afraid I can't, Raymond.

(Feda, *sotto voce.*—She can't do that.)

He wanted to know whether you could play Hulu—Honolulu.

Well, can't you try to ?   He is rolling with laughter [meaning that he's pleased about something].

He knows who he is speaking to, but he can't give the name.

[Here he seems to know that it is Norah and not Honor.]

L. L.—Should I tell him ?

No.

He says something about a yacht ; he means a test he sent through about a yacht.   Confounded Argonauts ! [2]

He is going.   Fondest love to them at Mariemont.

The sitting continued for a short time longer, ending at 1.30 p.m., but the present report may end here.

NOTE ON THE 'HONOLULU' EPISODE BY O. J. L.

In my judgement there were signs that the simultaneous holding of two sittings, one with Honor and Alec in Edgbaston, and one with Lionel and Norah in London, introduced a little harmless confusion ; there was a tendency in London to confuse Norah with Honor, and Alec was mentioned in London in perhaps an unnecessary way.   I do not press this, however, but I do press the 'Honolulu' episode—

(i) because it establishes a reality about the home sittings,

---

[1] This is the first mention of a Ralph—presumably the one whose people, not known to us personally, had had excellent table sittings with Mrs. Leonard.   See Chapter XII.—O. J. L.

[2] This is too late to be of any use, but ' Yacht ' appears to be the sort of answer they had wanted to ' Argonauts.'—O. J. L.

(ii) because it so entirely eliminates anything of the nature of collusion, conscious or unconscious,

(iii) because the whole circumstances of the test make it an exceedingly good one.

What it does not exclude is telepathy. In fact it may be said to suggest telepathy. Yes, it suggests distinctly one variety of what, I think, is often called telepathy—a process sometimes conducted, I suspect, by an unrecognised emissary or messenger between agent and percipient. It was exactly like an experiment conducted for thought transference at a distance. For at Edgbaston was a party of three sitting round a table and thinking for a few seconds of the word ' Honolulu '; while in London was a party of two simultaneously sitting with a medium and recording what was said. And in their record the word ' Honolulu ' occurs. Telepathy, however—of whatever kind—is not a normal explanation; and I venture to say that there is no normal explanation, since in my judgement chance is out of the question. The subject of music was forced in by the communicator, in order to bring in the word; it did not occur naturally; and even if the subject of music had arisen, there was no sort of reason for referring to that particular song. The chief thing that the episode establishes, to my mind, and a thing that was worth establishing, is the genuine character of the simple domestic sittings without a medium which are occasionally held by the family circle at Mariemont. For it is through these chiefly that Raymond remains as much a member of the family group as ever.

II. IMPROMPTU MARIEMONT SITTING

Once at Mariemont, I am told, when M. F. A. L. and Honor were touching it, the table moved up to a book in which relics and reminiscences of Raymond had been pasted, and caused it to be opened. In it, among other things, was an enlargement of the snapshot facing page 278, showing him in an old ' Nagant ' motor, which had been passed on to him by Alec, stopping outside a certain house in Somersetshire. He was asked what house it was, and was expected to spell the name of the friend who lived there, but instead he spelt the name of the house. The record by M. F. A. L., with some unimportant omissions, is here reproduced—merely, however, as another example of a private sitting without a medium.

Impromptu Table Sitting at Mariemont, Tuesday,
25 April 1916

(Report by M. F. A. L.)

I had been thinking of Raymond all day, and wanting to thank him for what he did yesterday for [a friend]. Honor had agreed that we might do it some time, but when I mentioned it about 10.50 p.m., she did not want to sit then—she thought it too late. We were then in the library.

Honor, sitting on the Chesterfield, said, " I wonder if any table would be equally good for Raymond?"—placing her hands on the middle-sized table of the nest of three. It at once began to stir, and she asked me to place mine on the other side to steady it.

I asked if it was Raymond, and it decidedly said YES.

I then thanked him with much feeling for what he had done for [two separate families] lately. I told him how much he had comforted them, and how splendidly he was doing; that there were quite a number of people he had helped now. We discussed a few others that needed help.

Then I think we asked him if he knew what room we were in—YES. And after knocking me a good deal, and making a noise which seemed to please him against my eyeglasses, he managed, by laying the table down, to get one foot on to the Chesterfield and raise the table up on it ; and there it stayed, and rocked about for a long time answering questions—I thought it would make a hole in the cover.

I don't quite remember how it got down, but it did, and then edged itself up to the other larger table, which had been given me by Alec, Noël, and Raymond, after they had broken a basket table I used to use there—it was brought in with a paper, " To Mother from the culprits."

(This was a year or two ago.)   Well, he got it up to this
table, and fidgeted about with the foot of the smaller table
on which we had our hands, until he rested it on a ledge
and tried to raise it up.   But the way he did this most
successfully was when he got the ledge of our small table
on to a corner of the other and then raised it off the
ground level.   This he did several times.   I took one hand
off, leaving one hand on the top, and Honor's two hands
lying on the top, *no part* of them being over the edge, and
I measured the height the legs were off the ground.   The
first time it was the width of three fingers, and the next
time four fingers.

Honor told him this was very clever.

I then tried to press it down, but could not—a curious
feeling, like pressing on a cushion of air.

He had by this time turned us right round, so that
Honor was sitting where I had been before, and I was
sitting or sometimes standing in her place.   Then we were
turned round again, and he seemed to want to knock the
other table again ; he went at it in a curious way.   I had
with one hand to remove a glass on it which I thought
he would upset.   He continued to edge against it, until
he reached a book lying on it.   This he knocked with such
intention, that Honor asked him if he wanted it opened.

YES.

> [This was a scrap-book in which I collect any-
> thing about him—photographs, old and
> new ; poems made *about* him, or sent to me
> in consolation ; and it has his name outside,
> drawn on in large letters.—M. F. A. L.]

So I opened it, and showed him the photograph of himself seated in the ' Nagant.' [A motor-car which Alec
had practically given him not long before the war, and
with which he was delighted.]

Honor asked if he could see it, and he said YES, and
seemed pleased.

She asked if he could tell her what house it was standing in front of, and he spelt out—

ST. GERMINS.

> [This was pretty good, as the name of the
> Jacques's house is ' St. Germains.']

(Honor had forgotten the name till he began,
and expected him to say Jacques's.)

We told him he had got it, but that his spelling wasn't
quite as good as it had been.

Honor talked to him then about the 'Nagant' and
the 'Gabrielle Horn,' all of which seemed to delight him.

We then showed him some other photographs, and the
one of his dog, and asked him to spell its name, which he
did without mistake—

LARRY.

He couldn't see the little photograph of the goats, as it
was too small. But he saw himself in uniform—the one
taken by Rosalynde and enlarged—and he seemed to like
seeing that.

We talked a lot to him. I asked if he remembered his
journey with me out to Italy, and the Pullman car, etc.
At this he knocked very affectionately against me.

We then thought it was time for us all to go to bed.
But he said No. So we went on telling him family news.
He listened with interest and appreciative knocks, and
he then tried his balancing trick again, sometimes with
success, but often failing to get the leg right. But he did it
again in the end. We tried to say good night, it being then
nearly one o'clock, but he didn't seem to want to go.

We said au revoir, and told him we would see him
again soon.

III. EPISODE OF 'MR. JACKSON'

A striking incident is reported in one of my 'Feda'
sittings—that on 3 March 1916—shortly after the death
of our peacock, which went by the comic name of 'Mr.
Jackson,' his wives being Matilda Jackson and Janet. He
was a pet of M. F. A. L.'s, and had recently met with a
tragic end. It was decided to have him stuffed, and one
of the last things I had seen before leaving Mariemont was
a wooden pedestal on which it was proposed to put him.

When I asked Feda if Raymond remembered Mr.
Jackson,. he spoke of him humorously, greatly to Feda's
puzzlement, who said at last that he was mixing him up
with a bird, about whom I had previously inquired;
because he said, ' Fine bird, put him on a pedestal.'

GROUP SUBSEQUENTLY TAKEN AT THE SAME TIME, BUT PRESSURE ON SHOULDER REMOVED

"CURLY" AND "VIX." CURLY BEING THE SHAGGY ONE.
VIX WAS THE MOTHER OF RAYMOND'S DOG "LARRY"

RAYMOND IN HIS "NAGANT" MOTOR, 1913. OUTSIDE A
FRIEND'S HOUSE IN SOMERSETSHIRE

If this was not telepathy from me, it seems to show a curious knowledge of what is going on at his home, for the bird had not been dead a week, and if he were alive there would be no sense in saying, ' put him on a pedestal.' Feda evidently understood it, or tried to understand it, as meaning that some man, a Mr. Jackson, was metaphorically put on a pedestal by the family.

The fact, however, that Mr. Jackson was at once known by Raymond to be a bird is itself evidential, for there was nothing in the way I asked the question to make Feda or anyone think he was not a man. Indeed, that is precisely why she got rather bewildered. See Chapter XXI.

IV. EPISODE OF THE PHOTOGRAPHS

It is unnecessary to call attention to the importance of the photograph incident, which is fully narrated in Chapter IV ; but he spoke later of another photograph, in which he said was included his friend Case. It is mentioned near the end of Chapter IV. That photograph we also obtained from Gale & Polden, and it is true that Case is in it as well as Raymond, whereas he was not in the former group ; but this one is entirely different from the other, for they are both in a back row standing up, and in a quite open place. If this had been sent to us at first, instead of the right one, we should have considered the description quite wrong. As it is, the main photograph episode constitutes one of the best pieces of evidence that has been given.

REMARKS BY O. J. L. IN CONCLUDING PART II

The number of more or less convincing proofs which we have obtained is by this time very great. Some of them appeal more to one person, some to another ; but taking them all together every possible ground of suspicion or doubt seems to the family to be now removed. And it is legitimate to say, further, that partly through Raymond's activity a certain amount of help of the same kind has been afforded to other families. Incidentally it has been difficult to avoid brief reference to a few early instances of this, in that part of the record now published. For the most part, however, these and a great number of other things are omitted ; and I ought perhaps to apologise for the quantity which I have thought proper to include. Some home critics think that it would have been wiser to omit a great deal more, so as to lighten the book. But one can only act in accordance with one's own judgement ; and the book, if it is to achieve what it aims at, cannot be a light one. So, instead of ending it here, I propose to add a quantity of more didactic material—expressing my own views on the subject of Life and Death—the result of many years of thought and many kinds of experience.

Some people may prefer the details in Part II ; but others who have not the patience to read Part II may tolerate the more general considerations adduced in Part III—the " Life and Death " portion—which can be read without any reference to Raymond or to Parts I and II.

PART III

LIFE AND DEATH

"Eternal form shall still divide
The eternal soul from all beside;
And I shall know him when we meet."

TENNYSON, *In Memoriam*

INTRODUCTION

IN this "Life and Death" portion a definite side is unobtrusively taken in connexion with two outstanding controversies ; and though the treatment is purposely simple and uncontroversial, the author is under no delusion that every philosophical reader will agree with him. Explicit argumentation on either side is no novelty, but this is not the place for argument ; moreover, the opposing views have already been presented with ample clearness by skilled disputants.

Briefly then it may be said that Interactionism rather than Epiphenomenalism or Parallelism is the side taken in one controversy. And the non-material nature of life —the real existence of some kind of vital essence or vivifying principle as a controlling and guiding entity— is postulated in another : though the author never calls it a force or an energy.

Philosophical literature teems with these topics, but it may suffice here to call the attention of the general reader to two or three easily readable summaries—one an explanatory article by Mr. Gerald Balfour, in *The Hibbert Journal* for April 1910, on the Epiphenomenon controversy, and generally on the alternative explanations of the connexion between Mind and Body, in the light thrown on the subject by Telepathy and Psychical Research ; while on the vitality controversy a small book embodying a short course of lectures by the physiologist and philosopher Dr. J. S. Haldane under the title *Mechanism, Life, and Personality*, or a larger book by Professor M'Dougal called *Body and Mind*, may be recommended. On this subject also the writings of Professor J. Arthur Thomson may be specially mentioned.

The opinions of the present author on these topics, whatever they may be worth, are held without apology or hesitation, because to him they appear the inevitable consequence of facts of nature as now known or knowable. Some of these facts are not generally accepted by scientific men ; and if the facts themselves are not admitted, naturally any conclusion based upon them will appear ill-founded, and the further developed structure illusory. He anticipates that this will be said by critics.

In so far as the author's manner of statement is in terms of frank Dualism, he regards that as inevitable for scientific purposes. He does not suppose that any form of Dualism can be the last word about the Universe ; but, for practical purposes, mind and matter, or soul and body, must be thought of separately, and it must be the work of higher Philosophy to detect ultimate unity—a unity which he feels certain cannot possibly be materialistic in any sense intelligible to those who are at present studying matter and energy.

It may be doubted whether Materialism as a philosophy exists any longer, in the sense of being sustained by serious philosophers ; but a few physiological writers, of skill and industry, continue to advocate what they are pleased to call Scientific Materialism. Properly regarded this is a Policy, not a Philosophy, as I will explain ; but they make the mistake of regarding it as a Philosophy comprehensive enough to give them the right of negation as well as of affirmation. They do this in the interest of what they feel instinctively to be the ultimate achievement, a Monism in which mind and matter can be recognised as aspects of some one fundamental Reality. We can sympathise with the aim, and still feel how far from accomplishment we are. Nothing is gained by undue haste, and by unfounded negation much may be lost. We must not deny any part of the Universe for the sake of a premature unification. Simplification by exclusion or denial is a poverty-stricken device.

The strength of such workers is that they base themselves on the experience and discoveries of the past, and, by artificial but convenient limitation of outlook, achieve practical results. But they are not satisfied with results actually achieved—they forget their limitations—and, by a gigantic system of extrapolation from what has been done, try to infer what is going to be done ; their device being to anticipate and speak of what they hope for, as if it were already an accomplished fact. Some of the assumptions or blind guesses made by men of this school are well illustrated by an exposition in *The Hibbert Journal* for July 1916, where an able writer states the main propositions of Scientific Materialism thus :—

1. The law of universal causation ;
2. The principle of mechanism—*i.e.* the denial of purpose in the universe and all notions of absolute finalism or teleology ;
3. The denial that there exists any form of 'spiritual' or 'mental' entity that cannot be expressed in terms of matter and motion.

These appear to be its three propositions, and they are formulated by the exponent "as being of the first importance in the representation of materialistic thought."

Now proposition 1 is common property ; materialistic thought has no sort of exclusive right over it ; and to claim propositions 2 and 3 as corollaries from it is farcical. Taking them as independent postulates—which they are —all that need be said about proposition 2 is that a broad denial always needs more knowledge than a specific assertion, and it is astonishing that any sane person can imagine himself to know enough about the Universe as a whole to be able complacently to deny the existence of any "purpose" in it. All he can really mean is that scientific explanations must be framed so as to exhibit the immediate means whereby results in nature are accomplished ; for whether, or in what sense, they are first or simultaneously conceived in a Mind—as human undertakings are—is a matter beyond our scientific ken. Thus Darwinian and Mendelian attempts to explain how species arise, and how inheritance occurs, are entirely legitimate and scientific. For our experience is that every event has a proximate cause which we can investigate. Of ultimate causes we as scientific men are ignorant : they belong to a different region of inquiry. If the word "denial," therefore, in the above proposition is replaced by the phrase "exclusion from practical scientific attention," I for one have no quarrel with clause 2 ; for it then becomes a mere self-denying ordinance, a convenient limitation of scope. It represents Policy, not Philosophy.

But attention may be more usefully directed to the extravagantly gratuitous guess involved in hypothesis 3. As a minor point, it is not even carefully worded ; for entities which cannot be expressed in terms of matter and motion are common enough without going outside the domain of physics. Light, for instance, and Electricity, have not yet proved amenable, and do not appear likely to be amenable, to purely dynamical theory.

Certain phenomena have been reduced to matter and motion,—heat, for instance, and sound, the phenomena of gases and liquids, and all the complexities of astronomy. And in a famous passage Newton expressed an enthusiastic hope that all the phenomena of physics might some day be similarly reduced to the attractive simplicity of the three laws of motion—inertia, acceleration, and stress. And ever since Newton it has been the aim of physics to explain everything in its domain in terms of pure dynamics. The attempt has been only partially successful : the Ether is recalcitrant. But its recalcitrance is not like mere surly obstruction, it is of a helpful and illuminating character, and I shall not be misleading anyone if I cheerfully admit that in some modified and expanded form dynamical theory in mathematical physics has proved itself to be supreme.

But does dominance of that kind give to that splendid science—the glory of Britain and of Cambridge—the right to make a gigantic extrapolation and sprawl over all the rest of the Universe, throwing out tentacles even into regions which it has definitely abstracted from its attention or excluded from its ken ? There is not a physicist who thinks so. The only people who try to think so are a few enthusiasts of a more speculative habit of thought, who are annoyed with the physicists, from Lord Kelvin downwards, for not agreeing with them. And being unable to gather from competent authority any specific instance in which dynamics has explained a single fact in the region of either life or mind or consciousness or emotion or purpose or will,—because it is known perfectly well that dynamical jurisdiction does not extend into those regions,—these speculators set up as authorities on their own account, and, on the strength of their own expectation, propound the broad and sweeping dogma that nothing in the Universe exists which is not fully expressible in terms of matter and motion. And then, having accustomed themselves to the sound of some such collocation of words, they call upon humanity to shut its eyes to any facts of common experience which render such an assertion ridiculous.

The energy and enthusiasm of these writers, and the good work they may be doing in their own science, render them more or less immune from attack ; but every now and then it is necessary to say clearly that such extravagant generalisations profane the modesty of science : whose heritage it is to recognise the limitations of partial knowledge, and to be always ready to gain fresh experience and learn about the unknown. The new and unfamiliar is the vantage ground, not of scientific dogmatism, but of scientific inquiry.

The expository or theoretical part of this book may at first appear too abstract for the general reader who has had no experience of the kind of facts already described. Such reader may fail to see a connexion between this more didactic portion and the illustrations or examples which have preceded it ; but if he will give sufficient time and thought to the subject, the connexion will dawn upon him with considerable vividness.

It has always seemed to the author legitimate, and in every way desirable, for an experimenter to interpret and make himself responsible for an explanation or theory of his observations, so far as he can. To record bare facts and expect a reader of the record to arrive at the same conclusion as that reached by one who has been immersed in them for a long time, is to expect too strenuous an effort, and is not a fair procedure. Such a practice, though not unusual and sometimes even commended in physical science, is not followed by the most famous workers ; and it has been known to retard progress for a considerable time by loading the student with an accumulation of undigested facts. The hypothesis on which an observer has been working, or which he has arrived at in the course of his investigations, may or may not be of permanent value, but if his experience has led him to regard it as the best solution so far attainable, and if he is known not to be a specially obstinate or self-opinionated person, his views for what they are worth should be set forth for the guidance of future inquirers. If he mauls the facts in his direction, he will be detected ; but such an accusation is a serious one, and should not be made lightly or without opportunity for reply.

The string on which beads are strung may not be extremely durable, and in time it may give place to something stronger, but it is better than a random heap of beads not threaded on anything at all.

The main thread linking all the facts together in the present case is the hypothesis not only of continued or personal psychical existence in the abstract, but a definite inter-locking or inter-communication between two grades of existence,—the two in which we are most immediately interested and about which we can ascertain most,—that of the present and that of the immediate future for each individual ; together with the added probabilities that the actual grades of existence are far more than two, and that the forthcoming transition, in which we cannot but be interested even if we do not believe in it, is only one of many of which we shall, in some barely imaginable way, in due time become aware.

The hypothesis of continued existence in another set of conditions, and of possible communication across a boundary, is not a gratuitous one made for the sake of comfort and consolation, or because of a dislike to the idea of extinction ; it is a hypothesis which has been gradually forced upon the author—as upon many other persons—by the stringent coercion of definite experience. The foundation of the atomic theory in Chemistry is to him no stronger. The evidence is cumulative, and has broken the back of all legitimate and reasonable scepticism.

And if by selecting the atomic theory as an example he has chosen one upon which supplementary and most interesting facts have been grafted in the progress of discovery—facts not really contradicting the old knowledge, even when superficially appearing to do so, but adding to it and illuminating it further, while making changes perhaps in its manner of formulation—he has chosen such an example of set purpose, as not unlikely to be imitated in the present case also. ⸙

CHAPTER I

THE MEANING OF THE TERM LIFE

" Eternal process moving on."—TENNYSON

THE shorter the word the more inevitable it is that it will be used in many significations ; as can be proved by looking out almost any monosyllable in a large dictionary. The tendency of a simple word to have many glancing meanings—like shot silk, as Tennyson put it—is a character of high literary value ; though it may be occasionally inconvenient for scientific purposes. It is unlikely that we can escape an ambiguity due to this tendency, but I wish to use the term ' life ' to signify the vivifying principle which animates matter.

That the behaviour of animated matter differs from what is often called dead matter is familiar, and is illustrated by the description sometimes given of an uncanny piece of mechanism—that " it behaves as if it were alive." In the case of a jumping bean, for instance, its spasmodic and capricious behaviour can be explained with apparent simplicity, though with a suspicious trend towards superstition, by the information that a live and active maggot inhabits a cavity inside. It is thereby removed from the bare category of physics only, though still perfectly obedient to physical laws : it jumps in accordance with mechanics, but neither the times nor the direction of its jumps can be predicted.[1]

We must admit that the term ' dead matter ' is often misapplied. It is used sometimes to denote merely the constituents of the general inorganic world. But it is inconvenient to speak of utterly inanimate things, like stones, as ' dead,' when no idea of life was ever associated with them, and when ' inorganic ' is all that is meant. The term ' dead ' applied to a piece of matter signifies

[1] See Explanatory Note A at end of chapter.

19

the absence of a vivifying principle, no doubt, but it is most properly applied to a collocation of organic matter which has been animated.

Again, when animation has ceased, the thing we properly call dead is not the complete organism, but that material portion which is left behind ; we do not or should not intend to make any assertion concerning the vivifying principle which has left it,—beyond the bare fact of its departure. We know too little about that principle to be able to make safe general assertions. The life that is transmitted by an acorn or other seed fruit is always beyond our ken. We can but study its effects, and note its presence or its absence by results.

Life must be considered *sui generis* ; it is not a form of energy, nor can it be expressed in terms of something else. Electricity is in the same predicament ; it too cannot be explained in terms of something else. This is true of all fundamental forms of being. Magnetism may be called a concomitant of moving electricity ; ordinary matter can perhaps be resolved into electric charges : but an electric charge can certainly not be expressed in terms of either matter or energy. No more can life. To show that the living principle in a seed is not one of the forms of energy, it is sufficient to remember that that seed can give rise to innumerable descendants, through countless generations, without limit. There is nothing like a constant quantity of something to be shared, as there is in all examples of energy : there is no conservation about it : the seed embodies a stimulating and organising principle which appears to well from a limitless source.

But although life is not energy, any more than it is matter, yet it directs energy and thereby controls arrangements of matter. Through the agency of life specific structures are composed which would not otherwise exist, from a sea-shell to a cathedral, from a blade of grass to an oak ; and specific distributions of energy are caused, from the luminosity of a firefly to an electric arc, from the song of a cricket to an oratorio.

Life makes use of any automatic activities, or transferences and declensions of energy, which are either potentially or actually occurring. In especial it makes use of the torrent of ether tremors which reach the earth from the sun. Every plant is doing it constantly. Admittedly life exerts no force, it does no work, but it makes effective the energy available for an organism which it controls and vivifies ; it determines in what direction and when work shall be done. It is plain matter of fact that it does this, whether we understand the method or not,—and thus indirectly life interacts with and influences the material world. The energy of coal is indirectly wholly solar, but without human interference it might remain buried in the earth, and certainly would never propel a ship across the Atlantic. One way of putting the matter is to say that life *times*, and *directs*. If it runs a railway train, it runs the train not like a locomotive but like a General Manager. It enters into battle with a walking-stick, but guns are fired to its orders. It may be said to aim and fire : one of its functions is to discriminate between the wholesome and the deleterious, between friend and foe. That is a function outside the scope of physics.

Energy controlled by life is not random energy : the kind of self-composition or personal structure built by it depends on the kind of life-unit which is operating, not on the pabulum which is supplied. The same food will serve to build a pig, a chicken, or a man. Food which is assimilable at all takes a shape determined by the nature of the operative organism, and indeed by the portion of the organism actually reached by it. Unconscious constructive ability is as active in each cell of the body as in a honeycomb ; only in a beehive we can see the operators at work. The construction of an eye or an ear is still more astonishing. In the inorganic world such structures would be meaningless, for there would be nothing to respond to their stimulus ; they can only serve elementary mind and consciousness. The brain and nerve system is an instrument of transmutation or translation from the physical to the mental, and *vice versa*.

STAGES OF EVOLUTION

Steps in the progress of evolution—great stages which have been likened by Sir James Crichton Browne to exceptional Mendelian Mutations—may be rather imaginatively rehearsed somewhat thus :—

Starting with

The uniform Ether of Space, we can first suppose
The specialisation or organisation of specks of ether into Electrons ; followed by
Associated systems of electrons, constituting atoms of Matter ; and so
The whole inorganic Universe.

Then, as a new and astonishing departure, comes—

The cell, or protoplasmic complex which Life can construct and utilise for manifestation and development.[1]

And after that

A brain cell, which can become the physical organ for the rudiments of Mind. Followed by
Further mental development until Consciousness becomes possible. With subsequent
Sublimation of consciousness into Ethics, Philosophy, and Religion.

We need not insist on these or any other stages for our present purpose ; yet something of the kind would seem to have occurred, in the mysterious course of time.

[1] See Explanatory Note B.

THREE EXPLANATORY NOTES

NOTE A.—MECHANICS OF JUMPING BEAN

The biological explanation of a jumping bean is sometimes felt to be puzzling, inasmuch as the creature is wholly enclosed ; and a man in a boat knows that he cannot propel it by movement inside, without touching the water or something external. But the reaction of a table can be made use of through the envelope, and a live thing can momentarily vary its own weight-pressure and even reverse its sign. This fact has a bearing on some psycho-physical experiments, and hence is worthy of a moment's attention.

To weigh an animal that jumps and will not keep still is always troublesome. It cannot alter its average weight, truly, but it can redistribute it in time ; at moments its apparent weight may be excessive, and at other moments zero or even negative, as during the middle of an energetic leap. Parenthetically we may here interpolate a remark and say that what is called interference of light (two lights producing darkness, in popular language) is a redistribution of luminous energy in space. No light, nor any kind of wave motion, is destroyed by interference when two sets of waves overlap, but the energy rises to a maximum in some places, and in other places sinks to zero. No wave energy is consumed by interference—only rearranged. This fact is often misstated. And probably the other statement, about the varying apparent weight—*i.e.* pressure on the ground—of a live animal, may be misstated too : though there is no question of energy about that, but only of force. The force or true weight, in the sense of the earth's attraction, is there all the time, and is constant ; but the pressure on the ground, or the force needed to counteract the weight, is not constant. After momentary violence, as in throwing, no support need be supplied for several seconds ; and, like the maggot inside a hollow bean, a live thing turning itself into a projectile may even carry something else up too. It is instructive also to consider a flying bird, and a dirigible balloon, and to ask where the still existing weight of these things can be found.

NOTE B.—DIFFERENCES BETWEEN A GROWING ORGANISM AND A GROWING CRYSTAL

The properties which differentiate living matter from any kind of inorganic imitation may be instinctively felt, but can hardly be formulated without expert knowledge. The differences between a growing organism and a growing crystal are many and various, but it must suffice here to specify the simplest and most familiar sort of difference ; and as it is convenient to take a possibly controversial statement of this kind from the writings of a physiologist, I quote here a passage from an article by Professor

Fraser Harris, of Halifax, Nova Scotia, in the current number of the quarterly magazine called *Science Progress* edited by Sir Ronald Ross :—

"Living animal bioplasm has the power of growing, that is of assimilating matter in most cases chemically quite unlike that of its own constitution. Now this is a remarkable power, not in the least degree shared by non-living matter. Its very familiarity has blinded us to its uniqueness as a chemical phenomenon. The mere fact that a man eating beef, bird, fish, lobster, sugar, fat, and innumerable other things can transform these into human bioplasm, something chemically very different even from that of them which most resembles human tissue, is one of the most extraordinary facts in animal physiology. A crystal growing in a solution is not only not analogous to this process, it is in the sharpest possible contrast with it. The crystal grows only in the sense that it increases in bulk by accretions to its exterior, and only does that by being immersed in a solution of the same material as its own substance. It takes up to itself only material which is already similar to itself ; this is not assimilation, it is merely incorporation.

"The term ' growth,' strictly speaking, can be applied only to metabolism in the immature or convalescent organism. The healthy adult is not ' growing ' in this sense ; when of constant weight he is adding neither to his stature nor his girth, and yet he is assimilating as truly as ever he did. Put more technically : in the adult of stationary weight, anabolism is quantitatively equal to katabolism, whereas in the truly growing organism anabolism is prevailing over katabolism ; and reversely in the wasting of an organism or in senile decay, katabolism is prevailing over anabolism. The crystal in its solution offers no analogies with the adult or the senile states—but these are of the very essence of the life of an organism. . . .

"The fact, of course familiar to every beginner in biology, is that the crystal is only incorporating and not excreting anything, whereas the living matter is always excreting as well as assimilating. This one-sided metabolism—if it can be dignified with that term—is indeed characteristic of the crystal, but it is at no time characteristic of the living organism. The organism, whether truly growing or only in metabolic equilibrium, is constantly taking up material to replace effete material, is replenishing because it has previously displenished itself or cast off material. The resemblance between a so-called ' growing ' crystal and a growing organism is verily of the most superficial kind."

And Professor Fraser Harris concludes his article thus :—

"Between the living and the non-living there is a great gulf fixed, and no efforts of ours, however heroic, have as yet bridged it over."

Note C.—Old Age

We know that as vitality diminishes the bodily deterioration called old age sets in, and that a certain amount of deterioration results in death ; but it turns out, on systematic inquiry, that old age and death are not essential to living organisms. They represent the deterioration and wearing out of working parts, so that the vivifying principle is hampered in its manifestation and cannot achieve results which with a younger and healthier machine were possible ; but the parts which wear out are not the essential bearers of the vivifying principle ; they are accreted or supplementary portions appropriate to developed individual earth life, and it does not appear improbable that the progress of discovery may at least postpone the deterioration that we call old age, for a much longer time than at present. Emphasis on this distinction between germ cell and body cell, usually associated with Weismann, seems to have been formulated before him by Herdman of Liverpool.

Biologists teach us that the phenomenon of old age is not evident in the case of the unicellular organisms which reproduce by fission. The cell can be killed, but it need neither grow old nor die. Death appears to be a prerogative of the higher organisms. But even among these Professor Weismann adopts and defends the view that "death is not a primary necessity, but that it has been secondarily acquired by adaptation." The cell is not inherently limited in its number of cell-generations. The low unicellular organism is potentially immortal ; the higher multicellular form, with well-differentiated organs, contains the germ of death within its *soma*. Death seems to supervene by reason of its utility to the species : continued life of an individual after a certain stage being comparatively useless. From the point of view of the race the soma or main body is "a secondary appendage of the real bearer of life—the reproductive cells." The somatic cells probably lost their immortal qualities on this immortality becoming useless to the species. Their mortality may have been a mere consequence of their differentiation. "Natural death was not introduced from absolute intrinsic necessity, inherent in the nature of living matter," says Weismann, "but on grounds of utility ; that is from necessities which sprang up, not from the general conditions of life, but from those special conditions which dominate the life of multicellular organisms."

It is not the germ cell itself, but the bodily accretion or appendage, which is abandoned by life, and which accordingly dies and decays.

CHAPTER II

THE MEANING OF THE TERM DEATH

" And Life, still wreathing flowers for Death to wear."—ROSSETTI

WHATEVER Life may really be, it is to us an abstraction : for the word is a generalised term to signify that which is common to all animals and plants, and which is not directly operative in the inorganic world. To understand life we must study living things, to see what is common to them all. An organism is alive when it moulds matter to a character-istic form, and utilises energy for its own purposes—the purposes especially of growth and reproduction. A living organism, so far as it is alive, preserves its complicated structure from deterioration and decay.[1]

Death is the cessation of that controlling influence over matter and energy, so that thereafter the uncontrolled activity of physical and chemical forces supervene. Death is not the absence of life merely, the term signifies its departure or separation, the severance of the abstract principle from the concrete residue. The term only truly applies to that which has been living.

Death therefore may be called a dissociation, a dis-solution, a separation of a controlling entity from a physico-chemical organism ; it may be spoken of in general and vague terms as a separation of soul and body, if the term ' soul ' is reduced to its lowest denomination.

Death is not extinction. Neither the soul nor the body is extinguished or put out of existence. The body weighs just as much as before, the only properties it loses at the moment of death are potential properties. So also all we can assert concerning the vital principle is that it no longer animates that material organism : we cannot

[1] See Note C at end of preceding chapter.

safely make further assertion regarding it, or maintain its activity or its inactivity without further information.

When we say that a body is dead we may be speaking accurately. When we say that a *person* is dead, we are using an ambiguous term ; we may be referring to his discarded body, in which case we may be speaking truly and with precision. We may be referring to his personality, his character, to what is really himself ; in which case though we must admit that we are speaking popularly, the term is not quite simply applicable. He has gone, he has passed on, he has " passed through the body and gone," as Browning says in *Abt Vogler,* but he is—I venture to say—certainly not dead in the same sense as the body is dead. It is his absence which allows the body to decay, he himself need be subject to no decay nor any destructive influence. Rather he is emancipated ; he is freed from the burden of the flesh, though with it he has also lost those material and terrestrial potentialities which the bodily mechanism conferred upon him ; and if he can exert himself on the earth any more, it can only be with some difficulty and as it were by permission and co-operation of those still here. It appears as if sometimes and occasionally he can still stimulate into activity suitable energetic mechanism, but his accustomed machinery for manifestation has been lost : or rather it is still there for a time, but it is out of action, it is dead.

Nevertheless inasmuch as those who have lost their material body have passed through the process of dissolution or dissociative severance which we call death, it is often customary to speak of them as dead. They are no longer living, if by living we mean associated with a material body of the old kind ; and in that sense we need not hesitate to speak of them collectively as ' the dead.'

We need not be afraid of the word, nor need we resent its use or hesitate to employ it, when once we and our hearers understand the sense in which it may rightly be employed. If ideas associated with the term had always been sensible and wholesome, people need have had no compunction at all about using it. But by the populace, and by Ecclesiastics also, the term has been so misused, and the ideas of people have been so confused by insistent concentration on merely physical facts, and by the necessary but over-emphasised attention to the body left behind, that it was natural for a time to employ other words, until the latent ambiguity had ceased to be troublesome. And occasionally, even now, it is well to be emphatic in this direction, in order to indicate our disagreement with the policy of harping on worms and graves and epitaphs, or on the accompanying idea of a General Resurrection, with reanimation of buried bodies. Hence in strenuous contradiction to all this superstition comes the use of such phrases as ' transition ' or ' passing,' and the occasional not strictly justifiable assertion that " there is no death."

For as a matter of familiar fact death there certainly is ; and to deny a fact is no assistance. No one really means to deny a fact ; those who make the statement only want to divert thoughts from a side already too much emphasised, and to concentrate attention on another side.   What they mean is, there is no extinction. They definitely mean to maintain that the process called death is a mere severance of soul and body, and that the soul is freed rather than injured thereby.   The body alone dies and decays ; but there is no extinction even for it— only a change.   For the other part there can hardly be even a change—except a change of surroundings.   It is unlikely that character and personality are liable to sudden revolutions or mutations. Potentially they may be different, because of different opportunities, but actually at the moment they are the same.   Likening existence to a curve, the curvature has changed, but there is no other discontinuity.

Death is not a word to fear, any more than birth is. We change our state at birth, and come into the world of air and sense and myriad existence ; we change our state at death and enter a region of—what ?   Of Ether, I think, and still more myriad existence ; a region in which communion is more akin to what we here call telepathy, and where intercourse is not conducted by the accustomed indirect physical processes; but a region in which beauty and knowledge are as vivid as they are here : a region in which progress is possible, and in which " admiration, hope, and love " are even more real and dominant.   It is in this sense that we can truly say, " The dead are not dead, but alive." οὐδὲ τεθνᾶσι θανόντες.

APPENDIX ON FEELINGS WHEN DEATH IS IMMINENT

PRELIMINARY STATEMENT BY O. J. L.

A lady was brought by a friend to call on us at Mariemont during a brief visit to Edgbaston, and I happened to have a talk with her in the garden. I found that she had been one of the victims of the *Lusitania*, and as she seemed very cheerful and placid about it, I questioned her as to her feelings on the occasion. I found her a charming person, and she entered into the matter with surprising fullness, considering that she was a complete stranger. Her chief anxiety seems to have been for her husband, whom she had left either in America or the West Indies, and for her friends generally ; but on her own behalf she seems to have felt extremely little anxiety or discomfort of any kind. She told me she had given up hope of being saved, and was only worried about friends mourning on her behalf and thinking that she must have suffered a good deal, whereas, in point of fact, she was not really suffering at all. She was young and healthy, and apparently felt no evil results from the three hours' immersion. She was sucked down by the ship, and when she came to the surface again, her first feeling was one of blank surprise at the disappearance of what had brought her across the Atlantic. The ship was " not there."

I thought her account so interesting, that after a few months I got her address from the friend with whom she had been staying, and wrote asking if she would write it down for me. In due course she did so, writing from abroad, and permits me to make use of the statement, provided I suppress her name ; which accordingly I do, quoting the document otherwise in full.

The Document referred to

" Your letter came to me as a great pleasure and surprise. I have always remembered the sympathy with which you listened to me, that morning at Edgbaston, and sometimes wondered at the amount I said, as it is not easy to give expression to feelings and speculations which are only roused at critical moments in one's life.

" What you ask me to do is not easy, as I am only one of those who are puzzling and groping in the dark—while you have found so much light for yourself and have imparted it to others.

" I would like, however, most sincerely to try to recall my sensations with regard to that experience, if they would be of any value to you.

" It would be absurd to say now. that from the beginning of the voyage I knew what would happen ; it was not a very actual knowledge, but I was conscious of a distinct forewarning, and the very calmness and peace of the voyage seemed, in a way, a state of waiting for some great event. Therefore when the ship was rent by the explosion (it was as sudden as the firing of a pistol) I felt no particular shock, because of that curious inner expectancy. The only acute feeling I remember at the moment was one of anger that such a crime could have been committed ; the fighting instinct predominated in the face of an unseen but near enemy. I sometimes think it was partly that same instinct—the desire to die game—that accounted for the rather grim calmness of some of the passengers. After all—it was no ordinary shipwreck, but a Chance of War. I put down my book and went round to the other side of the ship where a great many passengers were gathering round the boats ; it was difficult to stand, as the *Lusitania* was listing heavily. There seemed to be no panic whatever ; I went into my cabin, a steward very kindly helped me with a life-jacket, and advised me to throw away my fur coat. I felt no hurry or anxiety, and returned on deck, where I stood with some difficulty— discussing our chances with an elderly man I just knew by sight.

" It was then I think we realised what a strong instinct there was in some of us—*not* to struggle madly for life—but to wait for something to come to us, whether it be life or death ; and not to lose our personality and become like one of the struggling shouting creatures who were by then swarming up from the lower decks and made one's heart ache. I never felt for a moment that my time to cross over had come—not until I found myself in the water —floating farther and farther away from the scene of wreckage and misery—in a sea as calm and vast as the sky overhead. Behind me, the cries of those who were sinking grew fainter, the splash of oars and the calls of those who were doing rescue work in the lifeboats ; there seemed to be no possibility of rescue for me ; so I reasoned with myself and said, ' The time *has* come—you must believe it—the time to cross over '—but inwardly and persistently something continued to say, ' No—not now.'

" The gulls were flying overhead and I remember noticing the beauty of the blue shadows which the sea throws up to their white feathers : they were very happy and alive and made me feel rather lonely ; my thoughts went to my people—looking forward to seeing me, and at that moment having tea in the garden at ———— ; the idea of their grief was unbearable—I had to cry a little. Names of books went through my brain ;—one specially, called ' Where no Fear is,' seemed to express my feeling at the time ! Loneliness, yes, and sorrow on account of the grief of others—but no Fear. It seemed very normal,—very right,—a natural development of some kind about to take place. How can it be otherwise, when it *is* natural ? I rather wished I knew some one on the other side, and wondered if there are friendly strangers there who come to the rescue. I was very near the border-line when a wandering lifeboat quietly came up behind me and two men bent down and lifted me in. It was extraordinary how quickly life came rushing back ;—every one in the boat seemed very self-possessed—although there was one man dead and another losing his reason. One woman expressed a hope for a ' cup of tea ' shortly—a hope which was soon to be realised for all of us in a Mine Sweeper from Queenstown. I have forgotten her name— but shall always remember the kindness of her crew—specially the Chief Officer, who saved me much danger by giving me dry clothes and hot towels.

" All this can be of very little interest to you—I have no skill in putting things on paper ;—but, you know. I am glad to have been near the border ; to have had the feeling of how very near it is *always*—only there are so many little things always going on to absorb one here.

" Others on that day were passing through a Gate which was not open for me—but I do not expect they were afraid when the time came—they too probably felt that whatever they were to find would be beautiful—only a fulfilment of some kind. . . . I have reason to think that the passing from here is very painless—at least when there is no illness. We seemed to be passing through a stage on the road of Life."

CHAPTER III

DEATH AND DECAY

" All, that doth live, lives always ! "—EDWIN ARNOLD

CONSIDER now the happenings to the discarded body. In the first place, I repeat, it is undesirable to concentrate attention on a grave. The discarded body must be duly attended to when done with ; the safety of the living is a paramount consideration ; the living must retain control over what is dead. Uncontrolled natural forces are often dangerous : the only thing harmful about a flood or a fire is the absence of control. Either the operations must be supervised and intelligently directed, or they must be subjected to such disabilities that they can do no harm. But to associate continued personality with a dead body, such as is suggested by phrases like " lay him in the earth," or " here lies such an one," or to anticipate any kind of physical resuscitation, is unscientific and painful. Unfortunately the orthodox religious world at some epochs has attached superstitious importance, not to the decent disposal, but to the imagined future of the body. Painful and troublesome to humanity those rites have been. The tombs of Egypt are witness to the harassing need felt by the living to provide their loved ones with symbols or tokens of all that they might require in a future state of existence,—as if material things were needed by them any more, or as if we could provide them if the were.[1] The simple truth is always so much saner

---

[1] It is rash to condemn a human custom which has prevailed for centuries or millenniums, and it is wrong to treat it *de haut en bas*. I would not be understood as doing so, in this brief and inadequate reference to the contents of Egyptian tombs. Their fuller interpretation awaits the labour of students now working at them.

In the same spirit I wish to leave open the question of what possible rational interpretation may be given to the mediæval phrase " Resur-

and happier than the imaginings of men ; or, as Dr. Schuster said in his Presidential address to the British Association at Manchester, 1915,—" The real world is far more beautiful than any of our dreams."

What is the simple truth ? It can be regarded from two points of view, the prosaic and the poetic.

Prosaically we can say that the process of decay, if regarded scientifically, is not in itself necessarily repugnant. It may be as interesting as fermentation or any other chemical or biological process. Putrefaction, like poison, is hostile to higher living organisms, and hence a self-protecting feeling of disgust has arisen round it, in the course of evolution. An emotional feeling arises in the mind of anyone who has to combat any process or operation of nature,—like the violent emotions excited in an extreme teetotaller by the word ' drink ' : a result of the evil its profanation has done ; for the verb itself is surely quite harmless. Presumably a criminal associates disagreeable anticipations with the simple word ' hanging.' The idea of a rank weed is repulsive to a gardener, but not to a botanist ; the idea of disease is repellent to a prospective patient, not to a doctor or bacteriologist ; the idea of dirt is objectionable to a housewife, but it is only matter out of place ; the word ' poison ' conveys nothing objectionable to a chemist. Everything removed from the emotional arena, and transplanted into the intellectual, becomes interesting and tractable and worthy of study. Living organisms of every kind are good in themselves, though when out of place and beyond control they may be harmful. A tiger is an object of dread to an Indian village : to a hunting party he may be keenly attractive. In any case he is a lithe and beautiful and splendid creature. Microscopic organisms may have troublesome and destructive effects, but in themselves they can be studied with interest and avidity. All living creatures have their assuredly useful function, only it may be a function on which we naturally shrink from dwelling when in an emotional mood. Everything of this kind is an

rection of the body " ; a subject on which much has been written. What I am contending against is not the scholarly but the popular interpretation. For further remarks on this subject see Chapter VII below.

affair of mood ; and, properly regarded, nothing in nature is common or unclean. That a flying albatross is a beautiful object every one can cordially admit, but that the crawling surface of a stagnant sea can be regarded with friendly eyes seems an absurdity ; yet there is nothing absurd in it. It is surely the bare truth concerning all living creatures of every grade, that "the Lord God made them all" ; and it was of creeping water-snakes that the stricken Mariner at length, when he had learnt the lesson, ejaculated :—

> " O happy living things !
> A spring of love gushed from my heart,
> And I blessed them unaware."

For what can be said poetically about the fate of the beloved body, the poets themselves must be appealed to. But that there is kinship between the body and the earth is literal truth. Of terrestrial particles it is wholly composed, and that they should be restored to the earth whence they were borrowed is natural and peaceful. Moreover, out of the same earth, and by aid of the very same particles, other helpful forms of life may arise ; and though there may be no conscious unification or real identity, yet it is pardonable to associate, in an imaginative and poetic mood, the past and future forms assumed by the particles :—

> " Lay her i' the earth ;—
> And from her fair and unpolluted flesh,
> May violets spring ! "

Quotations are hardly necessary to show that this idea runs through all poetry. An ancient variety is enshrined in the Hyacinthus and Adonis legends. From spilt blood an inscribed lily springs, in the one tale ; and the other we may quote in Shakespeare's version (*Venus and Adonis*) :—

> " And in his blood that on the ground lay spilled,
> A purple flower sprung up chequered with white,
> Resembling well his pale cheeks and the blood
> Which in round drops upon their whiteness stood."

So also Tennyson :—

> " And from his ashes may be made
> The violet of his native land."
>
> *In Memoriam*

We find the same idea again, I suppose, in the eastern original of Fitzgerald's well-known stanza :—

> " And this delightful Herb whose tender Green
> Fledges the River's Lip on which we lean—
> Ah, lean upon it lightly ! for who knows
> From what once lovely Lip it springs unseen ! "

The soil of a garden is a veritable charnel-house of vegetable and animal matter, and from one point of view represents death and decay, but the coltsfoot covering an abandoned heap of refuse, or the briar growing amid ruin, shows that Nature only needs time to make it all beautiful again. Let us think of the body as transmuted, not as stored.

The visible shape of the body was no accident, it corresponded to a reality, for it was caused by the indwelling vivifying essence ; and affection entwines itself inevitably round not only the true personality of the departed, but round its material vehicle also—the sign and symbol of so much beauty, so much love. Symbols appeal to the heart of humanity, and anything cherished and honoured becomes in itself a thing of intrinsic value, which cannot be regarded with indifference. The old and tattered colours of a regiment, for which men have laid down their lives—though replaced perhaps by something newer and more durable—cannot be relegated to obscurity without a pang. And any sensitive or sympathetic person, contemplating such relics hereafter, may feel some echo of the feeling with which they were regarded, and may become acquainted with their history and the scenes through which they have passed.

In such cases the kind of knowledge to be gained from the relic, and the means by which additional information can be acquired, are intelligible; but in other cases also information can be attained, though by means at present not understood. It may sound superstitious, but it is a

20

matter of actual experience, that some sensitives have intuitive perception, of an unfamiliar kind, concerning the history and personal associations of relics or fragments or personal belongings. The faculty is called psychometry ; and it is no more intelligible, although no less well-evidenced, than the possibly allied faculty of dowsing or so-called water-divining. Psychometry is a large subject on which much has already been written : this brief mention must here suffice.

It seems to me that these facts,when at length properly understood, will throw some light on the connexion between mind and matter ; and then many another obscure region of semi-science and semi-superstition will be illuminated. At present in all such tracts we have to walk warily, for the ground is uneven and insecure ; and it is better, or at least safer, for the majority to forgo the recognition of some truth than rashly to invade a district full of entanglements and pitfalls.

Transition

Longfellow's line, " There is no death ; what seems so is transition," at once suggests itself. Read literally the first half of this sentence is obviously untrue, but in the sense intended, and as a whole, the statement is true enough. There is no extinction, and the change called death is the entrance to a new condition of existence— what may be called a new life.

Yet life itself is continuous, and the conditions of the whole of existence remain precisely as before. Circumstances have changed for the individual, but only in the sense that he is now aware of a different group of facts. The change of surroundings is a subjective one. The facts were of course there, all the time, as the stars are there in the daytime ; but they were out of our ken. Now these come into our ken, and others fade into memory.

The Universe is one, not two. Literally there is no ' other ' world—except in the limited and partial sense of other planets—the Universe is one. We exist in it continuously all the time ; sometimes conscious in one way, sometimes conscious in another ; sometimes aware of a group of facts on one side of a partition, sometimes aware of another group, on the other side. But the partition is a subjective one ; we are all one family all the time, so long as the link of affection is not broken. And for those who believe in prayer at all to cease from praying for the welfare of their friends because they are materially inaccessible—though perhaps spiritually more accessible than before—is to succumb unduly to the residual evil of past ecclesiastical abuses, and to lose an opportunity of happy service.

CHAPTER IV

CONTINUED EXISTENCE

" Sit down before fact as a little child, be prepared to give up every preconceived notion, follow humbly wherever and to whatsoever abysses Nature leads."—Huxley

P EOPLE often feel a notable difficulty in believing in the reality of continued existence. Very likely it is difficult to believe or to realise existence in what is sometimes called " the next world "; but then, when we come to think of it, it is difficult to believe in existence in this world too; it is difficult to believe in existence at all. The whole problem of existence is a puzzling one. It could by no means have been predicated *a priori*. The whole thing is a question of experience; that is, of evidence. We know by experience that things actually do exist; though how they came into being, and what they are all for, and what consequences they have, is more than we can tell. We have no reason for asserting that the kind we are familiar with is the only kind of existence possible, unless we choose to assert it on the ground that we have no experience of any other. But that is becoming just the question at issue : have we any evidence, either direct or indirect, for any other existence than this ? If we have, it is futile to cite in opposition to it the difficulty of believing in the reality of such an existence; we surely ought to be guided by facts. At this stage in the history of the human race few facts of science are better established and more widely appreciated than the main facts of Astronomy : a general acquaintance with the sizes and distances, and the enormous number, of the solar systems distributed throughout space is prevalent. Yet to the imaginative human mind the facts, if really grasped, are overwhelming and incredible.

The sun a million times bigger than the earth; Arcturus a hundred times bigger than the sun, and so distant that light has taken two centuries to come, though travelling at a rate able to carry it to New York and back in less than the twentieth part of a second,—facts like these are commonplaces of the nursery ; but even as bare facts they are appalling.

That the earth is a speck invisible from any one of the stars, that we are on a world which is but one among an innumerable multitude of others, ought to make us realise the utter triviality of any view of existence based upon familiarity with street and train and office, ought to give us some sense of proportion between everyday experience and ultimate reality. Even the portentous struggle in which Europe is engaged—

> "What is it all but a trouble of ants
> in the gleam of a million million of suns?"

Yet, for true interpretation, the infinite worth and vital importance of each individual human soul must be apprehended too. And that is another momentous fact, which, so far from restricting the potentialities of existence, by implication still further enlarges them. The multiplicity, the many-sidedness, the magnificence, of material existence does not dwarf the human soul ; far otherwise : it illumines and expands the stage upon which the human drama is being played, and ought to make us ready to perceive how far greater still may be the possibilities—nay, the actualities—before it, in its infinite unending progress.

That we know little about such possibilities as yet, proves nothing ;—for mark how easy it would have been to be ignorant of the existence of all the visible worlds and myriad modes of being in space. Not until the business of the day is over, and our great star has eclipsed itself behind the earth, not until the serener period of night, does the grandeur of the material universe force itself upon our attention. And, even then, let there be but a slight permanent thickening of our atmosphere, and we should have had no revelation of any world other than our own.

Under those conditions—so barely escaped from—how wretchedly meagre and limited would have been our conception of the Universe ! Aye, and, unless we foolishly imagine that our circumstances are such as to have already given us a clue to every kind of possible existence, I venture to say that " wretchedly meagre and limited " must be a true description of our conception of the Universe, even now,—even of the conception of those who have permitted themselves, with least hesitation, to follow whithersoever facts lead.

If there be any group of scientific or historical or literary students who advocate what they think to be a sensible, but what I regard as a purblind, view of existence, based upon already systematised knowledge and on unfounded and restricting speculation as to probable boundaries and limitations of existence,—if such students take their own horizon to be the measure of all things,—the fact is to be deplored. Such workers, however admirable their industry and detailed achievements, represent a school of thought against the fruits of which we of the Allied Nations are in arms.

Nevertheless speculation of this illegitimate and negative kind is not unknown among us. It originates partly in admiration for the successful labours of a bygone generation in clearing away a quantity of clinging parasitic growth which was obscuring the fair fabric of ascertained truth, and partly in an innate iconoclastic enthusiasm.

The success which has attended Darwinian and other hypotheses has had a tendency to lead men—not indeed men of Darwinian calibre, but smaller and less conscientious men—in science as well as in history and theology, to an over-eager confidence in probable conjecture and inadequate attention to facts of experience. It has even been said—I quote from a writer in the volume *Darwin and Modern Science*, published in connexion with a Darwin Jubilee celebration at Cambridge—that " the age of materialism was the least matter-of-fact age conceivable, and the age of science the age which showed least of the patient temper of enquiry." I would not go so far as this myself, the statement savours of exaggeration, but there is a regrettable tendency in surviving materialistic quarters for combatants to entrench themselves in dogma and preconceived opinion, to regard these vulnerable shelters as sufficient protection against observed and recorded facts, and even to employ them as strongholds from which alien observation-posts can be shattered and overthrown.

CHAPTER V

PAST, PRESENT, AND FUTURE

" How often have men thus feared that Nature's wonders
would be degraded by being closelier looked into ! How often,
again, have they learnt that the truth was higher than their imagination ; and that it is man's work, but never Nature's, which
to be magnificent must remain unknown ! "—F. W. H. M.,
Introduction to *Phantasms of the Living*

OUR actual experience is strangely limited. We
cannot be actually conscious of more than a single
instant of time. The momentary flash which we call
the present, the visual image of which can be made permanent by the snap of a camera, is all of the external
world that we directly apprehend. But our real existence
embraces far more than that. The present, alone and
isolated, would be meaningless to us ; we look before and
after. Our memories are thronged with the past ; our
anticipations range over the future ; and it is in the past
and the future that we really live. It is so even with the
higher animals : they too order their lives by memory
and anticipation. It is under the influence of the future
that the animal world performs even the most trivial
conscious acts. We eat, we rest, we work, all with an eye
to the immediate future. The present moment is illuminated and made significant, is controlled and dominated,
by experience of the past and by expectation of the future.
Without any idea of the future our existence would be
purely mechanical and meaningless : with too little eye to
the future—a mere living from hand to mouth—it becomes
monotonous and dull.

Hence it is right that humanity, transcending merely
animal scope, should seek to answer questions concerning
its origin and destiny, and should regard with intense

interest every clue to the problems of 'whence' and 'whither.'

It is no doubt possible, as always, to overstep the happy mean, and by absorption in and premature concern with future interests to lose the benefit and the training of this present life. But although we may rightly decide to live with full vigour in the present, and do our duty from moment to moment, yet in order to be full-flavoured and really intelligent beings—not merely with mechanical drift following the line of least resistance—we ought to be aware that there is a future,—a future determined to some extent by action in the present ; and it is only reasonable that we should seek to ascertain, roughly and approximately, what sort of future it is likely to be.

Inquiry into survival, and into the kind of experience through which we shall all certainly have to go in a few years, is therefore eminently sane, and may be vitally significant. It may colour all our actions, and give a vivid meaning both to human history and to personal experience.

If death is not extinction, then on the other side of dissolution mental activity must continue, and must be interacting with other mental activity. For the fact of telepathy proves that bodily organs are not absolutely essential to communication of ideas. Mind turns out to be able to act directly on mind, and stimulate it into response by other than material means. Thought does not belong to the material region : although it is able to exert an influence on that region through mechanism provided by vitality. Yet the means whereby it accomplishes the feat are essentially unknown, and the fact that such inter-action is possible would be strange and surprising if we were not too much accustomed to it. It is reasonable to suppose that the mind can be more at home, and more directly and more exuberantly active, where the need for such interaction between psychical and physical—or let us more safely and specifically say between mental and material—no longer exists, when the restraining influence of brain and nerve mechanism is removed, and when some of the limitations connected with bodily location in space are ended.

Experience must be our guide. To shut the door on

actual observation and experiment in this particular region, because of preconceived ideas and obstinate prejudices, is an attitude common enough, even among scientific men ; but it is an attitude markedly unscientific. Certain people have decided that inquiry into the activities of discarnate mind is futile ; some few consider it impious ; many, perhaps wisely mistrusting their own powers, shrink from entering on such an inquiry. But if there are any facts to be ascertained, it must be the duty of some volunteers to try to ascertain them : and for people having any acquaintance with scientific history to shut their eyes to facts when definitely announced, and to forbid investigation or report concerning them on pain of ostracism,—is to imitate a bygone theological attitude in a spirit of unintended flattery—a flattery which from every point of view is eccentric ; and likewise to display an extraordinary lack of humour.

On the Possibility of Prognostication

I do not wish to complicate the issue at present by introducing the idea of prognostication or prevision, for I do not understand how anticipation of the future is possible. It is only known to be possible by one of two processes—

(a) Inference—*i.e.* deduction from a wide knowledge of the present ;
(b) Planning—*i.e.* the carrying out of a pre-arranged scheme.

And these methods must be pressed to the utmost before admitting any other hypothesis.

As to the possibility of prevision in general, I do not dogmatise, nor have I a theory wherewith to explain every instance ; but I keep an open mind and try to collate and contemplate the facts.

Scientific prediction is familiar enough ; science is always either historic or prophetic (as Dr. Schuster said at Manchester in the British Association Address for 1915), " and history is only prophecy pursued in the negative direction." This thesis is worth illustrating :—That Eclipses can be calculated forwards or backwards is well

known.   A tide-calculating machine, again, which is used
to churn out tidal detail in advance by turning a handle,
could be as easily run backwards and give past tides if
they were wanted ; but always on the assumption that
no catastrophe, no unforeseen contingency, nothing outside the limits of the data, occurs to interfere with the
placid course of phenomena.   There must be no dredging
or harbour bar operations, for instance, if the tide machine
is to be depended on.   Free-will is not allowed for, in
Astronomy or Physics ;   nor any interference by living
agents.

The real truth is that, except for unforeseen contin-
gencies, past, present, and future are welded together in a
coherent whole ;   and to a mind with wider purview, to
whom perhaps hardly anything is unforeseen, there may
be possibilities of inference to an unsuspected extent.
Human character, and action based upon it, may be more
trustworthy and uncapricious than is usually supposed ;
and data depending on humanity may be included in a
completer scheme of foreknowledge, without the exercise
of any compulsion.   " The past," says Bertrand Russell
eloquently, " does not change or strive ;   like Duncan,
after life's fitful fever it sleeps well ;   what was eager and
grasping, what was petty and transitory, has faded away ;
the things that were beautiful and eternal shine out of it
like stars in the night."   My ignorance will not allow me
to attempt to compose a similar or rather a contrasting
sentence about the future.

REFERENCE TO SPECIAL CASES

It will be observed that none of those indications or intimations
or intuitions which are referred to in a note on page 34, Part I,
if they mean anything, raise the difficult question of prevision.
In every case the impression was felt after or at the time of the
event, though before reception of the news.   The only question
of possible prevision in the present instance arises in connexion
with the ' Faunus ' message quoted and discussed in Part II.   But
even here nothing more than kindly provision, in case anything
untoward should happen, need be definitely assumed.   Moreover,
if the concurrence in time suggests prognostication, the fact that
a formidable attempt to advance the English Front at the Ypres
salient was probably in prospect in August 1915, though not
known to ordinary people in England, and not fully carried out
till well on in September, must have been within human know-

ledge ; and so would have to be considered telepathically accessible, if that hypothesis is considered preferable to the admission of what Tennnyson speaks of as—

> "Such refraction of events
> As often rises ere they rise."

Prognostication can hardly be part of the evidence for survival. The two things are not essential to each other ; they hardly appear to be connected. But one knows too little about the whole thing to be sure even of this, and I decline to take the responsibility for suppressing any of the facts. I know that Mr. Myers used to express an opinion that certain kinds of prevision would constitute clear and satisfactory evidence of something supernormal, and so attract attention ; though the establishment of such a possibility might tend to suggest a kind of higher knowledge, not far short of what might be popularly called omniscience, rather than of merely human survival.

CHAPTER VI

INTERACTION OF MIND AND MATTER

"Spiritus intus alit, totamque infusa per artus
Mens agitat molem, et magno se corpore miscet."
Æneid, vi. 726

LIFE and mind and consciousness do not belong to the material region ; whatever they are in themselves, they are manifestly something quite distinct from matter and energy, and yet they utilise the material and dominate it.

Matter is arranged and moved by means of energy, but often at the behest of life and mind. Mind does not itself exert force, nor does it enter into the scheme of physics, and yet it indirectly brings about results which otherwise would not have happened. It definitely causes movements and arrangements or constructions of a purposed character. A bird grows a feather, and a bird builds a nest : I doubt if there is less design in the one case than in the other. How life achieves the guidance, how even it accomplishes the movements, is a mystery, but that it does accomplish them is a commonplace of observation. From the motion of a finger to the construction of an aeroplane, there is but a succession of steps. From the growth of a weed to the flight of an eagle,—from a yeast granule at one end, to the human body at the other,—the organising power of life over matter is conspicuous.

Who can doubt the supremacy of the spiritual over the material? It is a fact which, illustrated by trivial instances, may be pressed to the most portentous consequences.

If interaction between mind and matter really occurs, and if both are persistent and enduring entities, there is no limit to the possibilities under which such interaction may occur—no limit which can be laid down beforehand—we must be guided and instructed solely by experience.

Whether the results produced are styled miraculous or not, depends on our knowledge,—our knowledge of all the powers latent in nature, and a knowledge of all the intelligences which exist. A savage on his first encounter with white men must have come into contact with what to him was supernatural. A letter, a gun, even artificial teeth, have all aroused superstition ; while a telegram must be obviously miraculous, to anyone intelligent enough to perceive the wonder. A colony of bees, unused to the ministrations or interference of man, might puzzle itself over the provision made for its habitation and activities, if it had intelligence enough to ponder the matter. So human beings, if they are open-minded and developed enough to contemplate all the happenings in which they are concerned, have been led to recognise guidance ; and they have responded to the perception by the worshipful attitude of religion. In other words, they have essentially recognised the existence of a Power transcending ordinary nature—a Power that may properly be called supernatural.

Meaning of the Term Body

Our experience of bodies here and now is that they are composed of material particles derived from the earth, whether they be bodies animated by vegetable or by animal forms of life. But I take it that the real meaning of the term ' body ' is a *means of manifestation*,—perhaps a physical mode of manifestation adopted by something which without such instrument or organ would be in a different and elusive category. Why should we say that bodies must be made of matter ? Surely only because we know of nothing else of which they could be made ; but that lack of knowledge is not very efficient as an argument. True, if they were made of anything else they would not be apparent to us now, with our particular evolutionally-derived sense organs ; for these only inform us about matter and its properties. Constructions built of Ether would have no chance of appealing to our senses, they would not be apparent to us ; they would therefore not be what we ordinarily call bodies ; at any rate they would not be material bodies. In order to become apparent to us, a psychical or vital entity must enter the material realm, and either clothe itself with, or temporarily assimilate, material particles. ⸌

It may be that etherial bodies do not exist ; the burden of proof rests upon those who conceive of their possible existence ; but we are bound to admit that even if they did exist, they would make no impression on our senses. Hence if there are any intelligences in another order of existence interlocked with ours, and if they can in any sense be supposed to have bodies at all, those bodies must be made either of Ether or of something equally intangible to us in our present condition.[1]

Yet, though intangible and elusive, we have reason to know that Ether is substantial enough,—far more substantial indeed than matter, which turns out to be a rare and filmy insertion in, or modification of, the Ether of Space ; and a different set of sense organs might make the Ether eclipse matter in availability and usefulness. In my book *The Ether of Space* this thesis is elaborated from a purely physical point of view.

I wish, however, to make no assertion concerning the possible psychical use of the Ether of Space. Anything of that kind must be speculative ; the only bodies we now know of in actual fact are material bodies, and we must be guided by facts. Yet we must not shut the door prematurely on other possibilities ; and we can remember that inspired writers have sometimes contemplated what they term a spiritual body.

---

[1] That a great poet should have represented the meeting between the still incarnate Æneas and his discarnate father Anchises as a bodily disappointment, is consistent :—

"Ter conatus ibi collo dare brachia circum ;
Ter frustra comprensa manus effugit imago,
Par levibus ventis, volucrique simillima somno."
Æneid, vi. 700

It may be said that what is intangible ought to be invisible ; but that does not follow. The Ether is a medium for vision, not for touch. Ether and Ether may interact, just as matter and matter interact ; but interaction between Ether and matter is peculiarly elusive.

PERMANENCE OF BODY

But why should anyone suppose a body of some kind always necessary ? Why should they assume a perpetual sort of dualism about existence ? The reason is that we have no knowledge of any other form of animate existence; and it may be claimed as legitimate to assume that the association between life and matter here on the planet has a real and vital significance, that without such an episode of earth life we should be less than we are, and that the relation is typical of something real and permanent.

" Such use may lie in blood and breath."—TENNYSON

Why matter should be thus useful to spirit and even to life it is not easy to say. It may be that by the inter-action of two things better and newer results can always be obtained than was possible for one alone. There are analogies enough for that. Do we not find that genius seems to require the obstruction or the aid of matter for its full development ? The artist must enjoy being able to compel refractory material to express his meaning. Didactic writings are apt to emphasise the obstructive-ness of matter ; but that may be because its usefulness seems self-evident. Our limbs, and senses, and bodily faculties generally, are surely of momentous service; microscopes and telescopes and laboratory instruments, and machinery generally, are only extensions of them. Tools to the man who can use them :—orchestra to the musician, lathe or theodolite to the engineer, books and records to the historian, even though not much more than pen and paper is needed by the poet or the mathematician. But our bodily organs are much more than any artificial tools can be, they are part of our very being. The body is part of the constitution of man. We are not spirit or soul alone,—though it is sometimes necessary to emphasise the fact that we are soul at all,—we are in truth soul and body together. And so I think we shall always be ; though our bodies need not always be com-posed of earthly particles. Matter is the accidental part : there is an essential and more permanent part, and the permanent part must survive.

This is the strength, as I have said elsewhere and will not now at any length repeat, of the sacramental claims and practices of religion. Forms and customs which appeal to the body are a legitimate part of the whole ; and while some natures derive most benefit from the exclusively psychical and spiritual essence, others probably do well to prevent the more sensuous and more puzzling concomitants from falling into disuse.

CHAPTER VII

'RESURRECTION OF THE BODY'

"Never the spirit was born ; the spirit shall cease to be never."
EDWIN ARNOLD

IN the whole unknown drama of the soul the episode of bodily existence must have profound significance. Matter cannot only be obstructive, even usefully obstructive,—by which is meant the kind of obstruction which stimulates to effort and trains for power, like the hurdles in an obstacle race,—it must be auxiliary too. Whatever may be the case with external matter, the body itself is certainly an auxiliary, so long as it is in health and strength ; and it gives opportunity for the development of the soul in new and unexpected ways—ways in which but for earth life its practice would be deficient. This it is which makes calamity of too short a life.

But let us not be over-despondent about the tragedy of the present. It may be that the concentrated training and courageous facing of fate which in most cases must have accompanied voluntary entry into a dangerous war, compensates in intensity what it lacks in duration, and that the benefit of bodily terrestrial life is not so much lost by violent death of that kind as might at first appear. Yet even with some such assurance, the spectacle of thousands of youths in full vigour and joy of life having their earthly future violently wrenched from them, amid scenes of grim horror and nerve-wracking noise and confusion, is one which cannot and ought not to be regarded with equanimity. It is a bad and unnatural truncation of an important part of each individual career, a part which might have done much to develop faculties and enlarge experience.

Meanwhile, the very fact that we lament so sincerely this dire and man-caused fate serves to illustrate the view we inevitably take that the earth-body is not only a means of manifestation but is a real servant of the soul,—that flesh can in some sense help spirit as spirit can undoubtedly help flesh,—and that while its very weaknesses are serviceable and stimulating, its strength is exhilarating and superb. The faculties and powers developed in the animal kingdom during all the millions of years of evolution, and now inherited for better for worse by man, are not to be despised. Those therefore who are able to think that some of the essential elements or attributes of the body are carried forward into a higher life—quite irrespective of the manifestly discarded material particles which never were important to the body, for they were always in perpetual flux as individual molecules—those, I say, who think that the value derived and acquired through the body survives, and becomes a permanent possession of the soul, may well feel that they can employ the mediæval phrase "resurrection of the body" to express their perception. They may feel that it is a truth which needs emphasising all the more from its lack of obviousness. These old phrases, consecrated by long usage, and familiar to all the saints, though their early and superficial meaning is evidently superseded, may be found to have an inner and spiritual significance which when once grasped should be kept in memory, and brought before attention, and sustained against challenge : in no case should they be lightly or hastily discarded.

It seems not altogether fanciful to trace some similarity or analogy, between the ideas about inheritance usually associated with the name of Weismann, and the inheritance or conveyance of bodily attributes, or of powers acquired through the body, into the future life of the soul.

When considering whether anything, or what, is likely to be permanent, the answer turns upon whether or not the soul has been affected. Mere bodily accidents of course are temporary ; loss of an arm or an eye is no more carried on as a permanent disfigurement than it is transmissible to offspring. But, apart from accidents which may happen to the body, there are some evil things— rendered accessible by and definitely associated with the body—which assault and hurt the soul. And the effect of these is transmissible, and may become permanent. Habits which write their mark on the countenance— whether the writing be good or bad—are not likely to take effect on the body alone. And in this sense also future existence may be either glorified or stained, for a time, by persistence of bodily traits,—by this kind of " resurrection of the body."

Furthermore it is found that although bodily marks, scars and wounds, are clearly not of soul-compelling and permanent character, yet for purposes of identification, and when re-entering the physical atmosphere for the purpose of communication with friends, these temporary marks are re-assumed ; just as the general appearance at the remembered age, and details connected with clothes and little unessential tricks of manner, may—in some unknown sense—be assumed too.

And it is to this category that I would attribute the curious interest still felt in old personal possessions. They are attended to and recalled, not for what by a shopman is called their ' value,' but because they furnish useful and welcome evidence of identity ; they are like the *pièces de conviction* brought up at a trial, they bear silent witness to remembered fact. And in so far as the disposal or treatment of them by survivors is evidence of the regard in which their late owner was held, it is unlikely that they should have suddenly become matters of complete indifference. Nothing human, in the sense of affecting the human spirit, can be considered foreign to a friendly and sympathetic soul, even though his new preoccupations and industries and main activities are of a different order. It appears as if, for the few moments of renewed earthly intercourse, the newer surroundings shrink for a time into the background. They are remembered, but not vividly. Indeed it seems difficult to live in both worlds at once, especially after the life-long practice here of living almost exclusively in one. Those whose existence here was coloured or ennobled by wider knowledge and higher aims seem likely to have the best chance of conveying instructive information across the boundary ; though their developed powers may be of such still higher value, that only from a sense of duty or in a missionary spirit can they be expected to absent them from felicity a while in order to help the brethren.

Quotation of a passage from Plotinus seems here per-missible :—

" Souls which once were in men, when they leave the body, need not cease from benefiting mankind. Some indeed, in addition to other services, give occult messages (oracular replies), thus proving by their own case that other souls also survive" (*Enn.* IV. vii. 15).

As a digression of some importance, I venture to say that claims of thoughtless and pertinacious people upon the charitable and eminent, even here, are often excessive : it is to be hoped that such claims become less troublesome and less effective hereafter ; but it is a hope without much foundation. Remonstrances are useless, however, for only the more thoughtful and those most deserving of help are likely to attend to remonstrances. Nevertheless —useless or not—it behoves one to make them. We are indeed taught that in exceptional cases there may ulti-mately supervene such an extraordinary elevation of soul that no trouble is too great, and no appeal is unheard. But still, even in the Loftiest case of all, the episode of having passed through a human body contributes to the power of sympathising with and aiding ordinary humanity.

CHAPTER VIII

MIND AND BRAIN

" For nothing is that errs from law."—TENNYSON

IT is sometimes thought that memory is located in the brain; and undoubtedly there must be some physiological process at work in the brain when any incident of memory is recalled and either uttered or written. But it does not at all follow that memory itself is located in the brain; though there must be some easier channel, or some already prepared path, which enables an idea to be translated from the general mental reservoir into consciousness, with clarity and power sufficient to stimulate the necessary nerves and muscles into a condition adequate for reproduction.

Sometimes in order to remember a thing, one writes it in a note-book; and the memory may be said to be in the note-book about as accurately as it may be said to be in the brain. A physical process has put it in the note-book; there is a physical configuration persisting there; and when a sort of reverse physical process is repeated, it can be got back into consciousness by simply what we call ' looking ' at the book and reading. But surely the real memory is in the *mind* all the time, and the deposit in the note-book is a mere detent for calling it out or for making it easy of recovery. In order to communicate any information we must focus attention on it; and whether we focus attention on a part of the brain or on a page of a note-book matters very little; the attention itself is a mental process, not a physiological one, though it has a physiological concomitant.

This is an important matter, the keystone in fact of our problem about the connexion between mind and matter, and I propose to amplify its treatment further; for this is an unavoidably controversial portion of the book.

THE SEAT OF MEMORY

I am familiar with all the usual analogies drawn between organic habit and memory on the one hand, and the more ready repetition of physical processes by inorganic material on the other. Imperfectly elastic springs, for instance, which show reminiscences of previous bendings or twistings by their subsequent unwindings; and cogs which wear into smooth running by repetition; are examples of this kind. A violin which by long practice becomes more musical in tone, is another; or a path which by being often traversed becomes easier to the feet. A flower-bed recently altered in shape, by being partly grassed over, is liable to exhibit its former outline by aid of bulbs and other half-forgotten growths which come up through the grass in the old pattern.

This last is a striking example of apparent memory, not indeed in the inorganic but in the unconscious world; where indeed it is prevalent, for every one must recognise the memory of animals—there can be no doubt of that. And it would seem that a kind of race-memory must be invoked to account for many surprising cases of instinct; of which the building of specific birds' nests, and the accurate pecking of a newly-hatched chicken, are among the stock instances. No experience can be lodged in the *brain* of the newly-hatched !

That some sort of stored facility should exist in the adult brain, is in no way surprising; and that there is some physical or physiological concomitant of actual remembrance is plain; but that is a very different thing from asserting that memory itself, or any kind of consciousness, is located in the brain; though truly without the aid of the brain it is, as far as this planet is concerned, latent and inaccessible.

Plotinus puts the matter in an interesting but perhaps rather too extreme form :—

" As to memory, the body is an impediment . . . the unstable and fluctuating nature of the body makes for oblivion not for memory. Body is a veritable River of Lethe. Memory belongs to the soul " (*Enn.* IV. iii. 26).

The actual reproduction or remembrance of a fact—the demonstration or realisation of memory—undoubtedly depends on brain and muscle mechanism ; but memory itself turns out to be essentially mental, and is found to exist apart from the bodily mechanism which helped originally to receive and store the impression. And though without that same or some equivalent mechanism we cannot get at it, so that it cannot be displayed to others, yet in my experience it turns out not to be absolutely necessary to use actually the same instrument for its reproduction as was responsible for its deposition : though undoubtedly to use the same is easier and helpful. In the early Edison phonographs the same instrument had to be used for both reception and reproduction ; but now a record can readily be transferred from one instrument to another. This may be regarded as a rough mechanical analogy to the telepathic or telergic process whereby a psychic reservoir of memory can be partially tapped through another organism.

But, apart from any consideration of what may be regarded as doubtful or uncertain, there are some facts about the relation of brain to consciousness, which, though universally admitted, are frequently misinterpreted. Injure the brain, and consciousness is lost. ' Lost ' is the right word—not ' destroyed.' Repair the lesion, and consciousness may be restored, *i.e.* normal manifestation of consciousness can once more occur. It is the *display* of consciousness, in all such cases, that we mean when we speak of the effect of brain injury ; the utilisation of bodily organs is necessary for its exhibition. If the bodily organs do not exist, or are too damaged, no normal manifestation is possible. That is the fact which may be misinterpreted.

In general we may say, with fair security, that no receptivity to physical phenomena exists save through sense-organ, nerve, and brain; nor any initiation of physical phenomena, save through brain, nerve, and muscle. Apart from physical phenomena consciousness is isolated and inaccessible : we have no right to say that it is non-existent. In ordinary usage it is not customary or necessary to be always harping on this completer aspect of things : it is only necessary when misunderstanding has arisen from uniformly inaccurate, or rather unguarded, modes of expression.

In an excellent lecture by Dr. Mott on " The Effects of High Explosives upon the Central Nervous System," I find this sentence :—

" It is known that a continuous supply of oxygen is essential for consciousness."

What is intended is clear enough, but analysed strictly this assertion goes far beyond what is known. We do not really know that oxygen, or any form of matter, has anything to do with consciousness : all that we know, and all that Dr. Mott really means to say, I presume, is that without a supply of oxygen consciousness gives no physical sign.

Partial interruptions of physical manifestations of consciousness well illustrate this : as, for instance, when speech-centres of the brain alone are affected. If in such case we had to depend on mouth-muscle alone we should say that consciousness had departed, and might even think that it was non-existent ; but the arm-muscle may remain under brain control, and by intelligent writing can show that consciousness is there all the time, and that it is only inhibited from one of the specially easy modes of manifestation. In some cases the inhibition may be complete, —from such cases we do not learn much ; but when it is only partial we learn a good deal.

I quote again from Dr. Mott, omitting for brevity the detailed description of certain surgical war-cases, under his care, which precedes the following explanatory interjection and summary :—

" Why should these men, whose silent thoughts are perfect, be unable to speak ? They comprehend all that is said to them unless they are deaf ; but it is quite clear that [even] in these cases their internal language is unaffected, for they are able to express their thoughts and judgments perfectly well by writing, even if they are deaf. The mutism is therefore not due to an intellectual defect, nor is it due to volitional inhibition of language in silent thought. Hearing, the primary incitation to vocalisation and speech, is usually unaffected, yet they are unable to speak ; they cannot even whisper, cough, whistle, or laugh aloud. Many who are unable to speak voluntarily yet call out in their dreams expressions they have used in trench warfare and battle. Sometimes this is followed by return of speech, but more often not. One man continually shouted out in his sleep, but he did not recover voluntary speech or power of phonation till eight months after admission to the hospital for shell-shock."

Very well, all this interesting experience serves among other things to illustrate our simple but occasionally overlooked thesis. For it is through physical phenomena that normally we apprehend, here and now ; and it is by aid of physical phenomena that we convey to others our wishes, our impressions, our ideas, and our memories. Dislocate the physical from the psychical, and communication ceases. Restore the connexion, in however imperfect a form, and once more incipient communication may become possible again.

That is the rationale of the process of human intercourse. Do we understand it ? No. Do we understand even how our own mind operates on our own body ? No. We know for a fact that it does.

Do we understand how a mind can with difficulty and imperfectly operate another body submitted to its temporary guidance and control ? No. Do we know for a fact that it does ? Aye, that is the question—a question of evidence. I myself answer the question affirmatively ; not on theoretical grounds—far from that—but on a basis of straightforward experience. Others, if they allow themselves to take the trouble to get the experience, will come to the same conclusion.

Will they do so best by allowing their own bodies or brains to be utilised ? No, that seems not even the best, and certainly not the only way. It may not, for the majority of people, be a possible way. The sensitive or medium who serves us, by putting his or her bodily mechanism at our disposal, is not likely to be best informed concerning the nature of the process. Mediums have perhaps but little conscious information to give us concerning their powers ; we must learn from what they do, not from what they say. The outside observer, the experimenter, whose senses are alert all the time and who continues fully conscious without special receptivity or any peculiar power of his own, is in a better position to note and judge what is happening,—at least from the normal and scientific point of view. Let us be as cautious and critical, aye and as sceptical as we like, but let us also be patient and persevering and fair ; do not let us start with a preconceived notion of what is possible and what is impossible in this almost unexplored universe ; let us only be willing to learn and be guided by facts, not by dogmas ; and gradually the truth will permeate our understanding and make for itself a place in our minds as secure as in any other branch of observational science.

CHAPTER IX

LIFE AND CONSCIOUSNESS

THE limitation of scope which eminent Professors of a certain school of modern science have laid down for themselves is forcibly expressed by one of the ablest of their champions thus :—-

> "No sane man has ever pretended, since science became a definite body of doctrine, that we know or ever can hope to know or conceive the possibility of knowing whence the mechanism has come, why it is there, whither it is going, or what may be beyond and beside it which our senses are incapable of appreciating. These things are not 'explained' by science and never can be."
> —Sir E. RAY LANKESTER.

I should myself hesitate to promulgate such a markedly *non-possumus* and *ignorabimus* statement concerning the scope of physical science, even as narrowly and popularly understood ; but it illuminates the position taken up by those *savants* who are commonly known as Materialists, and explains their expressed though non-personal hostility to other scientific men who seek to exceed the boundaries laid down, and investigate things beyond the immediate range of the senses.

Eliminating the future tense from the statement, however, I can agree with it. The instrument of translation from the mental to the physical, and back from the physical to the mental, is undoubtedly the brain, but as to how the translation is accomplished, I venture to say, we have not the inkling of an idea. Nevertheless, hints which may gradually lead towards a partial understanding of psycho-physical processes may be gained by study of exceptional cases : for such study is often more instructive than continued scrutiny of the merely normal.

The fact of human consciousness, though it raises the

problem to a high degree of conspicuousness, by no means exhausts the difficulty ; for it is one which faces us in connexion with every form of life. The association of life with matter, and of mind with life, are problems of similar order, and a glimmering of understanding of the one may be expected to throw light upon the other. But until we know more of the method by which the simplest and most familiar psycho-physical interaction occurs—until we know enough to see how the gulf between two apparently different Modes of Being is bridged—it is safest to observe and accumulate facts, and to be very chary of making more than the most tentative and cautious of working hypotheses. For to frame even a tentative hypothesis, of any helpful kind, may require some clue which as yet we do not possess.

I have been struck by the position taken by Dr. Chalmers Mitchell in his notable small book *Evolution and the War*, the early chapters of which, on Germany of the past and present, I would like unreservedly to commend to the reader. Indeed, commendation of a friendly and non-patronising kind may well extend to the whole book, although it must be admitted that here and there mere exposition of Darwinism is suspended, and difficult and debatable questions are touched upon.

On these questions I would not like to be understood as expressing a hasty opinion, either against or for the views of the author. The points at issue between us are more or less fine-drawn, and cannot be dealt with parenthetically ; nor do I ever propose to deal with them in a controversial manner. The author, as a biologist of fame, is more than entitled to such expression of his own views as he has cared to give. I quote with admiration, not necessarily with agreement, a few passages from the part dealing with the relation between mind and matter, and especially with the wide and revolutionary difference between man and animal caused by either the evolution or the incoming of free and conscious Choice.

He will not allow, with Bergson and others, that the roots of consciousness, in its lower grades, go deep down into the animal, and even perhaps into the vegetable, kingdom ; he has no patience with those who associate elementary consciousness and freedom and indeterminateness not merely with human life but with all life, and who detect rudiments of purpose and intelligence in the protozoa. Nor, on the other hand, does he approve the dogmatic teaching of the 'ultra-scientific' school, which, being obsessed by the idea of man's animal origin, interprets human nature solely in terms of protoplasm. He opposes the possibility of this by saying :—

"However fruitful and interesting it may be to remember that we are rooted deep in the natal mud, our possession of consciousness and the sense of freedom is a vital and overmastering distinction."

On the more interesting of the above-mentioned alternatives Dr. Chalmers Mitchell expresses himself thus :—

"The Bergsonian interpretation does nothing to make consciousness and freedom more intelligible ; and by extending them from man, in whom we know them to exist, to animals, in which their presence is at best an inference, it not only robs them of definiteness and reality, but it blurs the real distinction between men and animals, and evades the most difficult problem of science and philosophy. The facts are more truly represented by such phraseology as that animals are instinctive, man is intelligent, animals are irresponsible, man is responsible, animals are automata, man is free ; or if you like, that God gave animals a beautiful body, man a rational soul. . . ."

And soon afterwards he continues :—

"Not 'envisaging itself,' not being at once actor, spectator, and critic, 'living in the flashing moment,' not seeing the past and the present and the future separately, this is the highest at which we can put the consciousness of animals, and herein lies the distinction between man and the animals which makes the overwhelming difference.

"Must we then suppose, with Russel Wallace, that somewhere on the upward path from the tropical forests to the groves of Paradise, a soul was interpolated from an outside source into the gorilla-like ancestry of man ? I do not think so, although I not only admit but assert that such a view gives a more accurate statement of fact than does either of the fashionable doctrines that I have discussed. I believe with Darwin, that as the body of man has been evolved from the body of animals, so the intellectual, emotional, and moral faculties of man have been evolved from the qualities of animals. I help myself towards the comprehension of the process by reflecting on two phenomena of observation [which he proceeds to cite]. I help myself, and perchance may help others ; no more ; could I speak dogmatically on what is the central mystery of all science and all philosophy and all thought, my words would roll with the thunder of Sinai."

Let it not be supposed for a moment that this distinguished biologist is in agreement with me on many matters dealt with in the present book. If he were, he would, I believe, achieve a more admirable and eloquent work than is consistent with the technically ' apologetic ' tone which, in the present state of the scientific atmosphere, it behoves me to take. To guard against unwelcome misrepresentation of his views, and yet at the same time to indicate their force, I will make one more quotation :—

" Writing as a hard-shell Darwinian evolutionist, a lover of the scalpel and microscope, and of patient, empirical observation, as one who dislikes all forms of supernaturalism, and who does not shrink from the implications even of the phrase that thought is a secretion of the brain as bile is a secretion of the liver, I assert as a biological fact that the moral law is as real and as external to man as the starry vault. It has no secure seat in any single man or in any single nation. It is the work of the blood and tears of long generations of men. It is not, in man, inborn or innate, but is enshrined in his traditions, in his customs, in his literature and his religion. Its creation and sustenance are the crowning glory of man, and his consciousness of it puts him in a high place above the animal world. Men live and die ; nations rise and fall, but the struggle of individual lives and of individual nations must be measured not by their immediate needs, but as they tend to the debasement or perfection of man's great achievement."

My own view, which in such matters I only put forth with diffidence and brevity, is more in favour of Continuity. I do not trace so catastrophic a break between man and animals, nor between animal and vegetable, perhaps not even between organised and unorganised forms of matter, as does Dr. Chalmers Mitchell.

I would venture to extend the range of the term ' soul ' down to a very large denominator,—to cases in which the magnitude of the fraction becomes excessively minute,—and tentatively admit to the possibility of survival, though not individual survival, every form of life. As to Individuality and Personality—they can only survive where they already exist ; when they really exist they persist ; but bare survival, as an alternative to improbable extinction, may be widespread.

Matter forms an instrument, a means of manifestation, but it need not be the only one possible. We have utilised matter to build up this beautiful bodily mechanism, but, when that is done with, *the constructive ability remains* ; and it can be expected to exercise its organising powers in other than material environment. If this hypothesis be true at all (and admittedly I am now making hypothesis) *it must be true of all forms of life* ; for what the process of evolution has accomplished here may be accomplished elsewhere, under conditions at present unknown.[1] So I venture to surmise that the surroundings of non-material existence will be far more homely and habitual than people in general have been accustomed to think likely.

And how do I know that the visible material body of anything is all the body, or all the existence, it possesses ? Why should not things xist also, or have ethereal counterparts, in an ethereal world ? Perhaps everything has already an ethereal counterpart, of which our senses tell us the material aspect only. I do not know. Such an idea may be quoted as an absurdity ; but if the evidence drives me in that direction, in that direction I will go, without undue resistance. There have been those who do not wait to be driven, but who lead ; and the inspired guidance of Plotinus in that direction may secure more attention, and attract more disciples, when the way is illuminated by discoverable facts.

Meanwhile facts await discovery.

Passages from Plotinus, it may be remembered, are eloquently translated by F. W. H. Myers, from the obscure and often ungrammatical Greek, in *Human Personality*, vol. ii. pp. 289–291 ; and readers of S.P.R. *Proceedings*, vol. xxii. pp. 108–172, will remember the development by Mrs. Verrall of the καὶ αὐτὸς οὐρανὸς ἀκύμων motto prefixed to F. W. H. Myers's posthumously published poem on Tennyson in *Fragments of Prose and Poetry*.

---

[1] I wish to emphasise this paragraph, as perhaps an important one.

My reference just above to teachings of Plotinus about the kind of things to be met with in the other world, or the ethereal world, or whatever it may be called, is due to information from Professor J. H. Muirhead that, roughly speaking, Plotinus teaches that things there are on the same plan as things here: each thing here having its counterpart or corresponding existence there, though glorified and fuller of reality. Not to misrepresent this doctrine, but to illustrate it as far as can be by a short passage, Professor Muirhead has given me the following translation from the *Enneads* :—

"But again let us speak thus: For since we hold that *this* universe is framed after the pattern of *That*, every living thing must needs first be There ; and since Its Being is perfect, all must be There. Heaven then must There be a living thing nor void of what are here called stars ; indeed such things belong to heaven. Clearly too the earth which is There is not an empty void, but much more full of life, wherein are all creatures that are here called land animals and plants that are rooted in life. And sea is There, and all water in ebb and flow and in abiding life, and all creatures that are in the water. And air is a part of the all that is There, and creatures of the air in accordance with the nature and laws of air. For in the Living how should living things fail ? How then can any living thing fail to be There, seeing that as each of the great parts of nature is, so needs must be the living things that therein are ? As then Heaven is, and There exists, so are and exist all the creatures that inhabit it ; nor can these fail to be, else would those (on earth ?) not be."

Enn. VI. vii.

The reason why this strange utterance or speculation is reproduced here is because it seems to some extent to correspond with curious statements recorded in another part of this book ; *e.g.* in Chapter XIV, Part II.

I expect that it would be misleading to suppose that the terms used by Plotinus really signify any difference of locality. It may be nearer the truth to suppose that when freed from our restricting and only matter-revealing senses we become aware of much that was and is ' here ' all the time, interfused with the existence which we knew ;— forming part indeed of the one and only complete existence, of which our present normal knowledge is limited to a single aspect. We might think and speak of many interpenetrating universes, and yet recognise that ultimately they must be all one. It is not likely that the Present differs from what we now call the Future except in our mode of perceiving it.

22

CHAPTER X

ON MEANS OF COMMUNICATION

"In scientific truth there is no finality, and there should therefore be no dogmatism. When this is forgotten, then science will become stagnant, and its high-priests will endeavour to strangle new learning at its birth."—R. A. GREGORY, *Discovery*

HOW does mind communicate with mind? Our accustomed process is singularly indirect. Speech is the initiation of muscular movements, under brain and nerve guidance, which result in the production of atmospheric pulsations—alternate condensations and rarefactions—which spread out in all directions in a way that can be likened superficially to the spreading of ripples on a pond. In themselves the aerial pulsations have no psychical connotation, and are as purely mechanical as are those ripples, though like the indentations on the wax of a phonograph their sequence is cunningly contrived ; and it is in their sequence that the code lies —a code which anyone who has struggled with a foreign language knows is difficult to learn. Sound waves have in some respects a still closer analogy with the ethereal pulsations generated at a wireless-telegraph sending station, which affect all sensitive receiving instruments within range and convey a code by their artificially induced sequence.

Hearing is reception of a small modicum of the above aerial pulsations, by suitable mechanism which enables them to stimulate ingeniously contrived nerve-endings, and so at length to affect auditory centres in the brain, and to get translated into the same kind of consciousness as was responsible for the original utterance. The whole is done so quickly and easily, by the perfect physiological mechanism provided, that the indirect and surprising nature of the process is usually overlooked ; as most things are when they have become familiar. Wireless telegraphy is not an iota more marvellous, but, being unfamiliar, it has aroused a sense of wonder.

Writing and Reading by aid of black marks on a piece of paper, perceived by means of the Ether instead of the air, and through the agency of the eye instead of the ear,—though the symbols are ultimately to be interpreted as if heard,—hardly need elaboration in order to exhibit their curiously artificial and complicated indirectness : and in their case an element of delay, even a long time-interval —perhaps centuries—may intervene between production and reception.

Artistic representation also, such as painting or music, though of a less articulate character, less dependent on purely linguistic convention and less limited by nationality, is still truly astonishing when intellectually regarded. An arrangement of pigments designed for the reception and modification and re-emission or reflexion of ether-tremors, in the one case; and, in the other, a continuous series of complicated vibrations excited by grossly mechanical means; intervene between the minds of painter and spectator, of composer and auditor, or, in more general terms, between agent and percipient,—again with possible great lapse of time.

That ideas and feelings, thus indirectly and mechanically transmitted or stored, can affect the sensitive soul in unmistakable fashion, is a fact of experience ; but that deposits in matter are competent to produce so purely psychic an effect can surely only be explained in terms of the potentialities and previous experience of the mind or soul itself. No emotional influence can be expressed, or rendered intelligible, in terms of matter. Matter is an indirect medium of communication between mind and mind. That direct telepathic intercourse should be able to occur between mind and mind, without all this intermediate physical mechanism, is therefore not really surprising. It has to be proved, no doubt, but the fact is intrinsically less puzzling than many of those other facts to which we have grown hardened by usage.

Why should telepathy be unfamiliar to us? Why should it seem only an exceptional or occasional method of communication? There is probably, as M. Bergson has said, an evolutionary advantage in our present almost exclusive limitation to mechanical and physical methods of communication; for these are under muscular control and can be shut off. We can isolate ourselves from them, if not in a mechanical, then in a topographical manner: we can go away, out of range. We could not thus protect ourselves against insistent telepathy. Hence probably the practical usefulness of the inhibiting and abstracting power of the brain; a power which in some lunatics is permanently deficient.

Physical things can reach consciousness—if at all—only through the brain; that remains true as regards physical things, however much we may admit telepathy from other minds; and, conversely, only through the brain can we operate with conscious purpose on the material world. To any more direct mental or spiritual intercourse we are, unless specially awakened, temporarily dead or asleep. There is some inversion of ordinary ideas here, for a state of trance appears to rouse or free the dormant faculties, and to render direct intercourse more possible. At any rate it does this for some people. For we find here and there, a few perfectly sane individuals, from whom, when in a rather exceptional state, the customary brain-limitation seems to be withdrawn or withdrawable. Their minds cease to be isolated for a time, and are accessible to more direct influences. Not the familiar part of their minds, not the part accustomed to operate and to be operated on by the habitually used portion of brain, no, but what is called a subliminal stratum of mind, a part only accessible perhaps to physical things through an ordinarily unused and only subconscious portion of the brain.

The occurrence of such people, i.e. of people with such exceptional and really simple faculties, could not have been predicted or expected on a basis of everyday experi-

ence ; but if evidence is forthcoming for their existence—
even although it be not quite of an ordinary character—
and if we can make examination of the subject-matter
and criticise the statements of fact which are thus re-
ceivable, there is no sort of sense in opposing the facts
by adducing preconceived negative opinions about impossibility, and declining to look into the evidence or
judge of the results. There were people once who would
not look at the satellites of Jupiter, lest their cherished
convictions should be disturbed. There was a mathematician not long ago who would not see an experimental
demonstration of conical refraction, lest if it failed his
confidence in refined optical theory should be upset.
And so, strange to say, there are people to-day who deny
the fact, and condemn the investigation, of any manner of
communication outside the realm of ordinary commonplace experience : having no ground at all for their denial
save prejudice.

Well, like other little systems, they have their day and
cease to be. We need not attend to them overmuch.
If the facts of the Universe have come within our con-
templation, a certain amount of contemporary blindness,
though it may surprise, need not perplex us. The study
of the material side of things, under the limitations appropriate thereto, has done splendid service. Only gradually
can mental scope be enlarged to take in not only all this
but more also.

In so far as those who are open to the less well-defined
and more ambitious region are ignorant or unresponsive
to what has been achieved in the material realm, it is no
wonder that their asserted enlargement of scope is not
credited. It does not seem likely that a new revelation
has been vouchsafed to them, when they are so ignorant
concerning the other and already recognised kind of
Natural knowledge. They cannot indeed have attained
information through the same channels, or in the same
way. And it is this dislocation of knowledge, this difference of atmosphere, this barely reconcilable attitude of
two diverse groups of people—though occasionally, by the
device of water-tight compartments, the same individual
has breathed both kinds of air and belonged to both
groups—it is this bifurcation of method that has retarded

mutual understanding. There are pugnacious members of either group who try to strengthen their own position by decrying the methods of the other ; and were it not for the occurrence from time to time of a Wallace or a Crookes, *i.e.* of men who combine in their own persons something of both kinds of knowledge, attained not by different but by similar methods—all their theses being maintained and justified on scientific grounds, and after experimental inquiry—the chances for a reasonable and scientific outlook into a new region, and ultimately over the border-line into the domain of religion, would not be encouraging. The existence of such men, however, has given the world pause, has sometimes checked its facile abuse, and has brought it occasionally into a reflective, perhaps now even into a partially receptive, mood. We need not be in any hurry, though we can hardly help hoping for quick progress if the new knowledge can in any way alleviate the terrible amount of sorrow in the world at present ; moreover, if a new volume is to be opened in man's study of the Universe, it is time that the early chapters were being perused.

It may be asked, do I recommend all bereaved persons to devote the time and attention which I have done to getting communications and recording them? Most certainly I do not. I am a student of the subject, and a student often undertakes detailed labour of a special kind. I recommend people in general to learn and realise that their loved ones are still active and useful and interested and happy—more alive than ever in one sense—and to make up their minds to live a useful life till they rejoin them.

What steps should be taken to gain this peaceful assurance must depend on the individual. Some may get it from the consolations of religion, some from the testimony of trusted people, while some may find it necessary to have first-hand experience of their own for a time. And if this experience can be attained privately, with no outside assistance, by quiet and meditation or by favour of occasional waking dreams, so much the better.

What people should not do, is to close their minds to the possibility of continued existence except in some lofty

and inaccessible and essentially unsuitable condition;
they should not selfishly seek to lessen pain by discourag-
ing all mention, and even hiding everything likely to
remind them, of those they have lost; nor should they
give themselves over to unavailing and prostrating grief.
Now is the time for action; and it is an ill return to
those who have sacrificed all and died for the Country
if those left behind do not throw off enervating distress and helpless lamentation, and seek to live for the
Country and for humanity, to the utmost of their
power.

Any steps which are calculated to lead to this wholesome result in any given instance are justified; and it is
not for me to offer advice as to the kind of activity most
appropriate to each individual case.

I have suggested that the new knowledge, when
generally established and incorporated with existing
systems, will have a bearing and influence on the region
hitherto explored by other faculties, and considered to be
the domain of faith.   It certainly must be so, whether the
suggested expansion of scientific scope is welcomed or not.
Certainly the conclusions to which I myself have been led
by one mode of access are not contradictory of the conclusions which have been arrived at by those who (naturally) seem to me the more enlightened theologians; though
I must confess that with some of the ecclesiastical over-
growth which has remained with us from a bygone day,
a psychic investigator can have but little sympathy.
Indeed he only refrains from attacking it because he
feels that, left to itself, it will be superseded by something
better and more fruitful, and will die a natural death.
There is too much wheat mingled with the tares to
render it safe for any but an ecclesiastical expert to
attempt to uproot them.

Meanwhile, although some of the official exponents of
Christian doctrine condemn any attempt to explore things
of this kind by secular methods; while others refrain from
countenancing any results thus obtained; there are many
who would utilise them in their teaching if they conscientiously could, and a few who have already begun to
do so, on the strength of their own knowledge, however

derived, and in spite of the risk of offending weaker brethren.[1]

[1] For instance, a book called *The Gospel of the Hereafter*, by Dr. J. Paterson Smyth, of Montreal, may be brought to the notice of anyone who, while clinging tightly to the essential tenets of orthodox Christianity, and unwilling or unable to enter upon a course of study, would gladly interpret eastern and mediæval phrases in a sense not repugnant to the modern spirit.

CHAPTER XI

ON THE FACT OF SUPERNORMAL COMMUNICATION

" But he, the spirit himself, may come
Where all the nerve of sense is numb."
TENNYSON, *In Memoriam*

HOWEVER it be accomplished, and whatever reception the present-day scientific world may give to the assertion, there are many now who know, by first-hand experience, that communication is possible across the boundary—if there is a boundary—between the world apprehended by our few animal-derived senses and the larger existence concerning which our knowledge is still more limited.

Communication is not easy, but it occurs ; and humanity has reason to be grateful to those few individuals who, finding themselves possessed of the faculty of mediumship, and therefore able to act as intermediaries, allow themselves to be used for this purpose.

Such means of enlarging our knowledge, and entering into relations with things beyond animal ken, can be abused like any other power : it can be played with by the merely curious, or it can be exploited in a very mundane and unworthy way in the hope of warping it into the service of selfish ends, in the same way as old and long accessible kinds of knowledge have too often been employed. But it can also be used reverently and seriously, for the very legitimate purpose of comforting the sorrowful, helping the bereaved, and restoring some portion of the broken link between souls united in affection but separated for a time by an apparently impassable barrier. The barrier is turning out to be not hopelessly obdurate after all ; intercourse between the two states is not so impossible as had been thought ; something can be learnt about occurrences from either side ; and gradually it is probable that a large amount of consistent and fairly coherent knowledge will be accumulated.

Meanwhile broken ties of affection have the first claim ; and early efforts at communication from the departed are nearly always directed towards assuring survivors of the fact of continued personal existence, towards helping them to realise that changed surroundings have in no way weakened love or destroyed memory, and urging upon their friends with eager insistence that earthly happiness need not he irretrievably spoiled by bereavement. For purposes of this kind many trivial incidents are recalled, such as are well adapted to convince intimate friends and relatives that one particular intelligence, and no other, must be the source from which the messages ultimately spring, through whatever intermediaries they have to be conveyed. And to people new to the subject such messages are often immediately convincing.

Further thought, however, raises difficulties and doubts. The gradually recognised possibility of what may be called normal telepathy, or unconscious mind-reading from survivors, raises hesitation — felt most by studious and thoughtful people—about accepting such messages as irrefragable evidence of persistent personal existence ; and to overcome this curious and unexpected and perhaps rather artificial difficulty, it is demanded that facts shall be given which are unknown to anyone present, and can only subsequently be verified. Communications of this occasional and exceptional kind are what are called, by psychic investigators, more specifically ' evidential ' : and time and perhaps good fortune may be required for their adequate reception and critical appreciation. For it is manifest that most things readily talked about between two friends, and easily reproducible in hasty conversation, will naturally be of a nature common to both, and on subjects well within each other's knowledge.

The more recent development of an elaborate scheme of ' cross-correspondence,' entered upon since the death of specially experienced and critical investigators of the S.P.R., who were familiar with all these difficulties, and who have taken strong and most ingenious means to overcome them, has made the proof, already very strong, now almost crucial. The only alternative, in the best cases, is to imagine a sort of supernormal mischievousness, so elaborately misleading that it would have to be stigmatised as vicious or even diabolical.

In most cases complete proof of this complicated and cold-blooded kind is neither forthcoming nor is necessary : indeed it can hardly be appreciated or understood by non-studious people. Effective evidence is in most cases of a different kind, and varies with the personality concerned. It often happens that little personal touches, incommunicable to others in their full persuasiveness, sooner or later break down the last vestiges of legitimate scepticism. What goes on beyond that will depend upon personal training and interest. With many, anything like scientific inquiry lapses at this point, and communication resolves itself into emotional and domestic interchange of ordinary ideas. But in a few cases the desire to give new information is awakened ; and when there is sufficient receptivity, and, what is very important, a competent and suitable Medium for anything beyond commonplace messages, instructive and general information may be forthcoming. An explanation or description of the methods of communication, for instance, as seen from their side ; or some information concerning the manner of life there ; and occasionally even some intelligent attempt to lessen human difficulties about religious conceptions, and to give larger ideas about the Universe as a whole,—all these attempts have been made. But they always insist that their information is but little greater than ours, and that they are still fallible gropers after truth,—of which they keenly feel the beauty and importance, but of which they realise the infinitude, and their own inadequacy of mental grasp, quite as clearly as we do here.

These are what we call the ' unverifiable ' communications ; for we cannot bring them to book by subsequent terrestrial inquiry in the same way as we can test information concerning personal or mundane affairs. Information of the higher kind has often been received, but has seldom been published ; and it is difficult to know what value to put upon it, or how far it is really trustworthy.

I am inclined to think, however—with a growing num-

ber of serious students of the subject—that the time is
getting ripe now for the production and discussion of
material of this technically unverifiable kind ; to be scrutinised and tested by internal consistency and inherent
probability, in the same sort of way as travellers' tales
have to be scrutinised and tested. But until humanity as
a whole has taken the initial step, and shown itself willing
to regard such communications as within the range of
possibility, it may be unwise to venture far in this more
ambitious direction.

It has nevertheless been suggested, from a philosophic
point of view, that strict proof of individual survival must
in the last resort depend on examination and collation of
these 'travellers' tales,' rather than on any kind of resuscitation of the past ; because, until we know more about
memory, it is possible to conjecture, as I think Professor
Bergson does, that all the past is potentially accessible to
a super-subliminal faculty for disinterring it. And so one
might, in a sceptical mood, when confronted with records
of apparently personal reminiscence, attribute them to an
unconscious exercise of this faculty, and say with Tennyson

!" I hear a wind
Of memory murmuring the past."

I do not myself regard this impersonal memory as a
reasonable hypothesis, I think that the simpler view is
likely to be the truer one, so I attach importance to trivial
reminiscences and characteristic personal touches ; but I
do agree that abstention from recording and publishing,
however apologetically, those other efforts has had the
effect of making ill-informed people—*i.e.* people with very
little personal experience—jump to the conclusion that all
communications are of a trivial and contemptible nature.

CHAPTER XII

ON THE CONTENTION THAT ALL PSYCHIC COMMUNICATIONS ARE OF A TRIVIAL NATURE AND DEAL WITH INSIGNIFICANT TOPICS

THAT such a contention as that mentioned at the end of the preceding chapter is false is well known to people of experience; but so long as the demand for verification and proof of identity persists—and it will be long indeed before they can be dispensed with—so long are trifling reminiscences the best way to achieve the desired end. The end in this case amply explains and justifies the means. Hence it is that novices and critics are naturally and properly regaled with references to readily remembered and verifiable facts ; and since these facts, to be useful, must not be of the nature of public news, nor anything which can be gleaned from biographical or historical records, they usually relate to trifling family affairs or other humorous details such as seem likely to stay in the memory. It can freely be admitted that such facts are only redeemed from triviality by the affectionate recollections interlinked with them, and by the motive which has caused them to be reproduced. For their special purpose they may be admirable ; and there is no sort of triviality about the thing to be proven by them. The idea that a departed friend ought to be occupied wholly and entirely with grave matters, and ought not to remember jokes and fun, is a gratuitous claim which has to be abandoned. Humour does not cease with earth-life. Why should it ?

It should be evident that communications concerning deeper matters are not similarly serviceable as proof of identity, though they may have a value and interest of their own ; but it is an interest which could not be legitimately aroused until the first step—the recognition of veridical intercourse—had been taken ; for, as a rule, they are essentially unverifiable. Of such communications a multitude could be quoted ; and almost at random I select a few specimens from the automatic writings of the gentleman and schoolmaster known to a former generation as *M.A.Oxon.*[1] Take this one, which happens to be printed in a current issue of *Light* (22 April 1916), with the statement that it occurs in one of M.A.Oxon.'s subliminally written and private notebooks, under date 12 July 1873—many others will be found in the selections which he himself extracted from his own script and published in a book called *Spirit Teachings* :—

" You do not sufficiently grasp the scanty hold that religion has upon the mass of mankind, nor the adaptability of what we preach to the wants and cravings of men. Or perhaps it is necessary that you be reminded of what you cannot see clearly in your present state and among your present associations. You cannot see, as we see, the carelessness that has crept over men as to the future. Those who have thought over their future have come to know that they can find out nothing about it, except, indeed, that what man pretends to tell is foolish, contradictory, and unsatisfying. His reasoning faculties convince him that the Revelation of God contains very plain marks of human origin ; that it will not stand the test of sifting such as is applied to works professedly human ; and that the priestly fiction that reason is no measure of revelation, and that it must be left on the threshold of inquiry and give place to faith, is a cunningly planned means of preventing man from discovering the errors and contradications which throng the pages of the Bible. Those who reason discover this soon ; those who do not, betake themselves to the refuge of Faith, and become blind devotees, fanatical, irrational, and bigoted ; conformed to a groove in which they have been educated and from which they have not broken loose simply because they have not dared to think. It would be hard for man to devise a means [more capable] of cramping the mind and dwarfing the spirit's growth than this persuading of a man that he must not think about religion. It is one which paralyses all freedom of thought and renders it almost impossible for the soul to rise. The spirit is condemned to a hereditary religion whether suited or not to its wants. That which may have suited a far-off ancestor may be

---

[1] The Rev. Stainton Moses (M.A.Oxon.) was one of the masters at University College School in London. He wrote automatically, *i.e.* subconsciously, in private notebooks at a regular short time each day for nearly twenty years, and felt that he was in touch with helpful and informing intelligences.

quite unsuited to a struggling soul that lives in other times from those in which such ideas had vitality. The spirit's life is so made a question of birth and of locality. It is a question over which he can exercise no control, whether he is Christian, Mohammedan, or, as ye say, heathen : whether his God be the Great Spirit of the Red Indian, or the fetish of the savage ; whether his prophet be Christ or Mahomet or Confucius; in short, whether his notion of religion be that of East, West, North, or South ; for in all these quarters men have evolved for themselves a theology which . they teach their children to believe.

"The days are coming when this geographical sectarianism will give place before the enlightenment caused by the spread of our revelation, for which men are far riper than you think. The time draws nigh apace when the sublime truths of Spiritualism, rational and noble as they are when viewed by man's standard, shall wipe away from the face of God's earth the sectarian jealousy and theological bitterness, the anger and ill-will, the folly and stupidity, which have disgraced the name of religion and the worship of God ; and man shall see in a clearer light the Supreme Creator and the spirit's eternal destiny.

"We tell you, friend, that the end draws nigh ; the night of ignorance is passing fast ; the shackles which priestcraft has strung round the struggling souls shall be knocked off, and in place of fanatical folly and ignorant speculation and superstitious belief, ye shall have a reasonable religion and a knowledge of the reality of the spirit-world and of the ministry of angels with you. Ye shall know that the dead are alive indeed, living as they lived on earth, but more truly, ministering to you with undiminished love, animated in their perpetual intercourse with the same affection which they had whilst yet incarned."

Any one of these serious messages can be criticised and commented upon with hostility and suspicion ; they are not suited to establish the first premise of the argument for continuance of personality ; and if they were put forward as part of the proof of survival, then perhaps the hostility would be legitimate. It ought to be clear that they are not to be taken as oracular utterances, or as anything vastly superior to the capabilities of the medium through whom they come,—though in fact they often are superior to any known power of a given medium, and are frequently characteristic of the departed personality, as we knew him, who is purporting to be the Communicator : though this remark is not applicable to the particular class of impersonal messages here selected for quotation. Yet in all cases they must surely be more or less sophisticated by the channel, and by the more or less strained method of communication, and must share some of its limitations and imperfections.

However that may be, it is proper to quote them occasionally, as here; not as specially profound utterances, but merely in contradiction of the imaginary and false thesis that only trivial and insignificant subjects are dealt with in automatic writings and mediumistic utterances. For such utterances—whatever their value or lack of value —are manifestly conclusive against that gratuitous and ignorant supposition. Whatever is thought of them, they are at least conceived in a spirit of earnestness, and are characterised by a genuine fervour that may be properlv called religious.

I now quote a few more of, the records published in the book cited above,—in this case dealing with Theological questions and puzzles in the mind of the automatic writer himself :—

" All your fancied theories about God have filtered down to you through human channels ; the embodiments of human cravings after knowledge of Him ; the creation of minds that were undeveloped, whose wants were not your wants, whose God, or rather whose notions about God are not yours. You try hard to make the ideas fit in, but they will not fit, because they are the product of divers degrees of development. . . ."

" God ! Ye know Him not ! One day, when the Spirit stands within the veil which shrouds the spirit world from mortal gaze, you shall wonder at your ignorance of Him whom you have so foolishly imagined ! He is far other than you have pictured Him. Were He such as you have pictured Him, were He such as you think, He would avenge on presumptuous man the insults which he puts on his Creator. But He is other, far other than man's poor grovelling mind can grasp, and He pities and forgives the ignorance of the blind mortal who paints Him after a self-imagined pattern. . . . When you rashly complain of us that our teaching to you controverts that of the Old Testament, we can but answer that it does indeed controvert that old and repulsive view . . . but that it is in fullest accord with that divinely inspired revelation of Himself which He gave through Jesus Christ—a revelation which man has done so much to debase, and from which the best of the followers of Christ have so grievously fallen away."

And again, in answer to other doubts and questions in the mind of the automatist as to the legitimacy of the means of communication, and his hesitation about employing a means which he knew was sometimes prosti-

:uted by knaves to unworthy and frivolous or even base
)bjects,—very different from those served by humorous
ind friendly family messages, about which no one with a
spark of human feeling has a word to say when once they
1ave realised their nature and object,—the writing continued thus :—

" If there be nought in what we say of God and of man's
ifter-life that commends itself to you, it must be that your mind
1as ceased to love the grander and simpler conceptions which it
1ad once learned to drink in. . . ."

" Cease to be anxious about the minute questions which are
)f minor moment. Dwell much on the great, the overwhelming
1ecessity for a clearer revealing of the Supreme ; on the blank
ind cheerless ignorance of God and of us which has crept over
the world : on the noble creed we teach, on the bright future we
·eveal. Cease to be perplexed by thoughts of an imagined Devil.
For the honest, pure, and truthful soul there is no Devil nor
Prince of Evil such as theology has feigned. . . . The clouds of
sorrow and anguish of soul may gather round [such a man] and
his spirit may be saddened with the burden of sin—weighed down
with consciousness of surrounding misery and guilt, but no fabled
Devil can gain dominion over him, or prevail to drag down his
soul to hell. All the sadness of spirit, the acquaintance with
grief, the intermingling with guilt, is part of the experience, in
virtue of which his soul shall rise hereafter. The guardians are
training and fitting it by those means to progress, and jealously
protect it from the dominion of the foe.

" It is only they who, by a fondness for evil, by a lack of
spiritual and excess of corporeal development, attract to themselves the congenial spirits of the undeveloped who have left the
body but not forgotten its desires. These alone risk incursion of
evil. These by proclivity attract evil, and it dwells with them
at their invitation. They attract the lower spirits who hover
nearest Earth, and who are but too ready to rush in and mar our
plans, and ruin our work for souls. These are they of whom you
speak when you say in haste, that the result of Spiritualism is not
for good. You err, friend. Blame not us that the lower spirits
manifest for those who bid them welcome. Blame man's in-
sensate folly, which will choose the low and grovelling rather than
the pure and elevated. Blame his foolish laws, which daily
hurry into a life for which they are unprepared, thousands of
spirits, hampered and dragged down by a life of folly and sin,
which has been fostered by custom and fashion. Blame the gin-
shops, and the madhouses, and the prisons, and the encouraged
lusts and fiendish selfishness of man. This it is which damns
legions of spirits—not, as ye fancy, in a sea of material fire, but
in the flames of perpetuated lust, condemned to burn itself out
in hopeless longing till the purged soul rises through the fire and
surmounts its dead passions. Yes, blame these and kindred

23

causes, if there be around undeveloped intelligences who shock you by their deception, and annoy you by frivolity and falsehood."

I suppose that the worst that can be said about writing of this kind is that it consists of ' sermon-stuffe ' such as could have been presumably invented—whether consciously or unconsciously—by the automatic writer himself. And the fact that with some of it he tended to disagree, proves no more than the corresponding kind of unexpected argumentation experienced by some dreamers (cf. L. P. Jacks, *Hibbert Journal*, July 1916). The same kind of explanation may serve for both phenomena, but I do not know what that explanation is.

CHAPTER XIII

ON THE MANNER OF COMMUNICATION

PERHAPS the commonest and easiest method of communication is what is called 'automatic writing' —the method by which the above examples were received—*i.e.* writing performed through the agency of subconscious intelligence ; the writer leaving his or her hand at liberty to write whatever comes, without attempting to control it, and without necessarily attending at the time to what is being written.

That a novice will usually get nothing, or mere nonsense or scribbling, in this way is obvious : the remarkable thing is that some persons are thus able to get sense, and to tap sources of information outside their normal range. If a rudiment of such power exists, it is possible, though not always desirable, to cultivate it ; but care, pertinacity, and intelligence are needed to utilise a faculty of this kind. Unless people are well-balanced and self-critical and wholesomely occupied, they had better leave the subject alone.

In most cases of fully-developed automatism known to me the automatist reads what comes, and makes suitable oral replies or comments to the sentences as they appear : so that the whole has then the effect of a straightforward conversation of which one side is spoken and the other written—the speaking side being usually rather silent and reserved, the writing side free and expansive.

Naturally not every person has the power of cultivating this simple form of what is technically known as motor automatism, one of the recognised subliminal forms of activity ; but probably more people could do it if they tried ; though for some people it would be injudicious, and for many others hardly worth while.

The intermediate mentality employed in this process

seems to be a usually submerged or dream-like stratum of the automatist whose hand is being used. The hand is probably worked by its usual physiological mechanism, guided and controlled by nerve centres not in the most conscious and ordinarily employed region of the brain. In some cases the content or subject-matter of the writing may emanate entirely from these nerve centres, and be of no more value than a dream ; as is frequently the case with the more elementary automatism set in action by the use of instruments known as ' planchette ' and ' ouija,' often employed by beginners. But when the message turns out to be of evidential value it is presumably because this subliminal portion of the person is in touch, either telepathically or in some other way, with intelligences not ordinarily accessible,—with living people at a distance perhaps, or more often with the apparently more accessible people who have passed on, for whom distance in the ordinary sense seems hardly to exist, and whose links of connexion are of a kind other than spatial. It need hardly be said that proof of communion of this kind is absolutely necessary, and has to be insisted on ; but experience has demonstrated that now and again sound proof is forthcoming.

Another method, and one that turns out to be still more powerful, is for the automatist not only to take off his or her attention from what is being transmitted through his or her organism, but to become comprehensively unconscious and go into a trance. In that case it appears that the physiological mechanism is more amenable to control, and is less sophisticated by the ordinary intelligence of the person to whom it normally belongs ; so that messages of importance and privacy may be got through. But the messages have to be received and attended to by another person ; for in such cases, when genuine, the entranced person on waking up is found to be ignorant of what has been either written or uttered. In this state, speech is as common as writing, probably more common because less troublesome to the recipient, *i.e.* the friend or relative to whom or for whom messages are being thus sent. The communicating personality during trance may be the same as the one operating the hand without trance, and the messages may have the same general character as those got by automatic writing, when the consciousness is not suspended but only in temporary and local abeyance ; but in the trance state a dramatic characterisation is usually imparted to the proceedings, by the appearance of an entity called a ' Control,' who works the body of the automatist in the apparent absence of its customary manager. This personality is believed by some to be merely the subliminal self of the entranced person, brought to the surface, or liberated and dramatised into a sort of dream existence, for the time. By others it is supposed to be a healthy and manageable variety of the more or less pathological phenomenon known to physicians and psychiatrists as cases of dual or multiple personality. By others again it is believed to be in reality the separate intelligence which it claims to be.

But however much can be and has been written on this subject, and whatever different opinions may be held, it is universally admitted that the *dramatic semblance* of the control is undoubtedly that of a separate person,— a person asserted to be permanently existing on the other side, and to be occupied on that side in much the same functions as the medium is on this. The duty of controlling and transmitting messages seems to be laid upon such a one—it is his special work. The dramatic character of most of the controls is so vivid and self-consistent, that whatever any given sitter or experimenter may feel is the probable truth concerning their real nature, the simplest way is to humour them by taking them at their face value and treating them as separate and responsible and real individuals. It is true that in the case of some mediums, especially when overdone or tired, there are evanescent and absurd obtrusions every now and then, which cannot be seriously regarded. Those have to be eliminated ; and for anyone to treat them as real people would be ludicrous ; but undoubtedly the serious controls show a character and personality and memory of their own, and they appear to carry on as continuous an existence as anyone else whom one only meets occasionally for conversation. The conversation can be taken up at the point where it left off, and all that was said appears to be remarkably well remembered by the appropriate control ; while usually memory of it is naturally and properly repudiated by another control, even when operating through the same medium ; and the entranced medium knows nothing of it afterwards after having completely woke up.

So clearly is the personality of the control brought out, in the best cases, so clear also are the statements of the communicators that the control who is kindly transmitting their messages is a real person, that I am disposed to accept their assertions, and to regard a control, when not a mere mischievous and temporary impersonation, as akin on their side to the person whom we call a medium on ours.

The process of regular communication—apart from the exceptional more direct privilege occasionally vouchsafed to people in extreme sorrow—thus seems to involve normally a double medium of communication, and the activity of several people. First there is the ' Communicator ' or originator of ideas and messages on the other side. Then there is the ' control ' who accepts and transmits the messages by setting into operation a physical organism lent for the occasion. Then there is the ' Medium ' or person whose normal consciousness is in abeyance but whose physiological mechanism is being used. And finally there is the ' Sitter '—a rather absurd name—the recipient of the messages, who reads or hears and answers them, and for whose benefit all this trouble is taken. In many cases there is also present a Note-taker to record all that is said, whether by sitters or by or through the medium ; and it is clear that the note-taker should pay special attention to and carefully record any hints or information either purposely or accidentally imparted by the sitter.

In scientific and more elaborately conducted cases there is also some one present who is known as the Experimenter in charge—a responsible and experienced person who looks after the health and safety of the medium, who arranges the circumstances and selects the sitters, making provision for anonymity and other precautions, and who frequently combines with his other functions the duties of note-taker.

In oral or voice sittings the function of the note-taker is more laborious and more responsible than in writing sittings ; for these latter to a great extent supply their own notes. Only as the trance-writing is blindfold, *i.e.* done with shut eyes and head averted, it is rather illegible without practice ; and so the experimenter in charge frequently finds it necessary to assist the sitter, to whom it is addressed, by deciphering it and reading it aloud as it comes—rather a tiring process ; at the same time jotting down, usually on the same paper, the remarks which the sitter makes in reply, or the questions from time to time asked. Unless this is done the subsequent automatic record lacks a good deal of clearness, and sometimes lacks intelligibility.

For a voice-sitting the note-taker must be a rapid writer, and if able to employ shorthand has an advantage. Sometimes a stenographer is introduced ; but the presence of a stranger, or of any person not intimately concerned, is liable to hamper the distinctness and fullness of a message ; and may prevent or retard the occurrence of such emotional episodes as are from time to time almost inevitable in the cases—alas too numerous at present— where the sitter has been recently and violently bereaved.

It is perhaps noteworthy—though it may not be interesting or intelligible to a novice—that communicators wishing to give private communications seldom or never object to the presence of the actual ' medium '— *i.e.* the one on our side. That person seems to be regarded as absent, or practically non-existent for a time ; the person whose presence they sometimes resent at first is the 'control,' *i.e.* the intelligence on their side who is ready to receive and transmit their message, somewhat perhaps as an Eastern scribe is ready to write the love-letters of illiterate persons.

As to the presence of a note-taker or third person on our side, such person is taken note of by the control, and when anything private or possibly private is mentioned —details of illnesses or such like—that third person is often ordered out of the room. Sometimes the experimenter in charge is likewise politely dispensed with, and under these circumstances the sitting occasionally takes on a poignant character in which note-taking by the deeply affected sitter becomes a practical impossibility. But this experience is comparatively rare ; it must not be expected, and cannot wisely be forced.

Another circumstance which makes me think that the more responsible kind of control is a real person, is that sometimes, after gained experience, the Communicator himself takes control, and speaks or writes in the first person, not only as a matter of first-person-reporting, which frequently occurs, but really in his own proper person and with many of his old characteristics. So if one control is a real person I see no reason against the probability of others being real likewise. I cannot say that the tone of voice or the handwriting is often thus reproduced—though it is, for a few moments, by special effort sometimes ; but the unusual physiological mechanism accounts for outstanding or residual differences. Apart from that, the peculiarities, the attitudes, the little touches of manner, are often more or less faithfully reproduced, although the medium may have known nothing of the person concerned. And the characteristic quality of the message, and the kind of subjects dealt with, become still more marked in such cases of actual control, than when everything has to be transmitted through a kindly stranger control, to whom things of a recondite or technical character may appear rather as a meaningless collocation of words, very difficult to remember and reproduce.

NOTE ON DIFFICULTY OF REMEMBERING NAMES

When operating indirectly in the ordinary way through a control and a medium, it usually appears to be remarkably difficult to get names transmitted. Most mediums are able to convey a name only with difficulty. Now plainly a name, especially the proper name of a person, is a very conventional and meaningless thing : it has very few links to connect it with other items in memory ; and hence arises the normally well-known difficulty of recalling one. Conscious effort made to recover a name seems to inhibit the power of doing so : the best plan is to leave it, and let subconsciousness work. An example occurred to me the other day, when I tried to remember the name of a prominent statesman or ex-Prime Minister whom I had met in Australia. What I seemed to recollect was that the name began with " D," and I made several shots at it, which I recorded. The effort went on at intervals for days, since I thought it would be an instructive experiment. I know now, a month or two later, without any effort and without looking it up, that the name was Deakin ; but what my shots at it were I do not remember. I will have the page in the notebook looked up and reproduced here, as an example of memory-groping, at intervals, during more than one day. Here they are :—D. Dering. Denman, Deeming, Derriman, Derring, Deeley, Dempster, Denting, Desman, Deering.

Now I knew the name quite well, and have known it for long, and have taken some interest in the gentleman who owns it ; and I am known by some members of my family to have done so. Hence if I had been on ' the other side ' and could only get as far as D, it would have seemed rather absurd to anyone whose memory for names is good. But indeed I have had times when names very much more familiar to me than that could not on the spur of the moment be recalled—not always even the initial letter ; though, for some reason or other, the initial letter is certainly easier than the word.

The kind of shots which I made at the name before recalling it—which it may seem frivolous to have actually recorded—are reminiscent of the kind of shots which are made by mediums under control when they too are striving after a name ; and it was a perception of this analogy which caused me to jot down my own guesses, or what, in the case of a medium, we should impolitely call ' fishing.' I think that the name was certainly in my memory though it would not come through my brain. The effort is like the effort to use a muscle not often or ever used— say the outer ear—one does not know which string to pull, so to speak, or, more accurately, which nerve to stimulate, and the result is a peculiarly helpless feeling, akin to stammering. In the case of a medium, I suppose the name is often in the mind of the communicator, but it will not come through the control. The control sometimes describes it as being spoken or shown but not clearly caught. The communicator often does not know whether a medium has successfully conveyed it or not.

CHAPTER XIV

VARIOUS PSYCHO-PHYSICAL METHODS

" If man, then, shall attempt to sound and fathom the depths that lie not without him, but within, analogy may surely warn him that the first attempts of his rude *psychoscopes* to give precision and actuality to thought will grope among ' beggarly elements '—will be concerned with things grotesque, or trivial, or obscure. Yet here also one handsbreadth of reality gives better footing than all the castles of our dream ; here also by beginning with the least things we shall best learn how great things may remain to do."—F. W. H. M., Introduction to *Phantasms of the Living*

I MUST not shirk a rather queer subject which yet needs touching upon, though it bristles with theoretical difficulties ; and that is the rationale of one of the most elementary methods of ultra-normal communication, a method which many find practically the easiest to begin with.

It is possible to get communication of a kind, not by holding a pencil in the fingers, but by placing the hand on a larger piece of wood not at all adapted for writing with. The movements are then coarser, and the code more elementary ; but in principle, when the procedure is analysed, it is seen not to be essentially different. It may be more akin to semaphore-arm signalling or flag-wagging ; but any device whereby mental activity can translate itself into movements of matter will serve for subliminal as well as for conscious action ; and messages by tilting of a table, though crude and elementary, are not really so surprising or absurd as at first sight they seem. The tilts of a telegraphic operator's key are still more restricted ; but they serve. A pen or pencil is an inanimate piece of matter guided by the fingers. A planchette is a mere piece of wood, and when touched it must be presumed to be guided by the muscles,—though there is often an illusion, as with the twig of the dowser, that the inanimate object is moved directly, and not by muscular intervention. So also we may assume that a table or other piece of furniture is tilted or moved by regular muscular force: certainly it can only move at the expense of the energy of the medium or of people present. And yet in all these cases the substance of the message may be foreign to the mind of anyone touching the instrument, and the guidance necessary for sense and relevance need not be exercised by their own consciousness.

When a table or similar rough instrument is employed, the ostensible communicators say that they feel more *directly* in touch with the sitters than when they operate through an intermediary or 'control' on their side,—as they appear to find it necessary to do for actual speech or writing,—and accordingly they find themselves able to give more private messages, and also to reproduce names and technicalities with greater facility and precision. The process of spelling out words in this way is a slow one, much slower than writing, and therefore the method labours under disadvantages, but it seems to possess advantages which to some extent counterbalance them.

Whether it sounds credible or not, and it is certainly surprising, I must testify that when a thing of any mobility is controlled in this more direct way, it is able to convey touches of emotion and phases of intonation, so to speak, in a most successful manner. A telegraph key could hardly do it, its range of movement is too restricted, it operates only in a discontinuous manner, by make and break; but a light table, under these conditions, seems no longer inert, it behaves as if animated. For the time it *is* animated —somewhat perhaps as a violin or piano is animated by a skilled musician and schooled to his will,— and the dramatic action thus attained is very remarkable. It can exhibit hesitation, it can exhibit certainty; it can seek for information, it can convey it; it can apparently ponder before giving a reply; it can welcome a new-comer; it can indicate joy or sorrow, fun or gravity; it can keep time with a song as if joining in the chorus;

and, most notable of all, it can exhibit affection in an unmistakable manner.

The hand of a writing medium can do these things too ; and that the whole body of a normal person can display these emotions is a commonplace. Yet they are all pieces of matter, though some are more permanently animated than others. But all are animated temporarily,—not one of them permanently,—and there appears to be no sharp line of demarcation. What we have to realise is that matter in any form is able to act as agent to the soul, and that by aid of matter various emotions as well as intelligence can be temporarily incarnated and displayed.

The extraction of elementary music from all manner of unlikely objects—kitchen utensils, for instance—is a known stage-performance. The utilisation of unlikely objects for purposes of communication, though it would not have been expected, may have to be included in the same general category.

With things made for the purpose, from a violin to the puppets of a marionette show, we know that simple human passions can be shown and can be roused. With things made for quite other purposes it turns out that the same sort of possibility exists.

Table-tilting is an old and despised form of amusement, known to many families and often wisely discarded ; but with care and sobriety and seriousness even this can be used as a means of communication ; and the amount of mediumistic power necessary for this elementary form of psychic activity appears to be distinctly less than would be required for more elaborate methods.

One thing it is necessary clearly to realise and admit, namely that in all cases when an object is moved by direct contact of an operator's body, whether the instrument be a pencil or a piece of wood, unconscious muscular guidance must be allowed for ; and anything that comes through of a kind known to or suspected by the operator must be discounted. Sometimes, however, the message comes in an unexpected and for the moment puzzling form, and sometimes it conveys information unknown to him. It is by the content of the communication that its supernormal value must be estimated.

There are many obvious disadvantages about a Table Sitting, especially in the slowness of the communications and in the fact that the sitter has to do most of the talking; whereas when some personality is controlling a medium, the sitters need say very little.

But, as said above, there are some communicators who object to a control's presence, especially if they have anything private to say; and these often prefer the table because it seems to bring them more directly into contact with the sitter, without an intermediary. They seem to ignore the presence of the medium on our side, notwithstanding the fact that, at a table sitting, she is present in her own consciousness and is aware of what goes on; they appear to be satisfied with having dispensed with the medium on their side. Moreover, it is in some cases found that information can be conveyed in a briefer and more direct manner, not having to be wrapped up in roundabout phrases, that names can be given more easily, and direct questions answered better, through the table than through a control.

It must be remembered that under control every medium has some peculiarities. Mrs. Leonard, for instance, is a very straightforward and honest medium, but not a particularly strong one. Accordingly anything like conversation and free interchange of ideas is hardly possible, and direct questions seldom receive direct answers, when put to the communicator through Feda.

I have known mediums much more powerful in this respect, so that free conversation with one or two specially skilled communicators was quite possible, and interchange of ideas almost as easy as when the communicator was in the flesh. But instances of that kind are hardly to be expected among hard-worked professional mediums.

I shall not in this volume touch upon still more puzzling and still more directly and peculiarly physical phenomena, such as are spoken of as ' direct voice,' ' direct writing,' and ' materialisation.' In these strange and, from one point of view, more advanced occurrences, though lower in another sense, inert matter appears to be operated on without the direct intervention of physiological mechan sm. And yet such mechanism must be in the neighbourhood. I am inclined to think that these weird phenomena, when established, will be found to shade off into those other methods that I have been speaking of, and that no complete theory of either can be given until more is known about both. This is one of the facts which causes me to be undogmatic about the certainty that all movements, even under contact, are initiated in the muscles. I only here hold up a warning against premature decision. The whole subject of

psycho-physical interaction and activity requires attention in due time and place ; but the ground is now more
treacherous, the pitfalls more numerous, and the territory
to many minds comparatively unattractive.   Let it wait
until long-range artillery has beaten down some of the
entanglements, before organised forces are summoned to
advance.

CHAPTER XV

ATTITUDE OF THE WISE AND PRUDENT

" The vagueness and confusion inevitable at the beginning of a novel line of research, [are] naturally distasteful to the *savant* accustomed to proceed by measurable increments of knowledge from experimental bases already assured. Such an one, if he reads this book, may feel as though he had been called away from an ordnance survey, conducted with a competent staff and familiar instruments, to plough slowly with inexperienced mariners through some strange ocean where beds of entangling seaweed cumber the trackless way. We accept the analogy ; but we would remind him that even floating weeds of novel genera may foreshow a land unknown ; and that it was not without ultimate gain to men that the straining keels of Columbus first pressed through the Sargasso Sea."—F. W. H. M., Introduction to *Phantasms of the Living*

IT is rather remarkable that the majority of learned men have closed their minds to what have seemed bare and simple facts to many people. Those who call themselves spiritualists have an easy and simple faith ; they interpret their experiences in the most straightforward and unsophisticated manner, and some of them have shown unfortunately that they can be led into credulity and error, without much difficulty, by unscrupulous people. Nevertheless, that simple-hearted folk are most accessible to new facts seems to be rather accordant with history. Whenever, not by reasoning but by direct experience, knowledge has been enlarged, or when a revelation has come to the human race through the agency of higher powers, it is not the wise but the simple who are first to receive it. This cannot be used as an argument either way ; the simple may be mistaken, and may too blithely interpret their sense-impressions in the most obvious manner ; just as on the other hand the eyes

of the learned may be closed to anything which appea
disconnected from their previous knowledge. For after ;
it is inevitable that any really new order of things mu
be so disconnected ; some little time must elapse befo
the weight of facts impel the learned in a new directio
and meanwhile the unlearned may be absorbing direct e
perience, and in their own fashion may be forging ahea
It is an example of the ancient paradox propounded
and about 1 *Cor.* i. 26 ; and no fault need be found wi
what is natural.

It behoves me to mention in particular the attitude
men of science, of whom I may say *quorum pars parva fu*
for in no way do I wish to dissociate myself from eith
such stricture or such praise as may be appropriate to m
who have made a study of science their vocation,—n
indeed the peaks of the race, but the general body. For
is safe to assume that we must have some qualities
common, and that these must be among the causes whi
have switched us on to a laborious and materially unr
munerative road.

Michael Foster said in his Presidential Address to tl
British Association at Dover :—

" Men of science have no peculiar virtues, no speci
powers. They are ordinary men, their characters a
common, even commonplace. Science, as Huxley said,
organised common sense, and men of science are comm
men, drilled in the ways of common sense."

This of course, like any aphorism, does not bear pressii
unduly : and Dr. Arthur Schuster in a similar Address
Manchester hedged it round with qualifying clauses :—

" This saying of Huxley's has been repeated so oft
that one almost wishes it were true ; but unfortunately
cannot find a definition of common sense that fits t
phrase. Sometimes the word is used as if it were identic
with uncommon sense, sometimes as if it were the sar
thing as common nonsense. Often it means untrain
intelligence, and in its best aspect it is, I think, th
faculty which recognises that the obvious solution of
problem is frequently the right one. When, for instanc

I see during a total solar eclipse red flames shooting out from the edge of the sun, the obvious explanation is that these are real phenomena, caused by masses of glowing vapours ejected from the sun. And when a learned friend tells me that all this is an optical illusion due to anomalous refraction, I object on the ground that the explanation violates my common sense. He replies by giving me the reasons which have led him to his conclusions; and though I still believe that I am right, I have to meet him with a more substantial reply than an appeal to my own convictions. Against a solid argument common sense has no power, and must remain a useful but fallible guide which both leads and misleads all classes of the community alike."

The sound moral of this is, not that a common-sense explanation is likely to be the right one, or that it necessarily has any merits if there are sound reasons to oppose to it, but that the common sense or most obvious and superficial explanation *may* turn out to be after all truer as well as simpler than more recondite hypotheses which have been substituted for it. In other words—the straightforward explanation need not be false.

Now the phenomena encountered in psychical research have long ago suggested an explanation, in terms of other than living human intelligences, which may be properly called spiritistic. Every kind of alternative explanation, including the almost equally unorthodox one of telepathy from living people, has been tried : and these attempts have been necessary and perfectly legitimate. If they had succeeded, well and good; but inasmuch as in my judgement there are phenomena which they cannot explain, and inasmuch as some form of spiritistic hypothesis, given certain postulates, explains practically all, I have found myself driven back on what I may call the common-sense explanation ; or, to adopt Dr. Schuster's parable, I consider that the red flames round the sun are what they appear to be.

To attribute capricious mechanical performance to the action of live things, is sufficient as a proximate explanation ; as we saw in the case of the jumping bean, Chapter I. If the existence of the live thing is otherwise unknown,

24

the explanation may seem forced and unsatisfactory. But if after trying other hypotheses we find that this only will fit the case, we may return to it after all with a clear conscience. That represents the history of my own progress in Psychical Research.

Apologia

Meanwhile the attitude of scientific men is perfectly intelligible ; and not unreasonable, except when they forget their self-imposed limitations and cultivate a baseless negative philosophy. People who study mechanism of course find Mechanics, and if the mechanism is physiological they find Physics and Chemistry as well ; but they are not thereby compelled to deny the existence of everything else. They need not philosophise at all, though they should be able to realise their philosophical position when it is pointed out. The business of science is to trace out the mode of action of the laws of Chemistry and Physics, everywhere and under all circumstances. Those laws appear to be of universal application throughout the material Universe,— in the most distant star as well as on the earth,—in the animal organism as well as in inorganic matter ; and the study of their action alone has proved an ample task.

But scientific workers are sometimes thought to be philosophising seriously when they should be understood as really only expressing the natural scope of their special subject. Laplace, for instance, is often misunderstood, because, when challenged about the place of God in his system, he said that he had no need of such a hypothesis,—a dictum often quoted as if it were atheistical. It is not necessarily anything of the kind. As a brief statement it is right, though rather unconciliatory and blunt. He was trying to explain astronomy on clear and definite mechanical principles, and the introduction of a " finger of God " would have been not only an unwarrantable complication but a senseless intrusion. Not an intrusion or a complication in the Universe, be it understood, but in Laplace's scheme, his *Systéme du Monde.* Yet Browning's " flash of the will that can " in *Abt*

Vogler, with all that the context implies, remains essentially and permanently true.

Theologians who admit that the Deity always works through agents and rational means can grant to scientific workers all that they legitimately claim in the positive direction, and can encourage them in the detailed study of those agents and means. If people knew more about science, and the atmosphere in which scientific men work, they would be better able to interpret occasional rather rash negations ; which are quite explicable in terms of the artificial limitation of range which physical science hitherto has wisely laid down for itself.

It is a true instinct which resents the mediæval practice of freely introducing occult and unknown causes into working science. To attribute the rise of sap, for instance, to a ' vital force ' would be absurd, it would be giving up the problem and stating nothing at all. Progress in science began when spiritual and transcendental causes were eliminated and treated as non-existent. The simplicity so attained was congenial to the scientific type of mind ; the abstraction was eminently useful, and was justified by results. Yet unknown causes of an immaterial and even of a spiritual kind may in reality exist, and may influence or produce phenomena, for all that ; and it may have to be the business of science to discover and begin to attend to them, as soon as the ordinary solid ground-plan of Nature has been made sufficiently secure.

Some of us—whether wisely or unwisely—now want to enlarge the recognised scope of physical science, so as gradually to take a wider purview and include more of the totality of things. That is what the Society for Psychical Research was established for,—to begin extending the range of scientific law and order, by patient exploration in a comparatively new region. The effort has been resented, and at first ridiculed, only because misunderstood. The effort may be ambitious, but it is perfectly legitimate ; and if it fails it fails.

But advance in new directions may be wisely slow, and it is readily admissible that Societies devoted to long-established branches of science are right to resist extraneous novelties, as long as possible, and leave the study of occult phenomena to a Society established for the purpose.

Outlandish territories may in time be incorporated as States, but they must make their claim good and become civilised first.

Yet unfamiliar causes must be introduced occasionally into systematised knowledge, unless our scrutiny of the Universe is already exhaustive. Unpalatable facts can be ruled out from attention, but they cannot without investigation be denied. Strange facts do really happen, even though unprovided for in our sciences. Amid their orthodox relations, they may be regarded as a nuisance. The feeling they cause is as if capricious or mischievous live things had been allowed to intrude into the determinate apparatus of a physical laboratory, thereby introducing hopeless complexity and appearing superficially to interfere with established laws. To avoid such alien incursion a laboratory can be locked, but the Universe can not. And if ever, under any circumstances, we actually do encounter the interaction of intelligences other than that of living men, we shall sooner or later become aware of the fact, and shall ultimately have to admit it into a more comprehensive scheme of existence. Early attempts, like those of the present, must be unsatisfactory and crude; especially as the evidence is of a kind to which scientific men for the most part are unaccustomed; so no wonder they are resentful. Still the evidence is there, and I for one cannot ignore it. Members of the Society for Psychical Research are aware that the evidence already published —the carefully edited and sifted evidence published by their own organisation—occupies some forty volumes of *Journal* and *Proceedings*; and some of them know that a great deal more evidence exists than has been published, and that some of the best evidence is not likely to be published,—not yet at any rate. It stands to reason that, at the present stage, the best evidence must often be of a very private and family character. Many, however, are the persons who are acquainted with facts in their own experience which appeal to them more strongly than anything that has ever been published. No records can surpass first-hand direct experience in cogency.

Nevertheless we are also aware, or ought to be, that no one crucial episode can ever be brought forward as deciding such a matter. That is not the way in which things of importance are proven. Evidence is cumulative, it is on the strength of a mass of experience that an induction is ultimately made, and a conclusion provisionally arrived at ; though sometimes it happens that a single exceptionally strong instance, or series of instances, may clinch it for some individual.

But indeed the evidence, in one form and another, has been crudely before the human race from remote antiquity ; only it has been treated in ways more or less obfuscated by superstition. The same sort of occurrences as were known to Virgil, and to many another seer—the same sort of experiences as are found by folk-lore students, not only in history but in every part of the earth to-day— are happening now in a scientific age, and sometimes under scientific scrutiny. Hence it is that from the scientific point of view progress is at length being made ; and any one with a real desire to know the truth need not lack evidence, if he will first read the records with an open mind, and then bide his time and be patient till an opportunity for first-hand critical observation is vouchsafed him. The opportunity may occur at any time : the readiness is all. Really clinching evidence in such a case is never in the past ; a *prima facie* case for investigation is established by the records, but real conviction must be attained by first-hand experience in the present.

The things to be investigated are either true or false. If false, pertinacious inquiry will reveal their falsity. If true, they are profoundly important. For there are no half-truths in Nature ; every smallest new departure has portentous consequences ; our eyes must open slowly, or we should be overwhelmed. I once likened the feeling of physical investigators in the year 1889 to that of a boy who had long been strumming on the keyboard of a deserted organ into which an unseen power had begun to blow a vivifying breath.[1] That was at the beginning of the series of revolutionary discoveries about radiation and the nature of matter which have since resounded through the world. And now once more the touch of a finger elicits a responsive note, and again the boy hesitates, half delighted, half affrighted, at the chords which it would seem he can now summon forth almost at will.

[1] *Modern Views of Electricity*, p. 408 of third and current edition.

CHAPTER XVI

OUTLOOK ON THE UNIVERSE

WHAT then is the conclusion of the whole matter? Or rather, what effect have these investigations had upon my own outlook on the Universe? The question is not so unimportant as it seems ; because if the facts are to influence others they must have influenced myself too ; and that is the only influence of which I have first-hand knowledge. It must not be supposed that my outlook has changed appreciably since the event and the particular experiences related in the foregoing pages : my conclusion has been gradually forming itself for years, though undoubtedly it is based on experience of the same sort of thing. But this event has strengthened and liberated my testimony. It can now be associated with a private experience of my own. instead of with the private experiences of others. So long as one was dependent on evidence connected, even indirectly connected, with the bereavement of others, one had to be reticent and cautious and in some cases silent. Only by special permission could any portion of the facts be reproduced ; and that permission might in important cases be withheld. My own deductions were the same then as they are now, but the facts are now my own.

One little point of difference, between the time before and the time after, has however become manifest. In the old days, if I sat with a medium, I was never told of any serious imaginary bereavement which had befallen myself—beyond the natural and inevitable losses from an older generation which fall to the lot of every son of man. But now, if I or any member of my family goes anonymously to a genuine medium, giving not the slightest normal clue, my son is quickly to the fore and continues his clear and convincing series of evidences ; sometimes giving testimony of a critically selected kind, sometimes contenting himself with friendly family chaff and reminiscences, but always acting in a manner consistent with his personality and memories and varying moods. If in any case a given medium had weak power, or if there were special difficulties encountered on a given occasion, he is aware of the fact ; and he refers to it, when there is opportunity, through another totally disconnected medium (cf. Chapter XXI, Part II). In every way he has shown himself anxious to give convincing evidence. Moreover, he wants me to speak out ; and I shall.

I am as convinced of continued existence, on the other side of death, as I am of existence here. It may be said, you cannot be as sure as you are of sensory experience. I say I can. A physicist is never limited to direct sensory impressions, he has to deal with a multitude of conceptions and things for which he has no physical organ : the dynamical theory of heat, for instance, and of gases, the theories of electricity, of magnetism, of chemical affinity, of cohesion, aye and his apprehension of the Ether itself, lead him into regions where sight and hearing and touch are impotent as direct witnesses, where they are no longer efficient guides. In such regions everything has to be interpreted in terms of the insensible, the apparently unsubstantial, and in a definite sense the imaginary. Yet these regions of knowledge are as clear and vivid to him as are any of those encountered in everyday occupations ; indeed most commonplace phenomena themselves require interpretation in terms of ideas more subtle,—the apparent solidity of matter itself demands explanation,— and the underlying non-material entities of a physicist's conception become gradually as real and substantial as anything he knows. As Lord Kelvin used to say, when in a paradoxical mood, we really know more about electricity than we know about matter.

That being so, I shall go further and say that I am reasonably convinced of the existence of grades of being, not only lower in the scale than man but higher also, grades of every order of magnitude from zero to infinity.

And I know by experience that among these beings are some who care for and help and guide humanity, not disdaining to enter even into what must seem petty details, if by so doing they can assist souls striving on their upward course. And further it is my faith—however humbly it may be held—that among these lofty beings, highest of those who concern themselves directly with this earth of all the myriads of worlds in infinite space, is One on whom the right instinct of Christianity has always lavished heartfelt reverence and devotion.

Those who think that the day of that Messiah is over are strangely mistaken : it has hardly begun. In individual souls Christianity has flourished and borne fruit, but for the ills of the world itself it is an almost untried panacea. It will be strange if this ghastly war fosters and simplifies and improves a knowledge of Christ, and aids a perception of the ineffable beauty of his life and teaching : yet stranger things have happened ; and, whatever the Churches may do, I believe that the call of Christ himself will be heard and attended to, by a large part of humanity in the near future, as never yet it has been heard or attended to on earth.

My own time down here is getting short ; it matters little : but I dare not go till I have borne this testimony to the grace and truth which emanate from that divine Being,—the realisation of whose tender-hearted simplicity and love for man may have been overlaid at times and almost lost amid well-intentioned but inappropriate dogma, but who is accessible as always to the humble and meek.

Intercommunion between the states or grades of existence is not limited to messages from friends and relatives, or to conversation with personalities of our own order of magnitude,—that is only a small and verifiable portion of the whole truth,—intercourse between the states carries with it occasional, and sometimes unconscious, communion with lofty souls who have gone before. The truth of such continued influence corresponds with the highest of the Revelations vouchsafed to humanity. This truth, when assimilated by man, means an assurance of the reality of prayer, and a certainty of gracious sympathy and fellow-feeling from one who never despised the suffering, the sinful, or the lowly ; yea, it means more—it means nothing less than the possibility some day of a glance or a word of approval from the Eternal Christ.

CHAPTER XVII

THE CHRISTIAN IDEA OF GOD

A PLEA FOR SIMPLICITY [1]

INVESTIGATION is laborious and unexciting ; it takes years, and progress is slow ; but in all regions of knowledge it is the method which in the long-run has led towards truth ; it is the method by which what we feel to be solid and substantial progress has always been made. In many departments of human knowledge this fact is admitted—though men of science have had to fight hard for their method before getting it generally recognised. In some departments it is still contested, and the arguments of Bacon in favour of free experimental inquiry are applicable to those subjects which are claimed as superior to scientific test.

If it be objected that not by such means is truth in religious matters ascertained, if it be held that we must walk by faith, not by sight, and that never by searching will man find out any of the secrets of God, I do not care to contest the objection, though I disagree with its negative portion. That no amount of searching will ever enable us to find out the Almighty to perfection is manifestly true ; that secrets may be revealed to inspired ' babes ' which are hidden from the wise and prudent is likewise certain ; but that no secret things of God can be brought to light by patient examination and inquiry into facts is false, for you cannot parcel out truth into that which is divine and that which is not divine ; the truths of science were as much God's secrets as any other, and they have yielded up their mystery to precisely the process which is called in question.

[1] *Hibbert Journal*, July 1911.

We are part of the Universe, our senses have been evolved in and by it ; it follows that they are harmonious with it, and that the way it appeals to our senses is a true way ; though their obvious limitation entitles us to expect from time to time fresh discoveries of surprising and fundamental novelty, and a growing perception of tracts beyond our ancient ken.

Some critics there are, however, who, calling themselves scientific, have made up their minds in a negative direction and a contrary sense. These are impressed not only with the *genuineness* of the truth afforded us through our senses and perceptions, but with its *completeness* ; they appear to think that the main lines of research have already been mapped out or laid down, they will not believe that regions other than those to which they are accustomed can be open to scientific exploration ; especially they imagine that in the so-called religious domain there can be no guides except preconception and prejudice. Accordingly, they appear to disbelieve that anyone can be conscientiously taking trouble to grope his way by patient inquiry, with the aid of such clues as are available ; and in order to contradict the results of such inquiry they fall into the habit of doing that of which they accuse the workers,—they appeal to sentiment and presumption. They talk freely about what they believe, what they think unlikely, and what is impossible. They are governed by prejudice; their minds are made up. Doubtless they regard knowledge on certain topics as inaccessible, so they are positive and self-satisfied and opinionated and quite sure. They pride themselves on their hard-headed scepticism and robust common sense ; while the truth is that they have bound themselves into a narrow cell by walls of sentiment, and have thus excluded whole regions of human experience from their purview.

It so happens that I have been engaged for over forty years in mathematical and physical science, and for more than half that period in exploration into unusual psychical development, as opportunity arose ; and I have thus been led to certain tentative conclusions respecting permissible ways of regarding the universe.

First, I have learned to regard the universe as a concrete and full-bodied reality, with parts accessible and intelligible to us, all of it capable of being understood and investigated by the human mind, not as an abstraction or dream-like entity whose appearances are deceptive. Our senses do not deceive us ; their testimony is true as far as it goes. I have learned to believe in Intelligibility.

Next, that everything, every single thing, has many aspects. Even such a thing as water, for instance. Water, regarded by the chemist, is an assemblage or aggregate of complex molecules ; regarded by the meteorologist and physiographer, it is an element of singular and vitally important properties ; every poet has treated of some aspect of beauty exhibited by this common substance ; while to the citizen it is an ordinary need of daily life. All the aspects together do not exhaust the subject, but each of them is real. The properties of matter of which our senses tell us, or enable us to inquire into in laboratories, are true properties, real and true. They are not the whole truth, a great deal more is known about them by men of science, but the more complex truths do not make the simpler ones false. Moreover, we must admit that the whole truth about the simplest thing is assuredly beyond us ; the Thing-in-itself is related to the whole universe, and in its fullness is incomprehensible.

Furthermore, I have learned that while positive assertions on any given subject are often true, error creeps in when simple aspects are denied in order to emphasise the more complex, or *vice versa*. A trigonometrical sine, for instance, may be expressed in terms of imaginary exponentials in a way familiar to all mathematical students ; also as an infinite series of fractions with increasing factorials in the denominators ; also in a number of other true and legitimate and useful ways ; but the simple geometrical definition, by aid of the chord of a circle or the string of a bow, survives them all, and is true too.

So it is, I venture to say, with the concept God.

It can be regarded from some absolute and transcendental standpoint which humanity can only pretend to attain to. It can be regarded as the highest and best idea which the human mind has as yet been able to form. It can be regarded as dominating and including all existence, and as synonymous with all existence when that is made sufficiently comprehensive. All these views are legitimate, but they are not final or complete. God can also be represented by some of the attributes of humanity, and can be depicted as a powerful and loving Friend with whom our spirits may commune at every hour of the day, one whose patience and wisdom and long-suffering and beneficence are never exhausted. He can, in fact, be regarded as displayed to us, in such fashion as we can make use of, in the person of an incarnate Being who came for the express purpose of revealing to man such attributes of deity as would otherwise have been missed.

The images are not mutually exclusive, they may all be in some sort true. None of them is complete. They are all aspects—partly true and partly false as conceived by any individual, but capable of being expressed so as to be, as far as they go, true.

Undoubtedly the Christian idea of God is the simple one. Overpoweringly and appallingly simple is the notion presented to us by the orthodox Christian Churches :—

A babe born of poor parents, born in a stable among cattle because there was no room for them in the village inn—no room for them in the inn—what a master touch ! Revealed to shepherds. Religious people inattentive. Royalty ignorant, or bent on massacre. A glimmering perception, according to one noble legend, attained in the Far East—where also similar occurrences have been narrated. Then the child growing into a peasant youth, brought up to a trade. At length a few years of itinerant preaching ; flashes of miraculous power and insight. And then a swift end : set upon by the religious people ; his followers overawed and scattered, himself tried as a blasphemer, flogged, and finally tortured to death.

Simplicity most thorough and most strange ! In itself it is not unique ; such occurrences seem inevitable to highest humanity in an unregenerate world ; but who, without inspiration, would see in them a revelation of the nature of God ? The life of Buddha, the life of Joan of Arc, are not thus regarded. Yet the Christian revelation is clear enough and true enough if our eyes are open, and if we care to read and accept the simple record which, whatever its historical value, is all that has been handed down to us.

Critics often object that there have been other attempted Messiahs, that the ancient world was expectant of a Divine Incarnation. True enough. But what then ? We need not be afraid of an idea because it has several times striven to make itself appreciated. It is foolish to decline a revelation because it has been more than once offered to humanity. Every great revelation is likely to have been foreshadowed in more or less imperfect forms, so as to prepare our minds and make ready the way for complete perception hereafter. It is probable that the human race is quite incompetent to receive a really great idea the first time it is offered. There must be many failures to effect an entrance before the final success, many struggles to overcome natural obstacles and submerge the stony products of human stolidity. Lapse of time for preparation is required before anything great can be permanently accomplished, and repeated attempts are necessary; but the tide of general progress is rising all the time. The idea is well expressed in Clough's familiar lines :—

> " For while the tired waves, vainly breaking,
>   Seem here no painful inch to gain,
>   Far back, through creeks and inlets making,
>   Comes silent, flooding in, the main."

So it was with the idea of the Messiah which was abroad in the land, and had been for centuries, before Christ's coming ; and never has he been really recognised by more than a few. Dare we not say that he is more truly recognised now than in any previous age in the history of the Church—except perhaps the very earliest ? And I doubt if we need make that exception.

The idea of his Messiahship gradually dawned upon him, and he made no mistake as to his mission :—

The word which ye hear is not mine, but the Father's who sent me.

As the Father gave me commandment, even so I do.

The words which I say unto you I speak not of myself the Father which dwelleth in me, he doeth the works.

The Father is greater than I.

But, for all that,

He that hath seen me hath seen the Father.

Yes, truly, Christ was a planetary manifestation of Deity, a revelation to the human race, the highest and simplest it has yet had ; a revelation in the only form accessible to man, a revelation in the full-bodied form of humanity.

Little conception had they in those days of the whole universe as we know it now.   The earth was the whole world to them, and that which revealed God to the earth was naturally regarded as the whole Cosmic Deity.   Yet it was a truly divine Incarnation.

A deity of some kind is common to every branch of the human race.   It seems to be possessed by every savage, overawed as he necessarily is by the forces of nature.   Caprice, jealousy, openness to flattery and rewards, are likewise parts of early theology.   Then in the gods of Olympus—that poetic conception which rose to such heights and fell to such depths at different epochs in the ancient world—the attributes of power and beauty were specially emphasised. *Power* is common to all deities, and favouritism in its use seems also a natural supposition to early tribes ; but the element of *Beauty*, as a divine attribute, we in these islands, save for the poets, have largely lost or forgotten—to our great detriment.   In Jehovah, however, the Hebrew race rose to a conception of divine *Righteousness* which we have assimilated and permanently retained ; and upon that foundation Christianity was grafted.   It was to a race who had risen thus far—a race with a genius for theology—that the Christian revelation came.   It was rendered possible, though only just possible, by the stage attained.   Simple and unknown folk were ready to receive it, or, at least, were willing to take the first steps to learn.

The power, the righteousness, and other worthy attributes belonging to Jehovah, were known of old.   The Christian conception takes *them* for granted, and concentrates attention on the pity, the love, the friendliness, the compassion, the earnest desire to help mankind—attributes which, though now and again dimly discerned by one or another of the great seers of old, had not yet been thrown into concrete form.

People sometimes seek to deny such attributes as are connoted by the word ' Personality ' in the Godhead—they say it is a human conception.   Certainly it is a human con-

ception ; it is through humanity that it has been revealed.
Why seek to deny it ?   God transcends personality, objec-
tors say.   By all means : transcends all our conceptions
infinitely, transcends every revelation which has ever been
vouchsafed ; but the revelations are true as far as they go,
for all that. ʼ

Let us not befog ourselves by attempting impossible
conceptions to such an extent that we lose the simple and
manifest reality.   No conception that we can make is too
high, too good, too worthy.   It is easy to imagine ourselves
mistaken, but never because ideas are too high or too good.
It were preposterous to imagine an over-lofty conception in
a creature.   Reality is always found to exceed our clear
conception of it ; never once in science has it permanently
fallen short.   No conception is too great or too high.
But also no devout conception is too simple, too
lowly, too childlike to have an element—some grain—
of vital truth stored away, a mustard seed ready to
germinate and bud, a leaven which may permeate the
whole mass.

I would apply all this to what for brevity may be called
Human Immortality.   It is possible to think of that rather
simply ; and, on the other hand, it is possible to confuse
ourselves with tortuous thoughts till it seems unreal and
impossible.   It is part of the problem of personality and
individuality ; for the question of how far these are dependent on the bodily organism, or whether they can exist
without it, is a scientific question.   It is open to research.
And yet it is connected with Christianity ; for undoubtedly the Christian idea of God involves a belief in human
immortality.   If *per impossibile* this latter could be authori-
tatively denied, a paralysing blow would have been struck
at the Christian idea.   On the other hand, if by scientific
investigation the persistence of individual memory and
character were proved, a great step in the direction of
orthodox theology would have been taken.

The modern superstition about the universe is that,
being suffused with law and order, it contains nothing
personal, nothing indeterminate, nothing unforeseen ; that
there is no room for the free activity of intelligent beings,
that everything is mechanically determined ; so that given
the velocity and acceleration and position of every atom

at any instant, the whole future could be unravelled by sufficient mathematical power.

The doctrines of Uniformity and Determinism are supposed to be based upon experience. But experience includes experience of the actions of human beings ; and some of them certainly appear to be of a capricious and undetermined character. Or without considering human beings, watch the orbits of a group of flies as they play ; they are manifestly not controlled completely by mechanical laws as are the motions of the planets. The simplest view of their activity is that it is self-determined, that they are flying about at their own will, and turning when and where they choose. The conservation of energy has nothing to say against it. Here we see free-will in its simplest form. To suppose anything else in such a case, to suppose that every twist could have been predicted through all eternity, is to introduce præternatural complexity, and is quite unnecessary.

Why not assume, what is manifestly the truth, that free-will exists and has to be reckoned with, that the universe is not a machine subject to outside forces, but a living organism with initiations of its own ; and that the laws which govern it, though they include mechanical and physical and chemical laws, are not limited to those, but involve other and higher abstractions, which may perhaps some day be formulated, for life and mind and spirit ?

If it be said that free-will can be granted to deity but to nothing lower, inasmuch as the Deity must be aware of all that is going to happen, I reply that you are now making a hypothesis of a complicated kind, and going beyond knowledge into speculation. But if still the speculation appears reasonable, that only the Deity can be endowed with free-will, it merely opens the question, What shall be included in that term ? If freedom is the characteristic mark of deity, then those are justified who have taught that every fragment of mind and will is a contributory element in the essence of the Divine Being.

How, then, can we conceive of deity ? The analogy of the human body and its relation to the white corpuscles in its blood is instructive. Each corpuscle is a living creature endowed with the powers of locomotion, of assimilation, and, under certain conditions now being inquired into, of reproduction by fission. The health and polity of the body are largely dependent on the activity of these phagocytes. They are to us extremely important; they are an essential part of our being.

But now suppose one of these corpuscles endowed with intelligence — what conception of the universe will it be able to form? It may examine its surroundings, discourse of the vessels through which it passes, of the adventures it encounters; and if philosophically minded, it may speculate on a being of which perhaps it and all its like form a part—an immanent deity, whose constituents they are, a being which includes them and includes all else which they know or can imagine—a being to whose existence they contribute, and whose purposes they serve or share. So far they could speculate, and so far they would be right. But if they proceeded further, and entered on negations, if they surmised that that immanent aspect of the universe in which they lived and moved and had their being was the sole and only aspect, if they surmised that there was no personality, no feeling, no locomotion, no mind, no purpose, apart from them and their kind, they would greatly err. What conception could they ever form of the manifold interests and activities of man? Still less of the universe known to man, of which he himself forms so trivial a portion.

All analogies fail at some point, but they are a help nevertheless, and this analogy will bear pressing rather far. We ourselves are a part of the agencies for good or evil; we have the power to help or to hinder, to mend or to mar, within the scope of our activity. Our help is asked for; lowly as we are, it is really wanted, on the earth here and now, just as much wanted as our body needs the help of its lowly white corpuscles—to contribute to health, to attack disease, to maintain the normal and healthy life of the organism. We are the white corpuscles of the cosmos, we serve and form part of an immanent Deity.

Truly it is no easy service to which we are called; something of the wisdom of the serpent must enter into our activities; sanity and moral dignity and sound sense must govern our proceedings; all our powers must be called out, and there must be no sluggishness. Impulses, even good impulses, alone are not sufficient ; every faculty of the human brain must be exerted, and we must be continually on guard against the flabbiness of mere good intentions.

Our activity and service are thus an integral part of the Divine Existence, which likewise includes that of all the perceptible universe. But to suppose that this exhausts the matter, and that the Deity has no transcendent Existence of which we can form no idea,—to suppose that what happens is not the result of his dominant and controlling Personality, is to step beyond legitimate inference, and to treat appearance as exhaustive of reality.

Always mistrust negations. They commonly signify blindness and prejudice—except when thoroughly established and carefully formulated in the light of actual experience or mathematical proof. And even then we should be ready to admit the possibility of higher generalisations which may uproot them. They are only safe when thrown into the form of a positive assertion.

The impossibility of squaring the circle is not really a negative proposition, except in form. It is safer and more convincing when thrown into the positive and definite form that the ratio of area to diameter is incommensurable. That statement is perfectly clear and legitimate ; and the illustration may be used as a parable. A positive form should be demanded of every comprehensive denial ; and whatever cannot be thrown into positive form, it is wise to mistrust. Its promulgator is probably stepping out of bounds, into the cheap and easy region of negative speculation. He is like a rationalistic microbe denying the existence of a human being.

I have urged that the simple aspect of things is to be considered and not despised ; but, for the majority of people, is not the tendency the other way ? Are they not too much given to suppose the Universe limited to the simplicity of their first and everyday conception of it ? The stockbroker has his idea of the totality of things ; the navvy has his. Students of mathematical physics are liable to think of it as a determinate assemblage of atoms and ether, with no room for spiritual entities—no room, as my brilliant teacher, W. K. Clifford, expressed it, no room for ghosts. ⁄

Biological students are apt to think of life as a physico-chemical process of protoplasmic structure and cell organisation, with consciousness as an epiphenomenon. They watch the lowly stages of animal organisms, and hope to imitate their behaviour by judicious treatment of inorganic materials. By all means let them try ; the effort is entirely legitimate, and not unhopeful. That which has come into being in the past may come into being under observation in the present, and the intelligence and co-operation of man may help. Why not ? The material vehicle would thus have been provided—in this case, without doubt, purposely and designedly — for some incipient phase of life. But would that in the least explain the nature of life and mind and will, and reduce them to simple atomic mechanism and dynamics? Not a whit. The real nature of these things would remain an unanswered question.

During the past century progress has lain chiefly in the domain of the mechanical and material. The progress has been admirable, and has led to natural rejoicing and legitimate pride. It has also led to a supposition that all possible scientific advance lies in this same direction, or even that all the great fundamental discoveries have now been made ! Discovery proceeds by stages, and enthusiasm at the acquisition of a step or a landing-place obscures for a time our perception of the flight of stairs immediately ahead ; but it is rational to take a more comprehensive view.

Part of our experience is the connexion of spirit with matter. We are conscious of our own identity, our own mind and purpose and will : we are also conscious of the matter in which it is at present incarnate and manifested. Let us use these experiences and learn from them. Incarnation is a fact ; we are not matter, yet we utilise it. Through the mechanism of the brain we can influence the material world ; we are in it, but not of it ; we transcend it by our consciousness. The body is our machine, our instrument, our vehicle of manifestation ; and through it we can achieve results in the material sphere. Why seek to deny either the spiritual or the material ? Both are real, both are true. In some higher mind, perhaps, they may be unified : meanwhile we do not possess this higher mind. Scientific progress is made by accepting realities and learning from them ; the rest is speculation. It is not likely that we are the only intelligent beings in the Universe. There may be many higher grades, up to the Divine ; just as there are lower grades, down to the amœba. Nor need all these grades of intelligence be clothed in matter or inhabit the surface of a planet. That is the kind of existence with which we are now familiar, truly, and anything beyond that is for the most part supersensuous ; but our senses are confessedly limited, and if there is any truth in the doctrine of human immortality the existence of myriads of departed individuals must be assumed, on what has been called " the other side."

But how are we to get evidence in favour of such an apparently gratuitous hypothesis ? Well, speaking for myself and with full and cautious responsibility, I have to state that as an outcome of my investigation into psychical matters I have at length and quite gradually become convinced, after more than thirty years of study, not only that persistent individual existence is a fact, but that occasional communication across the chasm—with difficulty and under definite conditions—is possible.

This is not a subject on which one comes lightly and easily to a conclusion, nor can the evidence be explained except to those who will give to it time and careful study ; but clearly the conclusion is either folly and self-deception, or it is a truth of the utmost importance to humanity—and of importance to us in connexion with our present subject. For it is a conclusion which cannot stand alone. Mistaken or true, it affords a foothold for a whole range of other thoughts, other conclusions, other ideas : false and misleading if the foothold is insecure, worthy of attention if the foothold is sound. Let posterity judge.

Meanwhile it is a subject that attracts cranks and charlatans. Rash opinions are freely expressed on both sides. I call upon the educated of the younger generation to refrain from accepting assertions without severe scrutiny, and, above all, to keep an open mind.

If departed human beings can communicate with us, can advise us and help us, can have any influence on our actions, — then clearly the doors are open to a wealth of spiritual intercourse beyond what we have yet imagined.

The region of the miraculous, it is called, and the bare possibility of its existence has been hastily and illegitimately denied.   But so long as we do not imagine it to be a region denuded of a law and order of its own, akin to the law and order of the psychological realm, our denial has no foundation.   The existence of such a region may be established by experience ; its non-existence cannot be established; for non-experience might merely mean that owing to deficiencies of our sense organs it was beyond our ken.   In judging of what are called miracles we must be guided by historical evidence and literary criticism. We need not urge *a priori* objections to them on scientific grounds.   They need be no more impossible, no more lawless, than the interference of a human being would seem to a colony of ants or bees.

The Christian idea of God certainly has involved, and presumably always will involve, an element of the miraculous,—a flooding of human life with influences which lie outside it, a controlling of human destiny by higher and beneficent agencies. By evil agencies too ? Yes, the influences are not all on one side ; but the Christian faith is that the good are the stronger.   Experience has shown to many a saint, however tormented by evil, that appeal to the powers of good can result in ultimate victory.   Let us not reject experience on the ground of dogmatic assertion and baseless speculation.

Historical records tell us of a Divine Incarnation.   We may consider it freely on historical grounds.   We are not debarred from contemplating such a thing by anything that science has to say to the contrary.   Science does not speak directly on the subject.   If the historical evidence is good we may credit it, just as we may credit the hypothesis of survival if the present-day evidence is good. It sounds too simple and popular an explanation—too much like the kind of ideas suited to unsophisticated man and to the infancy of the race.   True ; but has it not happened often in the history of science that reality has

been found simpler than our attempted conception of it ?
Electricity long ago was often treated as a fluid ; and a
little time ago it was customary to jeer at the expression
—legitimate in the mouth of Benjamin Franklin, but
now apparently outgrown.   And yet what else is the
crowd of mobile electrons, postulated by [not] the very
latest theory, in a metal ?   Surely it is in some sense a
fluid, though not a material one ?   The guess was not so
far wrong after all.   Meanwhile we learned to treat it by
mathematical devices, vector potential, and other recondite methods.   With great veneration I speak of the
mathematical physicists of the past century.   They have
been almost superhuman in power, and have attained
extraordinary results, but in time the process of discovery
will enable mankind to apprehend all these things more
simply.   Progress lies in simple investigation as well as
in speculation and thought up to the limits of human
power ; and when things are really understood, they are
perceived to be fairly simple after all.

So it seems likely to be with a future state, or our own
permanent existence ; it has been thought of and spoken
of as if it were altogether transcendental—something
beyond space and time (as it may be), something outside
and beyond all conception.   But it is not necessarily so
at all ; it is a question of fact ; it is open to investigation.
I find part of it turning out quite reasonably simple ; not
easy to grasp or express, for lack of experience and
language—that is true,—but not by any means conveying
a feeling of immediate vast difference and change.   Something much more like terrestrial existence, at least on one
aspect of it, than we had imagined.   Not as a rule associated with matter ; no, but perhaps associated with ether
—an ethereal body instead of a material one ; certainly
a body, or mode of manifestation, of some kind.   It
appears to be a state which leaves personality and character and intelligence much where it was.   No sudden
jump into something supernal, but steady and continued
progress.   Many activities and interests beyond our
present ken, but with a surviving terrestrial aspect,
occasionally accessible, and showing interest in the doings
of those on earth, together with great desire to help and
to encourage all efforts for the welfare of the race.   We

need not search after something so far removed from humanity as to be unintelligible. .

So likewise with the idea of God.

No matter how complex and transcendentally vast the Reality must be, the Christian conception of God is humanly simple. It appeals to the unlettered and ignorant; it appeals to " babes."

That is the way with the greatest things. The sun is the centre of the solar system, a glorious object full of mystery and unknown forces, but the sunshine is a friendly and homely thing, which shines in at a cottage window, touches common objects with radiance, and brings warmth and comfort even to the cat.

The sunshine is not the sun, but it is the human and terrestrial aspect of the sun ; it is that which matters in daily life. It is independent of study and discovery ; it is given us by direct experience, and for ordinary life it suffices.

Thus would I represent the Christian conception of God. Christ is the human and practical and workaday aspect. Christ is the sunshine—that fraction of transcendental Cosmic Deity which suffices for the earth. Jesus of Nazareth is plainly a terrestrial heritage. His advent is the glory, His reception the shame, of the human race.

Once more, then. Although there may be undue simplification of the complex, there is also an undue complication of the simple ; it is easy to invent unnecessary problems, to manufacture gratuitous difficulties, to lose our way in a humanly constructed and quite undivine fog. But the way is really simple, and when the fog lifts and the sunshine appears, all becomes clear and we proceed without effort on our way : the wayfaring man, though a fool, need not err therein. The way, the truth, and the life are all one. Reality is always simple ; it is concrete and real and expressible. Our customary view of the commonest objects is not indeed the last word, nay, rather, it is the first word, as to their nature ; but it is a true word as far as it goes. Analysing a liquid into a congeries of discrete atoms does not destroy or weaken or interfere with its property of fluidity. Analysing an atom into electrons does not destroy the atom.   Reducing matter to electricity, or to any other ethereal substratum, does not alter the known and familiarly utilised properties of a bit of wood or iron or glass, in the least ; no, nor of a bit of bone or feather or flesh.   Study may superadd properties imperceptible to the plain man, but the plain man's concrete and simple view serves for ordinary purposes of daily life.

And God's view, strange to say, must be more akin to that of the plain man than to that of the philosopher or statistician.   That is how it comes that children are near the kingdom of heaven.   It is not likely that God really makes abstractions and " geometrises."   All those higher and elaborate modes of expression are human counters ; and the difficulties of dealing with them are human too. Only in early stages do things require superhuman power for their apprehension ; they are easy to grasp when they are really understood.   They come out then into daily life ; they are not then matters of intellectual strain ; they can appeal to our sense of beauty ; they can affect us with emotion and love and appreciation and joy ; they can enter into poetry and music, and constitute the subject-matter of Art of all kinds.   The range of art and of enjoyment must increase infinitely with perfect knowledge. This is the atmosphere of God : " Where dwells enjoyment, there is He."   We are struggling upwards into that atmosphere slowly and laboriously.   The struggle is human, and for us quite necessary, but the mountain top is serene and pure and lovely, and its beauty is in nowise enhanced by the efforts of the exhausted climber, as he slowly wins his way thither.

Yet the effort itself is of value.   The climber, too, is part of the scheme, and his upward trend may be growth and gain to the whole.   It adds interest, though not beauty.   Do not let us think that the universe is stagnant and fixed and settled and dull, and that all its appearance of " going on " is illusion and deception. I would even venture to urge that, ever since the grant to living creatures of free will, there must be, in some sense or other, a real element of contingency,—that there is no dullness about it, even to the Deity, but a constant and aspiring Effort.

Let us trust our experience in this also. The Universe is a flux, it is a becoming, it is a progress. Evolution is a reality. True and not imaginary progress is possible. Effort is not a sham. Existence is a true adventure. There is a real risk.

There was a real risk about creation—directly it went beyond the inert and mechanical. The granting of choice and free will involved a risk. Thenceforward things could go wrong. They might be kept right by main force, but that would not be playing the game, that would not be loyalty to the conditions.

As William James says : A football team desire to get a ball to a certain spot, but that is not all they desire ; they wish to do it under certain conditions and overcome inherent difficulties—else might they get up in the night and put it there.

So also we may say, Good is the end and aim of the Divine Being ; but not without conditions. Not by compulsion. Perfection as of machinery would be too dull and low an achievement—something much higher is sought. The creation of free creatures who, in so far as they go right, do so because they will, not because they must,—that was the Divine problem, and it is the highest of which we have any conception.

Yes, there was a real risk in making a human race on this planet. Ultimate good was not guaranteed. Some parts of the Universe must be far better than this, but some may be worse. Some planets may comparatively fail. The power of evil may here and there get the upper hand : although it must ultimately lead to suicidal destructive failure, for evil is pregnant with calamity.

This planet is surely not going to fail. Its destinies have been more and more entrusted to us. For millions of years it laboured, and now it has produced a human race—a late-comer to the planet, only recently arrived, only partly civilised as yet. But already it has produced Plato and Newton and Shakespeare ; yes, and it has been the dwelling-place of Christ. Surely it is going to succeed, and in good time to be the theatre of such a magnificent development of human energy and power and joy as to compensate, and more than compensate, for all the pain and suffering, all the blood and tears, which have gone to prepare the way.

The struggle is a real one. The effort is not confined to humanity alone : according to the Christian conception God has shared in it. " God so loved the world that He gave "—we know the text. The earth's case was not hopeless ; the world was bad, but it could be redeemed ; and the redemption was worth the painful effort which then was undergone, and which the disciples of the Cross have since in their measure shared. Aye, that is the Christian conception ; not of a God apart from His creatures, looking on, taking no personal interest in their behaviour, sitting aloof only to judge them ; but One who anxiously takes measures for their betterment, takes trouble, takes pains—a pregnant phrase, takes pains,—One who suffers when they go wrong, One who feels painfully the miseries and wrongdoings and sins and cruelties of the creatures whom He has endowed with free will ; One who actively enters into the storm and the conflict ; One who actually took flesh and dwelt among us, to save us from the slough into which we might have fallen, to show us what the beauty and dignity of man might be.

Well, it is a great idea, a great and simple idea, so simple as to be incredible to some minds. It has been hidden from many of the wise and prudent ; it has been revealed to babes.

To sum up : Let us not be discouraged by simplicity. Real things are simple. Human conceptions are not altogether misleading. Our view of the Universe is a partial one but is not an untrue one. Our knowledge of the conditions of existence is not altogether false—only inadequate. The Christian idea of God is a genuine representation of reality.

Nor let us imagine that existence hereafter, removed from these atoms of matter which now both confuse and manifest it, will be something so wholly remote and different as to be unimaginable ; but let us learn by the testimony of experience—either our own or that of others —that those who have been, still are ; that they care for us and help us ; that they, too, are progressing and learning and working and hoping ; that there are grades of existence, stretching upward and upward to all eternity ; and that God Himself, through His agents and messengers, is continually striving and working and planning, so as to bring this creation of His through its preparatory labour and pain, and lead it on to an existence higher and better than anything we have ever known.

INDEX

Lightning Source UK Ltd.
Milton Keynes UK
UKOW04f1959120815

256848UK00001B/36/P